Parallel

LJ Bacon

Clink
Street

London | New York

Published by Clink Street Publishing 2019

Copyright © 2019

First edition.

ISBN:
978-1-913136-63-5 - paperback
978-1-913136-64-2 - ebook

I would like to say thank you to all those who have stood by me believing I could write this book.

Sam for helping spur me on when I doubted myself, my kids for putting up with me and my moody moments whilst constantly reading over and over checking as best I could for mistakes.

My mum; for if it wasn't for her taking a leap of faith in me, this book would probably never have been published, Thanks Mum.

Thank you to God, they say he works in mysterious ways and I am evidence he does, when the events happened and I suffered an injury I thought that's it what can I do now.

But then it became apparent to me, my injury had to happen, or I would still be working 10 to 12 hours shifts, some seven days a week, and this book would never have even been started.

This story has been in my head for many years, I was always wishing I could find the time to write it.

then it happened; although not the way I was looking for I.e having an injury and then loosing my job which I had been doing for over 30 years, but I believe God Said it's time to move on, sorry it has to be done.

And so my injury happened and I managed to write my book, my dream for years that I never thought I would actually achieve, has been achieved in the most strangest turn of events.

Never give up on your dreams, if it's meant to be, God will find a way, always have faith.

A final thank you, if you are reading this now I thank you for reading that which I have worked so hard to achieve, and I hope from the bottom of my heart you enjoy it.

Thank You

Chapter 1

The Realisation

Have you ever looked up at the nights sky and thought, with so many stars we can't be the only planet with life such as ours? What if I was to say our planet isn't the only one with life, in fact what if I was to say we are living part of a parallel life on ours! Unbeknownst to us we have a second existence on another planet in another universe, and what happens there affects us here, and vice versa, how do I know this, you may ask, well, until a month ago I didn't know any of these things, I was just like you going about my days like any other person.

I woke as normal, at 7 am Thursday morning, had a shower and then got myself dressed, then had a coffee with some toast and was ready for the day ahead.

I live and work in a Dojo, with Mr. Mechin, first name Sato.

After my parent's deaths, when I was only six, he took me-in and raised me as his own son, he is a very wise older man with long grey hair and thin goatee beard, slim in build and only 5/6 tall, but what an amazing martial artist, very disciplined respectful and full of honour. If all men were like this man, the world would be a much better place.

I'm not too sure how old he is, he has never said, I'm not too sure how it was he became my surrogate father, all he has ever said to me is that he knew my parents very well, and that their deaths were devastating to him, and thought it the right thing to do, to take me into his care and raise me. I can't remember much of my parents, even their faces are a blur to me now.

Anyway, I went downstairs to the Dojo, and as usual Sato was there preparing for the days lessons, he greeted me in his usual manner, "Good morning Jacob my son how are you this morning?" To which I replied, "I am very well thank you, apart from another strange dream last night!" Sato replied, "Oh really, explain it to me."

I had been having strange and very vivid dreams for about a week, Sato was very interested in them, and would have me try my best to recall them for him in great detail; it was as if they meant something to him.

So I closed my eyes and began to explain what I could remember; "It seemed so real. I was on another world the sky was dark and seemed to have two moons, the land was mountainous and black, there were these creatures, they looked almost human but were deformed."

"Their skin was dark and shining in the moon light, their heads were bald and disfigured, some had eyes of red and others of yellow, with bodies very muscular and powerful looking, with hands that have claws instead of fingernails."

"There was one standing in the center of a silver circle, then there was a huge flash of light which came from the sky, almost like a bolt of lightning but it lasted about a minute! And when it had raised back to the sky the creature was gone!

"The rest of these creatures started to go crazy in celebration, then I was back in our world, but now I wasn't me! I was a woman and I was fighting this creature that I had watched disappear into the light, I was wounded and running for my life! I had a sword in my hand, its blade was covered with what I can only explain as black tar, then the dream suddenly ended, and I woke sweating and feeling very afraid!"

When I opened my eyes, I could see Sato looked worried, almost afraid, his head and shoulders dropped as he said in a very quiet, almost a whispered voice; "Thank you for telling me." I replied, "What is wrong, you look concerned by what

I have told you, it's just a dream!" To which he replied in a very soft but concerned voice, "Yes just a dream, a dream, a nightmare," as he slowly turned and started to walk away with his head dropped and shaking from side to side, I placed my hand on his right shoulder and asked, "What is wrong?" He was silent for a few moments, then turned and said, "It would appear the time has come for you to know all I have to tell, I hope I have prepared you well for what is about to come." Then he said; "We should sit and I shall begin," as he said this I felt a shiver up my spine, I have never seen him like this, so much concern on his face and the tone of his voice was like that of a man who had the world on his shoulders.

We sat on a training mat, he looked at me and smiled saying; "Where do I begin?" Then continued; "This may be hard for you to except at first." Then with a deep breath; "I am not from your universe, I am from another planet much like earth, but in another dimension, in the past we visited your earth, to help your people evolve as we have."

Shocked I interrupted; "What do you mean, I don't understand," to which Sato replied; "The people of your world and mine are linked individually by the energies of the universe; our life force or spirit, we live a parallel existence, but lead different lives, the people of my world have always been more advanced spiritually, with true understanding of the workings of the universe, and their connection to the chakra energies of man."

"It was through these energies that we felt your worlds existence! And so using interdimensional portals; which naturally exist in certain positions on both our worlds, we found you! And when we did we taught you the ways of the universe and the power of the human mind. We are different in appearance, by which I mean here you are white-skinned and blue-eyed, and live and work in a Dojo, but on my world you are dark-skinned and brown-eyed, and the king of my people, a very powerful caring king at that, but unfortunately on my world as king you have grave concerns, you see, we are at war, we have been for many years."

"On my world, before the war, we lived happily as one people of one world, we shared it working together in harmony, we call our world the soul, as she is the mother of all things created, beast and human alike, in fact we can communicate with the beasts of our world through thought, amazing creatures of the air, land and sea, just as the people of your world did once, but you have lost your way, your brains have become lazy, you use less than half your brain's potential, because you see, when the war broke out on my planet we had to seal the portals which connected our worlds to protect your world; in an attempt to stop our enemies using them to destroy your world and your people also killing our people at the same time. You see if you are killed in your world, your parallel you or as we call you; soul mate also dies in my world."

Unfortunately the people of your world became concerned with power and wealth rather than spiritual wellbeing and loving their world and each other, this lead to wars and kingdoms fighting for more land, and the gifts you were given such as Telepathy and Telekinesis were outlawed, and anyone using these gifts was called a witch or wizard and put to death, only the most powerful of your people were allowed to use these abilities, and they did so to maintain their control of the people below them.

"And so your brains reduced their abilities with time, but you do have the abilities; you just have to learn how to unlock the parts of your brain that controls them, and you will with time, as I said, your soul mate is my king and he is very powerful both physically and mentally, with great abilities and so are you, we just have to unlock your mind!"

"Ok," I said; feeling totally shocked by what he had just told me. "Say I believe what you have told me, and believe me I'm finding this hard, what as this to do with my dream?"

Sato replied; some of us are seers, this gift enables us to see what is going to happen in the future, I have this ability as well as being a commander in my king's army, before I was sent here to protect you and your family; this is one of the reasons I was chosen; because I am a seer and can see the future and what you have dreamt I also dreamt. This means you have the ability to see what will happen.

"It would seem the changed have found or created a portal somehow and will use it to get here and attempt to destroy the bloodlines of the great and powerful of my world and enable them to win the war!"

"The woman in your dream is your sister, the princess and heir to the throne should the king perish!"

Now I was confused and had to say; "I don't have a sister!" To which Sato replied; "I'm sorry I couldn't tell you, we separated you to protect you both, I had visions that the changed might find a way to find you, and thought it best to separate you so if we were found they didn't get you both! This wouldn't be the first time they have found a way to get here, her name is Jasmine, and we have to find her before it's too late.

I replied in a state of shock trying to absorb what he had just said about my having a sister, and yet all I could think to say was; "Ok, please explain to me, if your world was so perfect what happened to cause all of this, and who are the changed?"

Sato replied; "I will tell you! But we don't have much time, we have to get to your sister before it's too late, I will tell you all I know once we have your sister safe, she will probably want answers to many questions as well, so when we are safe we can talk more."

"Ok," I said feeling confused almost lost, I've known this man my whole life, and knew this wasn't just a tale, and that scared me!

Sato got up and said, "We have to get a few things, I'm sure you will be ready, you have always trained hard.

Then he walked away to the storeroom and when he returned he had with him two samurai swords, he handed one to me saying, this is yours, it was forged in my world and has massive power, only you can call upon its powers, I will explain later but no time now.

When he passed the sword to me, I gripped it in my hand I felt a strange tingling in my hand and arm, which became quite powerful almost painful which made me wince! I then removed the sleeve of the sword and the sensation was amazing, it was like an unimaginable strength enveloped my entire body. I looked at Sato, he looked at me smiled and said; "Yes you have paired, feels good doesn't it?" To which I replied "Yes, amazing!" The sword seemed to hum, barely audible but I could hear it, I couldn't take my eyes off it.

But then my trance was disrupted by Sato's voice calling my name.

"Jacob, Jacob, we have to go, put your sword on your back!"

I replied; "I would if I had something to hold it there with!" Sato replied; "Put it back in its sleeve and just place it between your shoulder blades, it will stay, it is part of you now."

So I did as he said, and as I bent my arm to place the sword between my shoulder blades it felt like a magnet pulling it into place, so I let go and whoosh it stuck to my back, I couldn't believe it, I couldn't stop trying to twist my head to see it, I even jumped up and down, it didn't budge then I lifted my arm to reach for the handle and it shot into my hand, this was unbelievable, amazing, totally thrilling, suddenly! "Oi stop playing it's not a toy, we have to go!" said Sato. "Ok," I replied, "how does it do that?, it just flew into my hand before I even touched it." "Questions, questions," he replied; while scurrying around making sure he had all we would need. It is forged from Udriume a living metal or organism as one might say; when it was forged my king your soul mate added his blood to the molten mix, giving it your DNA, most of your DNA is identical to my king's apart from the strands which control skin tone and eye color, this sword is part of you now, it works by using telepathy, your brain is communicating with the living organism within the metal, it has also started to rebuild the muscles in your brain which are used for Telekinesis, this is how it knew you wanted to hold it and so helped your brain to put it in your hand before you actually grasped it! There is much more for you to learn but no time now, we have to get going!"

Totally bemused, yet excited to learn more, I agreed, "Yes

let's do this, I have a sister! But do you have any idea where Jasmine is?" "Yes-yes let's go! Put this on," he said; passing me what looked like an old monk's robe!

"It will hide your sword," he said. "We won't stand out then!" I replied; sarcastically putting the smelly old thing on. "That's the beauty of London, you see people of all walks of life, faith and dress, no one will take notice of two monks," he replied. "Yeah right," I murmured under my breath.

"I might be old, but I do have very good ears young man," Sato said. "Sorry," I replied, and off we set, we simultaneously took a last look at the Dojo; our home, our place of teaching, I don't know what Sato was thinking; but I felt sad, I felt as though I would never see this place again.

"Don't worry, this place will be fine, it's us I worry about, now let's go." "Thanks, fill me with confidence," I said, then we left, I was last out so got to lock the door, not for the last time I hoped!

We made our way to Brixton underground station, heading where? I did not know as yet, Sato said follow, so I did, but I couldn't stop looking around at the familiar shops and buildings with a real empty feeling in my stomach; it was as though I was saying good bye to the streets I knew so well for the last time, and at the same time my mind was going over what Sato had said, to be honest I couldn't quite get to grips with it all, this man raised me from a young age so I knew he wasn't crazy, which made things worse, if all he said was true what the hell were we heading in to!

One thought I found amusing was; he was right, no one was taking any real notice of us in our monk's robes, just a quick look and that was it, we arrived at the underground he bought our tickets then down the escalator we headed, the rush of air as we went down was like an awakening, this is really happening, and I have a sister! my god can't believe it! What does she look like, does she know about me? Then, "Are you ok?" Sato asked. "Yes, no, I'm not sure to be honest my mind is running wild, is this real? Am I dreaming again?" "No you are not dreaming my boy," said Sato, "When we have your sister I promise to explain everything from the very beginning, but for now I need you to focus on your training, especially your swordsmanship, we don't know what we may find!" Then a thought; "If I remember right it was night in my dream when I saw Jasmine, it's not even midday yet! So does that mean it's ok?"

"Let us hope so," he replied.

Our tube train arrived, we entered, it was full no place to sit, so we stood, no conversation, both of us contemplating what may await us.

We got off after five stops at Green Park, then got another which took us to Piccadilly Circus, where we got off and walked to the exit.

The closer we got to the exit, the stronger the feeling of anxiety grew, was I anxious about meeting my sister for the first time, how would we react to each other once face to face, especially if she doesn't know I even exist!

Oh yes, and the thought of impending dangers didn't help either, but even so I could not wait to get to our destination, wherever that may be.

I just needed to meet Jasmine and learn more about how we ended up in this situation from Sato. The thought of everyone in our world also existing on another world, in another universe was exciting; I had always felt there was more to my life than just teaching martial arts in a Dojo, I was happy; but maybe this parallel existence is why I have always felt there is so much more to life.

As we walked towards the exit, I asked Sato; "So where are we going exactly?" He replied; "Not far now, we will soon be there, hopefully all is well."

I thought about what he had said about being able to communicate with their minds on his planet, and so asked; "Can't you communicate with Jasmine's guardian via telepathy? Let them know what we have seen!" To which he replied, "No, we have to be careful, if the changed are here, they could pick up on our communication; as we would probably be the only ones using telepathy on this planet, and if they are scanning for us; hoping we might make that simple mistake, it would be easy for them; if we were on my planet it would be possible; as you focus on the person you wish to communicate with and it's like a private phone call; it is possible to listen in if you know who the two persons are using telepathy, but you would be sensed." He then continued; "But here it would be too easy to pick up our communication as they wouldn't need to focus on anyone in specific, as there wouldn't be mass communication, and so we would be very easy to sense."

Sato then said; "When we arrive, hopefully all is well, we need to act normal; as if we are just paying a visit to our friends, please don't say anything to Jasmine, I will need to speak with Jasmine's guardian alone, and then we will tell you both all there is to tell."

So, who is Jasmine's guardian? Have I ever met them?" "No," but you will soon!" he replied.

As we headed out of the station, he said, "Try not to look around as we walk, just follow me, the less you see the less the changed can see."

"What do you mean?" I replied.

He said "If the changed have focused on you they will see what you see, and this will make it very easy to find us, and we don't want that…

Now I was thinking, how am I going to do that, walk and not look, got to see where I'm going, I'll have to focus on his back, I thought to myself.

The streets were busy and the traffic very loud, everything seemed more intense than normal, I felt as if my senses were more sensitive and very responsive. As we walked I focused on Sato's back trying to keep up with him; for an older man he could walk fast, scurrying along weaving in and out of people, he must have forgotten I was trying to follow and not look where I was going, which I was finding very hard to do, so I said; "Can we please slow down a little, I'm bumping into people with all your weaving in and out so fast." Sato replied "You need to move faster then, don't you? Anyway we have arrived." My God the emotions I was feeling now he had said that were barely controllable, my legs felt like jelly and my stomach sick, I was so nervous!

I was still focused on Sato's back, scared to look, he opened a door and a bell rang, like you would get in a shop, he walked in and I followed still fixed on his back, as he walked I dared not look because of what he had said, then a soft voice said, "Hello how can I help you, is your friend ok?" The voice must have meant me, I must have appeared strange staring at Sato's back following his every move, to which Sato replied with a sigh and a shake of the head, "Sorry yes he is fine thank you," then turned to me and said; "You can stop being my shadow now! We are where we need to be, just don't look out the windows." "Ok! Oh, ok," I replied quite embarrassed.

I looked up and saw this young woman about my age – early twenties, with long brown hair big blue eyes and a strange look on her face as if to say, like – really?! Then I realised I was smiling like a Cheshire Cat, thinking to myself is this Jasmine? When I realised, I composed myself and said "Hello," to which she replied "Hello." I felt like a pillock! So, I started to look around what looked like an herbalist shop; advertising alternative medicine, massage, reiki and martial arts. I was impressed, and thought to myself, very cool!

Then Sato asked the young lady; "Is the owner here?, I would like very much to speak with her." The young lady replied; "Yes, I will see if she is free," and turned and walked toward the back of the shop and through a door.

As soon as she had gone through the door Sato turned and said; "Can you please try and act normal, and say nothing?" "Ok," I replied feeling incredibly nervous, then a tall slim oriental lady with incredibly long greying hair came through the door. I was the first she could see, so she said; "Hello how can—" She stopped halfway and with a shocked look, said, "Sato is that you?" to which he replied; "Yes my love it is me, we need to talk, can we come in? She instantly replied; "Yes, yes of course, you are so welcome so nice to see you, please come round," as she opened the counter door, and we walked through and followed her to the back of the shop which had a corridor with treatment rooms on both sides, and then ahead up a staircase which lead to a flat above.

As we walked I could hear the sound of a Dojo in session, commands being called out, and pupils responding, so I said to the lady, "You have a Dojo?" She replied; "Yes, I will show you around if you have time," to which Sato looked at me, put his forefinger on his lips rolled his eyes as if to say don't speak, so I just smiled and continued to follow.

When we reached the flat the lady opened the door and, said; "Please come in and sit, I will make us tea, are you going to introduce us Sato?" Sato replied; "Yes but you already know who he is."

"Yes, I do but he doesn't know who I am, does he?"

To which Sato replied; "No you are quite right."

And so, with a loving smile; as he looked at Syrah, Sato introduced us; "Jacob, this is Syrah; my wife and Jasmine's guardian."

Syrah then said; "That's better, you have grown Jacob, you look very much like your father, I am so happy we have finally met again, but is it good news you bring?" The fact you know of your sister leads me to think two possibilities, one our troubles are finally over, or two they are about to get worse, either way must be of the utmost importance for Sato to bring you here."

Sato then took a step forward; "It is indeed of utmost importance we speak, and I fear it is not good news I bring. I believe the changed may have found a portal to bring them here; where exactly I don't know, but both me and Jacob have been having the same vivid dreams of the changed using a portal and Jasmine fighting for her life."

"Oh God help us," Syrah replied, as she slumped into her seat her tea falling from her hand. "We must warn the others she said in an almost whispered voice staring out the window."

When I heard her say others I had to ask, "Others?! What do you mean others, it's not just me and Jasmine? "No," replied

Syrah, "and if the changed have managed to find a portal and reopen it, it effects every human on this world and ours, what has Sato told you about our world and the changed?" "Not a great deal, he said I would be told all I need to know once we found you and Jasmine!"

"It would appear the time is here for you and Jasmine to meet, we are so sorry we had to separate you; but it was for your protection, I hope you and Jasmine can forgive us, and understand why we had to do what we did," said Syrah. I replied; "So please tell me." I needed to know everything I was feeling so lost, and totally confused.

Syrah replied ; "We will, but I have to break the news to Jasmine, I have to tell her who you are, you will both have a lot of bonding to do, it won't be easy.

"Where do I start to explain to her?" she said reaching for Sato's hand.

"We will have to show them," Sato replied and smiled at Syrah softly.

"Show us how," I replied. Syrah said she would close the shop and Dojo early so we could be together all four of us, she wasn't looking forward to explaining things to Jasmine, she didn't quite know where to start but it had to be done.

With that Syrah continued; "No point in delaying, I'd best shut the shop now, you have both waited long enough, are you ready to meet your sister, Jacob?" To which I replied; I think I am, not to sure how I feel to be honest! I feel like I'm in a dream at the moment, but hopefully when we actually meet it will feel more real, I just hope she is ready to meet me!"

Then the door opened, and in walked the young lady who had greeted us at the counter, she was wearing a ZooBoo; a Chinese martial arts uniform, as was Syrah. "Never been more ready in all my life, I've been waiting a long time for this day to arrive, I've closed the shop, Aashif is tutoring at the moment in the Dojo, when the lesson as finished he will close the Dojo and inform all the pupils there will not be any further lessons until further notice." Then she turned and said, "Hello Jacob,

I've seen you in Syrah's thoughts, a lot younger, just a boy really, I've been longing to meet you."

Before I could reply, Syrah in a total state of shock said; "You've been reading my mind?, I haven't sensed you, only those with great mental strength can use Telepathy and not be sensed by other Telepathist's!

"Since when did you gain the ability, and why have you never mentioned it to me? Your connection to the princes must be very strong," said Sato, also shocked.

Jasmine replied; "The gift came to me about five years ago now, I was at a point where I needed to know about mum and dad, I was having vague memories of them, barely able to see their faces, wanting so badly to see them, I wanted to ask you about them, but felt you might feel I didn't appreciate you. I love you as a mother and didn't want to upset you by asking about my real parents, and I knew nothing could bring them back so accepted to live with the little I knew. Then one morning while preparing in the front shop, I started to have dizzy spells which seemed to fade as soon as they occurred, then straight after I started to have what seemed like pictures and sounds in my head, which with time became more vivid, and I soon started to realise that I was seeing someone else's memories and thoughts; which turned out to be yours, mother. I guess I haven't mentioned it to you because I didn't want to burden you with it, I grew used to it quite quickly and have it totally under control; it did scare me at first with some of the things I was seeing, but for some reason I've always felt safe! It's been nice to know I have a brother, and deep down I've known we would meet, as I've seen this day, this very moment in my dreams."

"Oh, my beautiful child I knew you would be gifted and you are," said Syrah, then she reached out and softly touched Jasmine's hair, with tears in her eyes. "You have such a wonderful soul just like your mother, I want you to know, you could have asked me anything you wanted, you could never hurt my feelings by wanting to know about your parents, as you must know I was always expecting the day you would ask," Syrah said with a gentle smile.

"I did yes, but I saw your memories and learned so much about you, your world, my parents and totally understand the reasons you have done the things you have done, and the huge sacrifices you have made for me and Jacob, I love you so much."

Then Jasmine turned to me and smiled and said, Hello my brother," then stepped towards me her arms open wide tears in her eyes and cuddled me, the feeling was amazing so warm, it was like an instant bond, our emotions got the better of us both, and we sobbed, and squeezed each other so tight, it was as though I'd never been complete, until now, as though until this moment meeting my sister and holding her, a part of me as been missing deep within me, and now as returned.

"Until this morning I didn't know you existed," I said sobbing uncontrollably, I couldn't believe the effect of meeting my sister for the first time was having on me, especially as I didn't even know about her until a few hours ago, the heart is an amazing thing and emotions so overpowering.

I thought on the way here, meeting Jasmine for the first time would be awkward and uncomfortable, as she was a stranger to me, but no it was as though I'd know her my whole life, amazingly wonderful to me she is my family.

I went on to say still sobbing like a baby; "You are my sister, my family, I feel complete now I have you in my life, my heart is singing, I promise no matter what the future holds, we will never lose each other again, I will protect you with my life."

"I know, I feel the same it's a wonderful feeling having you here, and I'm never going to lose you again," she replied.

"We have so much catching up to do," I said and smiled. Jasmine replied; "Yes we do don't we?" drying the tears from her eyes and smiling such a wonderful smile.

As I looked up I could see Sato and Syrah holding each other tight and looking at us, tears in their eyes and smiling at us, then we all joined in one big embrace, all of us so happy to be together it felt like a real family, wonderful, we all pondered silently, what lay ahead of us, not least me, as I didn't really have a clue as to what we faced, and wanted this moment to never end.

Then the silence was gently broken by Syrah's voice, "We have much to do, and it would seem that time may not be on our side, Jacob, there is much you need to know, we will need to show you things so you truly understand our situation, and you to Jasmine, we will show you to just to make sure you have seen everything completely."

We all raised our heads smiled unsteadily at each other in agreement.

Chapter 2

Let's go back

Once again, the silence was broken, this time by a knock on the door and a man's voice asking if he may enter, to which Syrah replied, "Is that you Aashif?" He answered; yes and entered the room; "I'm all done in the Dojo, and have informed all students there will be no lessons until further notice, what's going on?" he asked. Sato turned to Syrah and asked, "Who is this young man? Syrah replied, this is Aashif, he has been with us for many years, he was a fantastic student and now a brilliant master of martial combat. He was a young boy of eight when I found him wondering the streets, scared, alone and very hungry, and not able to speak much English, just the basics, he and his parents had fled their country to escape the terrible troubles happening there, but got separated in London, we tried to find his parents, took him to the authorities but even they were unsuccessful, so I took him in, he is like our own," she said as she looked softly at Sato, who in turn smiled shook his head in a loving manner and said; "I know why I married you, you have the most loving, caring heart my love." Aashif looked confused and asked Sato, "Who are you?" "I am Sato, Syrah's husband, nice to meet you Aashif and I guess welcome to the family, he will have to come with us Syrah," Sato said. Syrah replied, "Of course he will."

Aashif turned to Syrah and said, "Wow, I've lived with you as your son for twelve years and you never mentioned I have a stepfather," he laughed, shook his head and said, "What a day, did you know Jasmine?" "Yes and no," she replied, "What do you mean yes and no, don't confuse me even more please." Jasmine replied, "Long story, but you will understand shortly, I hope."

With that Syrah said, "I guess no better time than the present, shall we go to the Dojo?"

"Yes," we all said, Aashif looking confused like a lost puppy, saying; "I guess so, will someone please tell me what is going on! I'm confused and my brain is starting to hurt." He seemed quite a nice guy soft-natured and jokey, around the same age as me and Jasmine, he was quite tall, dark shoulder length hair and big brown eyes, he too was wearing his ZooBoo.

We left the flat and made our way down the stairs, as we did so I could hear Aashif whispering to Jasmine, "What is going on, and who's the younger guy? and what's with the smelly robes?" Jasmine replied, "Oh he's my brother." I looked back and smiled, Aashif look like he was going to melt with confusion, his eyes looking up, shaking his head in a stunned manner. "Surprise-surprise bloody hell what next?" he said. I turned back and chuckled in agreement. "I know exactly how you feel mate," I murmured.

We got to the bottom of the stairs and turned left, Syrah opened a door and we followed through into the Dojo, almost feels like home, I said to myself. Syrah said let's get some training mats out so we can sit on them, so we did, placing them together, me and Sato still had our lovely smelly robes on, so we took them off and placed them next to us.

Sato removed his sword and placed it on top of his robe, I thought I would do the same, but as I reached for my sword; it obviously thought I needed it for something urgent, and unsheathed itself as it flew into my hand, it must have looked pretty impressive though; as Aashif's mouth was wide open his eyes fixed on my sword; he looked like a mannequin frozen, I looked at him then at my sword then back at him and gave him an unsure smile.

Then suddenly as if someone had shocked him back to life, "BLOODY HELL, did that sword just fly into your hand?"

I didn't know what to say, just smiled nervously. "You need to get to grips with that boy!" said Sato; I just nodded, then re-sheathed my sword and put it on top of my robe.

We all sat in a circle; Sato explained what was going to happen next.

"We will sit with our eyes closed; I will need Jacob and Aashif to focus on my voice, try not to think of anything but my voice, you will be ok Jasmine as you already have the gift and will connect with me quite easily, we are going to go back to the beginning, back to before our worlds changed, to the days of our ancestors." Aashif and I took one last nervous look at each other then closed our eyes and cleared our minds focusing on Sato's voice.

Sato continued; "I'm going to take you back to the history of my world through the eyes of my ancestors." As Sato was saying this I was starting to experience what I can only explain as a tipsy sensation, then in my mind it was like a cloud dissipating in front of me, and images appearing out of focus and distant at first, but then becoming more focused and closer until it was as though I was there actually there!

I could hear Sato as he said we were seeing his home world Soul through the eyes of his great ancestor Julius, who was Advisor and close friend to King Stephen. Julius was Asian in appearance tall and broad, and wore a fine white linen robe.

I was up high, on a plateau looking down at what looked like a huge canyon; it was lush and green, with beautiful lakes, with what I could only assume at this distance to be wildlife drinking from them.

This world was so lush and green, as far as the eye could see was woodland and jungle in the distance; I've never seen so many trees, this land was truly untouched; as I turned to the east, well I presume it was the east as it was still early and the sun wasn't quite at midday; I could see snow-topped mountains, hundreds of them seemed to go on forever, when I turned to the west; there was more woodland and jungle, but further still on the horizon I could just make out the ocean.

"When I turned south; I could see settlements, the buildings weren't like what I'm used to seeing back home; these where beautiful wooden hand-crafted, with big beautiful pillars; so many in fact they went on for miles, there were people coming and going, everyone seemed happy smiley faced."

I could see they were still building and working together as one; but I couldn't see any form off scaffolding for them to work from as they got higher! Then it became clear they didn't need it as before my very eyes, a huge beast! At first I thought it was an elephant, but this was not, this beast looked like a mammoth! It was huge, bigger than any elephant I'd ever seen at the zoo, it walked past me with a huge shaved tree trunk held on its massive tusks, I couldn't help but stare, it walked to the structure that was being built and lowered this huge tree trunk carefully onto two other upright tree trunks which had grooves cut into them, it managed to line them up perfectly, then a man raised his hands and out of a big wooden container appeared a long length of rope which seemed to fly through the air as he moved his hands pointing to the meeting point of the timbers the mammoth had just put into place, and with a twist of his wrist the rope started wrapping itself around the timbers binding them tight.

Then another man looked at a big vat which was over a fire, it was filled with molten tar; and as he turned his head back towards the timbers which had just been bound together, a perfectly spherical and quite big ball of molten tar appeared out of the vat and floated through the air, not a drop falling from it, and then seemed to spread itself over the rope binding the timbers.

They then repeated this on the other end of the timbered structure, it was like magic I thought, then I heard Sato's voice. Not magic; this is Telekinesis you are seeing; these people are using Telekinesis to build, they have the ability to move anything with their minds, depending on the strength of their minds and the size of the object, the stronger the mind muscle the bigger the object.

He went on to say; the people of your world had this ability to as you will see!

Then I heard a voice; "Julius, my old friend pleased you are here, just in time for the roof timbers to be placed." And with that there was an almighty whooshing sound, whoosh, whoosh, whoosh, it was coming from above; and so I looked up, and what I saw took my breath away, as flying towards the structure holding this huge timber roof frame in its talons was a huge dragon, a beautiful silver dragon, this creature was the size of a football pitch, and on its back was a man holding reins, it was almost like he was riding a horse. The dragon and its rider hovered over the structure, lining the two structures up, then slowly lowering it into place perfectly, the men I had seen earlier did their bit again binding the structures together with the rope and tar.

Dragons! I thought to myself, these are things of myth, and yet I'm looking at one! "Yes, you are, and your world had these to but your ancestors killed them, as you can see we live side by side with all the beasts of our world in harmony, as did your world once." I had to ask, What happened on our world to turn us to killers of such beautiful beasts?"

Sato replied, "You will see."

"Let's move on," Sato said; and with that, I could hear Julius's thoughts, "Where are you horse?" to which I heard, "I'm on my way." All I could think was; did he just talk to his horse through thought, and what's really doing my head in is, the horse answered. "Yes," said Sato, "this is Telepathy, the ability to communicate with the mind, and even beasts have minds, they may not have vocal cords as we do, but are intelligent and are able to communicate with their minds, like when you tell a dog to do something; it understands, but just can't answer you verbally; but with Telepathy you can hear its thought.

Then Julius's horse arrived, "Sorry I was hungry, there's some lovely fresh grass over there!" "You're hungry, you don't stop eating," Julius replied and chuckled. "Funny," replied the horse, "I'm a growing stallion don't forget," then burped! "Hop on, where are we off to?" said the horse. To which Julius replied, "I have to meet the king at the temple."

"So, you are visiting Earth today?" the horse replied. "Yes," said Julius, and off they rode, heading south.

As they rode through the settlement, I could see all the different buildings were all different shapes and sizes and the land seemed quite arid, with patches of green and trees scattered around; not as lush as when I was looking down in the canyon. There were children fetching water from water wells; but not in the manner you would expect of dropping a bucket on a rope into the well then winching it back up pulling on the rope; no this was quite spectacular to watch as the children had what looked like leather satchels on their backs; as they got to the well they would remove the satchel and drop it into the well with nothing attached to it, then after a moment or two, the satchel would appear up out of the well full of water and dripping wet, just floating in the air; then the children would turn their backs to it put their arms through the shoulder straps and off they would go.

The people here were making the most of what green fertile land they had; there were areas which almost looked like allotments with vegetation growing, with people tilling these small areas. The way in which they watered the area was again spectacular; there was a lady with her arms stretched out in front of her; her hands palms up and her fingers closed; above her was a huge ball of water which was gently floating over this patch of land; and when it was in position she opened her fingers and the water reacted separating into millions of droplets at which point she turned her hands palms down and slowly lowered her arms; as she did so the water droplets fell moistening the ground below just like rain.

There was a slightly bigger area being ploughed, and for once I was seeing something I recognised; an actual plough being pulled by two bulls with a man sat on one of the bulls back, the funny thing was after all I had seen I thought; why is he using the bulls to plough, he could probably do it himself in some fantastic way, then I heard Sato say; "Remember most animals are intelligent, and just like you and me they don't like to be idle, so we give them jobs to do and they appreciate it; you see those bulls need lush green grass and know so, so it's in their interest to help till the land and help keep it fertile, as I said before we work as one with all the beast, we help with their needs and they help with ours." "So why is the man sat on the bull's back?" I asked.

"Oh, probably just having a conversation," Sato replied.

I found myself having to ask; "So if you communicate with all the animals, what do you do for food, do you eat them?"

"God no, that would be like eating a friend, would you eat me?" Sato replied laughing. "So, what do you eat here?" "We live of the land and sea, we eat fish and vegetables, nuts, fruit and insects, we have all we need to survive."

"insects; what like ants and spiders?"

"Yes, full of protein, quite yummy." The thought made me feel sick.

"Let's get back to our journey, you have lots to see and not much time," Sato said.

As Julius rode, I couldn't help but think how the land and settlements resembled, photos I'd seen of places such as Egypt, the further he rode the dryer the land became, and the dwellings were no longer wooden structures but looked to be made of sand and stone, and painted in all manner of colours, bright vibrant, whites, pinks, yellows all sorts and some just left unpainted; just sand, they were quite beautiful, some of the people had henna markings painted on their faces, and seemed very happy as if in celebration.

Then in the distance I could see a tall pillar; it looked as though it was quite a size, and as we got nearer I could see this structure was massive, it must have been still a mile away, and looked huge; a huge stone pillar in the middle of a desert.

I asked Sato, "Is that the temple?" "Yes," he said. I asked, "Why is the temple in the middle of a desert, so far from the settlements?"

He just replied, "You will see." "Ok," I said.

Then I asked about the people we had not long passed. "Who were those people with their painted faces," I asked. Sato replied, "They are guardians of the temple, and as we passed they were wishing us safe passage, blessing us, they are celebrating our journey."

"Ok, is it a dangerous journey from here to the temple then?" I asked.

"No," Sato replied, "The journey from here to the temple has no threats, that isn't why they bless us; you see the temple is a portal to Earth, and it is the journey which begins once we get to the temple they are blessing; They are blessing our safe arrival on Earth and the journey once we are there, but at this time you will see there is no need for any blessing, it is totally safe, there are no threats using the portal or on Earth at this time; but in the years that came after, things would change."

Sato continued; "You will see everything; I might have to jump forward as time isn't on our side."

And with that we were at the temple, this structure was huge, it must have stood two or three hundred feet tall, and an area big enough for a thousand people easily.

It had one entrance that I could see, but what was incredible about this structure was the silver metallic which seemed to be part of it; the metallic looked almost like veins running around the stone structure but not static; it was moving pulsating and rotating around the temple as if it was alive!.

Then I remembered what Sato said about my sward; it was made of Udriume, a living organism which could connect to my thoughts.

"You are correct," said Sato, "It is Udriume, and it is alive; it works with the temple to conduct and direct our thoughts to the portal, when we want to go to Earth we think where it is we want to go, and the Udriume picks up our thoughts and opens the portal."

Let's move on, he said.

Julius was entering the portal, and inside waiting was the king and several other men and women, must have been around twenty in total.

"Hello Julius," said the king, "how are you my friend?"

The king was dark skinned, tall and very muscular, he had long hair which was tied back like dreadlocks, and he to wore fine white linen robs.

"I am very well thank you my king, I hope all is well with you?"

"Thank you, Julius all is very well life is wonderful and the people are happy."

"Shall we proceed?" said the king.

And with that they all stood within a metallic circle much as the changed did in my dream, closed their eyes and thought of Earth; as they did so the Udrium began to glow bright; and now seemed to spread evenly over the temple, then whoosh a beam of bright light almost like lightning shot down from the sky, and now I understood why they had built the temple so far away from the settlements; the shockwave was immense and would of surely caused damage to the settlements if closer.

Then after a minute or two the light was gone and with it; Julius the king and the followers.

Then I was back with Julius and experienced everything, as Julius had closed his eyes and thought of Earth, I could feel a sensation of static energy tingling all over his body then a bright light, then within a minute or two it had gone.

When he opened his eyes, he the king and the others were standing in another silver circle, in the middle of a desert, surrounded by dunes, and on one of the dunes were people, they were dressed in Bedouin clothing, covered from head to toe in white, they were a greeting party for the king and his followers.

As Julius turned to the king he said, "It's a hot one today." "Yes," replied the king and smiled. "I wonder how they have fared since our last visit?" Julius asked.

To which the king replied, "They have been progressing wonderfully so far, we shall soon see. "Can't keep them waiting on a hot day such as this," the king continued, "Here they come."

The people who were standing on the dune had started to make their way down to meet the king, bringing with them horses and wagons for transporting those that had arrived with the king and Julius.

These people were very pleased to see the king and his people, they were waving and smiling, and when they arrived one of the men leaped off his horse and landed just in front of the king with a big smile and in a loud happy voice said, "King Stephen my friend I hope you and yours are well," reached out his right hand and clasped the king's right forearm in greeting. The king smiled, and said; King Kiptorias, "We are all well thank you, how are you and yours?"

To which King Kiptorias replied; "We too are well my friend and made especially happy you are here. We have refreshments waiting for you and yours, we have been busy since your last visit, new homes for our people, harvests have been very fruitful, we can never thank you enough for your teachings, we are a happy people."

King Stephen replied, "We are one people living on two different worlds but the same, your success is our success and we will always be willing to help in any way we can."

They made their way to the settlement al-lizah, on the way I could see it was true with regards to the amazing creatures that once dwelled on earth, amongst the hundreds of Bedouin tents there where huge eagles, and many other creatures I didn't have a clue as to what they were, but one in particular that was quite a sight to see, it was like a huge cat of some sort, and just like a cat people were petting it, this cat was black silky looking and stood as tall as a man, but seemed as gentle as a kitten, children were laying on it playing with it, what an incredible site.

When they arrived there was a large area encircled by the beautiful colorful tents, at the center was a large fire surrounded with stones and rocks, and on the edge of the stones were hand-crafted mats laid out, on which everyone sat and shared food and drink ,then they traded goods, clothing, fruits of their labours, I could see they were all as one almost like family.

Then Sato said, "Let's move on, as you can see our peoples have total peace love and respect for each other, this was the same all over our worlds, we learned from each other and grew together, I will show you a visit two another side of your world and mine."

With that we jumped to another visit, but this place was colder than the last, it was lush and green full of woodland, and quite wet, raining and cloudy, with mist-covered fields, the settlement consisted of small wooden huts of which the people dwelled, when I turned their were huge stones in a big circle, and these stones had a silver circle in the centre just as the other portals did.

Then it hit me, I think I know of this place, I've never actually been here but had read about it. "Is this Stonehenge?" I asked Sato, to which he replied, "Yes, you are right, we are at Stonehenge." He went on to tell me that Stonehenge was quite a new found portal and that the people here were very spiritual, but young to the ways of our people and those of this world, but they were learning very fast, their minds are very receptive to Telepathy and Telekinesis, they are a very loving happy people. Just like the other visit, there where people waiting to greet them, with welcoming smiles and arms open wide, and with them were three-horned dragons and four beautiful white unicorns, again a creature of myth standing before me, I had no words, I was truly mesmerised.

Again, they all greeted each other, as though they were family, shared drink traded stories and shared new skills practicing Telepathy.

They sat round a big unlit bonfire, then one of the men, turned to the biggest dragon and using Telepathy, asked, could you light the fire please, the dragon almost smiled and replied certainly, then took a big breath opened its mouth and as it breathed out, fire emerged from it and easily ignited the bonfire, they all gave out a, ah lovely. Time to eat said one very big bearded man.

Then we moved on, but now we were back on soul, at the furthest region to the north, again this region was very green wooded and, in some parts, mountainous with beautiful freshwater streams running down supplying the settlements.

It was quite beautiful very picturesque, with all these wooden almost hut like dwellings scattered around these acres of beautiful green land, and the wonderful sound of the streams flowing with children playing in them and fetching water.

This place had such a peaceful calming feel to it, I could easily live in a place like this I thought to myself.

As I looked to the sky I could see a large flock of birds, must have been a hundred or so, as they got closer I could see they were hunting birds; osprey, and they all had fish in their talons still wriggling like crazy, they were heading directly for the village, as soon as the children saw them they stopped what they were doing and started to run towards them excitedly screaming and laughing.

The osprey continued towards the children, then landed directly where they were waiting excitedly, these birds of prey were as big as the children that awaited them, but the children had no fear of them and the osprey let them stroke them and cuddle them, the osprey actually looked like they wanted to be petted rolling their heads back revealing their necks and opening their wings wide, and letting the children stand underneath, then wrapping their wings around the children like a cuddle, this was so wonderful to watch these beautiful powerful birds of prey playing with these excited children, you could see they adored each other, just like a puppy and a young child, wonderful!

After a time the osprey started leaving and we all watched them fly into the distance and out of sight, when we looked back they had left the fish they had brought with them, and the villagers started to collect them up, working together they prepared the fish for supper.

Then I heard Sato's voice once again, "I hope from what you have seen you can tell that your world and mine were wonderful places to live, only love and respect for all living things and our surroundings."

I replied "Yes, wonderful, so different from the world I'm used to, what went wrong, if only we could turn back time."

"Yes, if only," said another voice, it was Aashif, I'd almost forgot he was seeing all of this wonder with me, his voice was full of sadness as he continued to speak, all I remember of my world as a small child was war and fear, for centuries my country has been at war at one time or another, and I was borne into it, even now my country is at war, I couldn't imagine it ever being like what I have just seen, what happened to make man so cruel?

He was so upset you could hear the pain in he's voice, I felt so sorry for him, the things he must have experienced so awful, no one should experience such things, especially a child.

Sato then said, "The people of my world are at this very moment battling the evil which has changed our worlds, they will never give up as long as they have breath, we hope someday our worlds will be at peace, as they once were, stay strong of heart and true in faith we will prevail; you are all still so young, I'm sure your generation will get to experience the peace and harmony that once existed, and rebuild this world together as one," to which Aashif replied; "I would give my life to enable mankind to live as you have shown me."

To which Sato replied, "Honourable words Aashif, let's hope it doesn't come to that."

"Yes, let's hope, for all our sakes," I said.

"We must continue," said Sato. "Yes let's," I replied.

With that we were back at the beautiful village by the side of a stream, I thought to myself how nice it was to be back here, I had to ask Sato, "What is this place called?"

Sato replied; "this is Polaria of the northern hemisphere Europhia."

Who leads the people of this village?" I asked.

Sato replied, the head of the village is Aleksander, he is a good man and cares for his people very well.

Sato went on to say, "You have seen the beauty of our worlds, now it is time for you to see the time of the change!"

Chapter 3

The change

We were now back were we started up high on the plateau, looking down at the canyon below; it was night and the moons lit the land with such a beautiful silvery-blue light, you could see for miles.

There was music and laughter, people dancing and singing, everyone was sharing food and drink, it seemed as though all the inhabitants of the settlement were in celebration, children and all.

I asked Sato, what's the celebration in aid of?

Sato replied; it is the new year, the people are celebrating life and giving thanks, as you can see every inhabitant off Engypt is here beast and all.

"Engypt?" I asked. "Yes," replied Sato, you are back at the home of King Stephen and Julius. Engypt is part of the southernmost continent of Afcania.

"I'm pleased you said, I was about to ask the name of the king's home. You beat me to it," I said.

Stephen and Julius were walking together, talking to their people and joining in with the fun, making faces at the children who would laugh and pull a face back then run away.

"It's been a wonderful year hasn't it?" said Stephen, to which Julius replied; "Yes it as indeed my old friend, our people are flourishing and our settlement with them, we trade daily with the surrounding settlements, we have become quite the hub of trade."

Julius continued, "Many of our people from surrounding settlements are moving here to be part of our growth, hence the daily building of new homes."

King Stephen replied, "It is wonderful to be part of something so exciting isn't it? Our people are so happy, everyone so willing to help in any way they can."

"Yes indeed it is, what we do here today will benefit many generations to come, you are a great king and have done so much for your people, they, or should I say we, love you, and this is another reason why your people come from all around to settle where you are."

King Stephen replied, "I love them all, including you my old friend," and smiled a huge smile.

King Stephen was a mountain of a man, strong as a bull yet gentle and loving beyond belief, a man of his word, a strong belief in honour and honesty and his people loved him for it.

As they continued to walk, the people around them were stopping and point to the sky, pointing to the south gasping in amazement, the king and Julius were so engrossed in conversation they hadn't notice as yet.

But then the gasps became louder; some turning to screams, as the screams became louder, the music stopped, the ground below their feet was shaking! A bright light lit the entire area, Stephen and Julius looked to the sky, they too were stunned at what they saw, a huge ball of fire hurtling through the night sky, a huge trail of embers behind it.

As it hurtled over their heads heading north, the sound was deafening, an ear-piercing scream and booming, everyone clasped their ears in pain, even those holding their children had to let go and cover their own ears as it was so loud and painful.

People collapsed to the ground in fear and pain, after a few moments the ball of fire had passed over and continued north, it seemed to be heading towards Polaria, the beautiful village we had seen.

And now the screams of fear were being added to with shouts of "Fire! Fire!" The embers which trailed the ball of fire were now falling to the ground igniting everything they touched, including the poor souls below.

For as far as the eye could see was a trail of fire, the people were panicked and running for their lives to find cover from the embers still falling, and the fire which was spreading rapidly amongst the timbered buildings.

King Stephen turned to Julius with a look of readiness, not fear or anguish, this man was a born king, ready and able to do whatever needed to be done to secure his people, his mental and physical strength was steadfast.

"We have to pull together stop the panic," the king said to Julius in a raised voice fighting to be heard over all the noise.

Julius quickly agreed, "You will need to speak to the people at once, my king."

"Yes," said King Stephen, with that he surveyed the situation, he knew what had to be done in an instant, and so using Telepathy, he communicated with his people; "My people hear me, we have to have calm, we can't fight this with panic, we have to work as one."

Instantly the people heard his words and stopped running around like headless chickens, his words helped them to stop and think logically, he had never failed them, and they trusted him implicitly.

King Stephen continued; "We have to work in groups using our minds, children could you please stop the fire which is raining down, hold it above, men we need to move the burning buildings away from those that are not burning, place the burning timbers together in one pile, women can you please fetch water so we can extinguish the flames."

And with that the children seemed to no longer be fearful, not even the youngest was afraid, they had heard their king's words and acted immediately, thousands of them as if connected they simultaneously looked to the burning embers, raised their hands and opened their fingers, the embers stopped falling, they were being held exact no movement, just hanging in the sky.

Whilst the children held the embers above, thousands of men moved as close to the burning buildings as they dare, the heat was intense, the noise of fire was incredible, timbers cracking and exploding with the intense heat shooting shards towards the men, but they did not falter they stood fast, each choosing a blazing building and began to focus on it intently, they raised their arms out to the side then above their heads fingers open then after a moment began to slowly close their fingers, as they did the burning buildings started to make even louder cracking sounds, timbers were being scrunched up like paper snapping and exploding as they did so… I could see this was no easy task, as the men were grimacing teeth clenching, every muscle tensed and straining, they were moaning intently, they continued to close their fingers until they were clenched fists, although still burning the buildings had been completely crushed, then men lowered their clench fists to their chests and began to push their arms forward, as they did so the burning remains would slide ahead of them until their arms were fully extended, so now they had to step forward almost as if they were pushing a cart, and as they did so the still burning remains would slide ahead of them.

They did this until all the burning debris collided together to form one massive pile, a huge mile-circumference bonfire, then the men could relax for a moment.

While the men had been compressing the burning buildings into one manageable pile, the women had begun gathering water from wells, streams, and even drew moisture out of the sky above to form droplets and combined them, it was an amazing site to behold, there was water literally being pulled from the ground, any form of moisture was gathered to form a huge floating lake, and what I mean by floating, it was actually airborne, a huge lake of water stretching for at least two miles being magically guided through the air by all of the women, thousands of them working together their arms held high palms of their hands facing up fingers together, again this was not easy, and the strain was beginning to show.

Now they had to move this vastness of water high enough above the still burning embers of which the children were still holding in place, some of the younger children were now starting to flag and couldn't continue, they had become exhausted and fell to the ground and along with them hundreds of burning embers, just missing the men below who had cleared the burning buildings.

Now the men who had put so much energy into making the burning buildings safe had to help the children, they couldn't risk the embers falling again.

The women now had the expanse of water placed over the entire area, they now prepared to release it, but they couldn't just drop it in one mass, as the weight of all this water would be like a tsunami hitting land, totally devastating to the entire settlement and its population of thousands.

What they actually did was to open their fingers and with this motion the water separated into large droplets, they then turned their hands palms down and lowered their arms, the water fell as if a storm had started but without the wind, they were successful, the water extinguished the embers and burning timbers.

The children and men still focused on the embers, although no longer burning, they appeared to be stone and rock and would cause massive damage and death if just released, so had to be lowered cautiously to the ground.

They had been successful, and everyone sighed in relief and exhaustion, but! Just as everyone began to feel a little ease, there was an almighty flash of light and deafening boom the ground shook like an earthquake, everyone was screaming and yelling with pure fear clinging to one and other crying fearing the end was near. after a few moments the flash of light and boom disappeared, and the ground no longer shook.

The king and Julius quickly drew their attention to the point of impact and looked to the north were the explosion had come from.

The king with sunken heart murmured, "My god, that's Polaria, then both men were hit like a hammer with thoughts of their wives and children.

To which they both turned in despair, and began to look for their loved ones, luckily their families had been together preparing themselves for the evenings celebrations at King Stephan's home, which was untouched by the fire, but filled with smoke, that was where they decided to look first in the hope their families would still be there unharmed.

When Stephen and Julius entered the building they could barely see through the poor light and choking smoke, and could just make out there was a great amount of damage, timber supports had been torn apart by the force of the earthquake and lay in pieces blocking their paths, it would be hard to navigate these obstacles due to the thickness of the smoke, they moved cautiously unsure the structure wouldn't collapse on them, they dare not attempt to move anything, as the entire structure had been weakened, they managed to clamber over and under the fallen debris, and eventually found themselves in the main hall at the foot of the staircase which had in parts collapsed.

Unsure where to search first, Stephen called out to his wife and children; "NADIA, LUCAS, MAY!!" Julius looked on, praying they would answer, it was hard to hear with the noise from outside and the building creaking, they heard no response.

Then Julius shouted at the top of his voice starting to despair; "LAILA, OMAR, LIZET, please god let them answer," he said.

Still no answer!

Julius said, they must be here, maybe they can't hear us.

Then a voice in Julius's head, it was his wife, "Laila, we can hear you." "We are upstairs in May's bedroom with the children," then he could see through Laila's eyes they were all huddled together, crying with fear to scared to move.

Julius quickly replied; "It's ok, Stephen is with me, we are coming to get you."

Stephen focused on his wife, Nadia, "We are here, stay where you are, we will be with you soon."

Stephen and Julius looked to the staircase, which was partly collapsed, they knew they couldn't get up the stairs on foot;

they blocked any Telepathic ability not wanting to worry their families should they be listening in.

Quick thinking as ever, King Stephen said; "We need to get up there, but there is no way to clime the staircase; we need to find something to stand on, use it to levitate our way up, like we did as children."

Julius replied, "That's a good idea, just need something suitable to stand on."

With that Stephen spotted a broken circular table, so he picked it up, and snapped off the one leg that was still on it, this will do fine he said!

Julius noticed a floorboard that had been broken by a support beam falling on it, so he focused on what was left of the board using his mind; he managed to pull it away nails and all, then he removed the nails, "Yes that will do fine," he said.

"We will have to go one at a time," said Stephen. "I'll go first," he continued, and with that he stood on the tabletop, and with his arms slightly open began to focus on the tabletop, picturing it in his mind's eye leaving the ground, and sure enough it did, as it lifted a couple of inches he became a little unstable, opening his arms to regain balance and said; "I remember it being a lot simpler than this," to which Julius replied; "yes," having the same issue and trying to regain balance.

"We don't have time for this," said Stephen and with that placed his hands on the exterior wall and started to slowly guide himself as the tabletop glided up the broken staircase; he looked very unstable, but making good progress.

Julius used much the same method, it was a slow process, but they finally made it to the top of the stairs onto the landing where they gently lowered themselves not wanting to put any sudden pressure on the supporting timbers.

It was a mess; the roof supports had given way and parts of the roof had collapsed inwardly blocking their path to may's bedroom.

Julius said; "Now we are at the top of the building it should be safe for us to move these roof timbers out of the way, shouldn't it?"

To which Stephen replied, "I hope so, there isn't much left of the roof so the building shouldn't collapse as long as we take care."

With that Julius bent his right arm open hand fingers out straight, and started to move his arm forward and up very slowly, as he did so the fallen roof-timbers and tiles started to shift, the higher he lifted his hand the higher the debris were lifted, he continued cautiously until the debris were at a height that they could get under.

Julius then said, you go first, so with that Stephen walked slowly crouching under the hovering timbers, and when he was clear he turned to Julius and waved his hand beckoning him. Julius then followed still focusing intently, raising his hand as high as he could above his head as he walked under the timbers, finally approaching the end he had to turn keeping his hand held high, then slowly walk backwards until clear, then ever so slowly lowered the timbers back down on to the landing.

They could now get to May's bedroom, when they opened the door, they found waiting for them, still huddled together, their families.

All this time they had not moved, huddled together in fear the building would collapse on them, they dare not move a muscle, both Laila and Nadia trying their best to reassure their children, "It's going to be ok, your fathers are on their way to get us," the children took solace in their mothers words.

When the children saw their fathers standing there at the door, their first instinct was to jump up and run towards them, but before they could, King Stephen put his hand out and said, "Stop! Don't move we will come to you we can't have any sudden movements the building isn't very stable," and gave a reassuring smile as best he could.

With that Stephen and Julius moved slowly forward as the floor creaked and cracked, finally they reached them, they all stood and embraced so warmly, "Thank god your all ok," said Stephen holding his wife and children so tightly.

Julius's son Omar, said; "It's so good to see you daddy," with tears in his eyes, "I love you." "I love you too, all of you, now let's get you out of here," replied Julius and smiled at his wife.

With that Stephen said; "We are going to have to get something you can sit on so we can levitate it out of the windows with you on it one by one."

Julius found a chair, "This should do nicely," he said.

Then a very young voice said, "We don't need the chair daddy I can do it, it was little May, she was the youngest at only eight years of age.

Stephen's wife Nadia asked May, "What do you mean, May?" Sweet little May replied, "I can do it mummy, I can lift you out and down to the ground without the chair, look," she said, and with that stared at her mother and raised her head, as she did so her mother began to levitate.

With shock Nadia said, "Stop please," May did as her mother asked and lowered her gently down.

Everyone in the room was shocked, no one had ever been able to levitate another human being or themselves, and yet little May could!!

After everyone had stopped looking at each other in disbelief, Julius said; "It's a miracle, little May's control of Telekinesis is superior to anyone I have ever seen, how can this be?"

King Stephen replied; "I don't know, I didn't know she could," then he turned to May and asked; "Are you sure you are strong enough to move us all?"

May replied; "Yes, I'm sure daddy." "Have you done this before?" asked her mother Nadia. "No," replied May, "but I know I can do it."

"It's too risky," Nadia said to Stephen. "If she truly believes she can do it, we should at least let her try, she did lift you with ease, replied Stephen.

Then Stephen turned to May; "Ok May, we will start with Lizet as she is smallest, you can get her to safety first ok, but if you start to struggle bring her back and stop, and I will use the chair, ok?!" "Daddy, I can take everyone with me at once," May replied and continued; "There is a hole in the roof, I can get us all out through that." Just as May finished talking the building seemed to shift, it seemed they didn't have to long left; the building was becoming more unstable and they had to make a quick decision!!

May really believed she could get everyone to safety, and so this young girl who looked just as any other eight-year-old said; "Please trust me, I know I can do this, everyone put one hand on me."

With that everyone looked at each other unsurely, but as the building started to shift further, they realised they had to take the risk and have faith in little May.

Then May's brother Lucas said, "I believe in you May, and placed his hand on her shoulder.

Everyone else looked at each other, gave each other a nervous smile, then one by one turned to May saying, I believe in you May, and placed a hand on her.

May smiled a cheeky smile and said, "Hold tight." With that everyone held the hand of the one next to them forming a circle around May.

May looked to the hole in the roof and suddenly quicker than expected everyone's feet had left the ground, they headed up through the hole and out to safety, little May was giggling excitedly as she started to go faster, the wind in her face spurring her on faster and faster they flew over the settlement, a few people below and only a few witnessed as most were looking or helping to look for loved ones lost in all the panic of the fire.

Those that did witness this amazing feat couldn't help but stop and gaze in wonderment, never before has a human levitated without being sat or stood on something to lift them, let alone a group of eight.

More and more people were becoming aware of this amazing feat as others looked to the sky and caught their attention.

Julius, Stephen, Laila, Lizet, Nadia, Omar and Lucas; it could be said were quite excited too, with screams of; "Oh my god, this isn't happening, you're going to fast, I'm going to be sick from one or other."

Then it was time for them to return home back to the settlement, the king and Julius had issues of extreme importance to attend to, such as the devastation and loss of life within their community, the king asked may to take them home.

May knew her father was a very important man with a great many things to do and so immediately turned and returned home, as they flew over the settlement, they could see the vastness of the damage, it was devastating.

As they returned home there were many people waiting for the king, they didn't know what to do next, many had lost their homes, and some had lost loved ones, they looked to the king for guidance.

With a heavy heart the king spoke to his people as one using his mind.

They could instantly feel his deep heart-wrenching sadness just as he could feel theirs, it was almost overwhelming for him feeling so much pain, he could feel each person's loss.

But he had to be strong for his people, he had to show resolve, before him stood people with injuries that needed to be seen by healers urgently, but wanted to see their king first, that was the strength and loyalty of these people.

King Stephen started to speak; "What we have suffered this night as affected us all, we all feel each other's pain and will share the load and support each other as one family, we have lost family and friends, my words will not ease your pain, but remember you are not alone, we will never forget those we have lost they may not be with us in body, but will always remain in our hearts, tonight we mourn and say farewell, for tomorrow the sun brings a new day, a day to rebuild, we have to be strong, those we have lost wouldn't want it any other way."

With that the people agreed and worked through the night together lovingly laying their dead to rest and gave thanks for the lives they had led with songs of remembrance by candlelight; when the ceremony had finished those who had lost their homes were given shelter by their neighbors and family.

King Stephen and his family stayed with Julius's family, when morning broke Laila had prepared a porridge and fruit breakfast trying to continue with life as best she knew how, it was a solemn morning.

One by one they woke washed and dressed, barely a word was spoken apart from, "Morning."

They sat together at the table, which Laila had set for breakfast, none of them had an appetite for food, but out of respect for Laila's efforts they each had a small bowl of porridge and a piece of fruit.

When they had finished eating, King Stephen turned his attention to the children, he could see they were trying to be brave, holding back tears, memories of friends they had lost heavy in their hearts.

King Stephen said to the children; "If you feel the need to cry then do so, don't hold back your sorrow it will not help you move on, so let it out my children, it will take time to recover from the terrible events of last night, we are your parents and love you very-very much and will always understand, you can talk to us whenever you feel the need to get things off your chests."

With that Lucas asked; "Why did this happen father?" to which the king could only take Lukas's hand to comfort him and say; "I don't know my boy, it was a terrible, terrible thing, but we will recover I promise you, we will try our best to stop anything like this ever happening again, starting with the way we build our dwellings, the fire spread so fast I believe because of our use of timber and thatch for roofing, I will be speaking with our best architects to ensure we no longer build like this."

"In fact," the king continued, and turned to Julius saying, "would you agree Julius it is time our sons learned how communities are built, and the only way to do this is to assist you in overseeing the rebuilding processes?"

To which Julius replied; "I do indeed my king, they are young men now and as men they have responsibilities, I couldn't think of a better way for them to learn!"

With that the king replied; "It's settled then, Lucas and Omar will be your students, and I trust you will teach them well while I'm gone."

"While you're gone?" replied Julius.

"Yes," replied the king, "whatever it was in the night sky that caused this catastrophe, continued north and looked to impact near Polaria, I fear there may be many casualties, and as king it's my duty to assist in any way possible, so I intend to form a party of volunteers five hundred strong, Polaria is a big region and so I need as many men and healers as we can spare, and so my old friend I entrust to you the rebuilding of our once great home, and I'm sure with the help of these two such strong intelligent young men," and placed his left arm across Omar and Lucas's shoulders, "You will be very successful."

Lucas and Omar looked at each other and smiled now full of pride, they would be helping to rebuild Engypt, their beloved home they relished the responsibility they would be men just as their fathers.

We will indeed, Julius replied and smiled at the two young men.

"Before I make arrangements and speak with our people there is one thing that has left me in disbelief, although wonderful," said Stephen. "My darling beautiful daughter May" and looked at her with such love.

"Yes father?" she replied with a beautiful heart melting smile. "What you did last night, your ability was amazing a true gift from God, you said you had never done that before, how did you know you could lift us with you?"

May replied, "I don't know father, I can't explain it, I just knew I had to."

"Do you think it possible you could do it again?" asked her father.

"Easily, I found it so easy to do, I'm sure I could go further and faster if I needed."

"What are you thinking?" said the king's wife Nadia.

"Nothing for the moment I have to look into something first, I want to see if any other children among us can do as May did!"

"And why would you want to do that?" Nadia replied.

To which King Stephen replied with total honesty, "I know it is much to ask; but the people of Polaria may have experienced a catastrophic event last night and need our assistance, it will take days to get to them on foot, and they may not have days!"

"So, you are thinking, maybe to use anyone who as May's abilities to transport you there?" said Julius's wife Laila.

"Yes," said the king, "We don't have enough dragons to transport five hundred people in one journey, last night May transported seven of us to safety easily, so we would need seventy-two persons with the same abilities to transport all five hundred in one journey. The Dragons will transport any tools and provisions, we will have to build containers for them to carry. I know it's a big thing to ask, but that is what I intend to do, ask the people."

Then Laila asked the children to leave the room, she had to speak with the king and Julius.

Once the children left the room Laila began to explain. "After last night I had visions of Polaria, I found them very disturbing! I've never experienced visions such as these." "In which way disturbing?" asked Nadia.

"I can't make sense of them even now, they were very fast glimpses all I remember is the ground was covered in black thick ash, then flashes of people also covered in this thick ash, but, it wasn't like the ash was loose on their bodies and could be brushed off, no, this was more as though it was part of them, it was becoming thick and shiny black, the people themselves looked to be changing somehow, all I know for sure is these beings weren't good, I could see blood, blood they had spilled, please my King don't go to Polaria, I fear you may be in danger if you do."

The king looked to his wife and said, "What kind of king would I be if I left our people to suffer and die, I have to go, it is my duty!"

Nadia looked at him, knowing she could never change his mind, he cared too much for his people and she knew he would always put them before himself.

All she could say in reply was; "I know my love, but if there is danger such as Laila as said then you must return immediately for the sake of your people here."

"I will, I promise if there is as Laila as seen we will flee and return."

Julius felt he should be with the king at his side, but before he could say the king said; "No, Julius I know you my old friend, and if you wasn't needed here I would gladly have you at my side, but you have many duties here to attend too, I'm sorry, you must stay, and in light of Laila's vision I feel you should also start to build a defensive wall at the neck off the canyon, which would ensure no passageway to any foe, no chance of reaching us up here on the plateau.

Julius replied; "I understand, I will have a thousand men, and our best stonemasons make an immediate start once you have left."

King Stephen then turned to his wife; "My love I think it is time to speak with our people," and held out his hand, which she held so tight, and together they walked out to meet their people, Julius and his wife closely followed.

The people were already clearing the streets of debris and eager to rebuild.

King Stephen Telepathically connected with all his people and explained what was going to happen next, he explained how he wanted the architects to use brick stone and slate to rebuild Engypt so no more buildings that would catch fire so fast, and that with time they would be replacing every building with this new method.

He also made his people aware there was going to be a defensive wall built, and in doing so had to tell them the truth of what Laila had seen, he didn't believe in hiding things from his people and that is why they trusted him so.

He continued to inform them of his plans to help the people of Polaria and that he would be leaving that evening, and required five hundred volunteers, that must be very skilled at Telekinesis, to which over half the population offered assistance; as they had family or friends who lived there.

The king thought of the possible dangers and said; "it is wonderful so many of you are so willing to offer your assistance, but there may be dangers ahead of us, so I have to carefully consider those that may come, I think it best four hundred of you must be men, single with no children.

As for the hundred healers, male or female, but again have no children.

He then asked those who still volunteered to congregate at the head of the plateau, where Julius would select the five hundred.

The king then moved to the subject of what some may have seen in the night to which he referred his daughters ability to levitate herself and others, and asked; "Is there anyone amongst you which as the same abilities, to which there were gasps, as hundreds of little hands went up simultaneously, all children the age of ten and younger.

The king was stunned, amazed, and thought to himself, as the generations grow so do their abilities, what gifts, a blessing from god.

As there were so many the king said "Can only those who are eight years and above keep your hands up please."

And still there must have been around one hundred.

And now the king asked those children who still had their hands up, if they could levitate themselves and their parents to where he stood on the plateau as fast as they could, he wanted to see if they were strong enough and fast enough for this journey.

Many a parent was hesitant, totally unaware that the children had this gift, but faith in their children steadied them, and within moments groups of children and their parents were speeding through the air over the heads of fellow citizens, who stood a gasp watching, some saying "Oh wow I wish I could do that!" then a loud applause, and laughter, excitement was heard.

No one here was envious no such thing existed here these people applauded and were happy and excited for the children, what a gift they had.

When the last of the children and their families had landed the king explained he would only be needing seventy-two of the children, and that they would have to be the strongest among them, and so he would have to test their strength to make sure they would make the journey.

But he also asked the children if they would be willing to go on this mission of rescue, if selected, to which they all answered yes, they would.

So, then he asked the children's parents if they would be willing to let their children undertake such a journey, to which the answer was a resounding yes.

One of the parents approached the king, "We are all one people, it is our duty to care for one and other, I would be proud for my son to be chosen," he said as he looked at his young son smiling so proudly.

The king now set a test for the children, each child would have to levitate themselves and seven of the biggest men the king could find from where they stood at the head of the plateau to the far edge of Engypt and back, not forgetting this settlement was huge five miles long, it was big enough to be classed as a city. Oh, and they had to do this simultaneously.

The children now stood in a row facing south, along with them each had seven very nervous muscular men, each man placed a hand on the child they had been grouped with.

One man in particular looked at the child he would be levitating with and smiled so nervously that the child felt he had to console him, and asked his name, to which he replied nervously "I'm John." "Hello John, I'm Joshua, pleased to meet you, don't be nervous, as long as you are touching me you will be fine," he said and smiled. John replied, what if I lose my grip, my hands are sweating, Joshua looked at John gave him a big cheeky grin shook his head and said; "You don't want to lose your grip."

Now it was time, the king was connected to the children and those that were with them Telepathically, he now said to the scared-looking giant-sized men, "Keep one hand on the child and your other hand on the person next to you, to form a circle around the child, Children when I say go, you fly as fast as you possibly can, gentlemen hold tight."

With that, the children were looking at each other excitedly, some rubbing their hands as they looked at each other smiling, some running on the spot as fast as they could trying to psych themselves up, others standing legs slightly bent one slightly ahead of the other as if to start a race.

These children thought this was great fun, not so sure about the men though…

As the king counted down 10…9…8…7…6…5… the men were looking around as if looking for someone to help them out of this situation, one man was near to tears this man-mountain full of muscle, ready to cry…4…3…another saying, I don't think I…2 can do…1…GO this, as he shot of into the sky.

As the groups of children and men launched with great speed upward then south, there were these most unusual sounds, that seemed to come from the men, some were very squeaky and could be heard by all in close vicinity, which caused some to laugh out loud, the groups seemed to continue to accelerate some were going so fast it was barely possible to see them as they flew overhead, but the screams of the men could be heard clearly as they passed over, somewhere very deep sounding, and others quite a lot higher, more what you would expect of a lady.

In fact, some people could be heard, quite concerned, saying what on Soul was that?

This was an amazing sight to see, it had only been about ten minutes and several of the groups had reached the turnaround point and were now heading back, and in the lead was young Joshua who had the man mountain John latched to his right arm, screaming please stop, please stop, and on his left he had another gentleman not quite as big as john but still a size, who was laughing uncontrollably, tears in his eyes and barely able to breath he was laughing so hard.

All this just made young Joshua go faster and faster while smiling from ear to ear.

He was closely followed by a girl who seemed to be gaining on him at quite a rate, as they were about a mile from the finish they were nearly neck and neck, the young girl was very determined and as they reached the last hundred yards she pushed forward, but Joshua didn't give in, and with one last effort clenched his fist using every ounce of energy to push into the lead by a shoulder just as they reached the end and won.

The crowd below were ecstatically cheering and clapping, extremely thankful they had returned safely.

He then lowered his group to the ground, as the men finally touched solid ground they let go, their legs like jelly, barely able to stand, poor John collapsed to the ground kissing the soil and murmuring; "Solid ground thank god, I didn't think I was going to make it, it's good to be back."

The other gentleman that young Joshua had on his left arm was still laughing hysterically, and slowly crawled over to John saying, "I'm so glad I had you in my group, you totally took my mind off things, I've never heard a man as big as you make sounds like you can, what's your name big man?"

"John," he replied as he started to laugh, "to be honest I didn't know I could make sounds like that myself," and reached out his hand, "What's your name friend?" "My name is Samuel, nice to meet you John," they shook hands and just sat there laughing.

Next to return was the young girl who had so nearly beaten Joshua, as soon as she had lowered her group safely, Joshua ran over to congratulate her and her group, "That was close, you nearly had us," he said, "I'm Joshua, what is your name?" to which the young girl replied, "My name is Rose, yes it was very close you were just too fast, but it was great fun wasn't it?" "Yes, fantastic," Joshua replied.

After a time, all the groups had returned and the seventy-two had earned their places for the journey to Polaria.

The king told the children to go home and rest, they had a long journey ahead of them, he said the same to the men who would be going with them who all looked quite worse for wear and needed to rest after their mind-blowing experience.

While the children had been running the race, Julius had commissioned the carpenters to build three huge containers to transport provisions to Polaria, these would have to be carried by three silver dragons who had already arrived to assist the king.

The king was waiting for the containers to be completed before he could leave, and so was spending time with he's family.

Julius was having the provisions readied and stored waiting for the containers to be completed, once he had finished making sure all was in order, he met with the architects and stonemasons to ensure the building of the defensive wall would commence as soon as the king had left.

The architects had never been ask to design a defensive wall, defenses had never been required on Soul, this planet was a world of peace, and so the architects grew concerned they wouldn't have the knowledge to build a wall strong enough to withstand an attack, they had no idea of war and what type of weapons could be used in an attempt to breach such a wall.

Julius also informed them this wall would have to be manned night and day, and so would need a way to access the top of it, and would require cover for those manning it, it would also require strong doors which could be opened to trade, but withstand attack when closed.

One of the architects, Solomon was his name, he was one of the most inventive architects Engypt had, he stepped forward and proceeded to say; "This will be a true challenge and I happily accept."

He continued; "The neck of the canyon spans one hundred and twenty feet, and for this wall to be defensive it would need to be at least fifty feet tall, its foundations alone would need to be thirteen feet in depth, how long do we have?"

Julius replied; "the king said we should commence building as soon as he has left for Polaria, but didn't give a time scale for completion, I would presume as quickly as possible, how long would you say it will take to build something of this magnitude?"

Solomon replied; "How many men will we have, we will need stonemasons, carpenters, and blacksmiths, many of each!"

"I told the king I would have a thousand men working on this," Julius replied.

"That's a good number of men and should enable us to complete, hmm, all going well in around a month!" Solomon replied.

Julius was happy with this, he would have liked sooner but he knew this was going to be a real challenge, he said he would muster the thousand men and meet Solomon at the site of the wall after the king had left.

As he left the meeting, the head carpenter, Luke, Telepathically contacted him to let him know that the containers had been completed and waiting to be filled.

Julius then contacted the sixty or so people that he had given the task of loading the containers, letting them know it was time for them to start loading, which they immediately started.

As Julius continued back to see the king before he left, he checked in with the architects that had been tasked with rebuilding Engypt, he wanted to ensure they understood there would be no thatch used building the new homes, and that the walls would now have to be constructed of brick and stone.

The architects where already ahead of him and had already started designing a kiln for making the bricks that would be used.

In a way the rebuilding was helping the population recover from the catastrophe that had only happened the night before, they were all too busy now, concentrating on the tasks each had been set, every man, woman and child had a task of some sort, even if it was as simple as fetching water for all those doing the heavy tiring jobs, even using Telekinesis was a tiring thing to do, they were once again a huge unit working as one and happy in their labours.

Julius had now returned to his home where the king and his family were preparing for the king to leave.

As Julius entered, he said hello to everyone, kissed his wife and children, then turned to King Stephen and informed him that all was going well, the architects were all well on their way with the new designs for rebuilding Engypt and that the defensive wall would commence as soon as the King had left.

Julius continued; "The architect Solomon will be in charge of the wall construction and said that with the men we have available he hoped it would be completed in around a month."

The King replied: "That's great news but in all honesty, I hope it isn't actually needed."

"Yes indeed," replied Julius.

He then continued to inform the king the containers were complete and being loaded as they spoke.

Then from outside was a loud whooshing sound followed by a loud thudding, it was Egum, a silver dragon, not just any dragon, Egum was the largest dragon in the land and was leader to all the great silver dragons, when he had heard of the kings mission he didn't hesitate to offer his assistance. In fact, so close was the relationship between the dragons and the people of Engypt that his entire flight; which is the name for a family of dragons as a group, wanted to help so badly, not only with the king's mission but also help in any way they could to rebuild Engypt.

Along with Egum was his mate Symphet and their son Saturn, Egum's two brothers Bingwen and Deming, who along with them came their mates and their sons; Ai, the mate of Bingwen and mother of their son Gang, then there was Lifen, mate to Deming and mother to their son Ling.

As soon as the king and Julius heard the thudding sound outside they knew it was Egum and rushed out to greet him and his family, followed very closely by Omar, Lizet, Lucas, and little May, the children were so excited to see Egum, and Egum was so relieved to see their happy smiling faces.

As the children ran outside, quickly overtaking their fathers shouting Egum's name, he lowered his head to the ground and using Telepathy, said, "Hello children I am so pleased to see you, I hear that you little may can fly like me!"

"Yes, it's amazing, feel so free, the world looks so beautiful from above, are you here to help with our Mission to Polaria?"

"We are indeed, and you will be able to show me how well you can fly," Egum replied.

As for you two young men, Lucas and Omar, you will have to keep my nephews company, see to it they actually do some work! And not just play all day," Egum said as he looked to the right and sure enough on the edge of the plateau were these two young silver dragons; Gang and Ling running and jumping around grabbing each other's tails and saying your it. When the children saw this, they all laughed as did all the other children that were watching this spectacle.

"Sorry boys, you may have your work cut out for you with those two unfortunately," Egum chuckled.

"Don't worry, I'm sure they will be fine," said Lucas with a mischievous smile.

Then the king received a message Telepathically, telling him that the provisions had been stored safely in the containers and ready to take with him as soon as he was ready.

The time had passed quickly, the sun was now at three o'clock, although the days were long on Soul at this time of year as it was summer and the sun wouldn't set till at least nine of an evening, the king knew they would have to leave within the hour.

The journey would take at least a day even though they would be flying, they would need to stop at some point to rest the children and dragons, everyone would need to sleep at some point, so they would need to find somewhere to stop and make camp, and this would add to the time, of which the king believed the people of Polaria may not have if they had received the full force of the impact.

But even so he was not willing to risk the wellbeing of the children who would be transporting so many men, they only ever levitated the distance of the test he had set, and so the distance they could actually reach via levitation was quite unsure, especially at speed and carrying the weight of seven grown men.

With this in mind; the king decided he would have to make arrangements for a slight detour to the north-east, to a place called Bulgan, there they would be able to rest eat and sleep, if only for a few hours.

So, the king focused on the leader of Bulgan a good kind man called Bogumill.

Using Telepathy, the king spoke with Bogumill, Bogumill and his people were unaware of the king's situation and that of Polaria. Bulgan is set on low-lying land surrounded by mountains like a bowl and so obscured the lands around them, on that fateful night he and his people had been celebrating the new year just as the people of Engypt and Polaria had been, they had seen the ball of fire plunging through the night's sky, but were unaware of the trail devastation that lay in its wake, they had seen the bright light of its impact and felt the earth shake which also caused them structural damage to many properties and injuries to those inside, and so just as the king and his people they too were dealing with wounded citizens and repairs to their properties.

The king felt he had to help, to which Bogumill informed the king, he and his people had everything under control and didn't wish to concern the king.

The king then informed Bogumill of what had happened to the people of Engypt, and of his worries for the people of Polaria, how that he was sure that the ball of fire had, if not impacted Polaria directly then it was very close and he was sure they needed his help. He also continued to tell how he had been trying to contact Aleksander and his people via Telepathy but was unable to connect as though something blocked them.

To this terrible news Bogumill, with saddened heart offered assistance saying; My king this news saddens me, I would like to offer our assistance, I'm sure I can find many men to volunteer and assist you and yours.

The King was very happy for Bogumill's offer of assistance and replied; " I thank you my friend, but this journey may have dangers, I do not wish for anyone more than those I already have to be possibly risking their lives, if anything were to happen to your people I would never forgive myself, but I truly appreciate your offer, but would be truly thankful if me and those who follow me might find a place to camp, eat, rest and sleep."

To which Bogumill replied; "That goes without question my king, our door is always open to our king, when you arrive may we talk more of these dangers you speak?"

"Yes, once again thank you, all going well we should see you by sunset," replied the King.

Bogumill wished the king a safe journey and returned to his people to inform them of the king's arrival.

The king called a meeting of all those that would be journeying with him to discuss his travel plan.

When the five hundred and seventy-two strong party had arrived, the king informed them that they would be leaving within the hour, he continued he knew it was a long journey to much to ask it be made in one attempt, and that he had arranged for them to rest mid-journey at the settlement of Bulgan, where they would stay the night and continue on to Polaria at first sun.

This news was music to their ears, many of the men going on this mission had barely recovered from the morning's events and weren't really looking forward to the whole flying experience again, but knew it was the only way, so a respite would be so very welcome.

John the big man that would be traveling with Joshua said; "Thank the Lord for that! Don't think I could hold on the whole distance," to which Samuel, the man who found John hysterically funny, replied; "Yes I'll be pleased of a break from all your screaming and crying, don't get me wrong, I love a good laugh but don't enjoy earache," and began to laugh, as did John, saying; "You're a cheeky one, you."

The king continued, "Egum, Symphet and Saturn have kindly offered to accompany us and carry the provisions," the crowd cheered and clapped, the king continued, "Bingwen and Deming have said that they will help with the defensive wall," again the crowd cheered and clapped.

Again, the king continued; "Ai and Lifen, have said that they will help rebuild Engypt, along with their sons Gang and Ling," again the crowd cheered and clapped. "That is if Gang and Ling can break away from their playtime," the King continued sarcastically, the crowd laughed, Gang and Ling were still running around, jumping flying back and forth chasing each other all over the place, until they heard what the king said, at which they stopped what it was they were doing, looked at each other shrugged, then looked to the crowed feeling a little embarrassed smiled pushed out their chests and tried their best to pay attention.

The king continued to confirm that Julius would be staying to oversee the restoration and everyday care of Engypt and its people, the people were very happy with this news, as Julius like the king was a much loved and respected man.

With that it was now time the king and his party departed, and so said for them to say their farewells and be readied, the king shook Julius's hand and wished him good luck, Julius in turn wished the king a safe journey and to return swiftly and safely.

The king turned to his wife and family, kissed them and told them he loved them very much, then turned to little May and asked if she was ready, to which she replied; "Yes," and took her father's hand.

Together they walked to the centre of the plateau where they were joined one-by-one, by the brave volunteers, the king welcomed each and every one of them individually shaking their hands and embracing them, thanking them for their bravery which could be seen by all to lift and inspire them as they stood with pride.

The crowd that had gathered to see them off and wish them safe return must have been a hundred thousand strong, the whole of Engypt was there.

The king took little May's hand, as he did so the five hundred got to their groups, placed a hand on the child that was to levitate them, and the other hand on the person next to them all of them full of pride being watched by thousands, the Dragons, Egum, Symphet, and Saturn, also readied themselves clasping the huge containers in their massive talons hovering by just gently flapping their wings waiting for the king's signal.

There was a moments silence, then the crowd as one deafening voice – "FARE THEE WELL UNTIL YOU RETURN," they chanted.

Then the king and his party replied as one loud voice; "UNTIL WE RETURN."

Then lead by the king's group, they took to the sky at quite a rate, the crowd watched them disappear into the distance, and when they could see them no more the crowd slowly dispersed and went about the business of rebuilding Engypt and the Great Wall.

When the crowd had dispersed, Julius and his family stayed behind along with Nadia and Lucas still looking to the sky, they joined hands and said a prayer; "Please God watch over our loved ones, see them safely too their journeys end, and return them home to us speedily and well, Amen."

Then Nadia, Laila and Lizet said goodbye to Julius, Lucas and Omar, and that they would see them that evening, and went to help with the preparation of refreshments along with the other women.

Julius and the boys made their way down to the point where the wall was to be built, along with the one thousand men and two dragons they met on the way.

When they arrived, they were excitedly met by Solomon the architect who had already drafted his vision of the wall they would be building.

He proudly showed this to Julius, who agreed it looked perfect for the task, and then authorised the immediate start.

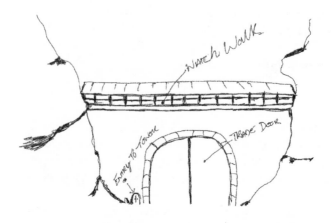

Solomon had it all planned out, and he had even brought a couple of helpers; two giant badgers, Donald and Ginger, he introduced them both to Julius, saying there is no human or beast that could dig as well as these two.

Before Julius, stood these two beasts, each stood as tall as a man, incredibly powerful looking and with huge claws perfect for digging.

Julius thanked them in advance and said, the people of Engypt will always remember them for being here in their moment of need, he too was so happy they could help.

To which Donald replied; "We all share this world, and if there is a threat to our way of life come to light, then it is in all our best interests to work together and keep it out, when do we start?"

"You're eager," replied Julius, "I like your work ethic, ask Solomon where he would like you to start, and once again thank you."

"You are welcome," Donald replied and off he thudded.

Solomon was with the dragons, giving them instruction as to what he required them to do first.

"We need to cut grooves into the rock face, I believe this would be made easier if you and Deming could super heat the rock thus making it crack, and therefore easier to be removed with your talons, is that ok?" he asked the two huge dragons.

"It will be a pleasure, no problem at all, just show us where and it will be done," replied Bingwen.

Whilst all this planning was well underway, the king and his brave five hundred and seventy-two were now well into their journey, maintaining a steady pace, no way as fast as when they took part in the race, they still had a distance to go until they would reach Bulgan, and so didn't want to tire the youngsters and have to find somewhere to rest, as time wasn't on their side, they only had approximately three hours of light left and it would be very unsafe to fly at night, as the regions around Bulgan are mountainous and would need to be navigated whilst they still had sun light.

From above they could clearly see the trail of devastation which had been left by the burning embers that had fallen from the mysterious fireball, which had ignited the woodlands and burned a line as far as the eye could see, strangely the fire wasn't still burning, and hadn't spread to the east or to the west, just a long charred line approximately a quarter of a mile in width.

As the king surveyed the devastation, he could only think the shockwave from the impact must have extinguished the fire before it could spread to the east and west.

Even so the damage done was extensive, and the king was concerned for the creatures and people who may have dwelled in the fires path.

"When we have completed our mission to Polaria, I think we should explore that region of devastation, there may be souls in need of assistance and it wouldn't hurt us to be sure," said the king to his followers Telepathically, it would seem they had all thought the same and agreed. That was the way of life here, these people truly cared for all that lived on Soul and would unselfishly do whatever it took to ensure the safety and care of all.

As they continued it became apparent that everyone was settling into this new flying experience and seemed quite relaxed enjoying the sights and sensations that came with soaring along at around five to six hundred feet above ground level.

Even John seemed to be quite relaxed enjoying the slower pace with the wind in his face, this did have an effect on one person, and that was Samuel, he was looking forward to being entertained by John with his screaming and crying, he did find that so funny, but not now, John was actually enjoying it, and said; "Why was I so scared earlier! I really don't know, this is quite wonderful, you are a lucky young man Joshua, when did you first realise you could do this?"

"Not till this morning when the king asked," he replied.

"Really?! Why would you volunteer for something that you didn't actually know you could do?"

"It's hard to explain, but when the king asked I had the most amazing sensation, a voice in my head said you are meant for this, you can do this, and with that I felt so light all of a sudden, in fact I have to focus more on staying on the ground than levitating," he said and laughed.

They were now nearing Bulgan and had to navigate around and between the clusters of mountains, some of which were thousands of feet high and to navigate them they would have to increase their altitude, they were currently at five to six hundred feet, which was fine, it was a summer's day and the cooling air that rushed over them as they sped along felt nice, everyone was at ease feeling amazingly free, and for that time they had almost forgotten what might lay ahead of them.

But then Egum brought a worrying issue to the Kings attention! And that issue was altitude! The fact was, they would have to gain a lot of altitude to clear the mountains, and the issue with that is, the higher you climb the colder the air becomes, and these mountains were covered with snow and ice at the altitudes they would need to reach to clear them, which indicated it would be well below freezing; this meant the groups wouldn't be able to fly as high as they needed and would have to plan a different approach, as they would freeze to death at such altitudes.

But It would take far too long to land and proceed on foot, they had to keep going…

They had to fly as low as they dare, in some places weaving in and out of very tight gaps between the mountains and watching for sudden changes in the rock formations.

This was proving to be far too difficult for the young children who had only just that morning come to the realisation that they could fly at all, let alone perform aerobatic manoeuvres between extremely jagged rock faces.

Also, all this sudden banking and turning this way and that was becoming a real issue for those trying to keep a grip of them, they were being thrown left, right, up and down and finding it hard to keep a grip without hurting the child, they were becoming scared, one slip would lead to certain death, the king had to come up with another plan, and fast!

The situation was rapidly worsening, Samuel had lost his grip on John with all the sudden movements and now the group around Joshua had become unstable as the bond had been broken, the bond is the invisible field that forms around the group and holds them stable as long as they maintain a grip of each other. Joshua was now struggling to maintain a steady turning ability as the men of his group now started to flap around like ribbons in the wind, panic was setting in for himself and his group…

Joshua had to fly extremely close to an overhang, literally just under it! just as the others ahead had done, he judged it as best he could in the situation, but Samuel's left leg swung up and just caught the rock which gashed his calf muscle, he grimaced in pain, but had to keep a hold of Joshua with his left arm, and was trying desperately to reach for John with his right, if he could just reach John the group would regain stability.

John wanted to reach out for his new friend so badly but knew, if he let go of Joshua to reach for Samuel it would destabilise the group even more and lead to disaster.

Then there was a girl's voice Telepathically telling the group to stay calm, she was on her way; it was Rose, thank god, please help I don't think I can keep control for much longer, said Joshua.

Rose replied; "Stay calm Joshua you can do this, as soon as we reach an opening, I will get alongside Samuel, and try to push him closer to John so he can regain a grip."

"Ok I'll try, there is an opening just ahead please hurry."

"Just hold on Samuel," said John.

They now reached the point at which the gap became wide enough for Rose and her group to get almost alongside, none of her group could let go of her to reach for Samuel, as they would also become unstable, and none had the Telekinetic power to move a human, Rose was the only one that could use her arms to reach out to Samuel, she wasn't strong enough to us Telekinesis for both flight and to move Samuel, so would have to physically grab his leg and pull him over to John.

Rose got just behind and slightly left of Samuel and reached for his leg which was still swinging around, she had to be so careful, if his foot was to hit her in the face or head it would have terrible consequences.

She reached out slowly but couldn't quite get a grip. His leg was swinging too much, Samuel please try and keep your leg as still as possible, "Ok," he replied grimacing with pain.

She then moved in close again reached out her right hand, she was just a few inches away, "Oh no hurry, it's starting to narrow again," said Joshua in a panicked voice.

So quickly thinking, she held out her left hand and pulled in directly behind Joshua, as she did so she grabbed Samuel's left leg and just managed to move him close enough that he could reach John, just in time, the way had narrowed, she had done it!

"Thank you, thank you, thank you," said Samuel.

Joshua's group was now stable thanks to Rose's bravery.

"We can't continue like this someone is going to get killed, we have to find another way," said the king.

Then Egum put an idea to the king, he said that they would all have to climb to the same altitude that himself, Symphet and Saturn were at.

"But you said we would all freeze at that altitude," said the king.

"I did indeed, but I have an idea that might just work," replied Egum.

And he continued to explain, "If I, Symphet and Saturn fly ahead and above you all at just the right distance, we could breathe fire of which the heat would be carried behind us in our wake, you could all fly in our wake and so be kept warm enough to survive the journey. There is only one slight issue! And that is for us to breath fire whilst in flight we have to keep our wings open and glide, we cannot breath fire and close our wings, so we would have to glide whilst breathing fire, and with the weight of the containers we carry, we will lose altitude quite quickly!! And so, we will have to get to an altitude that will allow for us all to descend safely."

"If you believe this will work Egum, then we will follow," replied the king.

"I believe we can only do but try my king," replied Egum. "The only way I think we can do this, is for me, Symphet and Saturn to take it in turn to lead and breath fire one at a time, spraying fire from left to right and when we have finished our breath, the next will then take the lead and do as before, you will have to gain height again to where we will be waiting in turn, then follow our descent until we have finished our breath, then you climb to the next as fast as you can, we will repeat this until we clear the mountains, it is the only way I can think of."

With that the king and his brave followers agreed they had to try, as it was becoming far too dangerous and had to do something, the route ahead was becoming more narrow and jagged.

So now they all ascended higher and higher, as fast as they possibly could, and as they did the air grew thinner and much-much colder, this was made worse by the wind speed chill as they soared to gain height.

Now they were feeling the effects of the thinning air, making it harder for them to breathe, and the cold causing pain to their extremities, fingers feeling as though they were on fire with such cold, but they had to continue, these poor young children being so brave and enduring such pains, their strength and determination with the thought of those in Polaria needing their help was all that spurred them now, and without the thought of them they could so easily give up, but no, they will make it or die trying.

They were now a-thousand feet above the mountains forming a row behind Egum, not to close though, as they would surely be burned by the great dragon's breath, so kept a distance behind and slightly below as he had said.

When they had formed a row Egum inhaled as deep as he possibly could, then opened his wings out wide and exhaled, spewing fire from left to right, and just as he said it would happen, the heat could be felt by all behind him, also as he said, they began to lose altitude quite quickly, they followed his descent trying to capture as much heat as they could, after around forty seconds Egum had to inhale, so it was time for them to climb again as fast as they could to where Symphet was awaiting them, as they drew up behind her she inhaled as deep as she possibly could then exhaled spewing fire from left to right, and again the king and his followers followed her descent feeling the wonderful warming heat.

And again, after forty to fifty seconds Symphet had to inhale, and so they repeated as they had done before and climbed to where Saturn awaited them, and again when they drew up behind him he inhaled as deep as he possibly could, and then he to spewed fire left to right, thankfully Egum's plan was working!

They continued with this procedure until finally as dusk drew in, they cleared the mountains and could now see Bulgan, what a sight it was, they had done it, and could now descend and feel the warmth of the summers night, and how good it felt, they all sighed a huge sigh of relief and thanked Egum, Symphet and Saturn, without whom they would never of made it.

As they drew closer to Bulgan the natural light was all but gone, they could just make out the light of lanterns which lit the paths below, they would just make it before the sun had totally set.

The people of Bulgan were still making the most of what little light they had whilst making repairs to the buildings which had been damage by the earthquake as a result of the impact, some of them had now noticed the unusual shapes in the sky heading toward there village, they were aware that the king and his five hundred and seventy-two followers would be arriving at some point, as Bogumill had informed them earlier that day, but not even Bogumill was expecting such a site as this, never before had a human been seen to levitate in such a way as this, and yet they were seeing groups of people flying toward them, being led by three huge silver dragons.

Some of the people of the village became unsure that this was the king and his party heading toward them and began to worry and look for somewhere to hide, thinking that what they were seeing was some strange beings coming to do them harm.

The king, being so Telepathically sensitive, began to sense their fears and so connected with them saying; people of Bulgan do not fear it is I your King, and those with me are your friends from Engypt you need not worry.

Hearing this the people sighed and relaxed and became excited by the king's visit and the spectacle of these people gliding through the air, they were eager to ask many questions.

There was a large area of green field, perfect for the king and his people to land and make camp for the night; as they approached the field the people of Bulgan ran to watch them as they landed, and as the groups landed one-by-one the people would give out a loud cheer every time a group set foot on the ground.

The first group to land was the mighty dragons, followed by the king and Little May, the king promptly walked over to the dragons holding his hand out wanting to touch and thank the dragons for all they had done to get the group to their journeys end safely.

The three mighty dragons lowered their heads to the king, allowing him to pet them; "We would never have made it without you, I am eternally indebted to you and yours," said the king.

"We are friends, there is no debt between friends helping each other," said Egum.

"Thank you," said the King and smiled.

Egum then asked the king if he and his family might burn a tree as they had used a lot of energy and needed nourishment.

"I'm sure Bogumill won't mind, just don't set the whole wood ablaze," laughed the king.

With that the three dragons turned to the woodland just west of the camp in search of a nice tasty tree to burn for supper.

After a time, most of the groups had landed except for Rose's and Joshua's, who were now making their approach. Rose's group would be the first to land, and when she finally touch down the other groups gathered to meet her, she was an heroine, this young girl with such bravery, if it wasn't for her Joshua's group would never of made it, and so the king and the other groups wanted to praise her.

Everyone gathered around her, even her own group stayed to praise her, they were there, and knew just how hard a task she had performed, and so felt so proud of her, one of the men in her group was Adrian, a big strong brave man, who would never shy away from a challenge, he couldn't believe this young child was so fearless.

He approached young Rose towering over her, he looked her in the eyes quite stern and said, that was very-very dangerous young lady…

Rose looked at Adrian as though she had just been told off and replied; I know but it had to be done!

With that Adrian burst into laughter, bent down picked her up and sat her on his shoulders saying; yes it did, and what bravery it took, many a grown man would not have had the heart and will to do what you have done to save our friends, you have the heart of a dragon, and so I will call you Little Dragon.

To which everybody cheered! Dragon, Little Dragon.

Rose, or Little Dragon, as she was now being called, noticed Joshua and his group were touching down and wanted to see them, so asked Adrian politely if he would please put her down and thanked him, to which he replied; of course, and gently lifted her to the ground, rose asked Adrian if he could come with her to see Joshua's group she wanted to make sure they were all ok, it would seem Rose and Adrian had formed a bond, her mother and father were far away and she looked to Adrian now as her guardian, she took his hand, he looked at her and smiled, and together they made their way through the crowd and headed to Joshua and his group.

When they arrived it was evident all was not well, poor Samuel who had caught his left leg on the rocks was laying on the ground, Joshua and John were bent knee over him looking at his leg, Rose was worried and asked; "Is he ok, what's happened?" to which John replied, "Yes he will be fine, big baby has cut his leg, probably needs a clean and a few stitches but he will live, he is just having a good moan, oh, and Rose, thank you so much, you were extremely brave, if it wasn't for you I don't think we would have made it."

"You are welcome," she replied with a big proud smile.

"My leg, Is it going to be ok? It looks nasty," Samuel was whimpering.

"Goodness me! It really isn't that bad Samuel, you haven't broken anything, it's just a cut, you're going on as though you only have half a leg left," said John sarcastically, and continued; "I'm actually finding this quite entertaining, big man like you crying over a small cut." Which was actually about five inches long and very deep.

I'm not crying, said Samuel and started to laugh as John couldn't hold back the laughter, and before you knew it the entire group was laughing. I think mainly the relief of making it through such an ordeal was like the world being lifted of their shoulders, they were commenting on each other's reactions to the situation, and now thinking back finding things to laugh about, one of the men was saying how he had never wanted his mum so much, another man jovially said I know, I could hear you calling for her; Mum-Mum-Mummy, you were going; which caused an outburst of laughter.

Then one of the healers came to see to Samuel's leg, she was a short round lady, quite a lot older, and sort of waddled along, as she looked down at Samuel's leg she tutted, goodness me is that it? To which she tore his leg garments to get a better look, then with no word of warning poured a liquid over the cut to clean it, which lead to a loud yelp from Samuel, "Ugh," he cried, too which the lady looked at him and said, "Hush now, big man like you crying out over a little healing fluid, tut-tut."

John and the others again laughed saying big baby. That stings, I'd like to see one of you try it, replied Samuel gritting his teeth.

Then he turned to the healer and asked her name, to which she said, "My name is Judith."

"Thank you for helping me Judith, is it going to be ok? Will I be able to continue with the mission?"

"It will heal, and you will be fine, but I think you should stay here and rest it," she replied.

"No!" said Samuel, I need to be able to continue I want to help, there may be people with much worse injuries than this cut out there that I can help.

"Can't we just bandage it up nice and tight?" asked Samuel.

Judith replied, "Well I'm going to stitch it and bandage it to keep it clean, the problem you have is, if you need to climb anything you could pull the stitches open, and we don't want that do we?"

"No," replied Samuel, "but I really want to help I don't want to let everyone down over a cut, there must be something you can do? Please!"

"Ok," Judith replied, "I can see this means a lot to you, you are determined, aren't you?"

"Yes, it means a lot to me and I will do whatever it takes to continue, please don't tell them I can't continue, please!"

"You're stubborn, I'll give you that, Judith replied. "What I'm going to do is use a Omiul leaf, it has great healing properties, I would usually use it on injuries much worse than this, I will place it over the cut after I have stitched it, you must not remove it, I will remove it in the morning and you should be fine to continue, but you must still take care of the leg, ok?"

"Thank you so much, I really appreciate your help and will repay you I promise," Samuel replied with a huge smile on his face.

"You hush there is nothing to repay it's what I do, you just make sure I don't have to come and see to you again, try and avoid sharp rocks," Judith chuckled.

"Don't worry I'll be sure to try and keep him out of harm's way," said John smiling.

With that Judith readied the needle and thread, she then placed her right hand over the cut and closed her eyes, as she did this Samuel could feel the cut and surrounding area becoming very cold, his leg was beginning to numb.

"Wow, I can't feel it anymore," he said.

"That's good," replied Judith, she then opened her eyes and pushed the needle into the edge of the skin around the cut, "Can you feel that?" she asked.

"No," replied Samuel.

"Good," replied Judith and proceeded to stitch the wound, when she had finished, she placed an Omiul leaf over the wound and bound it in place with lengths of grass woven together.

"There all done! I'll be back at first light to remove the bindings; in the meantime, you stay still and relax."

"Once again thank you," said Samuel.

"You're welcome, and of she went to check she wasn't needed by anyone else."

"How does it feel," asked John.

"It feels good, to be honest I can't feel a thing! Which is good, I guess," replied Samuel.

"Good," replied John, so you're be ok to continue at first light then, hopefully?

"Yes, I'll be fine, it feels so much better already."

"I'm going to get some food and drink would you like me to fetch you some?" John asked Samuel. "Yes please," he replied, "and thank you."

With that John went to the village where they had prepared refreshments for their visitors.

As he walked toward the village, he reflected on the day's events and how lucky the group had been that no one was seriously hurt, he was truly grateful his new friend Samuel had only suffered a cut and nothing more.

As he continued to walk toward the village he couldn't help but hope the rest of the journey might be peril free, he turned his thoughts to the people of Polaria, he truly hoped that the beautiful village had survived the impact of the fire ball, he hoped the people were unarmed, but he knew deep down this wouldn't be the case, the impact which he and the people of Engypt witnessed was huge and looked to be too close to Polaria for it to survive unscathed.

John also new people who lived in Polaria, and he would often speak with them via Telepathy, but now was unable to focus on them, it was like something blocking him, or they no longer existed, he tried to stay positive, he couldn't wait to get to Polaria to see one way or other.

He knew he would be having a sleepless night worrying about what may lay ahead.

John then changed his thoughts to food, there was lovely fresh cooked fish with lovely vegetables and rice, that looks so nice, that will be for me and Samuel he said to himself, there was a little old lady who was serving the food, as John approached she gave him a big heart-warming smile, and asked; "What would you like?" to which john said; "I would like two portions of the fish with rice and those lovely vegetables, thank you."

You must be hungry, said the lady with a cheeky smile. John felt embarrassed as he thought the lady must think it was all for him, and so said; it's not all for me, one is for my friend, he can't come and get it with me as he received an injury on the journey here.

Oh, I'm sorry to hear that, said the lady, I do hope he recovers quickly.

Thank you said John I'm sure he will be fine.

The lady served John his food on two big wooden dishes, and said, "Have a safe journey" and smiled, "Thank you," replied John, he collected his food and off he went back to his waiting friend Samuel.

When he got back to Samuel, he found him sleeping, and so gave him a nudge with his foot, and said, "Oi sleepy head, wake up, I have your food eat it while it's hot!"

To which Samuel moaned and groaned; as he woke from his slumber, "Aw I was having a nice dream, we were all back home before this all happened, having a great time at the celebrations, then boom your voice wakes me, but thanks for getting my food, you're a good man John."

"What are friends for, said John, if not to help a friend in a time of need, anyway enough of the sentimental stuff let's eat while our food is hot! Then get some rest, we have a long day tomorrow, and I do hope you will be fit to continue, it's strange but I feel quite a strong bond with you my friend, and feel we will be needing each other on this journey for some reason."

"Strange that," replied Samuel, "I have the same feeling to, in the pit of my stomach I feel all is not well in Polaria, in fact, I have a sense of danger, I've never felt it before, I knew people there, and since the occurrence I have not been able to make contact with any of them, it's like something is blocking me when I try to connect with them, I truly fear for them, I guess we shall see tomorrow."

"Yes," replied John, we shall see what tomorrow brings, hopefully our fears will be false."

And with that the two friends ate their food and settled down for the night on two small beautifully woven rugs and covered themselves with woolen robes.

Soon the rest of the group had fed and watered and began to settle for the night, but it was with heavy hearts they did so, as every one of them was unsure what the morning would bring them, they all knew someone in Polaria and pray they would find them well, but all shared a sense this was not going to be the case.

As the group tried to relax and get some needed sleep the king and Bogumill still stay awake talking.

They were discussing the mission, and Bogumill wanted to help, but the king kindly declined his assistance, saying that he was unsure what they would find, and began to inform Bogumill of Nadia's visions, and how she thought there could be danger ahead, and so didn't want to risk the wellbeing of Bogumill's people, and felt it best he should continue with his group of five hundred and seventy-two volunteers only. But if he found they needed assistance he would call on Bogumill for aid, to which Bogumill agreed, but with one concession, the king would have to contact Bogumill the moment they arrived in Polaria, and if they lost contact Bogumill would have no option but send aid, to which the king agreed, saying he would do as Bogumill asked.

The king and Bogumill, just as everyone else, also knew people who lived in Polaria, especially the king he would always stay in contact with the leaders of the settlements of Soul, but he too could no longer contact anyone whom dwelled in Polaria, or beyond, and grew worried for the worst, he felt restless, wide awake, and wanting to continue, he didn't really want to stop and rest, but knew he and his people had to, he felt that every minute they rest someone in Polaria could be closer to peril.

He felt guilty, that someone could be dying while he is resting, I guess he cared so strong for his people he couldn't help but feel this way.

Bogumill could see the king was concerned, he could see he was restless, agitated, full of sorrow, and tried to offer assurance, "My king you look tired and in need of rest, I can see you are worried, try to rest, tomorrow is a new day, and hopefully will bring good fortune to help you on your journey and find all is well in Polaria, so come lets settle and sleep."

"I guess you are right my old friend," replied the king and gave a halfhearted smile and nod of the head.

He then stood, shook Bogumill's hand and thanked him for being there for him and his party, "I wish you a good sleep, I will see you in the morning," then turned and began to walk back to the encampment where his brave volunteers were sleeping under the beautiful warm night's sky.

As he walked, he said a prayer asking god to watch over them all, keeping them safe, seeing them on their journey and back home to their loved ones safely.

When he arrived at his tent, he breathed deeply, taking in the beautiful warm sweet night air, he could smell the grass and the flowers, and for a moment his mind was at ease.

He then walked into the tent and laid down and tried to clear his mind, and within moments he was asleep, the stress had taken its toll he was exhausted, and finally at rest.

Now everyone in Bulgan was sleeping, the night was still and warm, what the morning would bring was unsure, but it wouldn't be too long till the sun would rise and the journey continues for the king and the brave volunteers.

Chapter 4

Friends in Need

When the morning came, the sun rose and along with it so did the people of Bulgan, preparing for the day ahead, making breakfast for themselves and their guests, lovely fresh fruits and bread, lemon and ginger tea with honey.

One by one the king and his brave party awoke refreshed after a good night's sleep, and when they did, the view that welcomed them was breathtaking, when they arrived in the dusk they couldn't fully appreciate the beauty that surrounded them, this beautiful settlement with its beautiful green fields, wonderful array of wild plants, flowers and woodland, all totally surrounded by the most awe inspiring snowcapped mountains with fresh melted snow streams and waterfalls, this place was truly beautiful.

"Oi wakey-wakey sleepy head," was the first thing poor Samuel heard while he still slept, John was trying to wake Samuel in a manner most would call heavy handed, but to him quite normal, shoving poor Samuel, "Oi! Wake up."

"Aw is it morning already?" replied poor Samuel feeling like he could sleep forever.

"I take it you didn't sleep well, was your leg playing up?" replied John.

"No not at all, I slept like a baby, my leg feels great wouldn't think anything had happened, I guess the stress of the journey as taken its toll, I just feel very sleepy, I'll be fine in a minute," replied Samuel.

"Ok I'll go get us breakfast, back in a minute," said John.

"Thanks John take your time; I'll be right here."

"You best be up by the time I get back, don't think we have long before we leave."

"I'll be up don't worry," replied Samuel and gave a weary smile.

With that John went to turn, but Samuel said "Wait, I'll come with you, need to stretch my legs make sure this cut is going to be ok, need the exercise."

And with that he stretched clambered out from under his nice warm robes, stood stretched as hard as he could almost tiptoeing, "Yep I'm awake, let's go…

With that they set off to get some breakfast, but before they could get ten feet, Judith the healer who had seen to Samuel's leg shouted out "Wait! I need to check your leg young man, you seem to be walking well, but I'd still like to take a quick look, do you mind if I take a look at it? Then I'll let you get on." "Sure," replied Samuel.

With that Judith bent on one knee removed the dressings and with a happy tone; "How wonderful looks great, no infection, you're be fine to continue on the mission, well done."

"Thank you so much for your help," said Samuel with a huge smile, and then grabbed the lovely little stout lady and hugged her.

"Steady, steady," said Judith, "don't want to crush me," she laughed. Samuel was so grateful he forgot just how strong he was, Judith did appreciate the gratitude, but at the time it felt like a bear had her in its arms."

"My you're a strong lad," she said, "best let me go now, need be on my way, have to get ready." "Ok," replied Samuel, then gave her a peck on the cheek, and loosened his bear-like grip. "Bye for now," and off she waddled.

"Bye for now," replied Samuel and John, then continued to get some much-needed breakfast.

When they arrived many of the group had already arrived and were eating, even little Rose had beaten them to breakfast, and alongside her like a personal bodyguard was Adrian. It was Adrian who first realised that it was Samuel and John and said aloud, "Here he is," then stood and walked toward Samuel with arms open in greeting. "It's good to see you are up and in good health, you had us all worried," he said as he wrapped his big arms around Samuel and gave him a brief but warm hug.

"Thank you," replied Samuel, "Must say I was a bit worried myself, but Judith did a great job looking after my leg, and I must say a huge thank you to Rose, what you did was incredibly brave, don't think we would have made it without you doing what you did, once again, thank you from the bottom of my heart."

"I hear that you have a nickname now," Samuel said to Rose, "Yes," replied Rose, "Adrian gave me the name, silly really," she said, "but he insists on it."

"Yes I do," said Adrian, "What you did showed the bravery of a dragon, you Little Dragon, and messed up her hair with his hand, Little Dragon did look a little embarrassed by her new hairstyle, but everyone laughed and so did she eventually, as she straightened her hair.

At that moment King Stephen arrived, and with him was Bogumill, the king greeted everyone wishing them a good morning, and continued that after everyone had eaten they would pack away there sleeping equipment and ready for the remaining journey, he felt it important they readied as soon as possible, hopefully within the hour they would be under way again.

He continued; please eat and drink plenty, as we still have a distance to cover, and with that he and Bogumill walked together to get food and drink.

As they walked the king asked Bogumill if there was a less dangerous route that could be taken through or over the mountains, as the journey there was incredibly dangerous.

Bogumill said there was a passage which would take them through the mountains safely, but they would need to be on foot, as like all the passages to and from Bulgan, they are narrow, and long, they are more like caves which lead directly under the huge mountains.

But luckily straight, just one path so no chance of getting lost, thankfully.

He continued; "The dragons would be too big to go through so they would have to fly over the mountains once again."

"Thank you," replied the king.

Bogumill then continued to ask the king to please let him send some of he's strongest men to assist the king, to which the king again replied; "I appreciate your wanting to help, but as I can't be sure as to what lay ahead, I can't ask you to risk the wellbeing of your people, but if once we arrive I decide we need your assistance I will call on you."

They then proceeded to obtain a nice big breakfast of beautiful fresh fruits and still warm bread.

The king spotted his daughter May sitting with her group eating, and as the king was also part of her group proceeded to join them and enjoy breakfast together, they were all in good spirits talking about the journey and remembering there first flight together, how scared they all were, well apart from May, she loved every moment.

Even the king admitted he was quite scared at first, but then did continue to say, "Nothing wrong with being scared of the unknown, as long as we still at least try to overcome our fear, and I think we can all say we have done that, can't we? To which everyone agreed with pride, nodding in agreement, and looking at each other with big smiles at the realisation that they had all conquered an unknown.

This seemed to fill them all with a confidence that they could achieve whatever it takes to complete their mission, and they became a little more excited by what challenges may lay ahead.

The king continued that they should all be very proud of themselves, as he was truly grateful for their selflessness in volunteering to assist on this quest, "I'm proud of everyone here."

Then one of the men of the group, Tim, returned the compliment saying; " I believe I speak for everyone here my king when I say it is us that are grateful to be allowed to assist you on this quest, to assist you is an honour, we would follow you anywhere and at any time, you are a great king and have always done the best for us your people, and it is a privilege to return your efforts."

The king smiled and said; "I appreciate your loyalty, thank you all, I'm sure the people of Polaria will be truly grateful to see us all. Hopefully we will find them well."

"Yes, please god," said May.

And with that they continued to eat and drink, ensuring they would have enough energy for the journey ahead of them.

Once everyone had eaten their full, they all started to gather up their belongings and met the king on the edge of the green fields, where everyone from Bulgan was awaiting them wanting to wish them a good safe journey, and see them off, the king was ready and waiting, they were on schedule, and to be honest he couldn't wait to get underway, he was truly thankful to the people of Bulgan and so thanked them, saying he appreciated the warm welcome he and his party had received, and the efforts the people of Bulgan had gone to, to provide food and drink, especially as they too were dealing with the after effects of the impact which occurred two nights prior. "I once again thank you all from the bottom of my heart, and wish you all well, we will be leaving now, until we return, fair thee well."

And with that the king and Bogumill made eye contact and nodded their heads with regard. The brave volunteers regrouped into their groupings, and once again placed one hand on the child who was their lead, and the other hand on the person next to them.

As they readied, Egum the silver dragon wanted to say a thank you to the people of Bulgan, and so started to talk with them Telepathically; "People of Bulgan I wish to thank you for letting me and mine feast on your beautiful woodland trees, we may have eaten more than expected, sorry! It was a tough journey here and we used more energy than first expected, which left us quite famished, so once again sorry!" And thank you. Then he gave a nervous smile, eyes wandering left to right."

The people of Bulgan could sense he was quite embarrassed and couldn't leave without saying something.

The crowd burst into laughter, and said they were welcome.

Egum thought to himself jokingly, "They haven't seen how many we've eaten yet," and sighed "Best be on our way then."

Then looked to the king and said, "When you are ready, my king," then he, Symphet and Saturn readied themselves on the huge containers once more.

The people of Bulgan then in loud voice said to the king and his followers, "May God watch over you see you safely to your journeys end and return you back to us unarmed, bless you and yours."

They then cheered and clapped the sound was deafening.

The king and he's brave followers looked to the sky, as they did the king asked, "Are we ready?" to which they all replied as one loud voice,

"WE ARE READY."

With that one by one, whoosh they took to the skies, but this time no screams or cries, they were now a confident, strong unit full of courage, fear was something they now embraced and conquered.

The people of Bulgan were aghast, they had not clearly seen this amazing feat, as when the group arrived it was night, and now to watch this incredible spectacle in bright day light was mind blowing for them, gasps and laughs of pure shock could be heard throughout.

Then as the last of the group took to the skies, sudden whooshes could be heard from all directions, and voices of parents in the crowd shouting come back, it would seem the people of Bulgan had many a youngster who unbeknownst to them and their families also had this incredible ability, it was amazing, like thousands of little rockets they took to the skies, little voices, wee, and laughing so loud, this is wonderful, a little girl shouted to her parents as she flew over their heads, "Wha-hoo!"

Purcha, stop that and get back here now please, your scaring me, her mother cried!

The parents of the children could do nothing, one parent caught the ankle of his nine-year-old son as he took to the skies, big mistake that was… although he was a big man this was nothing for his young son, so he just wound up going for a very excitable ride; his screams could be heard by all as they passed over head.

"Palo, please, take me back," the father asked he's son.

"This is amazing father," replied Palo, ever so excited.

Yes, it is," replied Palo's father in a terrified voice, eyes closed tight. "Please turn back now, I think it best you practice this flying before you take others," to which Palo replied, "Ok father, can I practice later?"

"Yes, yes," replied Palo's scared witless father.

And so, he did as his father asked and returned to the safety of the ground.

"Thank you , thank you," said his father, then there was another voice, it was Palo's mother, she was in quite a state of shock, anger, excitement, and happiness all at once, but could only say "Thank god you're back," and grabbed her husband and son so tight.

"Hi, my love, I need to sit for a moment," replied her very shaken husband, as his legs gave way from under him.

There was quite a bit of this going on in Bulgan on this day, shocked and scared parents, finding things hard to take in now.

But they would soon except and give thanks for this amazing gift their children had been given.

Bogumill couldn't believe what was happening, especially as his young daughter Yoana was amongst the swarm of children heading after the king, and swarm was the right word, the number of children with this amazingly strong levitational ability was so vast they looked just like a swarm of bees.

After a moment or several, Bogumill regained his senses and thought he'd best inform the king of what was happening, and that he would be having company very soon.

And with that he contacted the king using Telepathy, "My king it's amazing, all of the children of Bulgan are heading after you."

"What do you mean?" replied the king.

"Our children can fly just as you are now, in fact I believe you might see them soon."

"That is incredible," replied the King, "I will let them follow us until we reach the entrance to the path, then I will ask them to return to you."

"They are probably ever so excited by their new-found gift, let's let them enjoy the moment shall we?" replied the king.

"Yes, I will inform my people not to worry," replied Bogumill.

Bogumill then contacted his daughter, "Yoana, where are you! young lady?" he asked with a stern tone.

Yoana was now thinking she was in trouble with her father, and replied in a very nervous almost scared voice, "Hello father, sorry I couldn't help myself, it was like an uncontrollable sensation father, we are insight of the king's group.

Am I in trouble father?" she asked with her eyes half-open, squinting as she waited for a reply.

"No," her father replied in a sigh-full voice, "but we are all very shocked here! I have informed the king you are behind him, you are to follow them until they land at the entrance to the path, then he will ask you to return, I am making it your responsibility you all get back here safely, can you do this for me?"

"Yes, father I will, thank you father, I won't let you down, I'm sorry if I scared you and mother."

"Well, I said you're not in trouble with me, but I can't speak for mother," he chuckled. "See you soon."

"She isn't angry with me is she father?"

"I will talk with her," he replied, and sighed, he did this deliberately to leave her just a little worried she would have to face her mother when she got home, she wasn't too sure as to the welcome.

But it was too late, she would have to wait and see.

She then turned her attention to the king's group, she really wanted to catch them up before they landed, there was still a distance to be covered before they would reach the paths entrance, just as all the other children wanted to show the king and his group they could fly, so desperately she did to…

And so, she sped up, and as she did, she started passing the other children, and they in reaction also started to go faster to catch her, the children were now in a race, they were laughing loudly calling each other on…"

"Where do you think you're going?" said one of the boys, and flew alongside her then gently shouldered his left shoulder into hers, just a gentle nudge, to which Yoana reacted, "Jonathan, you little beast," and laughed, she couldn't be angry with him, Jonathan was seven years of age, but so cheeky, always laughing, very cute, he would melt your heart with his big blue eyes and dimple smile.

So, she gave him a gentle nudge back, then rolled left and under him then appeared on his right, and gently nudged him again, they both laughed, then she said your it! and sped away, Jonathan gave chase.

In her attempts to escape Jonathan, she was banking hard left, then hard right, and in between the other children, but Jonathan was hot on her heals, he was determined to catch her.

The other children saw this and thought this was great fun and began to shout! One it all it, and scattered this way and that, now poor little Jonathan didn't know what way to turn.

Next to him was a small boy who wasn't too sure what was going on, and so easy prey for him, so he quickly touched his left arm and said you're it with me, let's see how many others we can get before we catch up to the king, to which the little boy smiled, yes lets, he said and off he shot.

Jonathan then turned his attention back to Yoana, and returned to the chase, he did add those who were in his path, and by the time he caught up with her he had added ten other children, who in turn were chasing other children now, what fun this was.

Yoana looked back and sure enough, there was Jonathan now again hot on her heels, she could see the king's group just a short distance ahead, and so said to Jonathan Telepathically, "You're running out of time, once I reach the king I'm safe!" and laughed confident she would reach the king before he could get to her, and she laughed again teasingly.

Well this spurred Jonathan on immensely, to which he replied, "that's it you're mine!" gritted his teeth and accelerated as hard as he could, which was incredible, as Yoana had already sped up to make sure she would reach the king first, but Jonathan was catching her at an incredible rate, in fact within moments he was at her side, with that great big smile of his, and upside down, just to add insult to injury as he reached out his left hand and touched her left arm, you're it to, and laughed!

Although in disbelief, Yoana was very sporting and said, "Well done you, I thought I was safe, you are incredibly fast for one so small," and laughed, to which so did Jonathan, "Never judge a book by its cover," he said.

When they looked forward, they saw they had caught up with the king's group, and so said a big hello to the king and the group, to which the very shocked group replied, "Well hello."

The king continued; "Well you have caught us up, very well done to you all, I wasn't expecting so many of you" as he looked around him.

The children were all around them like a huge escort, the ground below was shadowed from the sun so huge the number, but it wasn't just the king and he's group or the people of Bulgan that were amazed by these incredible flying humans, the natural dwellers of the skies had heard of this phenomenon, and had to see for themselves.

All of the birds, from every breed had formed to see them, and amongst them was the biggest bird of the sky, they are the Birgumon, these incredible creatures are the real kings of the sky, as big as a dragon but much-much faster, they are incredibly beautiful, with feathers which seemed to change colour as the wind shifts them, the colours seemed to blend and change, from blues, greens, reds, gold, silver, and even mix to make almost rainbow-like effects.

As they approached, one of the Birgumon, a wise old bird, called Ti-at was in disbelief at the sight of these small humans soaring through the skies, and seeing the adults hanging on to them he found so funny, he couldn't help but burst into laughter, "Oh my-my do my eyes deceive me?" he laughed, and made sure to be heard by all, human and beast within range of him, "Ha-ha-ha, incredible, what a sight to behold, have I finally gone senile, and now live in a world of pure imagination?" he asked sarcastically, still laughing uncontrollably.

Then another voice joined him, it was Chip an old brown owl, his eyes looked huge as he stared with disbelief.

Well it must be catching, chip said to Ti-at, in a very sarcastic voice; as he flew between the children, hooting at them as he got close to them to make them jump! "I've always said these humans were peculiar looking creatures, just look at them ugh! beastly looking things, those silly little eyes," he said as he rolled his at one of the children, who proceeded to poke their tongue at him and say, "Look who's talking," Cheeky replied chip, and smiled at the child, then flew over to the king.

"Hello King Stephen, I do hope you are feeling ok being up here, quite out of your comfort zone I should think, don't look down!" the feisty old owl teased.

The king looked at Chip, hello Chip my old friend, must say at first yes, very uncomfortable, but now I think you might find we have grown accustomed to the sensation of not having the ground firmly under our feet, in fact it's quite exhilarating, such a sense of freedom, it's beautiful up here", smirked the king, knowing this would ruffle the old owl's feathers.

To which the owl replied, "Ok, I'm happy for you all, but how is this possible, you have no feathers or wings, how are you staying up here?" he asked, totally confused…

To which the king knew the old owl wouldn't understand if he tried to explain the workings of Telekinesis, and so thought it best to keep his answer simple. "It's magic," said the king, "We are using magic to fly, well, our children it would seem are the only ones with the magical abilities to fly, so us adults are, shall we say catching a ride to where we need to be…"

And at that moment, Ti-at interrupted "Well that's incredible, and where is it you have to be in such a rush?"

"We are on a quest to Polaria, there has been an occurrence, and I feel the people of Polaria, may need our assistance..."

"That's the origin of the light and wind two nights ago," replied Ti-at. "Yes," replied the king with sunken heart, Ti-at could feel the king's pain, and offered to assist in any way the king saw fit.

But before the king could reply: "No-no-no-no." It was Chip the owl, in a very concerned voice; "You must not go to Polaria my King, I came across a number of osprey in this region earlier today, which I thought was unusual as they usually prefer the rivers and seas of Polaria, so had to ask them what brought them here?, to which one of them told me they had to leave their home lands of Polaria, it wasn't safe there, they were very afraid almost in a state of shock, I asked what has happened?! But they just replied, bright light, dust , danger! I remembered the bright light of two nights ago, and thought this must have scared them, but I didn't understand 'dust'? But before I could ask them what they meant they had accelerated away, I couldn't keep up with them, and so I'm still unsure what they meant, but I got the distinct feeling it wasn't good! I don't think it's safe for you and yours to continue my King..."

Ti-at quickly offered to fly ahead and scout, check for danger, see what scared the ospreys, he and his kind are the fastest of all sky dwelling creatures, and could go and return in time to meet the king at the entrance of the passage to Polaria...

"I will take three of my fastest with me, my king, we will be back before you reach the passage..."

The king thought for a moment, then agreed, but insisted they didn't put themselves in arms way, to which Ti-at agreed and said, "Any sign of danger we will turn back immediately," then continued "Micah, Sush, Tornado, you're coming with me."

"With pleasure my lead," they replied, then whoosh they were almost out of sight in moments.

"Take care," said Chip, feeling quite worried for he's old friend.

The king then spoke to he's group using Telepathy, "My people hear me," to which the whole group focused on the king to hear his words.

"We will continue to the passage but will not enter until Ti-at and his group have returned, Egum!"

"Yes," my king.

"Would you, Symphet and Saturn please also land and wait at the entrance to the passage with us, I don't want you to continue until we have heard from Ti-at, is that ok?"

"Of course, my King…"

The king continued; "When we do arrive, I think it would be nice to contact our loved ones back home, just so they can be assured we are doing well, I'm sure they are thinking of us."

To which everyone agreed, "That would be nice." "Settled then," said the king.

And so, they continued as fast as they could, well as fast as the youngsters could carry them.

While the king and his group made their way to the passage, Ti-at, Micah, tornado and Sush had made great progress, and where passing the mountain peaks and now entering Polaria , they should have now been able to see it , but this was not the case, for as far as their eyes could see Polaria was enveloped by a dark cloud which was pulsating with electrostatic sparks or lightning, as they drew closer although they were at least a hundred feet above the cloud, the air became heavy and hard to breath, it was full of particles of black ash!! "This is what the ospreys must have meant when they said dust!" said Sush. "Yes," replied Ti-at, "This doesn't look hopeful does it?" he continued, "I best contact the King let him know what we have found so far," but as he tried to contact the king he found he was unable, something was blocking his Telepathic ability! What is happening?

"I can't contact the King, something is blocking me, it must be all this static, it must interfere with mind connection somehow! I think it best we turn back now! it's becoming hard to breathe!"

Then Micah asked, "Should I take a quick dive into the cloud to see if it is clear below? It might hopefully be just airborne!"

"No," replied Ti-at, "You could be killed by the static, or lightning could strike you, no definitely not, we shall turn back now."

"I don't believe anything human or beast could live in that!" said Ti-at, with a sad heart.

And so, they turned back to give the king the news of what they had seen.

The king and his people had now reached the entrance to the passage, and waited along with Egum, Symphet and Saturn, and as they said they would, they were all in conversation with their loved ones back home in Engypt, the people back home were so happy to hear the voices of their loved ones, to know they were safe was such a relief.

The king to was speaking with his wife Nadia, she was so happy to hear from him, she was still very concerned about the quest after the vision Laila spoke of , but was at ease for the moment, "How are you my love, is all going well? She asked, to which the king replied, "Yes, so far so good my love, how are you and Lucas?, Is he carrying out his duties?"

"We are doing well, and yes he is doing very well; he is reveling in his new responsibilities, he comes home every day excited by what he has learned that day, I think you will be very proud of him," she replied.

"I'm sure I will be, well I am already very proud of you both, you are both so strong and I love you very much, please don't worry my love we will be home soon enough, we are just about to proceed through a passage that will bring us out into Polaria, I will let you know what we find as soon as we arrive."

"I will try not to worry, but I will ask you please be careful, and at the first signs of danger, please don't hesitate to turn back, I want you and May back home unhurt my love," Nadia said lovingly.

"To which the king replied; of course my love, I promise you I will not risk the wellbeing of any of us, you can be rest assured, I am going to have to go now, I love you and will be back in your arms soon, bye for now my love."

The king was being a king, brave, not wanting his wife to be concerned, but he knew she would worry, and deep down he too was unsure, but had to be positive, and so he was putting on a brave face.

"See you when you get home my love, be safe, bye for now, love you."

The king then wanted to speak with Julius, he was feeling a little uneasy and wanted to ask how the defensive wall was coming along, and so contacted his old friend, Julius my old friend, "I hope you are well!"

"Great to hear from you my king, is all well?" he asked, "I sense a little unease coming from you."

"All is well my friend, just tired, didn't get much sleep, I'm too eager to get to Polaria I guess, I just wanted to check all is well with you, how is the defensive wall coming along?"

"What is wrong my king, you are concerned about something, I know this as you would never ask about defenses unless you felt we might be in danger, when you left, I felt we was just being cautious! But now I sense an air of fear, what is it my king?"

"It's probably nothing just Laila's vision playing on my mind I guess, I was just wanting to let you know all is well and we are making great progress, and also wanted to ask how things were proceeding with the wall and the restoration of Engypt, sorry if I have lead you to think the worst, but all is well so far my friend," replied the king.

"I'm pleased to hear it, my king, I am pleased to say all is going very well, we have been progressing better than first thought, I'm sure by the time you return you will see noticeable differences, my king."

"That's great news, I knew you was the man for the job, I'd best go now, give my love to your family, I will speak with you soon my friend."

"Safe journey, my king."

With that the king returned he's thoughts back to the group and said they should all relax for a while take some refreshments while they wait for Ti-at to return.

While they rested they took the time to take in the beautiful scenery that surrounded them, the sun shone so bright and warm, with a beautiful soft breeze which carried the smells of the plants and flowers around them, some of the children were laying on their backs staring at the beautiful blue sky, watching the light clouds moving so slowly, it made them feel as though it was them and not the clouds which were moving, everyone was so relaxed, talking and laughing, it was almost as though it was a family trip.

Even so the king wasn't as relaxed as those around him, he was desperate for Ti-at to return, he turned to Egum and said; "Shouldn't they be here by now?"

He then tried to contact them but was unable to contact them! "Something is wrong!" he said to Egum, "I can't contact them!"

Egum tried to put the king's mind at rest, "They will be here soon my king, it is quite a distance they have to cover, I'm sure they are fine, would you like me to scout for them?"

"If they don't arrive soon then yes that would be appreciated," but then Egum looked to the sky and said excitedly!! "Look there my king, it looks like them, told you they would be fine," and smiled.

"Thank God," replied the king.

Sure-enough it was Ti-at, Sush, Micah and Tornado, thankfully on their way back.

The king once again tried to contact them, he was so happy to see them, but he couldn't make contact, something isn't right he thought, Egum heard his thoughts and agreed, he too was unable to make contact!

So, all they could do was wait, they would be with them soon, and the king would have many questions for them!!!

Everyone turned to watch these four huge birds of prey approach, as they drew closer they seemed to look different, their once beautiful colourful feathers seemed to of lost their colour, in fact they now looked black! Maybe it was just the light, they were still very high, but as they came into land it was clear they were now in-fact black!

As soon as they landed, they shook as hard as they could, and totally unusual to see; they rolled over trying to drag themselves across the ground, Tornado could be heard to say, "It burns, get it off me please."

"My God what is wrong?" asked the king most concerned,

Everyone ran to see what was happening, they could hear the great Birgumon moaning, sounding so distressed; and when they joined the king, who looked helpless not knowing what was wrong! or how to ease their suffering; it was apparent these beautiful beast where suffering terribly, cries of "No, no, what's happening to them, poor-poor things." People were crying, the poor children were instantly terrified by what they could see and hear, the king asked the children to leave and wait by the passage, some of the children were besides themselves and crying. Adrian said he would escort the children and asked if john and Samuel would assist him, to which they did.

"We must help them," said the king, "Ti-at what is wrong describe what is happening so we may be able to help somehow!"

Ti-at replied; "It's the dust, its covered us it's burning into us, making it hard to breathe, feel like I'm suffocating, my skin is becoming hard, it's getting hard to move, ahh, ah, my king I think we are doomed…"

Then a voice could be heard, it was one of the healers; Babbyah. "We might be able to help them, Ti-at, did you say its dust that burns you?"

"Yes," he replied; "dust from the cloud, I thought we were safely above it, but fine particles must have been all around us and have stuck to us."

"Ok, if it's dust then surely we must be able to wash it off-of them somehow?" Babbyah replied.

"It is worth a try," said the king.

Babbyah, continued; "There are lemons growing over there,

which are a   great disinfectant," and pointed to a grove to her right, "We need their juice."

With that one of the men, Matthias was his name, turned to the group and pointed at ten men, "You are with me," he said. "We will get the lemon juice together," to which the men agreed, they stood in a row facing the lemon grove, and as Matthias led, they each put both hands together fingers stretched straight, then pushed their arms out straight ahead of them, and focused on the juice within the lemons, now they slowly began to bend their fingers as if they had a ball in their hands, and started to slowly open their arms sideways, as they did this the lemon groves began to shake, and the juice of the lemons started to drain from them, the lemons looked as though they were deflating like a balloon as the juice flowed from them.

While the men carried out the fetching of the lemon juice, Babbyah ask the rest of those standing there could they fetch water and clean cotton , luckily they were surrounded by snowcapped mountains which had streams of fresh melted snow running down them, so this made their task very easy indeed, so two hundred approximately stood in a row facing the mountains, arms out palms facing up focusing on the streams, and as they did sure enough water separated into droplets, and raised into the air, billions of them, like a storm had frozen midair. They worked together so well; this had only taken a few minutes to achieve.

The remainder of the group had gone and fetched clean cotton; this was to be used to wash the Birgumon down with the lemon juice.

Now on two sides of the Birgumon stood the groups with the lemon juice and cotton, and on the other stood the group holding tons upon tons of fresh clean water, above the desperate creatures, waiting for orders what to do next.

"Right!" said Babbyah, "Ti-at this might smart a little, but I believe it will work," she continued to ask the four desperate creatures if they could brace, and informed them; "We will need to clamber over you while we wash you down, this may hurt you but please refrain from biting or clawing us with your beaks and talons…"

To which Sush whimpered, "Whatever it takes, please just do it, get it over and done please. Tears of pain running along his beak, Babbyah wanted to cry seeing so much pain in this once beautiful creature's eyes, but steadfast she stayed, focused on what had to be done to save them, and so began to issue orders.

"Ok, here we go, we need to soak them with the water first," she commanded, and so those who held the water above now slowly allowed it to fall like heavy rain, as the water droplets touched down on the now black feathers, it sizzled and hissed and the more the water made contact the louder the sounds became, it wasn't just sounds the water was creating, unfortunately it was causing pain for the Birgumon, it was becoming unbearable, the poor creatures were screeching with the pain, it was deafening, but they did not lash out, their poor bodies were rigid their legs and talons stretched out, the muscles tensed and bulging, so intense was the pain.

Babbyah was becoming distressed by the effects this was having on the Birgumon, she wasn't expecting this reaction to be so intense, and so started to doubt they were doing the right thing, but Ti-at sensed her anguish, and told her to continue, he told her he had faith in her; to which she responded, "Very well."

Once they had truly soaked the Birgumon it was time to wash them down with the lemon juice, and so now the group of men who held the lemon juice began to lower it, saturating the four beasts, the purifying acids of the lemon juice burned them terribly, more intensely than the water had, so painful in fact the four Birgumon passed out.

In a way this was a Godsend, they now no longer felt the effects of the water and lemon juice, they were at peace for now, and so Babbyah and the people helping to clean them were able to do so without feeling so terrible for causing the Birgumon so much pain, and not just that! They could now clean them without the fear of the Birgumon lashing out in pain, which could be devastating, and cause instant death to a human.

But they were unsure as to how long the beasts would be unconscious, and so worked as fast as they could, they soaked the cotton in lemon juice and rubbed down along the shaft of the feathers, and outward so as not to cause damage to them, they carefully separated the feathers as they cleaned this almost shell-like substance which had cracked and started to separate like a scab.

Thankfully it was working! But the feathers had been slightly damaged, they didn't feel so soft as they once did, and so Babbyah said the Birgumon would have to be covered with Omiul leaf's, these leaves had incredible healing powers, but they would need to forage for more, as they would need far more than they had with them.

Luckily the Omiul leaf was abundant in the woodlands around them, "It would be faster if we send the children to fetch the leaves as they could fly to the woodlands and back with them," said the king.

And so, the King asked the children to fetch the leaves and bring them to where the Birgumon lay still unconscious.

The children were more than happy to assist and with most haste they participated; within the hour they had gathered enough Omiul leaves to completely cover the Birgumon and would still have plenty for the journey ahead should it be required.

Now everyone under the supervision of Babbyah lovingly covered the still Unconscious Birgumon with Omiul leaves, now all they could do was wait and pray it had all worked.

Matthias, had always had a passion for these beautiful beasts, even as a child would watch them in awe soaring through the skies, their beautiful colours glistening in the sun, to him they were the most beautiful wonderful creatures that lived, and had always dreamed of riding one, to be at one with such a beast soaring at incredible speeds was a dream of his, he hoped one day might come true.

With his passion for these Birgumon, he didn't want to leave them until he knew they had recovered, and so sat next to Ti-at gently stroking his beak, it was while he was doing this he could feel Ti-at's breath against his hand, but his breathing seemed to be stifled, and so Matthias became quickly concerned, he quickly called Babbyah.

"They aren't breathing properly, please come take a look Babbyah…"

Babbyah came as quick as she could, she placed her hand in front of Ti-at's nostril, she could barely feel his breath, "You're right! The dust must have got into their lungs, quickly, she said I need four hot head-sized rocks, wool, enough to cover the tips of their beaks, and boiling water, now!"

To which Matthias summonsed the help of three others, one he asked to fetch boiling water in a bowl, another he asked to fetch enough wool to cover the tips of each of the Birgumon's beaks.

The last he asked to assist him to make a fire and find head-sized rocks to heat on the fire.

They set the fire about five feet from the Birgumon, then ran to find rocks for the task, Samuel and John could see they were working frantically, and asked if they could help; "What do you need us to do?" asked John.

Matthias said they could help find head-sized rocks they needed four of them to be heated on the fire, to which they both agreed.

In no time the four had found the rocks and placed them on the fire to heat them till they glowed.

Now the two men Matthias had asked to fetch water and wool had returned, and asked Matthias what they should do, Matthias asked them to give the containers of water and wool to Babbyah.

Babbyah proceeded to wash the inside of the nostrils of all four Birgumon, with a piece of the wool and hot water, she'd mixed eucalyptus oil with the water, she hoped the eucalyptus would get into their lungs and help clear them.

Then once the rocks were glowing red, she asked the men to place a rock directly under the nostril of each of the Birgumon, to which they had to do using Telekinesis as they were far too hot to touch.

Once the men had placed the rocks, Babbyah tore the wool into pieces big enough to lay one end on the stones and place the other end up the nostril of the Birgumon, she then poured the hot water and eucalyptus mix onto the wool which was heated by the incredibly hot rocks, this caused the wool to steam and the vapour of the eucalyptus to travel along the wool and into the nostrils, it would then be inhaled by the Birgumon filling their lungs and cleaning them, freeing any gunk that may be inside them, and hopefully improving their breathing.

Once again all they could do now is hope, pray, and wait.

Matthias once again sat alongside his beloved Birgumon, and in turn gently stroked their beaks, and spoke to them, "Come on you guys, you can get through this, you're Birgumon! The kings of the skies, please don't let this beat you (I haven't ridden you yet!)," he chuckled to himself.

The rest of the group, including the king, had come to the acceptance that the journey had come to a halt, they would not proceed until the Birgumon had fully recovered, and so as it was coming up to midday they set about making food, they had nice dried fish, carrots, onions, garlic, all thrown together in big cooking pots, with water, black pepper and ginger, everyone was helping, including the king who was helping peel the potatoes, he did have quite a way of peeling the potatoes which a few of the group found quite funny and had to make sarcastic comments, "You're supposed to peel them my king," said Jamie, one of the volunteers who was also peeling potatoes and was laughing with disbelief at the kings total misunderstanding of how to peel a potato.

"I am" replied the king as another quarter of an inch of potato fell to the ground with a thud, which made Jamie and those who were witnessing this marvel of potato peeling burst into uncontrollable laughter!

"Not sure who is going to be eating better today! Us or the wildlife!" said Jamie still laughing! "Looks as though they are definitely getting more spuds than us!" replied Tim, laughing so hard his belly was hurting and eyes streaming.

"Ok, gentlemen, I'm obviously doing something wrong, so please enlighten me," said the king trying to keep a straight face, but finding it hard to do so with approximately ten men and women laughing so hard they could barely stand, tears streaming from their eyes..

You may ask, how could the Kings followers possibly laugh and be sarcastic towards him?

As after all he is their king!

Well a true king doesn't hold himself on high and think lower of the people he serves no, King Stephen was a king of the people, he was truly one of them, he would, play, laugh, cry, with his people, the people of Soul are completely as one, no one was lesser or higher than the other.

A king is one chosen to lead and care for their people, and King Stephen would even give his life for the good of his people if it came to it.

So with this in mind, the people around him would have no fear of having fun with their king, they would never be truly disrespectful, this was just playfulness, saying that the king was terrible at peeling potatoes, and someone would have to show him how it's properly done, as they didn't have an everlasting supply.

This single chore had lifted their spirits, they all needed a good laugh and the king knew this, and so played along.

And so, Jamie approached the king still laughing uncontrollably.

The king looked at Jamie with a slightly embarrassed demeanour, then looked back at his hand and what was left of the potato he had mutilated, then again looked back to Jamie and the potato he had in his hand that he had peeled so very well, it was perfect.

The king could only respond, "Well yours is a lot bigger than mine," and tilted his head.

Jamie then replied; "Well it's all down to how you use this," and showed the king the razor sharp short blade he was using to peel the potatoes, he then proceeded to take a fresh potato from the supply sack, and stood next to the King and started to explain how to peel a potato correctly. "You see the trick is to remove the skin only; then with a firm grip placed the edge of the blade into the potato at the top, with almost surgical precision, just under the skin and rotate the potato," the king was watching intently as Jamie peeled the potato so perfectly, and when he had finish the skin was still intact, Jamie then looked at the king and held the skin together, which formed the perfect shape of the potato, almost as if it hadn't been peeled, he then held the skin in one hand, and the perfectly peeled potato in the other, and said to the king "That's what it should look like" with a very proud, eyebrow-raised look on his face.

The king replied; "Ok, I'll try again." Then picked out a nice fresh potato and proceeded to place the edge of his blade into the potato, he was being cautious not to go to deep, then started to rotate the potato, the blade slid smoothly under the skin, for a moment he looked like he had control, but then, as he continued to rotate the potato he increased the pressure confidence growing, then with one slip of the thumb he cut the potato near in half.

"Wow, you're lucky to still have a thumb," said Jamie.

"It was close wasn't it?!" the king laughed, he then sighed "Think I'd best leave it to those who actually know what they are doing."

"I agree," said Jamie and laughed, it would be nice to have some potatoes left!

With that the king said, "I'll go check on the Birgumon," and hastily put the blade back into the leather wrap which kept all the cooking utensils and said, "I'll be off see you all soon."

To which they all chuckled, "See you soon, my king."

And off he went, when he arrived Matthias was still watching over the Birgumon. "Any change?" asked the King.

It had been over an hour now since Babbyah had place the wool over their beaks with the eucalyptus and water mix, the king was hoping it might have started to take effect by now.

"Hello, my king, it would seem their breathing is starting to become a little stronger, their lungs seem to be clearing, they have been coughing this horrible black mucus up, which must mean its clearing off their chest mustn't it?" Matthias replied.

"I'm not sure," replied the king, "I'll ask Babbyah to join us" and with that he called on Babbyah Telepathically, "Babbyah can you please join me and Matthias we are with Ti-at?"

"On my way," she replied.

Within a couple of minutes, she had arrived, and asked was there a problem?

"That's what we wanted to ask you," replied the king; "Matthias has been watching over the Birgumon, and says they are coughing up this black mucus, is this to be expected?" And pointed to the puddles by each of the four unwell beasts.

"Wonderful," she replied, "this is a great sign, the eucalyptus is breaking down the infection and forcing it out, so it's just what I wanted to see, it will still be a while before they are up and about I should think."

She then sighed, "I'd like to try something!"

"You're the healer," said the king; "Whatever you think is best, we have faith in your skills."

"Now that the eucalyptus as broken down whatever it is that is inside them, I should be able to speed the process, by dragging it out."

"How do you intend to do that?" asked Matthias.

"With my mind," she smiled.

And with that she knelt just under Ti-at's wing as close to his chest as she could get.

She then closed her eyes and focused on Ti-at's lungs trying to get a picture in her mind, she then started to rub her hands together and as she did so they began to glow, it was almost as if she had a bright light in her hands, they became almost transparent it was so bright, you could almost see the bones and veins.

She then began to hum, she hummed continuously raising and lowering the tone, then placed her glowing hands on Ti-at's chest, she could see the infection in her mind's eye, and so one lung at a time using the power of her mind began to scrape the now loosened substance into a ball.

Now she had to move the ball of mucus infection out of the lung, this would mean moving it out of the lung and pushing it through the Trachea, throat and out the mouth.

She'd have to try and do this as fast as she dare, but also not cause any further damage, she was now moving the substance along the trachea, this was the most stressful process, due to the fact that whilst she was doing this, the substance was completely blocking Ti-at's trachea and totally inhibited his breathing.

She had to continue, he was now fighting to get breath, and starting to lift his head; in an attempt to gasp for air; He was trying to move, this could be disastrous for Babbyah and Ti-at both.

Matthias sensed Ti-at was becoming distressed, and so crouched in front of him, holding his beak with both hands and gently rubbed it, saying, "Don't be afraid, try and stay calm," then suddenly Ti-at opened his eyes, and stared in to Matthias's eyes, "That's it, focus on me, you're going to be fine I promise," said Mathias.

Poor Ti-at's head was now raising and lowering, his neck trying to stretch as he reached for air, pulling Matthias's arms up and down...

Babbyah was now reaching the throat, this was causing poor Ti-at to retch, his eyes were so wide open they looked as though they were going to pop out, the poor beast was terrified, there was an amazing loud noise coming from is chest, like a groaning sound from deep inside him, his wings were starting to flap, he was losing control panic was taking over.

"Stay with me, stay with me," cried Matthias trying to help Ti-at regain focus, but the fear was to strong pure panic had taken over, Ti-at's eyes suddenly closed as he leapt up extending his wings fully, the sudden reaction knocked both Matthias and Babbyah flat on their backs wind-ing them both as Ti-at stumbled around almost falling, he just missed stepping on Babbyah who had been knocked on to her back and was now directly under the panic stricken Birgumon, she just manage to roll out of the way as his huge foot with huge talons thudded to the ground, she would have been crushed if she had hesitated, but before she could take a breath another stumbling foot was heading directly for her, she again rolled, there was a loud scream! One of Ti-at's talons had caught her in the waist, she was now pinned to the ground by the talon!

Matthias and the king both looked at each other terrified, and knowing they had to act quickly!

"I'll get to Babbyah shouted the king, you try and get Ti-at's attention."

The king then ran dodging Ti-at's huge flailing wings and managed to get under the beast and grab Babbyah by the hand, and readied to pull her from under Ti-at the moment he lifted his foot freeing Babbyah.

Matthias called out to Ti-at repeatedly trying to gain his attention, but to no avail, the creature was in such a state of panic…

But as Ti-at once again stumbled he lifted his foot freeing Babbyah, the king without hesitation pulled her as hard as he could and dragged her to safety.

Matthias was trying to stay in front of Ti-at to gain his attention moving this way and that calling his name constantly, then Ti-at opened his eyes, pure fear could be seen in his expression, then there was a huge bellowing as Ti-at released a huge cough which launched this thick tar like substance all over poor Matthias, he was knocked to ground with a wet thud.

"What on Soul?!" he shouted, as he ran his hands over his face to clear his eyes and mouth.

Then a huge inhale could be heard as Ti-at drew his first breath, coughing and splattering, "I can breathe, I can breathe," he repeated.

He then turned in the direction of the king and Babbyah, Babbyah was laying on her back clasping her waist in terrible pain, the king on bent knee over her, his hands on her shoulders, stay still, try not to move, I'll get help, you'll be fine I promise.

When Ti-at saw Babbyah his heart sank, "No, no, no, did I do this?" he said as he; with great haste thudded his way too them, feeling terrible at the thought he had hurt her, "I'm so-so sorry," he kept repeating.

"I'll be fine, it was an accident, please don't feel bad you couldn't help it, you had no idea I was under you."

"But even so I feel terrible," Ti-at replied.

"But nothing, she forgives you it was an accident," said the king, and smiled hoping to put Ti-at at ease.

Ti-at lowered his head sorrowfully, "Thank you, will she be ok?" he asked.

"Yes I'll be fine, it's a flesh wound, no internal organs or arteries have been damaged thankfully, just smarts a lot, besides I have to clear your other lung yet, and then I have to do the same for Sush, Tornado and Micah as yet, so I have to be!" she smiled at Ti-at.

Then Matthias arrived, "Thank god your alive," he said to Babbyah, "are you going to be ok?"

"Yes, I'll be fine, thank you Matthias. what happened to you?" she asked Matthias trying not to laugh, as it hurt.

That's great news," he replied, "I'll tell you what happened! Him, is what happened to me," he said as he pointed to Ti-at. "This is the thanks I get for watching over you, worrying about you, praying you're recover, and not leaving your side, thanks!" he said as he looked at Ti-at, who had his head lowered and eyes closed with shame.

Ti-at slowly opened his eyes and looked at Matthias with an almost sorry-full puppy eyed look, which just melted Matthias's heart, "no-no-no don't you look at me like that, I'm not letting you off, look at me, how am I supposed to get this off, it's so sticky!" as he tried to clear his ears and the substance stuck to his fingers, "blah it's on my mouth, and started to retch, I'm going to be sick!"

At this point Ti-at was looking at Matthias and couldn't help but say "My word no wonder I couldn't breathe, there was so much and that's just the one lung!"

And looked at Matthias with disgust then grimaced, ugh, then after a moment started to chuckle.

Don't you dare but before Matthias could finish, Ti-at, Babbyah and the king burst into laughter at the site of Matthias and his whining, he was a sight to see covered from head to toe in black goo.

"Ouch-ouch I don't mean to laugh," said Babbyah clasping her waist.

"Can't breathe," said Ti-at, laughing so hard and then started to cough, as he coughed the goo which was still in his other lung was starting to cause Ti-at to wheeze and gasp, the laughing came to a sudden stop, as he started to cough uncontrollably and retch, Matthias became instantly concerned, "Are you ok Ti-at," he asked fearing the worst…

Then an almighty cough, a real bellowing cough, followed by a loud sloppy thud.

"Oh my that feels so much better," said Ti-at as he spat out the remains of the goo, then inhaled a nice big deep breath of fresh air and exhaled, "how wonderful that feels!" he said, and with a look of elation turned to the king and Babbyah who both stood staring at him mouths open in gasp! They just looked at each other for a moment, then the king and Babbyah, not making it to obvious looked in the direction of where Matthias had been stood, Ti-at dare not look! And in a whispered thought; "I've done it again haven't I?" as he opened his eyes wide and started to look in the direction they were staring, he grimaced, as laying on the ground completely covered in a mound of black goo was poor Matthias, who was whimpering quietly, "You've done it again! I don't believe it," he moaned.

"O, o, o, I am so so-so sorry Matthias, please forgive me I had no idea. I am truly sorry. If it's any consolation I feel much better!" and smiled.

At this point members of the group had started to arrive as they had heard a commotion and saw Ti-at stumbling around, and so came to see if everything was ok.

The first person they approached was the king who was still staring with disbelief at what had just happened to Matthias, and when asked was everything ok, just replied; "Yes everything is fine, but please don't laugh he is upset enough as it is…"

To which the king explained what had just happened, and the group members just had to have a look, and so proceeded to get a closer look at Matthias, the king tried to stop them, "Please no, no, give him a moment, he is still in shock," the king said fighting back the laughter.

"But they had to see, ugh they exclaimed, that came out of you Ti-at?" one asked.

"Yes unfortunately," replied Ti-at…

As Matthias started to get to his feet, which was quite a struggle as he battled the sticky goo, and it would stretch then slap back against him, people could be heard to retch.

"That's disgusting," one said, "human handkerchief, ugh lovely."

As the others heard these comments, it was inevitable they could not help themselves and laughter broke out.

What a sight he was, poor Matthias stumbling around totally covered in this sticky goo, and as he tried to clear his mouth and eyes he was complaining "Once again, are you being serious, you've done it again I can't believe this, look at me!"

As his complaints became louder so did the laughter, everyone around him were in total hysterics.

Then suddenly a loud coughing could be heard, it was Sush he was regaining consciousness and the eucalyptus had worked perfectly as the black goo in his lungs had been completely broken down and was working its way out with his coughing, the coughing was becoming more intense, and Sush was now finding it hard to breathe, he stood trying to open his airways, stretching his neck as far as he could, the goo was now well in his trachea and cutting of his air supply and just as Ti-at did, he was now beginning to struggle and panic started to creep up.

Ti-at immediately jumped to Sush's aid and started to bang Sush's back with his powerful wings to free the sticky goo, "Stay calm, try not to panic you will be fine."

"It's the infection working its way out of you, you just need to stay calm and try to cough as hard as you can," but this was easier said than done as the goo being so sticky was almost stuck to Sush's wind pipe, and to cough he would need to take a breath and fill his lungs, but was unable too, he was starting to suffocate, his beak was opening as wide as it could as he gasped for air, then slamming shut making an incredible sound like two blocks of solid wood banging together.

He was in real trouble, his eyes were starting to roll as he was losing consciousness, Ta-at intently beat Sush's back, "Come on son, don't you give up, fight it please," Ti-at was starting to worry, he started squawking as he became overwhelmed with the situation, this was incredibly loud to those around, they clasped their ears in pain grimacing. Babbyah although in pain from her injury and now the deafening cries near bursting her eardrums leaped into action, running as fast as her injury would allow and rubbing her hands intently which once again began to glow.

Sush had now completely lost consciousness and fell to the ground with an earth-shaking thud, he was suffering convulsions, this was a terrible sign and Babbyah had to act quickly...

Ti-at was standing over Sush squawking continuously totally helpless.

He saw Babbyah running towards him he knew she was Sush's only chance, and stepped away giving her room, she slid into Sush's chest and placed her glowing hands on his upper chest at the base of his throat, she closed her eyes and focused intently, yes I can see it, she began to run her hands along his throat and towards his beak, his beak fell open and out started to pour this terrible sticky goo, there was so much, it must have been from both lungs simultaneously, and would explain the terrible difficulty to clear it.

She could see the last was nearing the end and gave it a swift hard push, to which it shot from his throat, and as it did there was a vacuum sound, it was the air rushing into his chest.

But still he was unconscious, unresponsive; Babbyah began to beat his chest as hard as she could, but nothing, she continued to beat his chest without success, his heart had stopped he was gone, Ti-at let out an almighty squawk it was an incredible pain-filled sound..

Then Judith the healer that helped Samuel, placed a hand on Babbyah, saying; "You're exhausted, let me try."

Babbyah agreed and stood aside, Judith began to chant and rub her hands, after a moment she looked to Ti-at and said when I say, I need you to slot your-beak into Sush's and exhale, can you do this? She asked, to which the distraught creature replied he would.

She then once again started to chant and placed her hands on Sush's chest, she was focused on his heart, and with her mind started to manipulate it, gently compressing and releasing it, she could see the blood flowing through Sush's veins as she did so, she would do three compressions then stop, Ti-at now please, then Ti-at placed his beak between Sush's open beak and exhaled filling Sush's lungs and expanding them fully, then Judith repeated the compressions, one, two , three, Ti-at again please, and again he placed his beak between Sush's and exhaled, again filling his lungs, then suddenly Sush gasped, and coughed, he was breathing heavily taking huge breaths, gulping as much air as he could, "My chest, it hurts so bad, what happened?" Ti-at just smiled and placed his right wing around Sush's back, and said "You're alive."

Everyone that had witnessed this incredible miracle just exploded with happiness grabbing each other, some crying so totally emotionally exhausted, "He's alive," some shouted!

Ti-at then turned to Judith and Babbyah; stood between them, they were both in tears of joy, he looked to them placed his huge wings around them and pulled them close to him and hugged them and said he could never thank them enough for what they had done to save Sush, he continued to tell them; "I will always be here for you if you ever need me in any way I'm here for you both."

"You are very welcome," replied Babbyah, "it's not over yet though! We still have Micah and Tornado to worry about yet! I'll be able to relax when they are both conscious and well."

With all that she had done, and the stress caused whilst fighting to help Sush, she had forgotten about her own injury, until Judith notice Babbyah was bleeding! "Babbyah you are bleeding, let me take a look at you please."

"If you could please, that would be wonderful, but first we still have work to do."

"No, you can't continue, you're bleeding and you look exhausted, you can't possibly," said Judith.

"I must, I have to see this through, and now I know what we have to do to remove the infection without causing distress to Micah and Tornado,"

Judith replied, asking Babbyah to tell her what had to be done so she could perform the procedure for her, and she could rest, "They will be in safe hands, I promise you."

"She is right," said the king, "your bleeding you have done enough, let Judith do this, we need you for the rest of our mission, we don't want you unable to continue do we?"

"Ok, you're right, I will explain to Judith, but with both of them likely to awaken any moment I think it best we have two healers, one for each Birgumon, working simultaneously, hopefully clear the infection a lot quicker before they wake."

"Ok, I will call Peter to join us, he is a very knowledgeable and wise healer, he should be just the man for the task," replied Judith.

With that, she Telepathically focused on Peter and asked him to join them, which he immediately did, and together Babbyah explained what had to be done, the Birgumon were suffering terribly due to the fact the infection had become so sticky it was taking too long to clear the windpipe, and trying to move it was difficult, so they needed to move it in much smaller sizes and so need to break it down into small slithers, so it would travel along the windpipe easier.

Peter suggested possibly breaking it down into minute particles almost like water vapour, "That way as the Birgumon exhales it would be carried out in the breath with a little help from them," he continued, "We would only be able to do a small area at one time, but it should be much more comfortable and easier for us to guide."

It is definitely worth a try they agreed, and so Judith cleaned and stitched Babbyah's injury, and then covered it with an Omiul leaf to speed her recovery, then with Peter, readied themselves for the task of removing the infection from Micah and Tornado! Hopefully while they were still unconscious.

They both sat next to the creatures, just under their wing, and focused on their lungs, they rubbed their hands until they glowed, then held them out in front of them, hands open as if ready to catch a ball in each, then turned them so their palms faced down.

Now they could see the infection, and using their minds it was as though they had stuck their fingertips into the infection while their hands were still open, and as they closed their fingers an area of approximately six inches was gathered by each finger clasp, they then pulled it away and off of the inner lining of the lung with a small arm motion backwards, as they did this the Birgumon gave a subtle cough, they must have been able to feel it being pulled off their lung! So Judith and Peter paused for a moment, the Birgumon both seemed at ease for the moment, so they proceeded, when it was clear of the lining of the lung they opened their fingers and the horrible sticky goo started to separate into minute particles, they could only of been the size of a pinhead, and now Judith and Peter, manipulated these tiny particles into a thin line and waited for the Birgumon to exhale, and as they did the pair guided the particles carefully, not letting them make contact with the lung or throat lining, up and out the beak, "Great it's working!" Judith said.

Now all they had to hope was that the Birgumon stay unconscious until they had finished the process.

So as soon as they had removed the first of the goo they immediately got straight back to it, and after a time they had succeeded in clearing the lungs of any infection, Both Judith and Peter were exhausted, it had actually taken them over two hours to complete the process, and both deserved a good rest and some food and drink, which was waiting for them both, as while they were healing the Birgumon the majority of the group had gone back to preparing the food, and saved Judith and Peter a nice big portion each.

Even the king and Matthias had taken turns to freshen up, eat and drink, then immediately returned just in case Judith and peter might have needed assistance should the Birgumon have woken.

As for Ti-at and Sush they stayed the whole time, watching the two healers working tirelessly to help their kin.

They also thought it best to stay just in case Micah and Tornado should wake, they would be able to hold them and try and comfort them, but fortunately this wasn't the case, the two Birgumon were still unconscious, but now their breathing had improved immensely, they were comfortable now.

And it would seem that the Omiul leaves had done a great job of almost restoring all of the Birgumon's feathers to their original beauty, the humans had performed an amazing feat and Ti-at and Sush would never forget this.

As for Babbyah she was so exhausted after her efforts she had fallen asleep, but now had woken and returned to the Birgumon, when she arrived the king, Matthias, Judith, Peter, Ti-at and Sush were all resting by Micah and Tornado, just waiting for them to wake.

As soon as the king saw Babbyah approaching he stood and walked towards her, she was still walking a little unsteadily due to her injury, and so the king offered his arm for her to put her weight, and so guided her to the group.

When Judith saw Babbyah she smiled a big all so happy smile. "It worked! We managed to clear all the infection from them both, we are now just waiting for them to wake, hopefully they will be fine!"

"I'm so pleased, they should wake soon!" replied Babbyah.

"I could always give them a nudge," said Ti-at, then thought yes I think I will, and so reached out his right wing and stroked

Tornado's head and said, "Wake up my boy, come on sleepy head, time to wake," then gave Tornado a nudge, which caused him to stir.

"That's it my boy, wake up," Ti-at was actually quite anxious about the pair, he wanted them to wake to put his mind at ease that they were ok, as it stood no one could be sure, so the longer they remain unconscious the more anxious Ti-at became, and so his nudges became heavy shoves, which seemed to work as Tornado opened his eyes and moaned; "What do you want I'm sleeping," then tutted and gave a big groan.

"He's fine," said Ti-at always loves his sleep this one, then rolled his eyes and chuckled with relief.

"Does anyone have any pai berries, one whiff of those and he will be up like a flash," said Sush.

Pai berries are an extremely juicy sweet fruit, purple in colour very soft, and almost explode when bitten, so for a human to eat they would usually cut into it carefully over a bowl to catch the juices and flesh, the flesh of the fruit was so nutritious full of vitamins and minerals and the Birgumon absolutely loved them, especially Tornado.

"Pai berries mmm," said Tornado, "I'd love some, why do I feel so tired, I had a terrible dream. You were all in it, me Sush, Micha and Ti-at were covered in this black dust." "That wasn't a dream I'm afraid, we have just recovered from that, it was real," said Ti-at.

"I remember the humans trying to help, then the pain! Then nothing," replied Tornado.

"It was an awfully painful experience for us all, we must have passed out, thankfully," replied Ti-at.

"Yes, so painful, I remember feeling as though I was being burned alive, I actually thought I was going to die, so I'm grateful we passed out, I couldn't have endured that being conscious," said Tornado.

"How is Micah?" Tornado continued looking at Micah who was still unconscious.

"Hopefully he will be fine, we are hoping he will wake anytime now," replied Matthias, still looking concerned…

Matthias then walked over to Micah, bent on one knee directly in front of the beautiful creature, he then reached out his right hand and began to stroke his beak and head with long gentle strokes, from the tip of his beak to the base of his head.

There was this big powerhouse of a man, and yet there he was stroking this beautiful creature with such love; it was easily visible to those around him; he resembled a small child stroking a sick puppy, so gentle and loving, it was easy to see he was fighting back many emotions, all he wanted was for Micah to wake, and so he would not move from Micah, and just continued to stroke him so lovingly.

The king could see that Matthias was truly concerned about Micah and so walked over to Matthias, he then bent on one knee opposite him and also began to stroke Micah, "Beautiful creatures aren't they?" the king said to Matthias, to which Matthias replied; as he ran his hand over the beautiful creatures head and ran his fingers through its wonderful feathers, "Yes truly wonderful."

The king then proceeded; "He will be fine, he is strong and young, he is just sleeping off and awful experience, I'm sure he will wake soon," he then smiled at Matthias, Matthias looked the king straight in the eye and asked "What could do this?! What lays in wait for us beyond these mountains?" he said as he looked at the beautiful snowcapped mountains. no one could imagine beyond them there lay something that could do something so terrible to these beautiful Birgumon, and if it could; what would it able to do to a human…?

The king swiftly replied, "Once Micah wakes, I will be asking Ti-at what happened to them beyond the mountains, hopefully he will be able to give us the answers we seek!

"We also have to consider what has become of our people, those souls whom live in Polaria, we can only hope they haven't succumbed to the same fate which nearly took the Birgumon from us, we have to proceed even more so now, as they may be in desperate need of our assistance to save them from this ghastly ash substance, that is if we aren't too late!

"But now due to what has happened I will not expect everyone to continue with me, if you want to turn back, I will understand Matthias," said the king.

"No my king I do not wish to turn back, I too know people of Polaria and turning back is out of the question for me my king, I would just like more information as to what caused this terrible infection so as we can plan and protect ourselves against it!

"I don't want us wondering blindly into what could be a very dangerous situation without a plan my king, not saying that you would lead us blindly my king, we all have faith in you, we know you are wise and hold our safety paramount, I mean no offence by my words."

"None taken," replied the king, "in fact I respect your words, you are a man of honour, you are also wise I can tell, you are a man who doesn't rush into something and that I like, in fact I believe I will be able to call on you to assist me in a strategy once we have gathered the information we need from the Birgumon, in fact I would like you to be my second, if anything should happen to me, you will lead the people back home."

"My king it would be my honour to assist you in any-way you see fit.

And I'm sure my king will be fine, But I give you my word if anything should happen to you, I will do my best to get us all home safely rest assured."

The two men then reached out their right arms and clasping each other's forearms and made a pact whatever happens they would do their best to get their people home safely.

As the king and Matthias made their pact, Micah began to stir, he began to make an almost hum like sound mmm, he started to lift his head ever so slightly, then after a moment he opened his eyes and just stared directly at Matthias; after several moments he asked Matthias; "What happened? I feel as though I've slept an eternity my head feels so heavy, and my chest aches so bad, what has happened?"

"Don't you remember?" asked Matthias.

"Remember what?" replied Micah.

"Ok, you're ok, everyone is ok, just let yourself wake up properly compose yourself, and hopefully you might remember, if not I'm sure we can refresh your memory for you," said Matthias.

After a few good yawns Micah stood and began to stretch, he stretched out his neck as far as he could and tilted his head back as far as possible; it looked as though he was going to snap his own neck he tilted it so far, he then puffed out his huge chest and stretched out his wings; and as he stretched, a shudder went right through him and out of his wing tips almost like a wave motion, causing the very tips of his wings to judder rapidly just for a second or two.

Then he lowered his wings looked around then; "I'm awake, who can tell me what happened?" to which Ti-at proceeded to explain what had happened and how the humans had worked so hard to save all their lives.

To which Micah looked around, and as he did, he thanked the king, Babbyah, Judith, Peter, and Matthias for their help, and continued he would always be in their debt.

"There is no debt, it was the least we could do," said Matthias, to which they all agreed. "We are just truly thankful you are all ok, we weren't too sure you would make it, but thank God you have," he said and smiled.

After the king and Matthias's earlier conversation they both felt it imperative to know what lay beyond the mountains, as they would have to have a plan of action to proceed to Polaria; as when the king first planned this mission it was simply a mission of aid, he was expecting to arrive at Polaria and find at the least, the region to of suffered massive structural and environmental damage with loss of life inevitable, as he was sure the impact area was if not Polaria its self then extremely close to it! And so was expecting to rescue the trapped and aid the injured back to health.

But he was not expecting anything which could have an impact on himself and those with him, such as what had happened to the Birgumon.

And so, if the mission was to continue, they now had to ask the Birgumon what they had seen and how they became covered in the deadly ash.

And so, the king asked Ti-at to explain what they had seen and how they believed they became infected.

Ti-at explained that they couldn't see the ground due to the whole region being covered by the deadly cloud, and couldn't be sure whether the infection was solely airborne or if it had made contact with the ground, he even explained how he thought that they were safely above the cloud, but it would seem that was not the case, as even the smallest particles where to be feared!

Now with this information the mission looked doomed, the king could not take his people into the seemingly deadly unknown! If only they could see the ground, they could get an idea of the situation, but he could not enter the path knowing this ash could be at ground level and easily be heading towards them being carried by the air which was flowing through the cave.

This now presented a new problem to be considered by the king and Matthias!

And that was they had to do something, and soon! Because the ash and cloud could easily be carried in their direction if the wind was to change direction, and that would mean Bulgan and even the king's homelands of Engypt could be in danger from the ash!

They would have to find a way to ensure the cloud could not become a danger to the lands to the south of Polaria.

The king, Matthias and Ti-at continued to ponder the situation.

"We have to find a way to stop the cloud being able to travel, but how?" asked the king.

Matthias turned to Ti-at, "You said this cloud is made up of ash and dust, am I right?"

"Yes, it is, the cloud itself seemed very dense with ash, but also the minuscule particles which we could not even see and that settled on us are extremely dangerous, how do you stop something you can't see!" Ti-at replied.

Matthias looked to the king; "I might have an idea my king!"

"What is it Matthias?" replied the king.

Ti-at said, "It is dust, the cloud is made up of dust and ash! And what happens to dust or ash when it becomes wet?"

With an expression of realisation and a muffled sounding voice, the king slowly replied becoming excited!; "It becomes heavy and falls to the ground, that's it! Matthias you're a genius," he then broke into laughter and grabbed Matthias, wrapping both arms around him and lifted him briefly off the ground with excitement! "It's obvious to me now what as to be done!!! To stop the cloud, we destroy it with water, we soak it with water, we make it rain, as it were," said the king.

"But to soak the cloud we have to be able to see it, in fact to be sure we soak every particle including those above the main cloud, we would have to be above it, my king, and that is the problem! how are we going to get above the cloud and dust?" replied Matthias.

"We could regroup using the children, once again they could lift us high enough above the cloud," replied the king.

They stood in contemplation for a moment or two, but then Matthias said it wouldn't work, and his head sank with disappointment.

"Why wouldn't it work?" asked the king.

"Well my king, to fly with the children we have one hand on them and the other on the person next to us, but for us to manipulate the water we would have to let go and so crash to the ground…"

The king thought for a moment, "You're quite right," said the king, "I didn't think about that," and sighed.

"We! can do it!" It was Ti-at. "We can take you up there, as high as you need, how many of you will it take to achieve this task?" he asked.

"What is it you are thinking Ti-at?" asked the king.

"If you need to be able to have your hands free to manipulate the waters, then you may ride on our shoulders and we will carry you," replied Ti-at…

To which the king replied, "It's too much too asked of you Ti-at, you have just recovered and I could never expect you to do this for us, plus to manipulate such a vast amount of water would take at least two hundred of us, and there is only three of you, but thank you my friend."

"My king it's the least we can do to stop this cloud from spreading to our homelands, I not only offer this opportunity just to assist you! I do it for the sakes of all living things on this world, for surely if we do not stop this cloud then we all perish, Man and beast both!... I can have as many of my kin here to assist as is needed within minutes, just give your word my king ... "

"You are right my old friend, we have the same purpose, and so we will work as one, thank you!"

Then there was another voice, it was Egum; "Well that sounds like a plan to me," he said, with a jovial persona, we are happy to oblige, don't want you getting all the praise for saving the world do we?!" he laughed and looked at Ti-at, Ti-at smiled back at Egum, "You are most welcome my friend," replied Ti-at.

"Yes, you are indeed," said the king, truly happy for the assistance.

They then set about devising a plan of action!!

The rest of the group were becoming anxious, they really wanted to get on and get to Polaria, but they did not as yet know what the king and the others knew, the king had not as yet explained the situation, and so they were becoming restless wondering why they were not proceeding, especially as the Birgumon were now healed and seemed in good health.

It was becoming obvious to the group that something wasn't right!

And so their curiosity began to run, they had now started to ponder the possibilities amongst themselves, some had even suggested that the king had grown fearful after the incident with the Birgumon, and that they would be abandoning the mission!!

"Nonsense," said John, "the king would never abandon his people, he has obviously formed a party to discuss whatever it is they are planning, and I'm sure they will let us know what actions we will be taking when they have made a decision, and is time for us to know, I'm sure."

The healers, Peter , Babbyah and Judith were making their way back to the main group, they had left the king in discussion with Ti-at, Egum and Matthias, as they approach the main group people were eager to know what was going on and what was being discussed; and so were trying to pry as to what Peter ,Babbyah and Judith may have heard!!

One of the other healers, a lady called Simone, approached them and asked "What's happening why have we not moved into the cave and on to the path to Polaria?"

Judith replied saying; "We don't know yet, but I'm sure when the time is right the king will update us all."

"We should have moved on by now as the Birgumon have recovered! What is the delay? People could be dying over there," gestured Simone pointing to the north.

Then Peter spoke; "Yes and I'm sure the king is more than aware of that, and I would say possibly more so than us, but you have to consider the weight he must carry, yes he must want to move on just as we all do, but he has to consider our safety too, our king loves all of his people, and I'm sure it pains him we are not in Polaria now!! But luckily for us he is wise and will not proceed blindly leading us into what could be a dangerous situation; without having a good plan to which we can follow as safely as possible, rest easy my friends we will be underway again, be patient please."

"You're right I'm sorry, it's just the not knowing I guess, but I'm sure as you say when the time is right all will be told, our king as never failed us and I'm sorry for doubting him, I feel like a fool," said Simone dropping her head forward, looking to the ground.

"Don't be silly, it's natural to become disconcerted especially as we all know someone, or have relatives in Polaria, so please you shouldn't feel foolish, honestly, just have faith in our king," replied Peter.

The majority of the group had heard what Peter had to say, and it seemed to help them, seemed to put their minds at east, so rather than gossiping and becoming agitated they took the time to pack away all of the cooking utensils and regather all the equipment in readiness for the kings commands when he was ready.

While the group were carrying out their chores, the king, Matthias, Ti-at and Egum were toiling over a plan, and the only option it would seem, was to go ahead with the plan they had discussed earlier, and that was to ride the Birgumon and thanks to Egum's offer of assistance, the dragons too.

Now that they had all agreed it was the only way, the king and Matthias would now have to explain to the group, and so they headed back to the group along with the dragons and Birgumon.

When they arrived the look of relief on the others faces was apparent, and the king thanked them for their patience, then asked them all the gather round, and so they did filled with relief, they so wanted to hear what the king had to say, they just needed to know what was happening and how they were to proceed.

Once everyone had gathered the king spoke with them all simultaneously using Telepathy.

"As you may be aware, earlier today we were warned there may be danger ahead of us on the other side of these mountains, and as you all know, Ti-at and his kin flew ahead to scout for us so we could be sure what lay ahead, and unfortunately what lay on the other side of those mountains infected them, and almost took their lives.

"Now that Ti-at and his kin have recovered he has been able to explain what happened, and it's not good news unfortunately," the king then began to explain what had happened to the Birgumon, and how it would seem the cloud was the cause of their illness, and that they would not be able to proceed to Polaria whilst the cloud was in their path, and also how they needed to be concerned if the cloud shifted direction, and the effects it could have on the other regions should it reach them.

And so he continued to explain that they would have to totally destroy the cloud so it would no longer be a danger; and the tactics they had devised to do so, he wasn't hiding anything from them and continued how dangerous this could be, and that he would understand if they wanted to turn back; and that they should not feel obliged to continue, no one would think any less of those who chose not to continue.

"So, if you do not wish to continue then please step forward now!" said the King.

But not one stepped forward, these brave souls wanted to see this mission through, and were willing to do whatever it took to keep their world safe from this all so real danger! plus they wanted to help those already effected in Polaria and so weren't going anywhere but onwards.

The king was overwhelmed by the bravery and loyalty of his people, and so thanked them, saying they were truly wonderful selfless people, and that he was truly grateful to have them by his side.

Now was the time for them to put the plan into action, and so the king turned to Ti-at and asked if he would be so kind as to summon his kin.

Ti-at was one step ahead of the king, and replied saying; "I have already summed them my king, I know we only have approximately five hours of light left and so I took the initiative while you spoke with your kin," and smiled, "They should be with us any time now," and so they all looked to the sky.

After approximately ten minutes, as Ti-at had promised the sun was blocked out as these beautiful colourful Birgumon appeared over the mountain tops coming from the south; there was approximately a hundred or so with more appearing out of the woodlands that surrounded them, what an incredible sight to behold.

The king and his followers were in a state of shock and awe at the sight, they had never seen so many Birgumon at one time.

People could be heard to gasp, and others couldn't help but say how beautiful they looked.

It was truly an incredible sight, with the beautiful lush woodlands which surrounded the huge fields of green on which they stood, then all around them stood these huge mountains with wonderful snow caps , with waterfalls and streams running down them, and now with the wonderful bright summers blue sky, the rays of the sun appearing as fine beams , as it fought its way through the spaces between the Birgumon which blocked its path to the ground below..

As the Birgumon made their way, Matthias couldn't believe his dream was about to come true; as he smiled from ear to ear, and looking all around at his kin so excitedly, he was getting some strange expressions in return, this may have been a life time dream of his, but for others around him the prospect was quite scary, the huge eagles are the fastest creatures of the sky's, a dragon would seem so slow in comparison, and so some were quite unsure, and it showed on their faces, so imagine you! Not feeling to confident and there is someone next to you smiling from ear to ear, so excited he can barely contain himself, just like a child when it receives its dream present, but the difference is Matthias is an adult.

Then one after another the Birgumon began to set down, and as they did the people had to step back as they were taking up a very large area, as each one stood as tall as a house and there were two hundred of them.

Even the king felt quite daunted by the prospect of riding one of these creatures, and so suggested to Ti-at that he and those who were going to be riding them should have a little practise as this was totally new to them all.

You imagine; you've never rode a horse before and yet their it stood towering over you, and this creature doesn't stay ground based, this Birgumon can reach speeds well in excess of a hundred miles an hour and thousands of feet high, quite a scary prospect...

And, they had to fathom out how the riders would stay on, what would they hold onto?

You see a dragon has hard scales completely covering it, so a rope around its neck while being ridden wouldn't cause it any discomfort. Where-as the Birgumon are just flesh and feathers and so anything around its neck could cause great discomfort.

And so, the king asked Ti-at how would they best posture themselves while riding them?

Ti-at suggested they sit on the shoulders of the Birgumon; leant forward placing their hands on the neck and press forward, there is a lot of strong muscle here and so wouldn't be uncomfortable.

He then continued; "But please don't pull on our feathers," and smiled. He then explained that the riders could; with their hands pressed forward grip the neck to help them balance, and use their legs to grip the chest of the Birgumon…

"It shouldn't be too long before you all get used to the sensation, and gain your balance, just like when you humans ride a horse, lean with us when we turn, just stay connected to us so we know what you wish to do, just tell us what you want and we will carry it out."

So now it was time for all those who had been chosen, to get to know their Birgumon, to have a chance to talk with them a little, time to build confidence in each other, you have to remember the Birgumon has never allowed humans to ride them, and so this was a totally new experience for them too, so getting to know the person that would be riding them was important they would have to feel comfortable with each other, trust each other with their lives.

The healers and children would not be participating in this exercise, they were too important if anything should go wrong; and when the king told them so, they were very disappointed but understood.

They would be remaining at the entrance to the cave, until informed it was safe for them to proceed into the cave and follow the path; which would lead them to the king, who would be waiting in Polaria.

Now it was time for the riders to be chosen by the Birgumon, yes the Birgumon would choose their riders, and they did this by walking between the humans, and when they felt drawn they would look to the one they chose, and then lower themselves placing their head on the ground so the rider could straddle their neck and shoulders.

Some of the Birgumon would actually sniff people as they walked around them, and if their smell wasn't to their liking they would give a short sharp nostril blow of disapproval; which was not the best for the human, as sometimes a small amount of snot could be received along with the disapproving blow.

And one such person was poor Samuel; this journey really wasn't going quite in his favour; first his leg and now being unsubtly told you smell by one of the Birgumon.

"Oh! You have got to be kidding me, you don't smell to great yourself you know, it is summer after all, said Samuel; subtly sniffing his armpits, "Ok I'm definitely not the sweetest," he mumbled, "but there is no need to blow your nose on me, yuk," as he wiped his cheek.

The Birgumon who had so insulted poor Samuel and left him with yucky snot on his face and hair, had heard his moans and thought him quite entertaining; and in a way brave, as he wasn't the first she had refused with a snotty decline, but! he was the first too actually say something about it, all the other refusals had just stood there almost in fear and not uttering a word, she liked his feistiness.

And so she turned around stared directly at him then; quite pace-fully walked towards him her head nodding back and forth as she did so, "What did you say?" she said to Samuel as she approached him, to which he replied saying "I said it is summer you know." "No the part before that," she replied, glaring at him, "something about my smell or something like that I believe!"

Samuel replied quite nervously but truthfully; "I said you don't smell to great yourself, but I didn't really mean it, I was a little upset that's all."

As he kept eye contact with her as she now stood over him looking him up and down left and right with jerky head movements.

"Hmmm, you humans are strange aren't you, guess that smell is just part of your makeup, can you do anything about it?"

"I haven't had a wash today if that's what you mean!" Samuel replied.

"So, when you wash you will smell better?" she asked.

"Yes, a lot better, talk about give someone a complex! It's been a long journey I don't always smell," he said snappily.

"Ok, as long as you promise to wash your mine! I'm Fanella, what's your name smelly?"

"I'm not smelly usually, it's just hot today and we haven't had a chance to freshen up properly as yet, and my name is Samuel," he said with a stern look.

"Well until you wash; your smelly to me," Fanella replied with a smirk on her face.

She then lowered herself and rested her head on the ground and said; "Come on smelly, climb on, sit on my shoulders and try to relax, we shall just walk about for a while to help you get comfortable."

Samuel couldn't believe what he was about to do, even though he had now quite got used to flying, and being high, he was feeling very precarious, the thought of riding a living creature and only having his legs to do the real gripping with was very un-easing.

But even so he knew he would again overcome another fear; and deep down he knew Fanella would look after him, and inspire him, and so he reached up with both hands placing them over the back of her neck and with a sideways leap and pull he managed to get his left leg half hooked around her neck, he wasn't quite there, and started to slide back down, and in trying to stop himself he tried to get a better grip with his left hand, "Ouch! Feathers, feathers , your pulling my feathers out," cried Fenella; in reaction Samuel instantly let go and fell to the ground landing on his back knocking the wind out of himself.

He lay there for a moment trying to catch a breath, Fanella turned to look at him and asked; "Are you ok smelly?"

After a moment and a huge gasp of air, Samuel replied; "Yes, I'm fine, I'm sorry if I hurt you, I didn't mean to grab your feathers so sorry I was losing my grip and just reached without realising, sorry!"

He was going to also say don't call me smelly, but he did smell and so just gave her a stern look.

Fanella knew calling him smelly teased him, it was evident on his face, and she loved it, and so smirked.

She then replied saying; "No damage done, let's have another go, you might have to really push with your legs to spring you up higher."

"Ok," he replied; "I'll give it another go!"

He then once again placed his arms over Fanella's neck and then bent his knees to hopefully get a good powerful spring up, he then pushed as hard as he could with his legs and pulled as hard as he could with his arms, hoping not to hurt her again though, and it worked a little better this time, he had managed to get his left leg quite a bit further around her neck this time, but still had to pull himself up so with a quick movement of his left arm he managed to wrap it almost around her neck, this was taking far more effort than he expected, but now that he had his arm around the other side of her neck he could now pull himself up and onto her shoulders, and this took a lot of effort, he was grimacing with his efforts, but had now achieved his goal, and with a big woo! "I did it!"

There he sat very proud of himself, and as he looked around, he could see he wasn't the only one that was struggling, so that made him feel most proud, he was one of the first to be sat on his Birgumon.

"I knew you could do it," said Fanella. "Are you ready for a walk!"

"Yes, I believe I am!" he replied slightly nervous but loving the moment.

And with that Fanella took a step forward, and as she did Samuel lurched back as she lifted her leg, and then as she lowered it he lurch forwards, so Fanella said for him to just relax, and just maintain his grip with is legs, she also told him not to worry he wouldn't hurt her so squeeze tight.

And so he did, and Fanella continued, "Samuel found this rocking motion quite fun" and began to laugh.

After a time, he was becoming quite confident and asked Fanella if she could go a little faster.

While Fanella and Samuel were building quite a bond, Matthias, the one person who had always wanted to ride a Birgumon had not yet been chosen, he couldn't understand why!!

He was standing hands by his sides, watching everyone else being chosen, but also was finding it so-so funny watching some of them struggling to mount their Birgumon, some falling off then trying again to mount them, and moaning as they did so.

He thought to himself; it can't be that hard surely!! Just hope I get the chance to find out firsthand; and watched intently those who seemed to be more accustomed to the process, it was easy to tell those who had ridden horses, they made it look so simple to mount the Birgumon, and also looked much more stable as the Birgumon moved around.

Their Birgumon were running around in no time, turning this way and that, their riders so comfortable, goading their Birgumon to go faster and faster.

As Matthias watched on he caught sight of the king and Ti-at who looked to be discussing something, and as he hadn't been chosen as yet he decided to head over too them, riskily crossing the paths of oncoming speeding Birgumon; out of the way, "Do you have a death wish?" one rider shouted at him as he barely missed him.

Matthias apologised as he leaped out the way, then having to swiftly avoid another, by rolling over forwards and straight back on his feet in one smooth motion; then another with a perfectly timed side step, then another from out of nowhere almost caught him unawares, and so without having to think, so instinctively he leaped through the air clearing the Birgumon and its rider easily, and as he landed he instantly sprinted clear, he was now safe and just feet from the king and Ti-at who both stood motionless in awe of the amazing gymnastic type feats Matthias had just performed in dodging the mass of speeding Birgumon.

"How on Soul did you perform such feats! I've never seen such incredible speed and agility; how did you jump so high?" the king asked Matthias.

"I truly don't know my King, I just did it, I didn't have time to even think, I'm quite shocked myself, didn't know I had it in me," replied Matthias.

"It was an incredible sight," replied the king.

"Thank you, my king, the reason I came over here was I saw you and Ti-at speaking, and just wondered if there was any way I could be of service to you both, as it would appear I'm free. It would appear that none of the Birgumon wishes me to ride with them, and so I'm free to assist you both," Matthias said feeling sad he wasn't chosen…

"What do you mean you haven't been chosen, of course you have," said Ti-at.

"No unfortunately I haven't, not one as even been near me," replied Matthias staring at all the others who had now been chosen, and looked to be getting to grips with riding their Birgumon very well; they were cheering and laughing, and racing each other…

"They haven't been near you, because they knew they didn't have to choose you as I told them so," replied Ti-at.

"What do you mean you told them so, you told them not to choose me, why would you do such a thing, I want to be a part of the group. I'm strategically minded, and I'm sure I would be of value," replied Matthias sounding quite upset.

"My dear fellow I told them not to bother with you, because you had already been chosen from the moment the plan was first hatched, by me, you are my rider," said Ti-at…

Matthias was speechless, not only would he be riding a Birgumon but, he would be at the fore, riding the biggest most powerful of them all, their leader Ti-at! This was the biggest privilege that could ever be bestowed on any human…

He was motionless while it sank in, his face was of total shock.

The king approached him and patted him on the left shoulder and said "I thought that would make you happy," then smiled and continued; "I'm riding Micah…"

Matthias could only exclaim wow! as he stood staring at Ti-at thinking how privileged he was…

Then his trance was broken by Ti-at's voice! "I think it's time we have our trial run, don't you," and smiled.

"Y-y-yes," replied Matthias nervously.

Don't be nervous said Ti-at, in a very calming voice, you were born for this, you were destined to be my rider I feel it within you, you have a free wild strong brave spirit, and you are instinctive which matches my consciousness, we are a perfect pairing…

With that Matthias approached Ti-at who lowered his head to the ground, and with such flowing grace Matthias placed his right hand on Ti-at's neck and with little effort at all seemed to glide onto his shoulders perfectly, "Ready when you are, Matthias said, sitting proudly on Ti-at's shoulders with his hands resting on his lap, he felt as one with Ti-at and Ti-at with Matthias, so strong was the bond with these two, they knew they didn't need to walk around to become comfortable with each other. No, they jumped straight to it, and with one huge powerful thrust of Ti-at's wings they were airborne, whoosh straight up, within moments they were hundreds of feet above ground, Matthias was at total ease just leaning into Ti-at's neck perfectly balanced, the wind in his face felt wonderful, he knew this was his destiny, the connection between himself and Ti-at was instantaneous, it was almost as though they were one being.

Ti-at began a hard roll left then over and upside down now heading directly down towards the ground and the group below who watched them, they were now going well in excess of two hundred miles an hour, Matthias made himself as aerodynamic as possible, leaning in as close as he could to Ti-at's neck with his arms tucked in so the speeding air would flow over him and not pull him off.

His heart was pounding but not with fear but exhilaration, and as they sped towards the ground, he let out a loud; "Wow this is wonderful!"

Ti-at then levelled out and flew directly over the heads of the group below, and at such speed the wind could be heard rushing over them so loud, whoosh! the people below could hear as they passed over head.

The other riders below had become quite excited by what they had seen and so wanted to get airborne, not quite as aerobatic as Ti-at and Matthias, this was visibly a special bond, but they just wanted to fly, they had fun walking and racing each other on the ground and now felt confident enough to fly with their Birgumon.

And so, one by one they took to the skies, just gently soaring turning this way and that, everyone was doing great and growing in confidence rapidly... They then practiced flying as a group; in formation and formed a row keeping it steady and well-spaced.

The healers and children below watched in awe wishing they might get the chance themselves someday.

After a time, led by Matthias and the king they headed back to their little base as it were; to quickly have some water and ready for the real flight.

They had lost a great many hours since the morning's events and the sun would start to set in approximately three hours, and so needed to get a move on as they didn't want to risk a sudden wind pushing the cloud in their direction.

So, on the king's order, the group drank water and filled their personal water satchels, and all wished each other luck, each turning to those around them and wished them well, then off they went back to their waiting Birgumon.

While everyone had been fetching refreshments the king had been in conversation with Egum the great dragon, the king had decided although he appreciated Egum's offer to assist on this mission he thought it best he and his kin stay and watch over the remaining group of children and healers, just in case something should come through the cave that wasn't friendly, there would be no one better than three fire-breathing dragons to defend them.

Egum saw sense in the king's decision and agreed telling him if danger came their way, he and his kin would protect the group, and get them to safety.

The king thanked Egum and said he hoped to see him soon, then parted making his way to Micah and the rest of the group, he then explained to the group his decision regarding the dragons staying behind, to which they all agreed he had made a wise choice, then turned to face Egum, Symphet and Saturn and nodded their heads with regard and thanks, which the three dragons did in return.

The king then mounted Micah turned to Matthias and Ti-at and asked they lead the way.

And so, they took to the skies one by one, the remaining group waving at them as they disappeared high into the sky.

When they had reached an altitude high enough to clear the mountains Matthias and the king thought it best they gather the water now, as the Birgumon had warned the cloud and fine dust was just the other side of the mountains, and so they had to be ready to start releasing the water the moment they see the dark clouds.

And so, the king gave the order to gather water from the mountain streams ahead of them. With that the Birgumon came to a hover allowing their riders to begin the process.

The riders now placed their hands out in front of them arms stretched, palms up fingers together and focused on the mountain streams, as they did sure enough once again water started to raise high into the sky, it looked as though it was being dragged from the streams, stretching to the sky.

After a time, there were approximately fifty huge lakes of water being held in the air.

They now moved them until they made contact and became one huge airborne river following along the length of the row they had formed, which must have spanned a mile, they skillfully held it a hundred feet ahead of them, they had to have it this far so that the water would make contact with the cloud long before they could, this would hopefully stop any of them coming in contact with the dust above the cloud, thus they could release the water safely.

Now they had the water gathered and under control the king gave the order to move forward, and so the Birgumon began to move forward steadily; there it was thousands of tons of water moving through the beautiful blue summers sky, this wall of water fifty feet in depth, quarter of a mile in width and a mile in length beautifully glistening in the sun, reflecting the ground below and the sky above like a mirror, it looked like a stretched miniature world, incredible!

And as it moved the reflection would change as they covered new ground, it almost seemed to be rolling just as a planet would.

This was no easy feat for the group, it was using a lot of mental strength to maintain control of such a large amount of water, and was starting to take its toll on the weaker members, they were starting to get bad headaches, the king had to think fast they were still about five minutes from reaching the clearing of the mountains, they could see the cloud ahead of them, but were not close enough to release the water they had to continue to hold for just another five minutes.

A few of the group were experiencing nosebleeds, and so the king made a suggestion that they relax and discontinue to hold the water until they arrived, this did put more pressure on the strongest of the group, but they had no choice, they couldn't take the chance on the weaker being injured, if they collapsed they would certainly fall to their deaths, and so they rested.

After they had cleared the mountains the king asked those that had rested to rejoin the group in holding the water, the cloud was now in range! The water would have to be separated into extremely fine vapour, this would be the only way to ensure every single particle of ash and dust would be soaked.

The already drained group would now have to focus even harder to separate the water correctly, if the droplets are too big, they could miss the fine dust particles, and so the water would have to be like fine drizzle

So now the group had to separate the water, and did so by opening their fingers which began to separate the water into minute droplets, but at this time the droplets were still too big, so they had to focus so hard to reduce the droplets even more, and they did this by quartering every droplet until they were so small the river of water now looked like a dense fog, pure moisture, they were now ready to lower this extremely dense fog into the black static filled cloud below.

The time had come so the king and Matthias looked to each other, the king saying "Let's pray this works." He then gave the order to lower the fog, and so the group working as one, turned their hands palms down, and began to lower their arms, as they did so the fine mist started to make contact with the fine dust which was above the main body of the black cloud.

As the moisture made contact, the dust started to become visible as it stuck to the moisture, forming bigger water droplets, it was working, the dust was being covered with moisture, and was so wet became heavy and started to fall to the cloud below as rain, as the rain made contact with the black static charged cloud it began to fizz and pop, and as the rain fall became heavier and heavier the louder it became, it became so loud it now resembled thunder, with flashes of lightning.

The group became unsettled by this unexpected occurrence, the king and Matthias could feel their fear, and so the king spoke with them using his mind, "Be calm my people we can't stop now we have to see this through," he said.

"But what about the lightning my king?" replied one of the group!

The king looked at the lightning and observed it was confined within the cloud shooting across it, it didn't seem to be heading up and towards them. So the king replied explaining what he had observed; "We should be fine the lightning seems to be confined within the cloud, it must be a reaction to the moisture making contact with the static sparks causing them to expand, but if the lightning should start to strike out in our direction we will have no option but to pull back."

The group looked to the cloud and saw the king was right and so agreed they would see it through. After a few minutes everyone began to feel a strange sensation! "What is this I'm feeling," said Matthias as his hair began to lift and stand on end, being pulled towards the cloud of moisture ahead of them. They all started to experience this strangeness, even the Birgumon were experiencing a tingling sensation! Ti-at grew concerned and asked the king, "What is happening?" to which the king could only answer he did not know!

Then before their eyes, clouds started to form approximately a hundred feet above the fog and black cloud, they began to expand rapidly and grow darker, then suddenly the entire group was enveloped within the clouds that formed so fast around them.

"My king, I think it best we retreat this doesn't look or feel good." It was Matthias, the cloud had grown so thick so fast they had all lost sight of each other, and now thunder could be heard in the distance. So quite rightly Matthias had grown concerned, he wasn't the only one, the king himself had also come to the conclusion; it was no longer safe.

Then suddenly it started to rain gaining momentum, in no time they were all soaked.

The king said, "God must be with us, this will surely destroy the cloud and make it safe for us to continue to Polaria once it stops, whenever that may be!"

Then Ti-at spoke in a very concerned tone; "My king we need to flee this rain, the cloud is becoming very dense, we could experience lightning!! We do not want to be around if lightning should start!"

No sooner had Ti-at finished his words when a bolt of lightning shot through the cloud just missing a member of the group, followed by deafening claps of thunder, so loud they nearly burst the eardrums of every member of the group, human and creature both.

With that the king using his mind gave the order to rapidly retreat to the rest of the group at the cave entrance. He didn't need to say it twice, instantly the group ceased to control the water vapour letting it fall free. The Birgumon turned back as fast as they could, Ti-at told the humans to hold tight as they accelerated rapidly.

Suddenly a bolt of lightning shot across the sky making contact with one of the Birgumon, instantly killing it and its rider! Due to the lightening illuminating the cloud this could be seen by the rest of the group, the terrible screams of the Birgumon and rider could be heard clearly, as they fell to the ground in a ball of flame.

There were screams of disbelief! Who was it? They asked one and other.

The king himself asked did anyone see who it was?

But before anyone could answer another bolt of lightning shot through the sky luckily missing the group.

They had no time to dwell, they had to get out of there and fast, they would have to discover who had perished once they were out of the clouds and back safe on the ground.

The lightning was becoming more intense, they had to dive straight down to get out of the weather as fast as possible. The Birgumon were now diving at speeds in excess of two hundred miles an hour nearing three hundred, their riders clinging on for dear life, this made worse by the Birgumon having to constantly roll hard left and right trying to avoid the lightning bolts which were now appearing one after the other, only seconds between them.

The riders tried desperately to look behind them so they could spot the lightning and warn the Birgumon, but every time they did the windspeed caused by the speeding Birgumon would almost rip them off.

John had tried to look back over his right shoulder, but as he did the wind got under him, and in a flash broke his grip and flung his top half of his body back the force of the wind was so great. He was now laid back just his legs clinging on for dear life, and unable to breath properly as the wind was rushing up his nose, his Birgumon instantly knew they were in trouble and said to John; hold on just a little longer, keep your legs bent tight, you can do it...

John could only reply using his mind, unable to speak as he couldn't exhale, "Please hurry I can't breathe!!!"

Just at that moment they broke out of the clouds, they had made it, but still wouldn't be totally safe until they had got back to the ground, and even then they would need shelter as the weather was fierce, and had become a storm, they could now see the tops of the mountains and had to get to the other side as fast as possible.

The weather had expanded rapidly and was now covering Bulgan.

The remaining group and dragons who were at the mouth of the cave had been watching in horror! They had seen the poor souls falling from the clouds in a ball of flame. When Egum saw the terrible sight he instantly knew what it was he was seeing! And just cried out, "Dear God – no!" which sounded like loud squawking to the humans around him, but they too had witnessed it also, and knew why he cried out so loudly.

The children were besides themselves, the adults tried their best to console them, they could now see the Birgumon and riders beginning to appear from the cloud with lightning striking around them, it was terrifying to watch, and so Egum decided this was to not be seen in case another Birgumon and its rider should be struck, he told the crying children and the adults with them to stand in a huddle facing each other, not to look up, and so they did.

Once they had all huddled together, the three huge dragons stood over them with their wings open wrapping around them forming a circle with their wings so they couldn't see the horrors above them. This is how they would stay until the Birgumon and riders would return.

Now the king's group had broken through the clouds they could now level out and headed directly for the mountain tops still having to dodge lightning bolts as they did so.

Now they were no longer diving the speed at which they traveled decreased, and so John could now lift himself beck into a seated position, this was much better, now he could finally breathe again.

For a moment he thought he was going to suffocate, and was now gasping for much needed breath, "Are you ok?" asked Tuniper; his Birgumon.

"Yes, thank you I'm fine now I can finally breathe," he replied.

"We aren't out of danger as yet, so hold tight," replied Tuniper as she banked this way and that.

The king using his mind told everyone there wasn't too far now; "Just hold on a little longer, we will make it," he said.

Although they were all so scared, his words spurred them on, each one soaked through and getting colder by the minute seemed to believe they were going to make it, they focused on the lightning, some now actually using Telekinesis to defend themselves from it, now they weren't diving they could look around spotting the lightning and redirecting it with a swipe of a hand and the power of their minds. This was quite a shock to them that they could actually do such a thing! They had never tried to control lightning before, and it would seem only the mentally strongest could actually do it; and so they tried their best to watch over the whole group, there was only about twenty of them that could actually control the lightning; and so this was becoming increasingly difficult as the lightning relentlessly struck after them.

John was fortunate enough to be one of those who could control the lightning, he had only realised this whilst acting in a defensive manner as a bolt of lightning struck after him and Tuniper; he literally put his hand up as though to block the lightning bolt, more of a reaction than intentional motion, but it deflected it, it was instinctive and he was incredibly shocked; "Did you see that Tuniper? I stopped the lightning hitting us!"

Tuniper replied saying; "Yes it was amazing, how did you do that?" she asked…

John wasn't sure himself and could only answer saying he didn't know, "It just happened as I saw the lightning I thought it was going to hit us, I just thought no and put my arms up, my mind must have instinctively taken over, thank god…"

"Well please continue to keep us safe," said Tuniper.

"I'll definitely be trying my best, you just fly true and get us back to safety," John replied…

He then looked to his left just in the nick of time, a bolt of lightning was headed after a member of the group who was unable to defend against it, and so John lifted his left hand up arm bent then straightened his arm out then down, as he did so he deflected the lightning bolt left then down towards the ground below, saving the helpless rider who just looked in shock at John and with his mind thanked John saying; "We owe you our lives thank you."

John just replied saying, "My pleasure," then continued to look all around him in the hope of spotting the lightning before it could reach anyone.

Just as John was trying his best to protect the group so to, were the king and Matthias, all those with this new-found ability were working tirelessly, some using both hands simultaneously to protect others one each side of them.

It was relentless and taking a huge toll on them draining them, you have to remember; they had just been holding a mass of water and now without reprieve where using their minds to defend the group, they surely wouldn't be able to continue like this, even the king and Matthias were beginning to flag.

They had to get to the other side of the mountains and to safety soon! Ti-at began to sense Matthias was weakening and knew he had to do something fast, although the Birgumon were themselves feeling quite drained they had to push harder, they needed to fly faster and get to safety before the humans defending them from the lightning started to pass out due to the strain..

And so Ti-at commanded his kin to pick up the pace, telling them they need to get a move on, they had to get the humans to safety as fast as possible as they were beginning to weaken.

And so, the Birgumon began to move their wings as hard and fast as they possibly could picking up quite a speed, they were working so hard they began to make a loud groaning sound with every stroke of their wings.

The speeds they were reaching made it hard for the riders to sit straight, they now had to lean into the wind, they now just prey the Birgumon could avoid the lightning as they could no longer look around and defend them, they were now just tired passengers.

After a period of time turning hard this way and that avoiding the lightning, they were now flying over the tops of the mountains and would soon be able to start making their descent, as they cleared the mountains the lightning seemed not to be reaching them now, it seemed as though the worst of the weather was somehow being held over Polaria. Although it was cloudy and raining hard over Bulgan there was no lightning, what a relief this was to see for the whole group, they could now begin to relax a little, they would soon be back with the rest of the group and safe.

As they descended the king could just make out a big silver dome like shape below them where they had left the remaining group.

He was unsure as to what it could be, and so asked Matthias if he too could see the silver dome shape below them. To which Matthias agreed he could indeed, what could it be? Matthias asked the king, to which the king could only reply; "I have no idea, that's why I'm asking you!"

And with that the king thought it best to check with Egum, so using his mind the king called out.

"Egum, Egum do you hear me!"

"I do my king, and so happy I am to hear your voice, we were afraid you had perished!"

"We are on our way back to you now, we are descending the mountains as we speak, we should be above you, but we can only see a silver dome, what is it, can you see it?" asked the king.

And as the king asked; the silver dome below seemed to change shape and move, at seeing this the king quickly said to Ti-at; "It's changed shape its moving, it must be very close to you…"

With that Egum lowered his wings and turned to look around to find what it was the king was speaking of, as Ti-at did this the king again said it is definitely moving, it has now separated, it would seem a part as started to move alone!

At that point the penny dropped! And Egum stopped, rolled his eyes tutted and began to chuckle; "My king I believe what you are seeing is us!"

"What do you mean?" replied the king...

"The silver dome is me and my kin, we formed a cover with our wings for your kin to shelter under, we didn't want the children to witness the horrors of your journey back, we saw someone falling in a ball of flame, this affected us all terribly and so I thought it better we not be able to see, and so the silver peace you say is moving, is actually me! as I'm looking for the mysterious dome you described, we are silver, remember," Egum replied and laughed...

"Oh, yes, ok," replied the king feeling quite embarrassed; "I didn't think! the journey as taken its toll on us all, feeling quite drained mentally and physically, we will hopefully be back with soon, we can talk when we arrive."

"Yes, my king, see you soon," replied Egum.

Egum then turned back to the huddled group with joy in his heart saying; they are safe, and on their way back. We should be able to see them. with that members of the group could be heard giving praise to god thanking him their kin were safe.

They all then turned their attentions skyward, and sure enough there they were. At that moment they appeared as small black dots in the sky, a hundred and ninety-nine of them looking like a swarm of bees, and how happy they were to see them.

The adults turned to the children hugging them with joy; "They are safe, look," said Babbyah as she held May close and they both looked to the sky watching the king's group growing larger as they drew nearer and nearer.

May couldn't wait to see her father she had to know that he was ok, and within the group that was returning.

And so, using her mind called out to him; "Father, father it is May."

"Hello, May I hear you," replied her father. "Are you with the group we can see?" she asked.

"Yes, I am my little May, I will be with you soon, can't wait to see you daughter," the king replied feeling a real sense of relief he will be seeing his daughter again.

"I can't wait to see you to, love you Daddy."

With that May turned to Babbyah and hugged her so tight saying, "He is ok, thank God..."

"Yes, thank god he is safe and those with him," replied Babbyah.

After five minutes or so the Birgumon began to touch down, the first being Ti-at and Matthias, followed closely by the king and Micah, as soon as they had landed they were greeted with cheers, hurray the waiting group would cheer as each Birgumon touched down one after the other.

After a time, all of the Birgumon had returned, and now their riders dismounted and were greeted with hugs from the waiting excited group, the riders although completely drained mentally and physically where so happy to of returned safely, they made extra efforts to return the affections of those who greeted them, then they turned to each other hugging each other, shaking hands saying it's so good to see you made it and asking if anyone knew who it was that had fallen.

At this point one of the riders a young man called Arban approached the king saying he thought he knew who it was that had fallen!

"My king now we are back I've looked hard and cannot seem to find my friend Simon, I believe his Birgumon was called Nar. I fear they were the ones that lost their lives."

"Thank you for letting me know, I'm so sorry for the loss of your friend, he will not be forgotten I promise," said the king.

"Thank, you my king, he was a good brave soul, and would always help others never considering himself," replied Arban with tears in his eyes and a slight smile on his face as he remembered his brave friend. He then turned and walked to the crowed.

The King then asked Matthias to confirm with Ti-at the identity of his kin that had not returned.

With that Matthias walked through the crowd and found Ti-at in conversation with his kin; they too had realised who it was that had lost their lives, and stood morning their loss, as Matthias approached, Ti-at turned and informed Matthias it was Nar that they had lost.

"We had come to the same conclusion," said Matthias, "One of our riders can't find his friend, His name was Simon and he was riding your Nar, we are so sorry."

Ti-at with sorrow replied; "We too are sorry for your loss, thankfully it was a swift death, hopefully they wouldn't have suffered, we will remember them together."

"Yes, indeed we will, it will be an honour to remember them together," replied Matthias.

Whilst the king had been having this solemn conversation with Arban the celebrations continued around them.

Even the three mighty dragons couldn't contain their happiness and so lead by Egum they to welcomed each rider, but also remembering their loss, gave condolences, saying their loss will not of been in vain, then turned to the Birgumon and walked to them, Egum approached Ti-at and told him he was deeply pleased to see him and his kin had returned safely, and that he and his kin felt so sorry for their loss, and asked did they know who it was that had perished!

At that point the king approached wanting to thank the Birgumon for their Bravery and their sad sacrifice, the king then continued; we could never of done it without you all, he then raised his right hand and placed it on Ti-at's neck and turned to face all of his people saying, today both us and our friends have lost good brave souls for the greater good of our kin on both sides of these mountains, they will never be forgotten we will give prays for their lives and remember them as one family, Human, Birgumon and Dragon together..

We will now make camp here and light two fires to remember our lost, we shall eat, drink and remember them, and let out our sorrows for tomorrow brings a new day, and we should rise with happy hearts in memory of them.

The king continued; the light fades fast so let's start making arrangements now.

With that the humans and beasts worked together in groups to find wood to make frames that could be covered for shelters for the night from the rain.

Others began to work on building the two fires, and another group worked preparing food and drink which they had brought with them for the journey.

The king now remembered his promise to Bogumill and so thought it best to keep him informed of the situation so far, knowing that Bogumill was a man of his word, and if he didn't hear from the king would probably send men, the king didn't want that to happen, he had lost two lives on this journey which he wasn't expecting to happen, and did not want to put even more lives in danger, the group he had with him was enough to worry about.

The king had no idea what awaited them on the other side of the mountains; even if the water and rain had washed away the ash and dust which filled the air, would it have dispersed that terrifying black cloud and lightning! He would have to wait till morning for the answer to that!

So, for now the king tried not to concern himself with what awaited them, and contacted Bogumill.

"Bogumill do you hear me?"

"My king, how is your mission proceeding?; I'm sensing a sadness what is wrong?"

"It's a long sad story, I have no time to go in to the details, but one of my men as died struck by lightning, and a Birgumon with him, so we have made camp for the night and will proceed tomorrow at first light into Polaria."

"My king you are not in Polaria as yet? I thought you would have arrived by now, what has held you up so?" asked Bogumill feeling concerned.

"We have had a number of obstacles to overcome, and the weather on the Polaria side of the mountains is to fierce for us to proceed now, we can only hope it as improved by morning."

"Do you wish me to send aid to you?; I have many strong men and healers I can dispatch to you instantly, my king."

"No, thank you; I just wanted to let you know we are ok and that I will contact you again tomorrow as soon as we arrive in Polaria, just as you asked. I didn't want you sending men in search of us, so my good friend I will say good night rest easy."

"My king! May I ask who it was that was lost, so myself and my kin can pray for them and the Birgumon?"

"Yes, of course my friend, the young man's name was Simon and the Birgumon was named Nar, your prayers will be appreciated my friend, goodbye for now."

"Thank you, my king, I will have my people light two fires for their souls, good night my King rest well."

"Thank you, my old friend, goodnight."

Bogumill then informed his people of what the king and he had just spoken, they were saddened by the news, he also asked them not to let anyone of Engypt know the sad news, it wasn't their place to inform the family, and he didn't want the king's people back home being panicked! They all agreed, and work together building two fires and would give prays through the night and ask for the king and his group to be guided safely.

The king then contacted his wife Nadia, not letting her know of the loss of young Simon and Nar, he didn't want her to be worried, he was torn whether to let her know or not; as he felt the young man's parents should be informed, but at the same time didn't want everyone including Nadia to start worrying or panic, they had enough to worry about trying to rebuild Engypt.

Plus, he felt it was his duty to inform family members of any such news and would do so when they returned home.

And so he kept his emotions controlled and hidden from Nadia, he spoke with her as if he was just checking in; "Nadia my love how are you and Lucas have you missed me and May?" he asked and chuckled trying to sound as normal as possible.

"My darling husband, you know I would be missing you terribly, and so does Lucas, is everything going as planned?"

"Not quite as planned, we have had a few obstacles to overcome which have put us back a day, but hopefully tomorrow will be a better day. What are you doing?" asked the king.

"Well at the moment my husband, I'm helping preparing supper with Laila, I do wish you were here with us!"

"I know my love, I wish that to, but I will be home within the next few days hopefully. I'd better get back to the group I will be in touch as soon as I can, please give my regards to Julius for me and let him know I will contact him soon, I love you bye for now."

"Please take care of yourself Stephen, I love you too."

The king then returned to the group to assist with preparations, and together they ate, talked and sat around the two big fires they had set in remembrance of the two souls they had lost earlier that day.

There was no sadness, only happy memories, those who had been close to Simon and Nar spoke of the times they had spent together remembering and sharing their memories Telepathically visually so all could see, almost like watching a video in their minds.

They all laughed at memories of Simon, he was a good young man with a big heart, but also liked to play and do things to help others, but his attempts didn't always go as planned, such as the time Simon and Arban were much younger playing in the back lands when they spotted an old man with a horse and cart, the old man was trying to load rocks onto the cart but they could see he was struggling trying to lift some quite sizeable rocks with his mind, but obviously his mind wasn't as strong as it used to be...

And so, the good-hearted youngster Simon suggested they help the old man, and so Simon respectfully approached the man and asked if he could assist him by loading the rocks on to the cart for him!

The old man was very appreciative of the kind young Simons offer saying; "I've been here for two hours and only loaded one large rock, so if you could be so kind, that would be very helpful young man."

147

Simon was only ten years of age and was so excited to help, he was getting very good with Telekinesis and could lift quite sizeable objects and noticed some nice almost perfectly round rocks he thought the old man would like. "What do you need rocks for?" asked Simon.

"I'm a stonemason and I like to sculpt using rocks."

"Sounds very skilled, will this one be big enough?" as he pointed to a rock half the size but one hundred times the weight of himself!

That would be perfect!; said the old man.

So with that, the young Simon focused on the rock, it was approximately ten feet from the cart, so with its size and weight would take quite a bit of mental strength of which Simon was sure he had, and so he began to lift it, gradually it rose up! Arban and the old man were quite impressed at this, it was rising and moving very smoothly towards the cart, he raised it about eight inches higher than the cart, and continued guiding it until it was now over the cart and ready to be lowered, it was at this point the old man said well-done young man; this filled Simon with such pride and he looked to the old man and Arban and smiled, instantly loosing focus on the rock which fell rather than being lowered, crashing onto the back of the cart with an almighty crash and crunch as the right wheel collapsed under the sudden weight...

Simon froze, a look of complete and utter horror on his face, he couldn't believe it! What have I done he said to himself? When he looked to the man who was staring at the collapsed wheel, he was filled with fear he was going to start shouting at him, but no the old man just stood for a moment then began to laugh; saying that will teach me to speak to soon, and in no time the three were laughing so hard their sides hurt, and the old man saying; the look on your face young man, priceless.

"Yes," said Arban, "I thought you was going to wet yourself."

"To be honest I nearly did and, if, I don't, stop laughing I might yet."

And with that they continued to laugh and when the laughter stopped the two youngsters stayed and helped that dear old man fix his old wooden cart, not leaving until it was completed, and he was safely on his way.

Seeing this everyone was filled with happiness and would remember Simon with fondness.

Now Tuniper showed one of her fondest memories of Nar. They too were quite young and gaining their skills of flight, and on this particular day they were practicing their diving and climbing skills, this would entail them flying at great height, then diving at as steep an angle as possible to gain as much speed as they possibly could, then at the last moment levelling out, if done correctly a Birgumon could judge it so well they could skim water with their talons an incredible sight to see, they would then climb as fast as they could gaining altitude rapidly, this took great skill and practice.

On this day Nar and Tuniper decided to fly above the mountains and then dive following a fresh snow stream which ran along the side of the mountain, they would attempt to get as close to the water as possible, ideally to skim the surface.

Nar had decided he would go first and Tuniper agreed, she would follow behind him, so as they approached the start of the stream Nar dived and carefully steered himself closer and closer to the stream, carefully avoiding large boulders which lay at the bank of the stream, there were even some protruding from the water's surface which he avoided very skillfully, as did Tuniper following approximately a hundred feet behind.

As they continued faster and faster, they would have to look a lot further ahead of them, looking for obstacles such as large rocks, and as they descended the greener the terrain became, and so brought new obstacles such as tree branches which hung over parts of the stream, which they would have to avoid skillfully, Nar would like to leave it to the very last moment then do some crazy aerobatics, such as when he approached a part of the stream which had large tree branches hanging from both sides, there was a branch on the left which hung very low just a matter of a couple of feet from the surface of the water, and opposite on the other side was a huge long branch which almost crossed the entire stream and overlapped with the one on the left, there was only just enough space for a Birgumon to fly over one and under the other, most Birgumon wouldn't risk it, as at speeds of over two hundred miles an hour they would surely be injured or worse if they clipped a branch.

But oh no not Nar; he loved the thrill, and squinted his eyes and stretched out his neck and beak and actually accelerated with a loud wahoo heading directly for the branches, which were set at an angle sloping left to right, this didn't deter Nar in the slightest he was now to close to back out, wings stretched out wide and level. Tuniper shouted you're crazy and pulled up and readied to fly over the branches, she continued to watch Nar with eyes half closed in fear he wasn't going to make it.

As Nar's beak passed the first lower branch he quickly banked right raising his left wing and lowering his right, this is going to be tight he thought as he whooshed between the branches brushing the leaves as he did so, and again "Wahoo, I did it, did you see that Tuniper?"

"Yes, I did you are crazy! What if you had misjudged it?!"

"But I didn't, did I?" Nar replied feeling ever so smug, he now slowed so he could tease Tuniper; "Was you worried about me then?" he asked with a big smile staring straight into Tuniper's eyes and raising his eyebrows!

Tuniper just smiled and said "Eyes front," but too late! Before he could react, he hadn't realised they had reached the base of the mountain and were heading into a field of pai berry bushes, and with a big crash and slide he tore through the field of pai berries coming to a halt a few hundred feet in...

"Oh dear," said Tuniper "That will teach you," she thought and flew to the point he had come to a stop, when she arrived she couldn't quite see him as he was completely covered in pai berry branches, but she could hear him moaning, mmm, mmm, mmm, she rushed to his aid fearing the worst calling his name, "Nar, are you ok?!" but when she arrived what she found was not what she quite expected!

Laying there was Nar covered in pai berry juice and pai berry flesh,

"My, my these are the best pai berries I've ever tasted, try some," he said scraping some off his beak and passing it to her.

"And there was I worrying you'd hurt yourself, grr," she exclaimed.

At that point her wonderful fun memory stopped, and she continued that Nar was the most fun-loving adventurous soul she had ever met, and he would be missed terribly.

Now they had reflected, they all said a prayer asking that Nar and Simon's souls will be at peace, and that they would meet them again in the next life.

It was now late and time for everyone, human and beast to get some much-needed sleep, and so they all settled for the night, the first to head off to their makeshift beds was King Stephen and little May. "Good night to you all, sleep well I hope tomorrow brings us some lovely warm sun, night."

And so, everyone wished one and other a goodnight and off to bed they went.

The night was not the best, as it was still pouring with rain, but it was warm under their makeshift shelters of wood and canvas.

The group settled with the sound of the rain droplets against the canvas, it was quite soothing, there wasn't another sound to be heard, just the rain; it seemed to ease them all, including the Birgumon and dragons, which had found shelter in the surrounding woods, they seemed to be so at ease and fell to sleep in no time at all.

Little May and her father the king were laying in their makeshift beds just listening to the sound of the rain, when little May said whilst staring at the canvas roof; "It sounds beautiful doesn't it father, it's relaxing isn't it, do you think Simon and Nar are sending us this rain, to help us relax and let us know they are with us?" She then looked to her father with her such sweet innocent eyes and loving smile.

"Is that what you believe my little May?" replied the king smiling at his sweet, loving daughter.

"Yes, I do father, in fact I know they are here with us, I can feel them, they are happy father, and that makes me happy to know, does it you, father?"

"Oh, my sweet wonderful daughter, yes it makes me very happy indeed, and you are so lucky you can feel their presence, they must be watching over you very closely indeed! The king continued; hopefully they will watch over us all, and guide us on our journey, but for now they will watch over us while we sleep, night-night May, sweet dreams," said the king and kissed her forehead.

"Goodnight, father sleep well."

And off to sleep they both drifted, it had been a long hard emotional day for the whole group, and it wasn't long before the physically and emotionally drained group fell into a deep slumber.

It continued to rain through the night and the group slept soundly, then in the early hours the rain began to slow, and as it did the king began to stir, it was as though the sound of the rain was helping him sleep, and as it slowed he was starting to wake, it was only three in the morning as the rain depleted, and when it had totally stopped the king awoke.

He lay for a moment, raised his head listening for the rain, he was almost disappointed the rain had stopped, the sound was so soothing it had helped relax his mind, which now since the rain had stopped once again became full of the days that had passed and what lay ahead.

As he lay there he looked out from the makeshift shelter, it was still dark outside with just the beautiful light of the bright moons, which gently lit the field of which they encamped, he could make out the hundreds of silhouetted shelters and surrounding woods, it was quite a beautiful night, he slowly rolled back the nice warm covers not wanting to wake little May, and slowly stood and began to put his damp robes on. Fortunately, his undergarments were dry and warm, he then stepped out from under the shelter and looked to the amazingly clear sky, it was quite incredible how clear the sky was, considering it had been raining so hard only moments ago.

As he looked to the sky he couldn't help but think how amazing the night looked, the stars seemed to be glistening, trillions of them forming wonderful shapes and colours, some clusters so dense they appeared as glistening clouds bright and colourful, then he took a deep breath as he stretched raising his arms out to the side then up and tiptoeing then relaxing, the smell of the damp grass was strong and wonderful.

Then in the silence of the night a deep hollow sound could just barely be heard, it was like the sound you get if you blow across the top of an open bottle, but quite eerie and continuous, the king was intrigued as to where the sound was coming, and so listening ever so carefully began to follow the direction of which it came.

Walking ever so carefully trying not to bump into the surrounding makeshift shelters, and not wake the others, the king continued, as he did so there was the sudden sound of a twig braking! But it wasn't the Kings steps that caused the sound, it seemed to come from the kings right!

The king stopped instantly and crouched, he was sure he was the only one awake at this time, and so the cracking sound made him slightly uneasy, the eerie sound he had been following had obviously made him feel uncomfortable, as a chill ran up his spine, and now this cracking sound added to his unease, and so in a whispered voice the king asked; "Who goes there?" To which a whispered voice answered, "It is me! John, who is that?"

"John, thank heavens, it's me your king, what are you doing awake at this hour?"

"I'm not sure my king, I just woke, and I can't get this sound out of my head, a low droning sound, I was trying to follow where its coming from!"

"Me too, we will follow it together, but I can't see you! Let's just follow the sound our paths should meet."

"Ok, my king," John replied.

And so the two continued cautiously following the sound and trying not to make any noise, which was proving hard in the dead of night, barely able to see ahead of them, the king stumbled on a protruding mound of soil, losing his balance he fell face first into a muddy puddle with a splat.

"Oh great!" he murmured to himself, still trying to be as quiet as possible, and scraping mud from his face and neck, he then picked himself up and continued heading for the origin of the droning whilst spitting muddy bits out of his mouth, luckily, he hadn't woken anyone.

As John continued; he was to the right and just behind the king and could now just make out the king's silhouette and so tried to gain the king's attention; "My king, my king," he was saying trying to keep his voice down.

The king didn't hear John's attempts to gain his attention! And so, John began to walk faster to gain ground on the king and hopefully catch up with him.

The ground below their feet was sodden, and as John picked up his pace, his steps began to make splashing and squelching sounds, it was also quite slippery and so he was having the odd slide or two in his attempting to catch up with the king.

As he drew closer to the king the sound of his wet slippery steps began to draw the Kings attention!

And so, hearing these wet sounds coming up on him from behind the king turned to face them unsure as to what was causing them; he said in a whisper; "John is that you?"

"Yes, my king I've been trying to gain your attention!"

"I'm pleased it's you," replied the king and continued; "I was beginning to feel a little uneasy, come we will continue together."

And so, he waited to allow john to catch up.

As John reached the king's side, they greeted each other, "Good very early morning to you John, I'm pleased you're here, if I'm honest, I was getting a little uneasy! But now I have you for company I'm feeling a little braver," he chuckled.

"Thank you, my king, it's a pleasure to be here," John replied jokingly. "Nothing quite like an extremely early, dark, unable to quite see where it is, we are going kind of walk is there! And oh yes, the extremely wet slippery muddy ground, and that sound make things much more enjoyable, wouldn't you say my king!"

To which the king replied in a jestful tone; "No, not really, no."

To which they both chuckled and together they slipped and slid their way in the direction of the sound that had them both quite intrigued, they were both happy for each other's company.

They were definitely heading in the right direction; as the sound they followed became more audible, "Definitely no turning back now!" said John to the king.

No definitely not, we have come this far so might as well see it through, replied the king.

"Yes, quite," said John.

They had been walking for about ten minutes, probably would have been less; if the ground wasn't so wet and muddy, when they reached what would seem to be the origin of the droning sound!

The sound was now quite loud, they found themselves at the mouth of the cave of which they would need to pass through to get to Polaria. Just as the king was about to speak there was another voice from behind them, it was Matthias and with him was Samuel.

"My king, it is you?" said Matthias.

"Yes," replied the king, "What are you doing here?"

"Probably the same as you my king, I heard that sound once the rain stopped, and for some reason found myself having to know where it was coming from, almost drawn to it!"

"What are you doing here Samuel?" asked John.

"I could ask you the same. I woke and found you had gone! I became concerned something had happened in the night, then I heard that sound, I knew you would have heard it, and would have to see its origin. And so, I followed it and bumped into Matthias on route, why didn't you wake me?"

"Well I know how much you like your sleep and didn't want to have you moaning at me if I did wake you," replied John.

"I wouldn't have moaned! You make me out to be a right miserable git!" replied Samuel.

Samuel then looked to the King and Matthias. "I'm not miserable, just haven't had a great start to this journey," he said with a sulky look, like a little boy who had just been told off.

The king and Matthias looked at each other sighed then simultaneously placed a hand on Samuel's shoulders, "No, you haven't have you my poor boy," said the king.

"Anyway, we are pleased to have you here," said Matthias, and patted Samuel's shoulder, and smiled.

"Right! Well it would seem we are at the origin of the eerie droning, what do you make of it, Matthias?" asked the king.

"It sounds like it's the wind rushing through the cave my king, which could mean the weather in Polaria could still be unsettled, but I guess we won't know until we get there!"

"That's what I was thinking, we shall have to pray the water and rain as washed the ash and dust away, we have to continue today, we have lost too much precious time as it is," replied the king shaking his head with uncertainty.

Then Matthias said he would be happy to scout ahead at daybreak, he offered to fly over the area with Ti-at and gain a view from above, and make sure it was safe to continue.

The king, John, and Samuel agreed this was a good idea, but the king didn't want Matthias to carry out this objective alone, and so asked Samuel to accompany Matthias, to which Samuel agreed with pride.

The wind rushing through the cave was quite intense, blowing their hair and robes around; it was quite an effort to take steps toward the entrance, they all looked to each other with heavy hearts fearing the weather at the other end of the cave would prevent them continuing.

"My king it is early yet, we have a few hours till daybreak so hopefully things may improve," said John.

"Yes, let's hope so!" replied the king.

Then suddenly there was a blast of wind, so powerful it knocked the men to the ground, as quick as it came it was gone! And when the four men picked themselves up and looked to each other, they noticed Matthias was stood staring at the entrance to the cave, a look of disbelief on his face, and as they too looked too the cave to see what held Matthias frozen, they to became frozen with shock and awe, as stood before them were two silhouettes; one a man and the other, a Birgumon.

It was hard to see them clearly, as they were almost transparent.

The king, frozen in his steps, tried to speak with Matthias, but Matthias was so drawn to what stood in front of him, he didn't hear the king's whispers.

"Matthias, Matthias, Matthias," the king continued, having to raise his voice to gain Matthias's attention!

Then when the king's voice became stern and almost a shout, "MATTHIAS!" the king called.

Matthias snapped out of his gaze and turned to the king; his expression was of shock as he heard the king's raised voice.

"M-m-my King," stuttered Matthias.

"Are you ok?" asked the king.

"I'm not sure my king, what manner of being are these that stand before us?"

"I honestly do not know," replied the king, then looked to John and Samuel, who were just as shocked as the king and Matthias; they could only respond with a shrug of the shoulders, as though to say they had no clue.

Then the king turned to face the figures who stood ahead of them and asked if they meant them harm.

There was no response for a moment, and in that moment a sensation of fear overcame the four men, as they did not know what response the king's question would bring.

Then a voice was heard in the four men's heads simultaneously saying; they had nothing to fear from those who stood before them, it was that which lay ahead of them beyond the mountains they had to fear!

The voice continued; "My king I urge you turn back, there is only death and wickedness lay beyond these mountains, those you seek are no more!"

At these words the four men looked to each other with disbelief. Matthias with his words now full of upset, almost angrily asked; "What do you mean those we seek are no more? Are you telling us the people of Polaria are dead?!"

The voice replied; "No not dead! But they are no longer those you seek, they are not as you knew them to be!" They are changed! you will no longer recognise them, and they will not know you anymore, and will hurt you and your people, stay away close your borders so they shall not be able to travel to your regions."

Matthias had family members and friends in Polaria, he was upset immensely by these words, and was not willing to give up on them, he wasn't alone as the king, Samuel and John also had family or friends in Polaria, they couldn't believe what they were being told; they struggled to accept it.

"So how is it they have become changed?, what is it that changes them?" asked the king. He continued, "Is it the ash and dust that as infected them in some way , just as it did with Ti-at and his kin? If so, we cured them of its effects, and so surely can do the same for those in Polaria! We have hopefully washed away the dust and ash with our efforts," continued the king.

"We know of your efforts we were there after all," replied the voice.

"What do you mean you were there?" asked the king.

"My king it is us Simon and Nar!" and as the voice spoke the human-shaped silhouette stepped forward to appear more clearly to the four men.

The four men gasped and stepped back with shock, cold fear shot up their spines as they realised that stood before them were the spirits of Simon and Nar. They could not rest in peace until they had warned the king of the dangers they had seen whilst their spirits walked the dark lands of Polaria where they had perished.

Although Simon's spirit was almost transparent, now that he had stepped closer, they could see his face, and Nar had now lowered his head and was visible to them also.

The four men felt such sorrow for the two lost troubled spirits that stood before them, "I'm so sorry I couldn't protect you," said the king with tears of sorrow.

"My king please feel no sorrow, it was our time and no man can stop time, when our time has come, it has come, we have to except it, I serve you now to warn you my king, and I hope you heed my warning, I know you are a good king, and truly care for your people, and I feel you will still try to save those who are lost, even though I warn you against it.

"As for your efforts to wash the sky clean of the ash and dust, you have been successful, but that doesn't make Polaria safe, there are greater dangers there now, I advise you do not enter Polaria!"

The king replied giving thanks for Simon and Nar's warning, but said; "as long as there was a chance they could heal the people of Polaria as they did the Birgumon, they had to continue," the other men supported their king, saying there is always hope, no matter how small.

At hearing this Simon could only smile and say, "You are a true king, and those with you are brave and loyal to you good King, they will follow you till their dying days, and as you make it clear you will not turn back I understand your reasons and so I to my king will follow you in my spirit form, I will assist you best I can, myself and Nar will watch over you and will not join our God until you need us no more."

"And so, my king, as you will not heed my warning! I can only offer you advice at this time, if you continue to Polaria you must do so at the light of day and be sure to be gone before the sun sets!"

"I was planning to proceed into Polaria at first light, and if needs be stay until our assistance is needed no more," replied the king.

Simon replied informing the king that no matter what; he and his kin must leave Polaria before nightfall, even if they found souls they felt they could save they must take them with them, but if they hindered their retreat they should leave them. "You must be gone by nightfall," he said in a very stern tone.

"Heed this my king, you will be in danger even by daylight, but once night has come dangers beyond comprehension will surround you, and you will all perish, It is time we leave you now, but we will be watching over you and shall try our best to assist!"

Before the king or any of the other men could reply the spirits were gone!

The king, Matthias, John and Samuel stood looking around them as though to see where the spirits had gone, but they were nowhere to be seen, then Samuel said for them all to listen!

And as they stood listening Samuel said, "The sound has gone!"

"Yes," replied the king, "You're right, it must have been Simon and Nar, they must have known we would follow the sound to them!"

"So, what do you think my king?" asked Matthias.

"What do I think? Do you mean about what they have just warned us of?" replied the king.

"Yes, my king, how do we best proceed knowing there is danger ahead, we as a people have never faced anything such as Simon as warned! It would appear our own kin would be willing to take our lives!"

John interrupted; "Yes! He said they are not as we remember them; it would sound as though they are unwell, he said they have changed! It would seem the ash and dust as made them unfamiliar to us, just as it did with Ti-at and his kin, and we managed to save them! So, what's to say we can't do the same for our kin in Polaria."

"You're right, it was changing them, it even changed their feathers, but we managed to save them before it was too late for them, remember it was suffocating them, and if we hadn't of acted when we did they would have died," replied Matthias.

John quickly replied asking; "What if it wasn't suffocating Ti-at and his kin, what if it was changing them inside just as it did outside, it wasn't killing them but changing them!"

He continued; "Well our healers saved them, and I'm sure even if they had changed in some way inside, our healers would have still brought them back, look at them now, they are just as they were before the ash and dust took hold of them... There must be hope for our people!"

The king then said; "We can't be sure of anything, but myself, I can't just walk away, I have to believe there is hope for our kin, but if we proceed, we are possibly putting the lives of the whole group in danger! If what Simon has said is true; and this infection as rendered our kin unrecognisable to us, and that they will not know us as they did, it may be that they become fearful of us as strangers, and possibly aggressive as a defensive response, and so with this in mind I think best the children don't proceed with us."

"So, my king you think that Simon meant that our kin would want to hurt us because they wouldn't recognise us, and think we want to hurt them?"

"Yes! I think just as Ti-at and his kin were rendered unconscious by the infection, I believe the same must be happening to our kin, and because they have been left untreated, when they wake they are left with some form of amnesia, unable to remember anything or anyone, and so could become easily agitated or scared thinking they have to protect themselves."

The king continued; "And so I hope that if we should recognise anyone, we should try and somehow help them remember us, say our names to them, and tell them their names, in the hope it may jog their memories and enable us to treat them. We can but try!"

"You could be right my king; I say we continue at sunrise just as planned," said Matthias looking to John and Samuel who nodded in agreement.

Matthias continued, "But if we are wrong and our lives are at threat, we will need a quick means of retreat, and so I believe we may need the children to lift us out of harms clasps and back to safety. I believe it best the children continue with us my king…"

Then Samuel spoke reminding them that they all knew there could be danger on this mission, and that the king mentioned that fact back home in Engypt, and that not one person as wanted to quit; "Child or adult, we all knew the risks before we left home, and so I say continue with the children, they may be young but they are fearless, and we just might need their abilities to get us out should the worst happen!"

"Yes, we may need their abilities, and yes they are fearless but! They are children and probably seeing this whole journey as just as an exciting adventure; what would happen should they come face to face with a disfigured being trying to harm them? That I can't allow, they aren't like us, we are grown men and much stronger physically, and able to defend ourselves should we have to, they would not be able to, I know their parents also knew there could be risks! But they trust in me and my judgment to keep their children safe, and after having an unimaginable experience of two spirits acutely warning us, we could perish! What kind of king would I be to take children into an almost certain; life threatening situation! It's bad enough I ask you to risk your lives!"

For a moment there was silence while they thought about the king's words.

Then Matthias respectfully responded to the king, saying he didn't see that they had an option but to take the children, if they did leave the children behind and the adults where to perish, what was to stop whatever lay on the other side of the mountains coming through the cave into Bulgan, and God forbid taking their lives, and those of the people of Bulgan, and even further afield!

Matthias continued; "One way or another my king we need to see what it is we are up against! And if they pose a threat to the surrounding regions, we are at present in a easily defendable region surrounded by mountains with only two entrances, unless airborne as we were, unlike the rest of the surrounding regions most of which have no walls, no way of defending themselves, and so my king we have to be sure we do not perish! As we may be the only one's able to warn the regions around us, and the only way to insure we can escape if needs be, is the power of flight which the children possess, they are the only ones that can get all of us out simultaneously. So, you see my king we don't really have an option!"

"Unfortunately my king, Matthias is right!" said John looking to the ground wishing there was another way.

The King drew a deep breath and exhaled heavily, a heavy sigh as his shoulders and head dropped, he felt anguish knowing Matthias was right!

The children were the only ones able to get them to safety.

There was silence while the king thought long and hard, then he spoke!

"You are right! They have to come, and if we do need to flee, they will not be able to go over the mountains, that was too dangerous last time, we will have to go the long way around to the south entrance to Bulgan. And I want two men for every child who will not leave their sides ready to defend them while we are in Polaria... So, we are in agreement?" asked the king.

Yes, they all agreed, the children will accompany them and will be under guard for their safety, it was to be Matthias's job to select the strongest most fearless men to protect the children.

So now that they had agreed, they turned back toward the camp, while they were walking back the sun began to rise and what a beautiful moment that was to behold. The sky was still black and littered with stars, the moons bright against the black background of space, and now as the sun began to rise the beautiful purple and orange rays began to illuminate the eastern most edge of the sky, subtly lighting the beautiful mountains in the fore, making the mountains appear somehow split, one side still dark with only the moon's light, and the other beautifully glistening as the rising sun reflected off of the snowy caps.

"It warmed the hearts of the four men luckily witnessing natures beauty at work."

And so, they stood in wonderment watching the sun rise, and with it bringing a warmth that felt so soothing on their faces, they stood eyes closed allowing the sun's rays to warm their faces and sooth away their worries, if only for a moment.

And when they opened their eyes the sky was no longer dark; it was now a beautiful pale blue with the moons still ever so slightly visible like balls of haze in the distance.

The king was the first to speak as he surveyed the beautiful surroundings with the little makeshift shelters dotted around amongst the dewy flower filled uncut long grass fields, and their beautiful woodland and mountainous backdrop.

"Isn't this beautiful?!" said the king, he then continued; "This world is truly beautiful?, and we will protect it and those who share it no matter the cost."

"It most certainly is my king, it's incomprehensible a ball of fire in the nights sky should threaten such beauty," replied Matthias.

"Well today we shall see if there is a threat or not!" replied the king, he then continued; "I pray for all our sakes what we find today will present no real danger, nothing more than a treatable infection which grips our kin, of which we will contain and cure."

"Yes!" replied Matthias, who then noticed those of the group who had been sleeping were now waking, and rising as they started to appear from their makeshift shelters and helping each other prepare breakfast, starting small camp fires to heat water and cook, "That's good my king, they are starting to rise and ready for the day ahead! Looks like we will be arriving just in time for breakfast!"

On hearing Matthias's observations, the men looked to each other and smiled, John saying that's great as he was famished and in need of a good hearty breakfast, and some lovely lemon and ginger tea, "Mmm!" he exclaimed.

As they drew closer to the camp, they could see the children were happily running around, being as children should be.

As the king saw the children his expression changed, his smile had dropped, although watching the children playing made him happy, he couldn't help but be concerned for them, and this was easily visible on his face, Matthias saw this and put his right hand on the king's shoulder and told the king the children will be fine!

The king whilst still watching the children play, with a heavy heart replied saying he truly hoped so, then continued, "Let's get some breakfast then ready ourselves."

And so that is what they did, the king found his daughter May, and together they ate talked and even laughed together at her father's silly jokes.

John and Samuel sat together enjoying a hearty breakfast and talking of what may lay ahead of them, promising each other they would watch out for one and other, although they had only known each other a few days, they had become good friends, and had a strong bond almost like that of which two brothers might have.

John felt such a strong bond with Samuel that he actually admitted to him how fearful he was feeling, and that having Samuel by his side filled him with confidence they would be ok!

After hearing this from John, Samuel felt he too could be totally honest; and admitted; he too was feeling ever so fearful and just wanted to be back home, but even so he wouldn't be anywhere else! As he felt a duty to the king and the poor souls of Polaria, he then continued, "Besides I have to be here to watch out for you! I've only just met you my good friend, and I don't intend to lose my friend no matter what!" He then laughed saying "Not that I think you can't look out for yourself, but you do scare easily and make some of the funniest sounds a man could ever make! And I don't want to miss out on hearing them, do I?"

"You're not going to let me forget about that are you?" replied John.

"No! Never ever," replied Samuel and together they laughed.

It would seem this breakfast was unlike any other; members of the group had formed bonds with one and other over the days they had spent together, and all had a sense this might be the last breakfast they shared together; and so talked to each other in a way which was quite personal to them, letting each other know that they cared for them, and if anything should happen to one or other, they would always remember them.

But the mood wasn't solemn as you might expect, no! they were all laughing and joking making fond memories that would last a lifetime.

After they had their fill, Matthias and the king went to see Ti-at, they wanted to check Ti-at and his kin had slept well and eaten, they also wanted to wish Ti-at and his kin a safe journey home, as the Birgumon wouldn't be joining them on this part of the mission, Ti-at had wanted to see the mission through to the end, but the king and Matthias had spoken and they had decided it best the humans continued as one group through the caves, the Birgumon had already helped them enough, and suffered a loss in their efforts; the king and Matthias didn't wish to burden the Birgumon, especially as they knew there was a real chance of danger, and couldn't bear the thought of the Birgumon suffering anymore losses, the king felt anguish enough having to have the children follow him into the unknown, he would need to have his mind on the task in hand and those who follow him.

And so, felt the Birgumon would just be another distraction for him, another worry for him.

It wouldn't be long now before the Birgumon would leave, and so the whole group wanted to say their goodbyes, especially those who had ridden them, and so they all got their chance to say farewell.

Samuel was looking for Fanella but couldn't seem to find her, He was saddened as he thought she had already left and he hadn't had the chance to say farewell and wish her a safe journey, he proceeded to ask the other Birgumon if they had seen Fanella, but unfortunately they hadn't, and just as he had given up hope a voice from behind him! "Oi smelly! You, looking form me...?"

He had never been so happy to be called smelly!

His face lit up so bright with a smile from ear to ear, he spun around and just grabbed her with both arms around her neck and squeezed her, there was silence between the two for a moment.

They just enjoyed the moment, he could feel and hear her heart beating and the sound it made was beautiful to his ears, and as she breathed he felt so comforted, a tear ran from his eye, he feared he may never see her again, he had never had such affection for a creature before, the bond that had formed between them was so-so strong, she could feel his emotions, and he felt hers, they both felt a sadness in the pit of their stomachs.

But then Fanella being Fanella "Oi smelly, you aren't going all soppy on me are you?" which made Samuel chuckle, "Who me! No never," he replied and smiled, you have a safe journey home won't you, you cheeky big bird you."

"Thank you I will," she replied with a big grin, "You be safe and look after yourself, we will see each other again I'm sure!"

"Ok, goodbye for now then Fanella," he replied and let go of her neck, and just as he was about to turn away, "Oh no my neck feels damp! You didn't rub your armpit against my neck! did you?" she said with a shake of the head and a cheeky grin.

"Well look at it like this, you have my sweet smell to remember me by" Samuel replied and smiled, then off they went in opposite directions smiling!

Now that everyone had said their goodbyes the king and his group stood and watched as the Birgumon took flight and headed home, they watched them until they could no longer be seen, then the king said, "I guess we should get heading off ourselves!"

The journey through the caves would take approximately two hours before they would reach Polaria, and it would only take the dragons with the huge containers approximately thirty minutes to reach Polaria by air, and so it was agreed, the dragons wouldn't start their journey until the King contacted them Telepathically letting them know they were nearing the end of the caves, the King didn't want the dragons waiting for them in Polaria knowing it could be dangerous.

So now the king and his followers said their goodbyes to the Dragons and turned to the entrance of the caves. The path through the caves was very wide, approximately twenty feet in width, but did narrow in places, and in some spots had sheer drops, so they would have to be careful as it was poorly lit inside the caves.

Although the caves were quite wide, the roof of the caves was quite shallow, approximately fifteen feet at the point they stood with stalactites and stalagmites scattered throughout, some reached from the roof of the cave to the ground forming pillars, and it was from these the source of a dim silvery light emanated, just bright enough to illuminate the crystals imbedded in the walls and floor of the cave, they sparkled like stars dimly lighting a path for them to follow.

As they proceeded deeper into the cave, the sunlight which lit the entrance behind them faded dimmer and dimmer, until the only light remaining was the dim silvery light of the stalactites stalagmites and the glistening crystals of the walls and floor, the star like glistening from the walls, floor and in parts roof of the cave began to have an effect on the group, a sensation as though they were walking through space itself, just as the sensation you would get if you lay in a field at night staring at the stars of clear nights sky, stare long enough and you begin to feel you are floating into the star-filled sky itself.

This sensation was starting to effect their judgment, it was becoming hard to walk as they normally would! it seemed every step they took they would have to take so slowly in this strange lighting, they were becoming disoriented, as the light almost appeared holographic appearing as three-dimensional shards of dim light, making it hard for them to judge were the ground below their feet lay, it was as though they were all tipsy.

"This is quite an unusual sensation isn't it?! There wasn't any wine in our morning tea this morning was there?" the king said jokingly, as he searched for the ground with his foot lowering it slowly unsure where the ground lay, and focusing as hard as he could with his eyes.

Matthias on hearing this let out a laugh ha-ha, "It certainly feels as though I've had a glass or two! That's for sure."

Others behind them could be heard laughing and commenting; "This is unbelievable ha-ha-ha!"

John was using his left hand to guide himself, running it against the wall of the cave for extra stability, he then suggested the others did the same as it was helping him a lot.

And so, they took John's advice and now reached for the wall of the cave, which was easier said than done! Because of the way the light reflecting off the crystals appearing three-dimensional protruding from the wall of the cave, it appeared the wall of the cave was closer than it actually was! And so, lead to members of the group reaching for the wall only to realise it was actually further away than the light would make it seem, and so lead to members of the group stumbling reaching for a wall which wasn't there!

Again, they were finding this quite funny, laughing at one and other as they heard members exclaiming damn, I've missed the wall, I can't find it!

Eventually after a time and a few bumps and bruises, they had all managed to find the wall, even so, they continued very gingerly.

Then suddenly! "Ugh that's freezing!" the king could be heard to exclaim as he came across a stream of freezing water, which as his fingers made contact ran instantly down his hand and arm to the elbow, leaving his sleeve soaked and very cold, he then warned those behind him, "Watch out for that, there is water running down the wall and it is freezing cold…"

But as it was so poorly lit in the cave the water running down the wall couldn't be seen, and so inevitably there where a great many exclamations of shock, as one after the other came across the freezing cold water. "Woohoo! Found it," exclaimed little May.

"Ah-chi-wow! Great that's going to take ages to dry," exclaimed Simon.

And so, it continued until every member of the group now had a soaking wet left arm and sleeve. It was quite funny hearing all the different reactions as each of the now five hundred and seventy-one strong party encountered the water, it seemed to go on forever!

The laughter echoed throughout the cave as did the moans of shock.

This had really lifted the spirits of the entire group; it was exactly what they needed! A good side-splitting laugh, and as for the wet sleeve, it would dry.

As they continued deeper into the cave the air became damp and very cold, they could hear the trickle of water as it ran into pools which had formed over many-many years; they could just make the pools out, thanks to the formation of the crystals in the floor of the cave which lit the edges of them, and as their eyes could barely see, their other senses had become quite sensitive such as their ears, they could hear the droplets of water falling from the roof of the cave into the pools below, which gave them a good indication they were approaching the pools, and they would become cautious not to fall into one.

Now they had become more reliant on their ears to help guide them, they started to notice strange scampering sounds! They seemed to come from every direction!

"What is that sound?!" asked little May.

"I think it could be cave rats, but don't worry they will always run from us, they are quite shy creatures, although they are quite a size! they are scared of most other living things and are rarely seen!" replied the king.

"Have you ever seen one, father?"

"No, I've never seen one, but then I've not been in many caves!" he laughed.

"So, nothing to fear then, father?"

"No nothing to fear," replied the king.

They had now been in the cave for quite some time and would hopefully be reaching the exit to Polaria shortly, they couldn't contact Egum until they could see the exit!

But at this time the exit was not in sight, they had hoped to see some sunlight anytime now, but it wasn't to be, for now!

The journey was taking longer than first expected, this could be due to the fact they had never used this cave before, and had been a little overly cautious, better late than never; the king would say.

As they continued, the scuttling sound they had been hearing now seemed to be coming from directly in front of them, and much slower now!

This didn't worry them as they had a good idea it was cave rats, and they were very shy and totally harmless creatures!

In fact, if they did get to see one it would be quite a privilege! And so, continued confidently, the king said to little May; that he would actually like to see one, as they are supposed to be quite a sight to see!

He then continued; "The main reason that not many people had actually seen one, was due to the fact they are exceedingly fast-moving creatures constantly scurrying around and only rest when it was time to sleep!"

"Really Father? Faster than the Chu-Chun? They are very fast!"

"I believe the cave rat may be faster!" replied the king.

"Now that I'd really like to see!" replied little may now excited and wanting to see a cave rat.

They were now nearing the end of the cave and could just make out a small speck of sunlight in the distance. "Finally!" said the king, "not far to go now!"

"Yes thankfully, I will be happy to feel the sun on my face once again!" replied Matthias.

"Me too, I'm starting to feel like a mine-mule! Just hope my eyes work correctly after being in the dark so long!" laughed John.

"Not too far now!" announced Samuel, to which members of the group exclaimed hurray!

As they neared the exit; which was still approximately three hundred feet ahead of them, a big roundish figure appeared from one of the smaller caves from the left of the main path! This figure was quite a size! They couldn't quite make out what form of creature it was but had an idea it was a cave rat as it appeared to have a very long tail, which was wagging slowly left to right repeatedly! And so, they continued undeterred, knowing it would probably scamper away before they got too much closer to it.

As they got closer, the eyes of the creature appeared green; as its pupils reflected what little light there was in the cave.

"I hope that is a cave rat!" said the king under his breath; "those are big eyes! And at the height those eyes would appear, that is a big rat! and it doesn't appear to be moving away from us! Matthias, have you ever seen a cave rat…?"

"No, my King I have not, I've been told they are big beasts! But that figure looks very big indeed!"

"Yes, it does, doesn't it?! and from what I have heard of them I would have expected it to run away by now!"

And with that the king put his right hand on little May and asked her to walk behind Matthias who was behind her.

Samuel overheard the king ask May to walk behind Matthias, and so offered to watch over her; saying she could hold his hand.

The king replied thanking Samuel, and so little may took Samuel's hand and together they continued to follow behind Matthias and the king, who were becoming a little concerned as this creature that stood a distance ahead of them wasn't doing as expected of a cave rat. And so, continued nervously! Neither the king nor any of his followers had weapons should this creature attack them! Weapons hadn't even been invented in this world; they had never been required the people of soul have never known war!

The only things that they had which could be used to defend themselves, were now safely packed away, with all the rest of the cooking utensils...

It was of little consolation, but Matthias liked to carve wood and always had his wood carving knife with him, the blade was only three inches long, but was very, very sharp!

He offered the knife to the king saying; "It's not the biggest knife my king, and will not kill a beast as big as whatever that may be, but it would cause pain, hopefully enough to cause the creature to run away if it should attempt to cause us harm."

"Thank you, Matthias, but no thank you, if whatever that is ahead of us should attack, we be doomed knife of no knife! So, let's just pray this is just a cave rat that is used to seeing people traveling through these caves, as it is the only way into and out of Bulgan from Polaria, and so it sees us as no threat."

"Yes! I hadn't thought of that!" Matthias replied with a sense of relief! And promptly re-sheaved the knife in its wooden hip sleeve.

And so, they continued, although very cautiously.

The cave became brighter as they neared the exit, and now they could make out the creature which stood before them! And indeed, it was a cave rat, but even so they kept their wits about them! As this particular rat didn't look to be in any way afraid of them as they drew closer to it, it just stood looking at them and occasionally running its front paws over its face as if cleaning itself.

As they approached the creature the king asked that everyone be quiet! He didn't want to startle it, he continued he didn't believe it meant them harm, but just didn't want anyone to make any sudden noises in case it became scared, they had no idea how it might react!

The rat stood on its hind legs sniffing the air as the group approached it, it now stood as tall as the king at around six feet tall.

"My they are big aren't they?" said the king to Matthias.

"Yes! That is one very big rat, look at its claws! Thankfully it doesn't seem aggressive! Quite the opposite I'd say," replied Matthias.

"Yes! Thankfully, but why is it standing there like that, as though it's waiting for us?" replied the king.

"We will soon find out I'm guessing my king," replied Matthias. "We could always ask it my king…"

"Do you think they have the intelligence to communicate with us?, they aren't the most sociable creatures are they?!"

"No, indeed they are not, this is the first I've ever seen one!" replied Matthias.

Before the king could reply, the cave rat lowered its front quarters as though to bow before the king! You must be King Stephen! I heard you would be heading this way and so wanted to meet you! It is such an honour to be able to stand before you good King…

The honour is mine, I feel privileged to actually meet you, you and your kin are quite elusive! You are the first cave rat I have ever met, and you are a lot bigger than I ever imagined! What are you called?" asked the king.

The Rat became excited that the king actually wanted to know his name, as no human had ever asked his name before, he moved forward towards the king and stretched out his neck, putting his nose only inches from the king's nose, and began to sniff at the king, with a huge smile and eyes glistening he was so happy! "You want to know my name?!" he said in an almost shocked state, then turned his back to the king, stood on his hind legs, stretched his neck towards the roof of the cave sniffing intently and rolling his head left and right excitedly!

He then turned his head over his left shoulder to look back to the King, stared for a moment, then turned and again almost nose to nose with the king, "You really want to know my name?!" the rat asked in an overly excited manner, it was almost as if the rat was slightly mentally unstable, not in a harmful way, just a very excitable way possibly quite eccentric! "Whoop-whoop! the king wants to know my name!" the rat said as he turned and started to skip and hop about in a circle.

As the rat was skipping and hopping around in circles whoop-whooping! Matthias and a few of the other members of the group tried their best to refrain from laughing at the rat, Matthias turned to whisper to the King "I don't think he is quite the full loaf my king," smiled with disbelief and shook his head.

Then suddenly the rat stopped and turned to the king, as it did the king and the group gasped! And quickly stepped back a step, so sudden was the rat's movement...

"So sorry didn't mean to startle you good king," said the rat, at realising he had caused everyone to jump!

With eyes wide open excitedly the rat said; my name is "Mit! Mit-Mit-Mit," he said repeatedly as he lowered himself back down onto all fours, and continued, "How can I be of service to you good King, I will serve you proudly..."

The king replied; "Thank you Mit, it's good to meet you, thank you for your offer of service, I must ask you! Are you always this excited when someone asks your name...?"

"Well my king other than my own kin, no human as ever

spoken with me, let alone asked my name! So please forgive my excitement...!"

"Well maybe if you and your kin weren't so shy you would actually get to meet people," said the king and continued; "Do you ever leave these caves?"

"Occasionally we do at night!" Mit replied, "but since the bright light we haven't roamed from our caves, and no humans have passed through! In fact no creature as passed through since the bright light! And today is the first time since the bright light that we have been able to see into Polaria! After the bright light came darkness! Like a cloud of black! The black cloud as finally gone...! But! The land is stained, we dare not venture out into Polaria, I fear it's unsafe to do so!"

Chapter 5

It's A Dangerous World

Mit continued; "Since this morning we have been watching the land, but nothing stirs! It is as-though the land as died, we haven't seen any form of life out there, and these caves would normally be filled with those passing through to trade with one and other at either Bulgan or Polaria, this has always been good for me and my kin, as there would always be plenty of fish and fruits all sorts of good things that had fallen from carts, and just left for us to forage at night... But now nothing!

"I was actually shocked and excited to hear you were here in these caves," Mit said, looking about him and fidgeting with his front paws, he then continued; "my good King, we thought we were the only living creatures left, so you can imagine my relief when I saw you! Is this all of your kin that have survived the light?" Mit asked...

The king then replied informing Mit that there are thousands upon thousands of his kin alive and well, and that he and those with him have come to assist those who may need help in Polaria.

In hearing the king's words Mit's expression became one of shock! "You are intending to go out there?"

"Yes, we do indeed, we intend to search for our kin, we bring aid for them," replied the king...

Almost in a state of shock at the king's words, "No-no-no! My king you cannot go out there!" said Mit almost laughing with shock!

He then turned looking out of the cave at the land that lay beyond, and with a heavy heart, "No, my king you can't go out there! Look at it! It's barren! Nothing lives there anymore, only danger lay beyond these caves now; turn back it is folly to continue…"

As Mit spoke, the king and the group approached the mouth of the cave to look on the world outside, and what they saw was a shock to them all. They had all thought it might be bad! But what they saw now shook them all!

The once so beautiful land of Polaria with its beautiful fields of lush green grass speckled with wonderful flowers of every imaginable colour and beauty was now black! Covered with a shimmering black crustaceous surface! The once beautiful mushroom shaped low-hung trees were now shimmering black, the leaves although surprisingly; still attached to the branches were now solid, they now resembled scales of black!

No matter how far they looked to the distance it was the same, even the mountains very tips shimmered black in the sunlight.

Where there had once been properties of all manner of shape and size, farms, blacksmiths, homes and stables; now stood ruins, barely recognisable as they once were beautiful wooden structures…

With this sight came so much pain to all those who beheld it; even the king was brought to tears, Matthias dropped to his knees crying, the king could only place his right hand on Matthias's head in an attempt to console him while staring in disbelief at the unrecognisable land he once loved.

Little May, sobbing, ran to her Father throwing her arms around his waist and pressed her face to his chest; as she impacted against the king, his numb body just rocked, his head just gently moving, his eyes full of tears and yet empty and numb slowly lowering to look to his daughter, he had no words to speak, all he could do was place his left arm around her and hold her tight to his chest as they cried.

John and Samuel stood motionless side by side not a word spoken, then after several minutes John in a barely audible voice; this is a nightmare beyond my wildest imagination!

Simon could only stand numbly looking, he had no words to respond.

The cries and screams of the group echoed throughout the caves; Adrian was bent on one knee cuddling Rose who had her arms around his neck sobbing into his shoulder, "They're all gone!" she said in floods of tears.

He didn't know what to say to ease her pain, he could only utter; "I know I know," as he looked out at the black land that lay before him. Then suddenly, from out of the blackened woodland appeared a Chu-Chun! It sped across the mouth of the cave at great speed! as it did so the ground beneath its paws made a cracking sound as each paw impacted on it breaking it, and parts flung into the air with the speed of the Chu-Chun's powerful strides! in moments the beautiful white-scaled cat-like creature was gone!

It had reached a blackened shrub-land and all that could be seen was the shrubs rustling at speed as the Chu-Chun smashed its way through and out of sight…

At the sight of the beautiful beast there were gasps; "Did you see that?!" Adrian shouted to gain the groups attention!

"Yes-yes," replied John.

"Me too," said Simon.

The king and many others had also seen the Chu-Chun, if only momentarily!

But this was enough to give them all hope! Surely if the Chu-Chun had somehow survived then there was hope for the other inhabitants of Polaria, including their kin.

Matthias stood and turned to the king in a very emotional state saying; "There is hope my king, we must search for our kin!"

Even Mit with his eccentricities rolling his eyes and saying: "Well I wasn't expecting that!" as he referred to the Chu-Chun, there may be hope after all…!

The king could feel the sense of hope emitting from his people, as he looked around at those with him, he could see they had a determination not to give up!

And so, they would continue, he was totally unsure as to what they would find, but even if they found one living person that would make their efforts worthwhile.

The king didn't answer immediately, he thought about Simon's words warning him to be sure to leave before nightfall!

He then nodded his head in agreement; "Yes there is hope! If our kin have survived this horror then we will find them! No matter how few we save, even if it's only one soul we save then we have achieved our goal. I'm not going to fill you with false hope, you can see for yourselves it is bleak out there; so please do not expect to find many, I pray with all my heart I am wrong, and that we find many of our kin safe! Only time will answer, and all we can do is our best, so with that in mind we will continue if you really truly wish to? So how say you all? Do you wish to proceed! Think for a moment if you need…"

It was unanimous! The whole group agreed, they had come this far and no matter how bleak the outlook, they had a duty to at least try!

Even Mit was holding on to the hope there would be someone still alive out there somewhere!

He even offered to join them in their search, saying he had a great nose, and could help to sniff them out! and if needs be, dig with his huge claws and teeth!

As he looked to the king quite excitedly the king said he would be happy to have him join them, but added; "Are you sure? A moment ago you were saying for us not to proceed! You were saying only danger lay ahead…"

Mit swiftly replied with his usual eccentric manner; rolling his eyes and rapidly shaking his head as he said; "Well that was before the Chu-Chun appeared! And I can tell you now, that beast didn't come through these caves! So it must have had shelter from the bright light, and so if it did, then you're kin may have also…"

Hearing Mit's words the king smiled and then placed his left hand on Mit's head, and said he was very welcome; he then continued to warn Mit that there may still be danger lurking! And that he had to be sure he was willing to risk himself! As the king and those with him had already accepted their fate, he didn't want Mit to continue with them unless he was sure.

The huge cave rat replied saying he appreciated the king's honesty and consideration. He then gave a big crazy-eyed smile, showing his huge fangs as he did so, then continued I could bring a number of my kin if it would help in our search, and should needs be, we may be shy, but if we have to defend ourselves we will! We are very powerful," he said, almost boasting!

To which the king smiled and said that he would truly be thankful for any assistance Mit and his kin could offer…

"Settled then," said Mit, he then continued, "Give me a few moments I'll fetch some of the strongest of my kin…"

"Thank you! But please be sure they understand there may be risks ahead, I wouldn't want anyone to feel obliged to join us, so if your kin prefer not to join us, then please don't feel you are letting us down, because you are not, we would understand," replied the king and smiled at Mit.

The king then continued to explain to Mit, that he and those who followed him knew first hand that there was a real danger in Polaria, and that it could spread to other regions, and so their mission wasn't just a rescue mission, but had now also become a mission to see just what dangers there may actually be, and gain knowledge of them, so as to warn others and hopefully protect against them!

"Yes, good idea, always good to know what threats may lay in that black land, but let's hope we find none!" replied Mit… "Right I'll go fetch my boys."

"Your boys!" replied the King.

"Oh yes! All the rats in these caves are my sons and daughters!" replied Mit very proudly!

"Oh, how many offspring to you have?" asked the king.

Mit thought for a few moments, rolling his eyes left and right and nodding his head as though he was counting. "Four hundred and fifty," Mit replied as he smiled and took a deep breath of pride.

"Your poor mate!" said Judith when she heard how many offspring there were.

"Oh, bless you no, that would be far too many for one mate," replied Mit, and continued to inform Judith with a big proud smile he actually had nine mates.

"Oh, ok," replied Judith with a look of disbelief.

"Anyway, I'll go fetch a few of my kin now," said Mit excitedly...

The King then replied, "Ok; but not too many! Five should suffice."

"Yes," replied Mit, and in a flash he had scurried off into the smaller cave to the left of the main path...

While the king and group waited, the king asked the group if they could attempt to contact whoever it was, they had known in Polaria. He was hoping that now they were actually at Polaria's doorstep they should be able to contact anyone who still survives!

So, using their Telepathic abilities the entire group tried to make contact, but none was successful!

In the hope of keeping hope alive, Matthias began to say, "Any survivors could be hidden in other caves, and that the materials within the walls of the caves could be blocking Telepathy! So let's not give up hope," and forced a smile...

"Quite right, if there is lead within the walls, it will block us making contact," said the king.

While the group had been trying to contact friends or loved ones, the King had contacted Egum, letting him know they had arrived at the mouth of the cave, and that Egum and his kin should now make their way, he also said for Egum to be prepared for a shock as the land they had all known, was no more!..

Egum with saddened heart replied; "I take it things are worse than we feared!"

"Much worse! It's barren! Covered in a crustaceous coating, it's unbelievable my friend, you will see for yourself!" replied the king.

He then continued, "We have hope still; we have seen a Chu-Chun! And so, would search the ruins and caves, there had to be someone still alive, and that they would find them!"

Egum replied to the King, "Well if you have seen one living creature there is always hope! we will be with you shortly my King and together we will search…"

"Thank you, see you soon old friend, travel safe," said the king.

After a period off about ten minutes Mit appeared from the cave which he had disappeared into earlier, and promptly scampered to the king, and proudly said "My king these are my strongest sons, as he turned to the entrance of the cave only to see there was no one there!"

And so with a cough of embarrassment; "Forgive me good king, these are my sons," he said again, although talking Telepathically with the king, the rest of the group could only hear loud squeaks as they looked to the cave expectantly! But again no one appeared.

The king and the group looked to each other quite bemused and trying not to laugh as they all thought the old Rat had totally lost his mind.

By now the old rat was feeling ever so embarrassed and so apologised to the king once more, then went to the cave and entered it!

He was obviously having a very stern conversation with whoever was inside! Very loud fast squeaks could be heard echoing from inside the cave, this went on for a minute or two before he reappeared…

As the poor old Rat reappeared the group were laughing, but not at him directly, it was the loud squeaks that had been echoing from the cave that had set them off; they sounded so funny to the group even though they could tell by the severity of the squeaks someone was getting a real telling off.

And so, as the king spotted him, he felt it best to explain that the group wasn't laughing at him, it was the echoing of the caves they found funny and hoped he didn't think otherwise.

"Oh no I understand!" replied the old rat, these caves can make the most unusual sounds, I quite understand!

"Oh, I am pleased, I didn't want you to think it was you that bore the brunt of our laughter and cause offence," replied the King.

"Definitely not! No offence taken good king, I would like to once again attempt to introduce my sons to you," said Mit…

And with that Mit once again looked to the cave and said; "I'd like for you all to meet my five strongest sons!" And called their names one by one, and as he did, they would appear!

The first being; Mash who promptly appeared on hearing his name. Mash seemed quite shy, and approached his father nervously as everyone welcomed him, saying hello and welcome Mash…

Next as his father called his name was Patch! it was obvious he had been named after his appearance, as he was a black rat with the cutest white circular patch around his left eye, hence the name Patch…

Next to be introduced was Fidget! Who was a brown colour unlike his brothers and father who were black, as Fidget stood nervously next to his father; it once again became apparent as to why he was given the name Fidget, he didn't stop! If he wasn't rubbing his face with his paws he was constantly looking around, he just couldn't stay still…

Again, everyone welcomed, Fidget and Patch, who just nervously smiled in return.

Now it was time for everyone to meet Short Tail!

As Mit said his name, Short Tail confidently walked out from the cave and stood on his hind legs, and continuing to walk to his father and nodding as the group welcomed him, and yep he had the shortest tail you would ever see on a Rat, it could only have been five inches in length, so his name was quite apt…

Some of the children could be heard to say; "Where is his tail? He looks strange without a tail doesn't he?!"

Then there was a voice, it was Babbyah, "Children please don't be rude, I think he is very cute."

The children chuckled and agreed, "Yes, I guess he is isn't he?" said Rose.

Now was the time to meet the fifth son, everyone looked on with anticipation, as the previous rats' names all seemed to fit their appearance the group couldn't wait to hear the next name!

And so Mit proudly introduced the last of his sons who would be joining them!

"Now I would like to introduce my second eldest son, Anchor!"

He then turned to the cave once more; as did the king and the group with anticipation.

The group thought this name rather strange! and so couldn't wait to see him, and they weren't disappointed as before them slowly appeared a beast of a rat, he was enormous!

Anchor was so large he could easily be mistaken for a bear! As he moved from the cave to join his father every step he took could be herd as a thud, so big and heavy was he, with every step the muscles of his legs could be seen to bulge then relax, even relaxed his muscle tone was incredible!

When he reached his father, he stood on his hindquarters and what a sight! He must have stood over seven feet tall and nearly the width of two of his brothers combined, and yet he was so shy he wouldn't lift his head to look at the group who stood in awe of him…

"Wow!" said Matthias, if danger does lurk out there, I want to be with him! I feel safer already, look at him, magnificent beast…"

"Yes," replied the King; thank heavens he is on our side he said with a smile of relief…

Now that Mit had introduced his sons, the group took a minute or two to gather themselves and ready to step out from the mouth of the cave. The king now informed them that Egum and his kin were making their way to join them and shouldn't be too much longer now!

He continued they shouldn't stray too far from the cave, as they would have to wait until Egum arrived before looking further afield.

He then continued; once they had all cleared the mouth of the cave they should form six groups of approximately eighty-three adults, twelve children and one rat to every group, the king's idea was seen by all as a very safe way to work in such groups, and to have the children with them just in case a quick escape was required, essential.

So now the time had come for the King and the group to take their first steps from out of the relative safety of the cave and into the now unknown land of Polaria!

King Stephen and Matthias would be the first to step from the caves and as they did so both felt a real sense of anxiety! The landscape was enough to send chills down the back of the bravest; it just appeared evil, and totally unwelcoming, they looked to each other as they together took their first steps onto the black crustaceous ground which crunched and cracked giving way as their feet made contact with the surface, their feet sank up to the ankle which caused them both to lose balance and take another quick step too right themselves which also broke through the surface and sank!

As each step broke through the crustaceous surface it released a plume of dust; on noticing this the king turned his head to Matthias and said for him to stop! "Don't take another step, as we break the surface small amounts of dust are being released, I think this could be what effected the Birgumon! I think it best we cover ourselves making sure to cover our nose and mouth so we don't ingest it…"

So, with that the king told everyone to turn back and stay in the cave whilst they put on clothing to cover every inch of their bodies, and to make face bandanas to cover their noses and mouths out of cotton strips…

And so, everyone began to do as the king asked!

When everyone had done as the king had asked, covering themselves from head to foot, and wearing the bandanas for their faces, they again readied to proceed once more, as the king was about to give the order Matthias called to the king…

"My king we have an issue!"

"What issue is it that concerns you Matthias?" asked the King.

"My king it's the cave rats! They cannot proceed with us, as they have no clothing to cover their bodies or faces!

And so would fall fail to the dust, we have to tell them they cannot proceed…"

My God! You're right Matthias I didn't consider the rats, I could have led them to their deaths! The King replied in a state of shock at the thought of what would have happened if it wasn't for Matthias's quick thinking!

The King continued; "I will inform them this instant! I'm so glad you are here Matthias; you see what I do not! Come we will tell Mit together."

And so, they walked together through the bodies of people readying to leave and found Mit and his sons being stroked fondly by a group of children.

"Children can you leave us please we have to speak with Mit and his sons for a moment, thank you," said the king.

Once the children had left and joined the main group the king began to explain the situation to Mit.

The king explained; "Unfortunately you will not be able to proceed with us, you see as we walk we are creating dust, and this dust I believe is the same that caused our friends the Birgumon to become unwell, in fact near to death it brought them! It covered them, but we washed it off them, but that wasn't the worst of it! The worst was it got into their lungs and nearly suffocated them! And so you cannot proceed as you have no way to cover yourselves, and would surely become incredibly unwell, possibly die! And so I ask you to stay and wait for our return."

"Of course, good king we will do as you ask, we thank you for bringing this to our attention, we could have so easily roamed out there unknowingly, so thank you," replied Mit.

Mit was so truly thankful for the King and Matthias's realisation, and was happy to watch and wait, he actually thought how lucky it was that the king and his kin had come by the caves, if they had not, then Mit and his kin would be unaware of the dangerous dust, and might after a time of left the caves and roamed Polaria, that would have been a big mistake.

The time had come for the king and his people to venture out into Polaria once more, after the king and Matthias's first attempt, they had both become aware of just how awkward the ground below them was to traverse, with its crumbling surface leading them to struggle to balance!

And so; with this in mind; they thought it best that no one should be carrying anything that could carry them over should their weight shift as their steps become unsteady.

The king said for everyone to leave their haversacks behind, as the weight could make it hard for them to traverse the already unstable, possibly changeable terrain.

He then continued; "Take nothing but your water pouches! And if you should need to drink, be sure the nozzle is clean of dust or dirt, and do not remove your face bandanas, drink from the nozzle from under the bandana, store the pouches within your outer garments so dust doesn't settle on it…"

Now it was time for the king and his group to once again leave the relative safety of the cave! But before they left the king and Matthias told everybody to check one another, making sure that only their eyes were visible from under their garments they could not have any skin visible that the dust might settle on.

And so they all stood covered from head to foot in beautiful white linen robes and leg garments, they even covered their footwear with strips of linen wrapping it around their feet and ankles, and halfway up their shins to be sure dust could not penetrate! and for their hands they cut linen into lengths and wrapped it around them to form mittens totally covering their skin.

Just as they were about to set off Mit approached the King and said; "Good king if it is so important that you are covered then surely your eyes should be covered! for if the weather was to change, becoming windy dust will be thrown into your eyes would it not!"

"To which the king said yes it very well would! But we need to see! And we have nothing that we can wear around our eyes that will not block our vision!" he said raising his arms and looking around, then continued; "The weather for the moment looks to be fine, barely a breeze! So we should be safe."

"Yes, that may be the case now, my king, but you and I know no one can predict the weather! And it can change rapidly! If you are out there in the barren land and the weather should change you would be caught in the midst of it! So my king I believe it would be best to cover your eyes! And I may have just the thing! Remember this is a trade path leading from Bulgan to Polaria and as I said, many a time goods have fallen from carts, unknown by the traders and so left for us to forage.

"And it would appear you're very lucky, my third mate is a hoarder! And we have rolls of fabrics, one of which you may be able to be used to protect your eyes and still let you see where it is you are going! I can show you if you wish."

Babbyah had overheard the conversation and butted in! That would be a great idea! Sorry my King I didn't mean to eavesdrop, but it would be an idea to have our eyes covered providing we can still see! May I have a look at what it is that Mit has to offer?!"

"Of course, hopefully you may find something that will be of use, would you like to take someone with you?"

But before Babbyah could reply there was a voice, "This should serve your purpose!!"

"Ha, here she is!" said Mit, as he turned to Babbyah. "This is my third mate, her name is Sibby, and she thinks she may have just what you need!"

As Babbyah turned, there was a white Rat walking towards her on its hindquarters, carrying a roll of white fabric in her front paws! "Hello, my dear, is this for you?" she said to Babbyah.

"Yes, thank you, you must be Sibby! Mit mentioned you might have some fabric we could use to cover our eyes, is that it? I'm Babbyah," she continued with a welcoming thankful smile.

"Nice to meet you Babbyah! Yes I am! And yes this is it! I think this could be perfect for your needs," she said as she unrolled the fine mesh like fabric onto the floor of the cave...

As the fabric rolled onto the floor, Babbyah could see it was a fine cotton mesh which looked fine enough to stop the dust penetrating it, but also not so fine that it could not be seen through, she asked Sibby if it was okay to cut a length so she could see if she could see through it! Sibby agreed "Yes of course," with that Babbyah asked Matthias for his knife, and cut a length of the fabric approximately two feet in length, she then placed it over her eyes and tied it at the back of her head, "That's great I think it will do the job perfectly, I can see fine."

With that Sibby said; "I am pleased, please take as much as you require if needs be, take it all, I have no use for it."

Babbyah replied; "Thank you so much, this is very kind of you, and very much appreciated, once again thank you."

With that Babbyah proceeded to continue cutting the fabric into strips, enough for everyone, and by the time she had finished her hands were quite sore with the continues gripping and cutting, and as for Matthias's carving knife, well it would definitely need to be sharpened before he could ever use it to carve again…

Now third time lucky, everyone was ready! Not a speck of skin could be seen, the king and Matthias were now confident it would be safe to proceed, and so again they would be the first to step out once more into the dark barren land, but this time they were well prepared or so they thought!

As the king went to take his first steps from the mouth of the cave something felt different!

Everything seemed incredibly bright, so bright it hurt his eyes, so much so, he had to raise his right hand partially covering his eyes; in an attempt to reduce the brightness! "Wow!" exclaimed the king, Matthias does it seem unbearably bright to you?

"Yes, it does my king," he replied trying to shield his eyes from the glare, it also feels so much hotter than before, but that could be due to all this extra clothing!

"No!" replied the king, it is definitely hotter! Incredibly so! It must be the heat from the sun reflecting off this shiny crustaceous surface which is everywhere! The shell-like surface is reflecting the sun like a mirror! I can barely see…"

The king continued to slowly take steps forward away from the mouth of the cave, with Matthias by his side.

As other members of the group approached the mouth of the cave, they could be heard to exclaim "Ah! Wow why is it so bright?" they asked.

As they left the caves and their cooling drafts, the heat outside hit them as though a huge oven door had been suddenly swung open, releasing its heat with one almighty gust, the air instantly stifling them!

The conditions were unbearable, what with the incredible glaring sun's rays reflecting everywhere they looked half blinding them, and this intense heat stifling their breaths, made worse by having to cover their mouths and noses with cotton bandanas, which in themselves inhibited their breathing.

Within minutes they were all soaked in sweat, their clothing sticking to them as they try to move and feeling so uncomfortable, but even so they all continued slowly one unstable step after another, the ground crunching and braking, releasing deadly dust with every step they took.

As they walked the king and the others were intrigued by their surroundings! the king so much so; he had to look closer at what was once a beautiful orchid, and would have been beautifully fragrant and diverse in colours; whites, pinks, purples, blues, so divers but now blackened! The petals hard and shiny, and as he touched it looking closely, he could see each petal had sharp edges.

Holding the blackened flower at the stem he wanted to pull it gently closer, but as he did it just cracked then snapped, it was so brittle.

He now held the broken flower in his hand and squeezed it and as he did it crumbled into fragments.

The king turned to Matthias "This land is truly dead!" he said in a saddened voice.

Matthias replied "yes, it is, everything one touches just snaps and crumbles, what could do this? It's evil!"

"I agree, whatever that was that burned through the nights sky and ended up here, must have been full of evil to do this to such a once so beautiful region," replied the king.

"This is nothing like I expected! Why isn't everything burned after that explosion? Instead, it's almost as though it's all been frozen black the way it's so brittle…"

They had been walking approximately twenty minutes and now stood only a hundred feet or so from what appeared to be the remains of the once beautiful home of Aleksander and his kin.

The king and Matthias got everyone into their groupings, as now they would separate into six groups to speed the search, Polaria is a big region and they would want to be as thorough as possible, this would mean shifting rubble and entering unstable buildings, this in itself could prove to be very risky and this is why they would work in sizeable groups, should anything go wrong they would have enough support to quickly respond.

Now all they required was for Egum and his kin to arrive with the supplies.

The king thought he would contact Egum to inform him of their location, and so he did, Egum informed the king he and his kin should be with them momentarily.

The king thanked Egum saying he looked forward to seeing him soon.

The king then realised that as they had broken the crustaceous ground releasing dust with their footsteps, this could be a danger to the great dragons, and would have to come up with an idea to stop the dust from being blown around by the force of the dragons wings flapping! And he would have to do so before they arrive!

"Matthias!" the king called.

"Yes, my king, what is it?"

"The dragons are on their way here, and will be with us shortly! But we may have a problem! Replied the king...

"Oh! What kind of problem my king?"

"The dust that we have caused by walking here will be blown around by the dragons and we can't risk the health of the dragons, we need to soak this whole area!"

"Well we don't have enough water with us! We will need to find a source for us to gather from," replied Matthias...

"Yes, we will, this place used to be surrounded by streams, and yet, can't see one!" replied the king...

Then suddenly there was a loud crunching and cracking sound followed by loud splashes and calls for help!...

One of the group had wandered only twenty feet of where the groups stood, heading towards the settlement when he crashed through the blackened surface, which had covered one of the narrow rivers that flowed through the settlement, he was hanging on just his arms and shoulders visible, with his arms bent on the edge of the hole trying to pull himself back up and out, they had to act quickly before the water could drag him under the crustaceous surface, for he would surely be lost...

The king quickly responded, calling twenty of his group to form a human chain by linking arms, and as they did Matthias would be the last link and closest to edge of the hole where he reached for the panicked man, "Calm down! And reach for my hand," said Matthias calmly offering the man his hand...

The man quickly reached for Matthias's hand clasping it tight, Matthias now had a firm grip and called to the rest of the chain to pull as hard as they could...

The chain off people simultaneously took a big step back and pulled the man slithering to safety!

Thank you, thank you!" said the frightened and soaked young man.

Matthias quickly said for the man to be escorted back to the caves, and for him to get out of his soaked and now black stained clothing, Matthias continued; "Make sure you wash yourself in one of the caves pools, your clothing to…"

"Yes-yes, I will, thank you," replied the young man.

One of the healers, Peter, said he would escort him and stay with him; in case the river water affected him in some way, to which Matthias agreed, "Good idea! Both of you leave now."

With that the two headed back to the caves as fast as they could, no one knew if the water could carry a contamination of some sort as it was black, just as the ash and surrounding area…

"Well there's our answer to our water issue, as long as we don't get it on us, we should be able to use it to soak this area for the arrival of the dragons!" said the king.

And with that the kings group using Telekinesis started to draw water from the blackened river guiding it through the air and commenced with soaking the entire area that the king had selected.

As the group were drawing water from the blackened river one of the members thought he could see the crustaceous surface moving! He wasn't too sure, and thought it could just be something to do with the way the sun was reflecting off of the shiny surface, so he crouched and just watched the ground, and as he did, sure enough the ground ahead of him ever so slightly moved! It was like a pulsating motion barely noticeable!

Thinking it might be his eyes, as it was hard to focus properly due to the blinding brightness, and heat-haze distorting the ground, he closed them shook his head, counted to five then opened them again.

Now he looked again with eyes slightly fresher, and now he was sure! The ground ahead was definitely pulsating! not the whole area, but pockets of ground rising like mounds for a second or two, then deflating for a second or two, then repeating!!

The young man was shocked, becoming concerned at the sight; and so in a state of fear, eyes fixed, reached his right hand out to a young lady working next to him, and tugged on her leg garments, "What are you doing?" she replied in a stern tone, not impressed at having her garments tugged on...

"Look-look," he replied trying to keep his voice down and pointing just a few feet ahead of him! Can you see that!" he said, nervously still pointing.

The young lady noticed he was quite nervous and so asked if he was ok as she crouched next to him.

"I'm not sure! Can you see the ground moving or are my eyes deceiving me?" he said as he looked to her with an expression of concern.

As she heard his words she laughed "Ha-ha-ha, is your brain melting in this heat," she said jokingly...

"Please don't, I already think I'm going crazy!" he replied as he turned his head back to look once more at the anomaly!

As he turned his gaze, the young lady turned with him to see what it was that had him quite shook!

As they gazed at the ground ahead the young man asked, "Can you see it?"

"Give me a chance I'm looking, can't believe you have me gazing at the ground, I mean really as..." before she could finish her sentence she saw it with her own eyes! "You're not going crazy!" she said in almost breathed words as she exhaled confused by what she saw...

While the two stayed crouched, focused intently on the anomaly the rest of the groups were working tirelessly to soak the landing site before the dragons arrived, they were totally unaware as to what was happening to the ground around them!

We have to show the king, she said anxiously, and was just about to contact the king, but before she could focus the young man grabbed her left arm, "Look its getting bigger, isn't it?" he said with a raised scared voice, his hands trembling as he pointed! "What can it be?!" he said to her now feeling more fearful!

As she looked once more, she could see he was right! The pockets of ground were expanding like black scale coated balloons, hundreds of them, getting bigger and bigger rapidly!

The young man and lady still crouched at this time began to slowly stand, almost scared stiff as they watched the areas of ground before them expanding!

Fear clasping them both unable to speak or move, they stood trembling, as the ground now started to make subtle cracking sounds as it continued to expand and separate the crustaceous scale like surface, until suddenly with loud sounds almost like glass exploding, each of the hundreds of pockets exploded open with such ferocity sending shards of broken hard shell like shrapnel flying through the air, followed by what appeared to be black shiny scale covered humans! heading directly at them and the rest of the unsuspecting groups!

The unsuspecting members of the king's groups didn't know what hit them! It all happened so fast! The shrapnel fell cutting down those closest to the hole over the river of which were eight adults and one child, instantly killed!

Screams could be heard from every direction as the shrapnel fell wounding and killing many more! As the shrapnel continued to fall, those that hadn't been hit, tried their best to get back to the king and his group.

Now that they could see what it was that was injuring and sadly killing members of their group; some quickly raised their hands stopping the remaining still-airborne shrapnel midflight, holding it hanging in the air enabling others to safely get to the king.

As they held the shrapnel they could not move! They were using their energies to focus on the shrapnel and would have to do so until the others had reached the king and could stop and take over.

There were twenty members of the group whom took it upon themselves to stop and hold the shrapnel back; they knew it would be a risk! But the risk had just become much greater; as heading towards them were the human like creatures of black!

Those holding the shrapnel would have to pray the others would soon reach the king, and be able to hold back the shrapnel before these terrifying creatures reached them, but they had all been spread out in groups, and it was taking some a time to reach the king!

Two of the twenty or so that were holding back the shrapnel were; Rose and Adrian, they were with the group that were to the west and furthest away from the king, and would take the longest to reach him, with this in mind and seeing the terrifying creatures that headed towards him, Adrian told Rose to leave him and run to the king.

But she would not! "No!" she cried! "I'm not leaving you; you need me to fly you out of here!" she said; crying and full of fear, but she would not leave…!

"You have to, you have to go! The others need you to, we can't risk you dying here! Please go Little Dragon," Adrian shouted tears running down his cheeks.

No! I'm not going to leave you! So please don't ask again! Rose said getting angry, she really was a fiery little one…

Adrian grew very frustrated with Rose, and felt he had to be cruel to be kind, and so in an extremely angry tone; "This is not the time for your stubbornness! Now do as you are told and go, now!" he shouted.

As Adrian said these words to Rose, one of the creatures was nearly upon him! only thirty feet or so.

In response to Adrian's sternness Rose had an outburst, so angry was she; "I said don't ask me again!" she shouted! And with rage she very quickly lowered her hands and looked to the creature that was about to make a dive at Adrian!! With a swift movement of her arms she raised her fist in front of her, knuckles touching knuckles and then quickly pulled them apart from each other opening her fingers rapidly!! As she did so the creature shattered into a million pieces!!!

After realising what she had done, she gasped with shock!

She looked at her hands almost in horror, "I killed it!" she said.

"Rose!" Adrian shouted, "Snap out of it! There are more coming for us! I don't know how you did that but you really need to do it again! Please!" he almost begged.

On hearing Adrian's voice she snapped out of her gaze, and turned to face the oncoming creatures, they were incredible looking things, the shape of a human! And yet not human, they were big and very muscular powerful looking, with black scales from head to foot which shone in the light, their toes and fingers had claws instead of nails!

And yet as they drew closer, she could see they had human eyes of blue and brown! For a moment she almost felt they were humans! (were these creatures once the people of Polaria, but changed somehow, she thought!) she shouted to Adrian; "Look at their eyes."

"Really! I'd rather they didn't get close enough thanks!" Adrian replied scared and so sarcastically!

"I think they are the people of Polaria! Changed as the Birgumon so nearly were, we might be able to change them back somehow, their eyes are still human, I'm not killing another," she said thinking to kill these creatures would be the same as to kill her own kin, as she truly believed they were still human deep down, she saw it in their eyes.

And so, with that, rather than destroy them she would throw them back, away from herself and Adrian, giving themselves a chance to run.

She shouted to Adrian to push the shrapnel away from them and to bring it to the ground, as she kept the creatures at bay by bringing her hands to her chest arching her back slightly, then in a rapid motion launching her top half and arms forward in a wave motion, as she did so the energy from her body could be seen like a shockwave distorting and rippling the air as it headed at incredible speed into the oncoming creatures, it impacted six of them with such force knocking them off their feet and launching them backwards through the air a good thirty feet or so…

Once the creatures had been knocked back, she shouted to Adrian to run to her!

And so, Adrian brought the shrapnel that hung over them both to the ground, then ran as fast as his feet could carry him to Rose.

And together they ran eastward towards the king, as they ran the creatures were running towards them from all along the north, so for as far as they could see on their left, were rows of these creatures getting closer by the second, they wouldn't reach the king before the creatures would; on foot!

It was as though in her despair she had forgotten she could actually fly, but soon realised and said to Adrian put your hands on me and hold tight, as he gripped her shoulder with his hand whoosh! They were airborne, just as they thought they would now be safe, sharp objects buzzed them just missing Adrian! "What are those?!" Rose cried.

As she looked down, a handful of the creatures were aiming their fingers at her and Adrian, then suddenly more of the sharp objects were whizzing past them once more only just missing them!

"My God they are shooting their claws at us," shouted Adrian "How can this be…?"

Then! "Ugh! My arm," it was Rose, she had been hit!

Luckily, they were just a hundred feet from the main group and so managed to get to them and land safely.

"Quick-quick! We need a healer!" shouted Adrian as Rose stood clutching her left arm, which had a big black claw like thing hanging out of it, approximately two inches in length.

But his calls could not be heard amongst the sheer chaos, everyone around them was in a state of complete and utter shock, unable to think logically; they had never experienced anything like this!

They were like sheep surrounded by wolves just waiting for the end!

The creatures had begun to encircle the king and his people, the king felt helpless; "Have I lead my people to their deaths?" he cried as he looked around him watching his people being herded into one compacted group screaming and crying…

These people had no idea of aggression, they were meek mild-mannered people, and so had no idea of how to defend themselves in such a situation, they wouldn't know how to fight each other let alone these unbelievably powerful creatures…

There was one among them who was not willing to just give up and except their fate! Mathias approach the king, "We can't just stand here doing nothing my king; they mean to do us harm anyway, so we had might as well fight back! At least if we die, we died trying…"

As Matthias spoke with the king, one of the children and her group tried to flee, as they took to the skies, the beasts around them fired a barrage of claws after them, and because the group hadn't the time to reach a high altitude they were an easy target; and swiftly brought down! Only one of the group survived the impact, but was severely injured! And was crying out in pain; when one of the creatures approached him while he lay on the ground unable to move, the creature showed no mercy and drove its clawed fingers through his chest killing him instantly.

The group that remained with the king were helpless and could only watch this evil episode unfold with tears and screams of sorrow, loss and anger.

Adrian turned to Rose and asked her; although she was wounded, could she do as she had done before to the creature she killed?

To which she replied; "I will try!"

With that she worked her way through the group to the front, as she did, she said to Adrian; "Surely, I'm not the only one that can do this! There must be others?"

With that Adrian used his mind to talk to the whole group, explaining what Rose had done to the creatures and said he thought the other children might have the same abilities!

He then continued to ask them to try as it was their only chance!

When the king heard this, he agreed they must try! None of the adults had this ability to move living things, only the children did and so everyone's lives would be in their hands…

What a thing to have to ask of the youngsters, no child should have to experience such brutality let alone perform it!

The children made their ways to the front of the circle they had all been herded into, a child stood at every direction north, east, south and west, every angle of attack from the creatures was now covered by the children...

Rose communicated to the children on how it was she killed the creature describing how she pulled it to a million pieces, saying they had to envisage their fingertips pulling it apart rapidly, and how it took so much energy to do so, she had to pull every ounce of energy from within her, the energy of every chakra had to be used simultaneously and diverted to her very fingertips, and directed with her mind's eye which was focused on the creature.

The time was now the other children would need to try it for themselves, as the creatures were now moving in on them closing the circle.

So as one, led by Rose, the remaining seventy children focused on a creature closest to them and began to focus intently! Forming fists and pulling their fists together knuckle to knuckle, then pressing their clenched hands palm side too their chests, drawing every ounce of energy while staring at their intended targets physically shaking as they focused so hard!

Then suddenly simultaneously as though connected as one they unleashed their deadly energy, throwing their arms outstretched ahead of them and rapidly opening their fingers; as they did-so sixty-nine creatures from around the circle simply exploded into a million pieces with sounds that resembled that of glass exploding! They were turned to dust!

Seeing this the king and the adults of the group were aghast, they could never of imagined such destructive power lurked within their young! But at this present moment in time they were truly grateful it did...

One of the youngsters had a slight issue with his intended target; the problem was the young lad didn't quite have the power to destroy his target! Instead the creature was trapped legs and arms stretched out looking like a starfish and unable to move as the youngster held it there!

"Hello!, it's not working for me!" he shouted as he stared at this terrifying creature, which was snarling at him showing its teeth, and struggling to break free from the child's magical grip.

"You need more practice," said a voice, it was Joshua. "Just focus a little harder envisage in your mind's eye the terrible thing turning to dust as you open your fingers! Give it a try! While you have it in your grasp, quickly close your hands into fists then open them again quickly as you see it clearly in your mind explode…"

"God really! I have to see it?" the young man replied, feeling giddy at the thought…

"Unfortunately, yes!" replied Joshua looking concerned the lad might throw up.

"Ok! I'll give it a try." With that the young lad focused with all his might…

"Can you see it?" asked Joshua.

"Yes!" the lad replied as he closed his fists, as he did the creatures legs closed together and its arms fell to its sides, then the lad quickly open his fingers as fast as he possibly could…

But all that happened was the creature's arms swung up above its head as before, and it's legs wide open as before, the creature made strange growling sounds as this happened, the poor lad with embarrassment and frustration repeatedly closed and opened his hands, the creature looked as though it was doing star jumps… "Oh, this is cruel, let me do it," said Joshua and quickly put the creature out of its misery.

"I'm sorry!" said the lad, looking very embarrassed.

"Don't be," said Joshua. "Do you think you could hold them back instead?"

"Yes; I should be able to do that," replied the lad who then focused on two creatures that stood looking confused as to what had just happened to one of their kind, and so the boy held them their so Joshua could swiftly destroy them one after the other…

After seeing their kind explode into thin air the creatures stopped and stood for a moment, looking at each other, then began to make an incredible roaring sound, they just stood staring at the king and his group roaring…

After a few moments of roaring and staring at their human prey the creatures began to run at them…

"Here they come!" shouted the king…

The children again stood fast ready to destroy as many as they could, to try and defend the adults.

One of the creatures broke, through killing two adults as it did so, it now stood breathing heavy claws extended directly in front of Matthias…

Matthias quickly drew his wood carving knife with his right hand, and readied himself legs bent, left hand forward in a defensive posture, and his right hand gripping the knife arm bent back ready to strike.

The creature lunged forward arms out wide, Matthias crouched low and leading with his left foot stepped in and under the great creature, grabbed its chest with his left hand and swung his right hand as hard as he could, in an attempt to drive the knife into the creatures abdomen…

As the knife made contact the blade snapped with the force Matthias used to drive it! The creature's scale-like exterior was like armor impenetrable to the steel blade, the blade didn't so much as scratch the surface…

Matthias instantly realised the blade had broken! This man mountain of a man six feet tall and solid muscle knew he was no match for this creature!!

And so, whilst under the creature's bent torso, all he could do was continue through with his right arm gripping the creature's abdomen, whilst still having his left hand gripping its chest and lift with all his might. He lifted the creature up and over his head and together they fell backwards to the ground, Matthias landed backwards his head and shoulders on the creature's stomach, but quickly leapt to his feet before the creature could, he turned to face it as it scrambled to its feet, it looked Matthias in the eye and roared at him, then went to rush Matthias, but before it could, from behind it, the king wrapped his right arm around its neck and bent his back into its back and lunged forward and down throwing the creature over his shoulder; "Down you stay!" shouted the king as it hit the ground. "May, quickly my girl…" he said as little May shattered the creature with her mind….

Matthias quickly thanked the king and continued; I don't know how we are going to get through this my king; their bodies are impenetrable! Not even sharp steel can penetrate them!

The king replied "I saw your blade break, that's how I knew you needed a little assistance!" and smiled.

The king then turned to May and told her to stay with himself and Matthias, he continued they had a better chance if they stay together, himself and Matthias would draw the creatures in so that May could destroy them…

The king then communicated to the group to defend the children at any cost! The adults would have to try and hold the creatures off long enough that the child with them could lock their minds on the creatures…

With that the adults formed groups around each child, encircling them as the creatures headed towards them at speed…

Suddenly the creature's attentions were drawn south of the group, as the king looked to see what it was that had suddenly caught their attentions he could see the creatures being thrown through the air like rag dolls! Not just one or two either, several at a time were being knocked or thrown around, but what could it be thought the king, feeling thankful the creatures were now being distracted away from himself and his people, and whatever it was, seemed to be doing the creatures some damage…

Not all the creatures were deterred by the attack's their kind were receiving, and continued to attack the king's group from the north…

The king was unsure as to what direction to move next! Seeing the creatures to the south being attacked, the king was tempted to head to the south back towards the caves but! couldn't be sure that whatever it was that was attacking the creatures wasn't just some other changed beast that would kill anything in its path, and so was hesitant to give the command…

Then suddenly a voice connected to the king's mind, saying; "Good king we heard your cries and couldn't just listen and do nothing! We have cleared a path for you and your kin, head towards the south we will be waiting but please hurry! I don't know how long we can hold these things off! No matter how hard we hit them they get back up! Hurry…"

The king sensed it was Mit and his sons! They had left the caves to help!

"What have you done Mit, you have doomed yourselves to the effects of the dust and ash that is kicking up…"

"Don't worry my king we have taken precautions, no time to chit-chat, good king; just move as fast as you can please," replied Mit…

With that the king communicated the order to turn and withdraw south as fast as possible.

Without hesitation the king's people turned and ran as fast as they could south, the creatures hot on their tails from the north and now the northeast and northwest, they were heavily outnumbered and if they didn't get back to the caves soon they would all be doomed, rats and all…

As they headed south one of the groups thought they would fly to safety, and so held the child of their group, and took to the skies but once again the creatures swiftly brought them down with a barrage of claws…

"No!" cried the king seeing these poor souls being instantly brought down and killed, he then quick-thinking communicated that no one was to attempt to take flight, as they couldn't get to a safe height quick enough, and were easy targets, they had to continue on foot as fast as possible…

As the king and his kin continued south, true to his words, there was Mit and his five sons, running around bashing into the creatures sending them flying creating a clear path for the king…

The smart cave rats had used cotton to wrap around their snouts and paws in an attempt to protect themselves from the ash and dust, and so did look most peculiar, but! this also left them at huge disadvantage with regards to defending themselves against the creatures, as they had covered their mouths, and so couldn't use their huge fangs to bite, and also in covering their paws could not use their claws to rip and shred, they could only run at the beast at great speed and ram them, which was proving most effective, but they still had to be sure not to be grabbed by the creatures, as that would be their doom!

As the king reached Mit, Mit quickly told the king not to stop! Keep running we will defend your rear, he said...

And so they did as Mit said, but as the king looked back he could see the rats would be overrun, the creatures were gaining ground rapidly, and so he had to now try and buy the rats some time, he couldn't let them sacrifice themselves!

And so, the king communicated to his people to stop and turn to face the creatures, and for the children to focus on those creatures that would reach the rats first and destroy them!

The king and his people were far enough ahead to turn eliminate a good few of the creatures then turn back south and continue to run. On seeing the creatures that were about to pounce on them suddenly shatter, Mit realised this was the kings doing and knew he had just bought them time to turn south and run to the caves, and so Mit and his sons now turned and ran...

The rats were much faster than the humans and so caught up to them in no time, but they hung back just in case they should have to defend the stragglers; as the creatures were continuing to gain ground on the king rapidly, nothing seemed to deter these ghastly things...

As the rats had slowed to stay just behind the king and his kin, this had enabled the creatures to catch up with them once more, and in doing so one of the creatures was close enough to make a dive for Patch!

As the creature dived arms stretched ahead of it, it caught Patch on the hindquarters digging its claws into his hips, poor

Patch instantly let out an almighty scream with the pain of the creatures claws penetrating deep into his rear. On hearing this Anchor, the biggest of the rats turned to see his brother being brought down! "No!" he screeched, as he turned and accelerated headed directly for the creature that was just about to rip into poor Patch in an attempt to finish him off, but before it could Anchor hit it with such force the creature was thrown approximately twenty feet crumpled and not moving, Anchor had shattered its bones, it was unable to move…

Anchor than turned to his brother telling him to get up, but poor Patch's hip muscles had been torn he was unable to move, he told Anchor to leave him as he could see the creatures were nearly upon them, but Anchor would not and turned to face the creatures saying "We die together little brother…" Mit, Short Tail and Fidget all turned watching in despair for a moment, then: "We aren't letting my boys die alone!" said Mit, and with that the three ran to aid their family knowing they would all surely perish, but at least they would die together…

As Mit and his three sons headed to Anchor and Patch, the creatures had nearly reached them when a huge shadow appeared, followed by a massive container which was swiftly used as a battering ram, as Egum glided over the row of creatures about to attack Anchor and Patch flattening them with the container which hung form his talons, smashing into them knocking them flat to the ground, he then released it, allowing the container to impact the ground and as it began to breakup as it rolled over several times flattening a number of the creatures ten or so…

Now Egum turned to Anchor and Patch and communicated to them, let me take you in my talons! I will not hurt you I will get you to safety, I promise you no harm! The two terrified rats looked to each other as this's huge dragon hovered over them!

"What do you think?" Anchor asked Patch, to which Patch replied, "Well if he was hungry I think he would have had us by now! I think we can trust him, don't really have an option either way, unless we want to be ripped to shreds by the next wave of those creatures, so I say let's do this!"

And with that the two thanked Egum, and he ever so slowly lowered himself low enough to gently wrap his huge talons around the two rats midriffs and carry them away to safety passing over the king and his group, who cheered at the sight of this huge dragon and the two rats who appeared dwarfed in size clasped in his talons…

On seeing this, poor Mit who had completely forgot that the king had Dragons amongst his group, and that they had been waiting for them, misread what he had just seen, saying; "My poor boys, survive the clutches of those blackened beasts, only to be carried off and eaten by dragons! How can this be," he said with tears in his eyes! And before they would be out of his range of Telepathy, he called to them; "My boys I'm so sorry I couldn't save you!"

"Save us?! Father we are going to be ok!" replied Anchor.

"How can that be? I've just seen you carried off in the talons of a dragon!" replied Mit; feeling confused and emotional.

"Oh, father they mean us no harm, he is carrying us to safety, he rescued us!" and with that Mit burst into laughter of joy, thank God, he laughed.

He then turned as did the king and the group to watch the remaining two dragons, Symphet and Saturn, dropping their containers into the creatures wiping out many as they broke up rolling end over end landing on the creatures as they did so, there were still approximately three or four hundred of the creatures pursuing the group, but they were far enough behind that the two dragons could now fly over to the three remaining cave rats; and swiftly but gently Symphet picked up Mitt in one set of talons and Fidget in the other and off she went taking them off to the safety of the caves, then Saturn began his descent to pick up Short Tail, who for some reason was running nervously as fast as he could towards the king and his group, and shouting, "It's ok I can make my own way thank you very much," which just sounded like a load of very load squeaks to the huge dragon who gave chase…

"I mean you no harm my little rat friend, you need not run from me, I only wish to get you to safety as fast as possible, so why tire yourself, when I can carry you?" said Saturn laughing at the sight of this rats legs moving so fast. "You're a fast little thing aren't you?!"

"Not so much of the little!" replied Short Tail, and continued; "Honestly, I'm fine! No need to burden yourself with me, I'll be fine honestly!"

But Saturn wasn't taking no for an answer, and so swooped in low behind Short Tail who was repeatedly looking back over his shoulders as he ran as fast as he could, but not fast enough to escape Saturn, who was smiling intently, he couldn't believe the rat was so afraid of him, and wanted to show him he had nothing to fear from him!

And so, continued lower, just behind Short Tail and extended his legs out forward talons wide open, and ever so skillfully and gently in one smooth motion continued directly over him, and placed his talons around Short Tail's

midriff holding him securely and lifting him with ease saying; "See, nothing to be frightened of, you will be home safe in no time…"

Poor Short Tail was petrified and squeaking so loudly the group below could hear him clearly and thought he had been injured such were his cries, and so they looked up thinking the worst and saying poor Short Tail, "Hope he will be ok!" some said.

"Am I hurting you?" asked Saturn.

"No!" replied Short Tail.

"Then why are you squeaking so?" asked Saturn.

"Well if I'm honest at first I thought you meant me harm, and with your size you are quite terrifying! Imagine if I was the size of you, and you me! I'm sure you would find it quite daunting, a huge beast wanting to pick you up and take you off! But must say I'm happy I was wrong, this is most enjoyable! And I was getting a little out of breath so, thank you…"

"You are most welcome," replied Saturn feeling happy to help!

And so, they continued to the safety of the caves….

Chapter 6

War Is Upon Us

After ten minutes or so the king and what was left of the group, were approaching the caves with only two hundred or so feet until they would be inside, but it wasn't time to feel secure yet, as the creatures were still in pursuit, and actually gaining ground, and would possibly reach the group as they reached the caves, this wouldn't be good as they would be able to catch and kill the king and his people, if not outside, then they would be able to follow them into the caves and have them almost cornered, and once they had done with the king and his group they would have a direct path into Bulgan and its unsuspecting people; who would be easy prey, and once they had done there could easily unchallenged proceed on through the one other set of caves; which lead out into the many other regions of Afcania…

The king was considering all of his options as he was running with the group, he knew he could not allow the creatures to kill himself and his people, he also had to stop them having the ability to roam unchallenged into the other unsuspecting regions around them…

He needed a way to hold them off; he needed to gain time to warn the people of the surrounding regions of the horrific fate that comes for them.

He now knew what it was he had to do, he would have to gain some time for his people to reach the safety of the caves and seal the caves behind them, although this would stop the creatures gaining direct access to Bulgan, it would not stop them being able to proceed around The mountains of Bulgan into other regions, but it would at least slow them!

The king whilst running spoke with Matthias informing him of the actions he felt he had to take. "Matthias we need to seal the caves once we are inside, but too do this we need to buy some time, as the creatures are nearly on us! would you join me in riding the Dragons and burning these ungodly things before they reach us?"

"Of course I'll help you my king, nothing, I'm sad to say would give me greater pleasure than ridding us of these ungodly things, it does sadden me to have to think of doing such things to living creatures, but we have no option! There is no reasoning with these things, they are inhuman!"

"It's settled then, may god forgive us for what we are about to do!" said the king.

He then spoke with Egum asking if he and Saturn could join him immediately, it was most urgent!

No sooner than said the two dragons had arrived, they had already been heading back thinking the king might need their assistance…

The king and Matthias quickly mounted the two dragons, and then the king told the dragons of his intent and asked would they be comfortable doing such a terrible thing!

Egum quickly replied; "We will do whatever it takes to save you and your kin from these terrible creatures, they have no spirits, only evil dwells within them, they have no place in this world, so please good king lead and we will follow…"

And so, with that the king told his people to continue to the caves, himself and Matthias would join them shortly, and off they took to the skies heading directly at the evil creatures below.

Once they were in range the king gave the order for Egum and Saturn to let their flame loose; "Let's not leave one alive!"

And with that he guided Egum on their attack, approaching from the east, gliding in, approximately sixty to seventy feet above the creatures, Egum exhaling flame as they did so, taking out the forward most rows of creatures, it was a terrible sight, both the king and Matthias were horrified by the sight, and sickened to their stomachs that they had been forced to do such a thing; they both felt as though they had lost a part of themselves, a part of their humanity had left them the king cried tears of anguish! He now felt he had become a monster, but it had to be done! His hand had been forced…

After the king and Egum had made their pass, Matthias and Saturn followed attacking the second rows, again gliding from the east unleashing terrible fire, but this time the creatures weren't so unsuspecting; and fired a barrage of claws at them, narrowly missing Matthias, some had hit Saturn, but were ineffective against his hard armour like scales, when they had finished their pass the king and Egum banked hard right and began another approach from the west, but as they approached the creatures stopped and turned north running for the blackened woodland disappearing out of sight, and so the king ceased his attack saying "I cannot kill them while they retreat, I'm not monster enough for cold-blooded murder!"

"I understand my king, we have done what had to be done no matter how monstrous our acts, we did them to protect our people," replied Matthias… trying to justify their actions to himself, knowing they had no other option… but still he felt horrified at himself…

Matthias continued; "But I fear this is not the last we shall see of these evil creatures! I believe what we have experienced today is just a taste of things to come my king, I believe life as we knew it is over!"

"I make you right my friend, we now live with a constant threat at our door! And so we have to think as we have never thought before, we had no way to defend ourselves! If it wasn't for the gift, although a truly terrifying gift, but a gift all the same that god as given our children, and our good friends the rats and dragons, we would have perished this day!" said the king with a heavy heart.

As the two flew back to the caves, Egum could feel the kings anguish, he could feel that the kings heart was broken, one of the reasons King Stephen was such a good king, and his people truly loved him, was his ability for understanding and compassion, you could say he was a gentle giant, this man who could look quite intimidating to those that didn't know him, standing six foot plus tall, built like a warrior, dark-skinned with long dreadlocks and yet eyes that showed nothing but love for all living creatures, in fact his smile could calm any man or beast, he truly had a beautiful spirit, and when in his presence those around him felt loved and protected, just as a child does in the arms of their father.

But now the king was doubting himself, he knew deep within himself, those creatures were once his own, people that he had visited, eaten with, shared stories with, and played games with the beautiful children, and now he felt such guilt! Wishing there could have been another way, what kind of man burns creatures that were once his people?! he thought to himself, feeling torn. He prayed to god asking for god not to let his spirit be destroyed, not to become dark and uncaring...

On feeling the king's pain, and knowing the king so well, Egum communicated with the king, with an empathetic tone saying; "To be a king comes with heavy responsibilities, and in times such as these, you will have to make choices that will lay heavy in your heart, but this will not change you as a man, your spirit is to strong, so please good king, mourn those you once knew as they are gone, these creatures are not them! Their spirits be with god now, they died nights ago, so you need not feel you have done wrong, what we have done was justified in the defense of your people! You have shown fortitude, which becomes a true king.

"Thank you Egum, your words strengthen my spirit! But the pain still lays heavy with my heart! Something tells me this is a feeling I will have to grow to accept, and for the sakes of my people, I must!" replied the king finding solace in Egum's words.

They had now reached the mouth of the caves were the kings people waited inside nervously!

As they touched down on the ground and dismounted the dragons, the king and Matthias turned to each other, both felt pain at the task they had just performed, and so walked to each other and embraced tearfully, in a tight embrace Matthias spoke softly and saddened; "Have we become monsters?"

To which the king thought of Egum's words and then replied; "No we are not monsters, we are two men that have done what had to be done, or our people in those caves would now be dead! And us along with them, as long as we feel the pain of our actions we are not monsters, a monster such as those we have just slain, acts without feeling, it is selfish and bloodthirsty, shows no mercy! So I say no, we are not monsters and shall never become so."

Matthias nodded silently for a moment then loosened his embrace, stepped back placing his hands on the king's shoulders and looking him in the eyes and tearfully said; "I will do whatever it takes to protect and serve you and our people, no matter how much it breaks my heart! As long as the cause is just…"

"I know you will, and I know you feel as I feel, and this makes us the right men to protect our people without becoming monsters, we shall not thirst for blood, we only do what we must for the greater good, when we get home I will have choices to make and I want you to play a part in assisting me, we will discuss it more once we are home safe, but be warned! If you accept the role I offer, it will come with heavy a burden, and call on your inner most strengths, say nothing now, we will speak in depth soon! But for now, let's dry our eyes, put on our brave faces and get back to our people, and seal these caves…"

The king then turned to Egum and Saturn; in turn he placed his head against theirs and thanked them.

Symphet had been waiting outside the caves and now joined Egum and Saturn, "Thank god your all back and in one piece!" she said smiling so happily.

The king then turned to Egum saying; "There's no time to waste, I'd like you, Saturn and Symphet to fly to Bulgan, I fear you may have dust from this horrid land on you and it needs to be washed off of you as soon as possible! I will notify Bogumill of your arrival, and be sure he has healers awaiting you, should you need them by the time you arrive there...

Egum replied thanking the king, and continued he and his kin felt fine, he felt that their hard scales would protect them from the dust as they are not absorbent like that of human skin or other beasts skins, and was sure they would be fine and said for the king not to worry...

The king wasn't willing to take a chance, and so asked the dragons to do as he asked just to be safe! He also said they may have ingested the dust, which took time before the effects took hold, and so wanted the healers to check their lungs, just to be safe! "Better safe than sorry," said the king with a smile...

Egum laughed and said to the king, "Since you put it like that! We will do as you ask good king, all being well we will see you when you arrive in Bulgan.

"Yes, you will indeed old friend, god speed to you, now off you go see you soon," replied the king smiling at his stubborn old dragon friend...

"Fare-thee-well, see you soon!" replied Egum, and with that the three mighty dragons took to the skies.

The king and Matthias watched the dragons fly into the sky and over the mountains and out of sight, then as he said, the king connected with Bogumill and informed him the dragons would be arriving ahead of the him and his group, and asked if Bogumill could have his healers wash them with lemon juice and steam eucalyptus to be sure the dragons lungs were clear of any possible infection. He then continued to tell Bogumill he would explain more when he arrived, but warned he did not have good news...

On hearing this Bogumill became concerned and wanted to know more, but the king refused to say, all he would say was that he would speak in depth with him when he returned...

"I will hopefully see you soon my friend, I will tell you all there is to tell, but for now I have to go! Goodbye for now my friend."

"God speed, my king, see you soon."

And with that Bogumill fetched six of his best healers explaining what the king had asked, and so they set about making preparations.

The king and Matthias now made their way into the caves, and when they arrived, there was an almighty cheer from his people who waited within...

They were very relieved to see them both, they had been waiting in the dark unsure they would see their king and Matthias again. So concerned were they; that they had just huddled in waiting, fearing the worst and expecting the evil creatures to enter the caves to finish them! And so, you can imagine their elation at the sight of their king's return.

Amongst the cheers people were asking what had the king done to defeat the creatures; the odds seemed not in their favour, they weren't expecting to see them again, and began to say it was a miracle, God was with their king...

The king didn't want to tell of the horrendous scenes he and Matthias had to commit in the defense of them, and so solemnly said; let's just say they were no match for our dragon friends! Then he looked to the roof of the cave...

With that Matthias,, sensing the king's pain solemnly spoke to the group; "Although we are most happy we are back together considering the odds against us! this is no time for celebration! Lest we forget we lost friends today! We lost children today! And those creatures were once our friends that we will never see again! Today as been a horror, and I fear there may be more days such to come! So please be thankful we all survive this day, but it is no time for cheer."

With that John spoke out; "We are sorry, we did not mean offence! It is just seeing you both overwhelmed us with joy, we do not take this day's events lightly.

"I know!" replied the king, he then continued; "I'm sorry I do not wish to sound ungrateful for your happiness in our return, let's try and put this day behind us, we have much to do, we need to seal these caves and move on. But firstly, we need to wash our clothes and our rat friends free of this dust! And once we are cleaned can we see to our wounded, we don't want dust from our cloths infecting their wounds! So it is best we are cleaned first."

With that; the king suggested they use the sizeable pools within the caves to submerge themselves while they were still clothed, then remove their clothing while they were wet, then wash themselves down once they had removed all of their clothing. With that the king thought it best he test the waters and sat on the edge of one of the pools then slowly lowered himself into it feet first, as his feet made contact with the water he was pleasantly surprised how warm the water was! "Mmm that's quite nice!" he said to himself as he lowered himself deeper into the pool. He was now submerged up to his chin, and yet his feet did not reach the bottom of the pool, he then fully submerged himself to soak every part of clothing, he removed the bandana whilst submerged, as now it was wet! and when he would surface he wouldn't be able to get breath through the soaked cotton.

Now that he had soaked his clothing, he proceeded to pull himself up and out of the pool, which was quite a struggle with his layers of soaked garments, and so John offered his hand, and pulled the king up and out of the pool to its edge.

Once the king was stood, he then said for everyone else to do as he had done, there are three pools but the king said to only use the two nearest the mouth of the cave for soaking their clothing, the third which was further in the caves would be used to wash themselves without clothing, to ensure no dust that sat on the surface of the water in the other two pools could be carried to the third and contaminate it, thus ensuring no wet dust could make contact with their skin.

Once everyone was clear on what it was they were to do, ten persons at a time entered each the first two pools, and those that stood waiting to enter the pools would assist those wishing to get out of the pools whilst still dressed and soaked, and so this continued until the last few had entered the pools, and those before them had to wait soaked and fully clothed to assist them before they could undress and proceed to the last clean pool.

Once they had all cleaned and changed it was time for the rats who were covered in dust to enter the first of the pools, to soak themselves and remove the makeshift coverings they had made from cotton for their paws and faces, once this was done the healers poured lemon juice over them and rubbed it into their fur ensuring they were completely coated, then the rats rinsed themselves in the clean pool.

Now clean the healers saw to Rose and Patch's wounds!

They poured lemon juice in the wounds which was very uncomfortable for the two, Patch let out several loud squeaks as the juice made contact with the open wounds on his hindquarters.

Although it was painful, it had to be done, it was the only way to ensure the wounds would be totally clean and disinfected before they could be stitched, and poor Patch had ten very long deep gashes on his rear quarters.

Where the creature had grabbed him with its claws, Patch received five gashes on each of his – what we would call hips – it was easy to see where the clawed fingers and thumbs of the creature had dug deep into him, and tore his flesh and muscles, it was almost the perfect shape of a hand – a very big hand at that!

With the size of his wounds it would be quite a time before he would be able to move, while Babbyah worked on them, she firstly numbed the first of the wounds with the power of her healing hands, which glowed so bright, then she would ask could he feel her prodding him with the needle. To which he replied; "No not at all my right side is numb but my left is so painful!"

"That's fine I'll get to the left hip shortly," replied Babbyah; and then commenced stitching the first of the gashes…

Poor Patch looked so sorrowful lying flat out with his chin on the ground and his eyes wondering but unable to move.

Rose was having her arm seen too, she had a deep circular hole in the side of the top of her left arm where the claw had pierced her, she was receiving attention from Judith, and was sitting next to Patch.

She too was in pain, which was made tenfold by the lemon juice, her father was busy in conversation with Matthias regards the sealing of the caves; and so was unavailable to comfort her at this moment.

And so, feeling discomfort and sorry for herself she wanted some comforting; and as she looked to her right she noticed how sorrowful patch looked, and said; "Oh bless you, you poor thing, and reached out her right hand and took Patch's right paw to comfort him – and herself!

The two smiled at each other as the healers saw too their wounds, Rose's wound was cleaned and stitched in a matter of minutes, but poor Patch would have to be seen too for much longer, and so Rose stayed with him holding his paw and talking with him, stroking his head as she did so.

She didn't move from his side until his wounds had been cared for, even then they stayed as they were enjoying each other's company – since there was nothing else to do; so made the most of the time to talk and relax, while around them members of the group were still getting dressed and preparing to move on – eventually!

The king, Matthias and Mit were in conversation, they had to seal the caves at the Polaria entrance.

The king was wanting the cave rats to leave the caves once they had been sealed, he wanted them to follow him and resettle in Engypt, as he felt although the cave entrance would be sealed, what if the creatures found a way to remove the rubble and gained entry, the rats would be at such high risk! And the king wanted to be sure they would be safe – it was the least he and his people could do for them, as they owed their lives to them!

The king knew it would be hard for the rats to leave the home they had known for probably hundreds of generations.

But all the same he had to ask; and hopefully get them to see the sense in relocation.

"If you stay here there will always be the risk of the creatures gaining entry, and what of your young kin?!" said the king trying to get Mit to see the sense in his words.

"Yes, I know!" replied Mit, in a soft voice of contemplation.

He knew the king was right and only had their best interests at heart, and so deeply considering the king's offer asked; "Do you have caves in Engypt?"

"Well we live on a plateau, with amazing canyons below and within those canyons there lay caves of all shapes and sizes! I'm sure you will find several suitable for you and your kin, and you would be more than welcome to visit or even live with us on the plateau, it stretches for miles and miles, with only one entry so we can well defend should we have too! You and you kin would be much safer and I would feel much more at ease knowing you are safe! It's the least we can do for you and your kin, my new found friend!" said the king with a huge warm smile and holding out his right hand.

With a look of pride, Mit stood tall and proud on his hindquarters and continued; "You called me friend! I have never been called friend by a human! Really you see me as a friend?" as he reached out his right paw and placed it in the king's hand.

"But of course! We all do, only a friend would have risked their life and the lives of their kin for us!" replied the king as he took Mit's paw and shook it with great respect…

The king then continued; "You will always be held with high regard by me and my people, and your young will grow and play with our young, forming new bonds that will last a lifetime! So is it settled my friend, will you come and be part of our world and live alongside us?"

Before Mit could reply, a soft voice said; "Sounds wonderful! I don't know about you hubby, but I would definitely like new surroundings, instead of these old damp caves which we have lived in for so many years, and to be able to actually stop hiding as we have always done, and to mix with the rest of the creatures and humans of this world would be a great future for our young!

We must accept the kind king's offer, mustn't we?" she said head tilted slightly left eyes wide open staring intently at Mit's pouted mouth; it was more than enough to scare any beast or man to agree!

"Yes-yes, my love! Good king, Matthias, I would like you to meet my first mate Nibbles! It would appear we will be joining you and your kin, good king."

With that both Matthias and the king in turn shook Nibbles paw; saying they were so happy they had decided to join them. The king then asked Nibbles; "How long do you require to prepare before we can leave?"

"We can be ready when you are; oh, you do know there are four hundred and fifty-nine of us don't you?" asked Nibbles with a tired smirk on her face!

"Yes! We do indeed," replied the king with a smile of sympathy, and nodding his head...

"Oh good! Just wanted to be sure you knew what you was letting yourself in for! I'll go fetch them now! Won't be long, see you in a mo," and off she went into one of the smaller caves, with a huge smile on her face...

What a wonderful mate you have there, said the king to Mit with a warm smile.

"Thank you, good king, she can be a little bossy at times, but a wise male knows when to do as he is told!" replied Mit trying to be sure she wasn't listening, and looking nervously over his left shoulder...

"Not too different from humans after all! A human male also knows when its best to be quiet and do as his told, rather than be the recipient of the wrath of his wife! You must, as I like my ears as they are!" said the king light-hearted and humorously – as Mit continued looking over his shoulder checking the coast was clear. With that Mit and the king burst into laughter! and as the two laughed so loudly Mathias was left looking unsure as to what it was they found so funny.

On seeing the young man's face the king and Mit looked to each other then back at Matthias, Mit couldn't help himself, and in his moment of laughter couldn't help but say; "You must be single my boy! Don't you worry, the day will come when you will understand what it is we laugh about!"

"Yes indeed," laughed the king…

Then after a few moments the still chuckling king said; I guess we had better get on and get these caves sealed, for all we know those creatures may have run into the woodlands to regroup!

"Yes, I agree!" said Matthias fighting back laughter after finding the king and Mit's laughter quite infectious…

"How do you intend to carry out the sealing of the caves?" he asked.

"Well I think it best, as we can't be too sure as to how safe this will be, to have myself, you and two of our strongest members of the group stay behind whilst the rest of the group including Mit and his kin move on ahead of us; making their way to a safe distance possibly the exit to Bulgan, before the remaining four of us attempt to bring down the roof of the mouth of the cave, as when we dislodge the boulders in the roof at the mouth, we could spark a chain reaction in which the entire cave could collapse!" said the king, and then continued as he look to the roof of the cave, but unable to see a great deal as it was quite dark, "This could be more challenging than we anticipate!"

To which Matthias replied quite concerned; "Yes it could well be my king, and the last thing our people need is to lose their king! And so my king, may I suggest you proceed ahead with the group and I will stay and carry out what needs to be done here?!"

"Matthias, I appreciate your concerns, but I will never ask anyone to do that which I can do myself… No, I will stay with you, I'm sure it will be fine!" said the king.

"Good king! Matthias is right! It is too risky! You should leave for the good of your people," said Mit…

"Gentlemen! Please! I will be staying. The discussion is final!" replied the king in slightly stern tone.

"Ok! Then I'm staying too, I might have to burrow you out from under the rocks!" replied Mit rather sarcastically…

To which the king looked at him and laughed, "You might just yet... Anyway; I believe we could control the ceiling's collapse; we should be fine!" the king said.

Then there was a voice, it was Nibbles, "We are ready when you are!" she said, with hundreds of reflecting eyes stood behind her!

She had gathered all the rats who now peered out from the darkness of the side caves, with their eyes reflecting what little light there was.

What a sight it was, so many green reflective circles appearing out of the darkness, like green fireflies, but attached to these where some very large rats, who even though they knew they had nothing to fear still remained very shy, they had never been in such close proximity to humans; but with time they would become accustomed to living together.

As the rest of the group saw these shy creatures slowly appearing they approached them welcoming them, especially the children, they were most excited to see so many of these big furry cave rats, and would walk up to them and offer their hand in friendship, wanting to lead them to the rest of the group.

The rats in turn looked nervously at these little people, then after a moment or two one of the younger rats smiled stood up on its hindquarters and placed its paw in the hand of little May, saying; "Pleased to meet you! I'm Rudolph;" he said in a very soft shy tone.

"Very pleased to meet you Rudolph, let's take you to meet everyone," replied little May, and slowly off they went to introduce Rudolph to the remaining group, both with big smiles on their faces...

It wasn't long before the main path of the cave had become quite crowded and so the king asked Adrian to lead the group to the Bulgan end of the caves. He then asked John and Samuel if they would stay behind...

Once the main group and their new rat friends had made their way along the path and were no longer in sight, the king explained to those that remained with him how he thought it best to collapse the roof of the cave without bringing the entire cave down on them…

Whilst he had been looking at the roof of the caves; he notice that at the entrance; in the roof was an almighty boulder which was wedged, and so he led them to look closer, and sure enough there in the roof was a boulder which would easily seal the entrance, all they had to do was free it somehow!

The boulder looked to be wedged between three much smaller rocks, one at each third of the boulder…

As they looked at the huge boulder Matthias said; "If we can dislodge those smaller rocks the boulder should hopefully fall free!"

"That was my thinking too!" replied the king. "I think it best we remove the rocks one at a time; see what effect this might have, see if the boulder does loosen; in a controllable fashion hopefully!"

"What do you think?" asked the king looking to the other men and Mit, just in case they might have better ideas!

They all stood and stared for a moment; "My king I think it's the only safe way, shall we have a go?!" said Matthias, feeling a little anxious!

"Ok, is everyone agreed?" asked the king.

"They all nodded in agreement, yes indeed," said Samuel.

"Right! Let's give it a try then see what happens!" said the king, and with that, following the king's lead, all four men raised their hands and began to focus on the rock to the left of the boulder.

As they held their hands out, fingers half bent as though gripping, and arms stretched, they envisaged the rock was being gripped by their hands, they then began to slowly pull their arms back and as they did a crunching sound echoed through the caves.

On hearing the loud crunching sounds coming from the rock, Mit became a little concerned and took a few steps back; I think I'll just stand over here, he said staring nervously at the roof of the cave and stepping backwards ever so slowly...

As the four continued to pull with their minds the noises became louder, they then as one began to rotate their arms left and right as though they were twisting the rock left and right, and sure enough the rock began to shift, ever so marginally at first, and as they continued to pull and twist with their minds the more it started to shift, it was now beginning to rotate with their hand movements and slowly move from its recess inch by inch...

Then suddenly bright sparks started to flash out from around the rock with loud sparking sounds, snap-snap, fizz-fizz, sizzle...

"STOP-STOP!I It was Mit, "You must stop, I've seen this before, and it didn't end well, please stop!" he said looking petrified!

Unbeknownst to the group there was a phosphorus which had formed between the rock formations, which they were now disturbing!

On hearing Mit's petrified voice the men instantly stopped, but it was too late; a chain reaction had now started, the phosphorus was now igniting!

The king, Matthias, John and Samuel quickly stepped back watching the phosphorus sparking brighter and brighter, it started to travel quickly across the roof of the cave, "RUN!" shouted the king!

They all turned and ran as fast as their feet could carry them! They had reached a hundred feet or so when; BOOM! The Phosphorus deep within the roof of the cave ignited and exploded with an almighty Bang!

The shockwave hit them so hard it knocked them off their feet, throwing them through the air thirty feet or so, the king landed on his back the wind knocked out of him!

Matthias, John and Samuel were blown forwards, landing on their fronts sliding along the ground, cutting their hands and knees, Samuel rolled over onto his back as he was sliding along, just as well he did! As following them were large debris of rock being thrown in all directions and ricocheting off of the walls of the cave and floor, thousands of much smaller but just as deadly particles of rock also headed after them!

Samuel quickly raised his hands shouting "No!" and as he did so with sheer panic; he stopped the particles of rock and stone directly after him.

Matthias slid hard into a stalagmite hitting his right shoulder, the impact spun him over onto his left side, he was now sliding along on his side in an almost curled posture, he then came to an abrupt halt as he slammed into another stalagmite!

As he hit the stalagmite his head was thrown back and his eyes thrown opened wide just in time for him to see a piece of rock as big as himself just about to impact on him! With absolute fear he instinctively held his hands out in front of him! And as he did so his mind must have instinctively gone into protection mode; as the rock was stopped just as it touched his hands, he had shut his eyes thinking the end had come. With his eyes still closed tight he became full of disbelief in the fact he wasn't dead, he could feel the rock pressed against his hand! and so breathing very heavily almost panting, he slowly opened his eyes seeing before him this rock the size of him! It must have weighed at least two tons! and yet there it was being held just inches from his face!

With pure elation he let out a cry "I'M ALIVE!" as he; using his mind threw the rock to one side and along with it fell the hundreds of other fragments which had been headed his way but luckily his mind had stopped them without him even thinking about it consciously!

With the realisation of just how close he had escaped death he burst into nervous laughter! And just lay there...

Whilst John was sliding along, he impacted against the wall of one of the smaller caves to the right off the main path, in which Mit had scampered into! John ended up lying face down unconscious in the cave as parts of rock and stone smashed to the ground just at the entrance...

It was over! the debris had stopped, the air was full of dust, it was now pitch black in the cave, Samuel now realised it was safe to release his hold on the debris and allowed them to fall to the ground! "Hello, is everyone ok?!" shouted Samuel shaking as the adrenaline rushed through his body...

Only one voice replied! it was Matthias; "I can hear you, who is it?" he asked still shaken and breathing heavily...

"It's me Samuel! I can't see a thing! Are you ok...?"

"I think so!" Matthias replied running his hands over himself knocking the dust off and checking he wasn't bleeding as he still lay against the stalagmite...

"I can't see a thing either! Stay where you are, and keep talking I'll try and follow the sound of your voice!" said Matthias...

"Where is the king?" asked Samuel, he then began to call for the king, "My king! My king!"

"I'm here!" replied the king barely audible, still struggling to get breath, "I'm ok, just had the wind knocked out of me!"

"Thank God!" replied Samuel, "Stay where you are we will come and get you! There are many debris and it's so dark with this dust, it's blocking what little light the crystals give off, so best you stay put sire..."

Then other voices could be heard, it was Adrian! When the explosion occurred the ground outside of the caves shook! And the sound of the explosion was so loud that the group that had left ahead of the king had been shaken by its suddenness – and the fact they were not expecting an explosion!

Just as the king had thought; they too thought; the king and the small group with him would be blocking the caves by shifting the roof boulders!

None expected an explosion!

And as the group turned to look back to the caves, all they could see was a huge plume of black dust and debris of rock and stone being thrown from the mouth…

They instantly feared the king and those with him had been killed! And so stood momentarily letting what they had witnessed sink in, it seemed almost surreal! As they stood in an almost lost gaze, then Adrian broke free from the shock which held his body fixed…

Once he had regained his faculties, he instantly tried to contact the king and others of the group using Telepathy! But was unable to make contact, it must be the rock and stone of the mountain blocking my transmissions! Adrian thought to himself…

And so, with that he turned and pointed to ten men and four healers, saying "You are coming with me! We need to go and see if anyone as survived that! Let's pray they have, let's go! …"

As they were about to move off back to the cave, Rose asked if she could go with them, but Adrian said she could not, it may not be safe! "If we need assistance I will call for you all to join us, but for now think it's best just a small group of us go, just in case there is a landslide due to the force of that explosion!"

He then continued; "We must hurry!"

And so off they set, when they arrived at the cave; nothing could be seen as the dust filled the cave, and so Adrian called out "Hello! Can you hear me?!"

On hearing Adrian's voice, the three men shouted back, "Yes! We are here!" "Don't enter, it's not safe!" shouted Matthias, as rocks still fell all around them…

"Are any of you hurt?, Adrian asked, feeling a little better at hearing their voices…

"A few cuts and bruises, apart from that we are ok!" replied Matthias.

"Wait a moment we haven't heard from Mit or John, God I hope they are ok!" said Samuel as his slowly and unsteadily got to his feet shaking dust from his hair and brushing himself down…

"Oh god, John I hope you are ok!" Samuel said under his breath, filled with concern for his friend…

Once he had got to his feet he began to call out for John and Mit; "John, Mit!" he then waited and listened intently, there was no reply! And so using his mind he continued to call out to John and Mit, but could not connect with either of them; could it possibly be the cave somehow was blocking his Telepathic ability? he thought to himself; well that is what he hoped, as the other option was they were not replying as they are injured or worse, and that didn't bear thinking about…

He had to find them one way or another! But first he had to regroup with the king and Matthias, but no one could see a thing, there would be no chance of finding each other in this pitch darkness, he had an idea! He had seen the healers make their hands glow bright white light when healing the Birgumon, if he could do the same then the king and Matthias would be able to see it and have a source of light to head for, or if he could do it, then they could too, none of them had ever tried it before! but he would have to give it a go, they had to have light…

Samuel shouted out to the king and Matthias; "We have all seen the healers hands light up with a bright light haven't we?" To which they both replied saying; "Yes." Samuel then continued that he was going to attempt to do the same with his hands, and if he was successful then they could see the light and make their ways to him…

"That sounds like a good idea! But I thought only healers could do so, I thought that was all part of their healing gift, and not wanting to state the obvious, but that's what makes a healer a healer isn't it?"

Samuel replied unsurely; "Yes, it is, but I believe I can do it, it's worth a try anyway isn't it?"

And with that Samuel focused all his energies into his hands rubbing them together and with his third eye pictured his hands glowing brightly...

Samuel was shocked as his hands began to dimly emit light, and as he continued to focus seeing with his mind's eye the light become brighter and brighter, it did!

"It's working," he shouted ever so excitedly, and smiling from ear to ear...

"This is amazing!" he said to himself quietly but excitedly, as he continued rubbing his hands, the light became so bright he could barely face it, and was having to avert his eyes to the right slightly...

Although his hands were emitting such an intense light there was no heat or any kind of pain involved, all he could feel was a tingling sensation!

He now stopped rubbing his hands together and they continued to emit light, still so very bright, but the light wasn't just emitting from his hands it was now beginning to appear from his forearms! Samuel was focused so intently he was now seeing just how far he could expand the light, he was beginning to picture his entire body as one bright light, he was commanding the light with his mind, expanding it all along his arms, and now his entire body was one mass of bright light, which lit a large area of the caves, he now expanded the light to his head and face, his features could still be made out, barely...

As the light continued, he began to feel an amazing sensation of energy, a pure bright energy coursing throughout his entire body and with it a power beyond imagination!

Matthias and the king could now see this amazing bright light starting to light the caves as though the sun was within the caves with them, the light was pulsating, it was almost rhythmic, it seemed to beat like a heart...

"My God! Is that Samuel?" Matthias said unable to move in awe...

"I believe it is!" replied the king, also, in shock at what they could see, the king was still laying on the ground just watching the light expanding throughout the caves, I've never seen anything like it!" said the king…

Samuel turned to face the location of the king and Matthias, as he turned he could see the path to them was blocked by some sizeable rocks, he could see the king still laying on the ground to the left of the path, and he could just make out Matthias just ahead still leant against a stalactite.

He called to them, "I can see you both, but the path is blocked! It might take some time to get to you both, can you see me?" he asked! To which they both replied almost simultaneously, "Yes!" "How could we not, you're lighting the entire cave, almost!" said the king… "I never thought it possible! You look incredible and at the same time terrifying, such energy, I can actually feel it from here! Are you in control of it?"

"It is strange my king, but although I've never even thought of performing such an act of directing my energies in such a way! I believe I can say yes! Although new and wondrous it feels I have total control, it's part of me, from deep within me, it's the pure energy of all seven of my chakras combined to form one mass energy! It feels incredible!" Samuel said as he looked at his hands and down his body to his feet, every part pure energy, he felt incredible.

He then looked up and back to the king, he then began to walk forward and as he did so the rocks which blocked his path began to shift as the brightest of the light which emitted approximately six feet in circumference from his centre made contact, he wasn't thinking about moving the rocks, they just moved away with the energy of the light it was that strong…

As Samuel walked the rocks continued to slide and separate to the left and right of the circle of light, within moments the path had been cleared and Samuel walked unhindered lighting the caves at a distance of thirty or so feet in all directions, and whatever the brightest of the light came into contact with was instantly moved and in some cases broken, as it made contact with some low hanging stalactites which hung lower than six feet above him they were instantly snapped by the energy of the light at the brightest most circumference, the parts that broke away didn't just fall to the ground, no they rode the edge of the light following the circumference down to the ground, just sliding like ice on the side of a bowl…

As the caves ahead of him became brightly lit, the light entered the smaller caves to the left and right of the main path, it was at this moment he noticed what looked like a foot…

My God is that John?! he said to himself and quickened his pace to the mouth of the smaller cave to gain a better look, and sure enough laying there, unconscious with Mit stood over him, not knowing what to do was John!

Samuel instantly shouted to the king and Matthias; "I've found John, he looks hurt!" And as he continued into the small cave he could see John had a cut to his head which had bled on to his face making it look much worse than it actually was… but not knowing this Samuel began to panic! "He is going to need help! There is blood all over him, and he is unconscious! Please come and help!" Samuel shouted to the king and Matthias.

On hearing Samuel's cries for help Matthias got to his feet as fast as he could! And now that the caves were lit by Samuel's light he and the king could see each other, so Matthias's first instinct was to get to the king, and now being able to see Matthias the king brushed the debris which surrounded him to one side with a swipe of his right arm and the power of his mind, and then commenced to stand, "Ow!" yelped the king on trying to get to his feet, his left ankle gave him pain as he attempted to move it, it would appear that as the king was thrown by the blast his left ankle had clattered against a rock or something, it wasn't broken but very swollen, bruised and painful.

Matthias could see and hear the king's anguish; and so made haste to his aid, "Samuel I'll be with you as soon as I can, the king is injured and unable to move I'll get him comfortable then be with you straight after, is John's breathing strong or weak?"

"Not sure I'll check, Samuel replied and continued; "Not sure I should touch him while I'm emitting such energy, I'll have to reduce it! But then you won't be able to see where you going, I'll have to wait till you reach the king, then I'll check John over, just let me know when you have the king comfortable please…"

I will, replied Matthias and moved swiftly climbing over rocks which separated him from the king…

While Matthias made his way to the king, Samuel and Mit stood watching over John, when Mit; "Sorry but I have to ask! How is it you have become light?! I can barely look at you! You shine so bright it hurts my eyes to look directly upon you, how can this be?"

"It's a long story, I will tell it to you when we are all away and safe from these caves, you have nothing to fear I promise you my friend," Samuel replied and smiled.

"Oh I know I have nothing to fear from you, I know it's you Samuel, you are a good kind man, and that is why God as let it be that your light can be seen, how it came to be is what intrigues me, we are all colour and light within us, they are our life energy colours, but never before have I seen the spirit's light shine outside of a living being, so yes when we get out of here please tell," Mit smiled…

Then Mit said he believed John would be ok! and that he had only been knocked unconscious; just needs time is all.

"I hope you are right, he is a good friend to me," replied Samuel looking down at John.

Whilst this was all going on deep within the caves, Adrian and those with him had seen the light within the cave, and could hear the calls of help as they echoed throughout the caves, and became concerned for those inside; and so Adrian took it upon himself to make the decision to enter the cave and head towards the light, and so just as Matthias reached the king, there could be heard multiple footsteps getting ever closer, and so on hearing these steps Matthias turned to the king and said; one moment sire, he then turned to the direction of the steps, and from the shadows he could just make out a group of people heading slowly towards them; "Who is that?" he asked in a raised voice...

"It is I, Adrian, we have come to aid you, we heard cries for help! I know you said for us not to enter, but once we saw the light and heard one of you cry for help, we had too, sorry Matthias."

"No, don't be sorry, I'm pleased you ignored me, the king and John are both hurt!"

"Do you have healers with you?" Matthias asked urgently; with worry for John, as he was unconscious!

"Yes, there are four healers with me, we will come to you."

"There are some rocks blocking our path we will have to climb them to get to you, we shouldn't be too long, is the king in a serious condition?" asked Adrian with a hasty tone, concerned for the king's wellbeing...

"The king has hurt his ankle and is unable to put weight on it, but other than that he is good! My main concern is for John, Samuel is with him, but he is unconscious, please send three men and a healer of your group to me, and the rest of you please aid Samuel with John, just make your way to the light and you will find Samuel!"

Adrian agreed and did as Matthias had asked, and so now the group split; four making their way to Matthias and the king, and the remaining ten to Samuel and John...

The paths for both groups were strewn with debris, rocks of all sizes block their paths, but at least with the cave now lit enough to make out what lay ahead of them it was safe to continue, although slowly, it was quicker to climb over the obstacles than to move them.

While the groups made their ways, Mit and Samuel grew restless waiting for John to regain consciousness, they were beginning to become slightly concerned about his condition, it had been a while now that he had been unconscious! and they both began to doubt whether poor John was just knocked unconscious or was something far worse going on with him, he had lost quite a lot of blood from the gash on his head...

Growing with concern Mit thought they were wasting time and that they should try and move John, and so Mit suggested they lay John on Mit's back and he carry him from the caves; we can't just stand here doing nothing, I fear his condition isn't as I first thought! He is still losing blood, and I fear he may have a serious injury to his head, more than just a cut, we need to get him to a healer as quick as we can, will you lay him on my back, asked Mit looking at John and feeling saddened…

"Yes, of course I will you're quite right we have to get him out of here, for all we know these caves may be about to collapse around us, the roof of the cave continues to lose stability, rocks continue to fall, we may not have much time…"

"I will lift him, but not sure I can as I am, I may have to stop the light, I'm not sure the energies I'm emitting won't hurt him! But then we won't be able to see a thing!"

"Your energies you are emitting will reflect your emotions, you are not angry so therefore your energies are calming and will not damage! If you were feeling angry or very negative then yes, your energies would reflect that and would be very negative and damaging! I believe you will be fine! Look how close I am to you, I can feel your energies, but they are not harming to me," said Mit, confident Samuel wouldn't hurt John, and gave a reassuring smile…

With that, Samuel crouched down and put his arms under John and lifted him, he was totally unconscious and non-responsive, Samuel's fears of causing him more damage with his energies were proven otherwise, he was doing him no harm, which gave him great comfort to know.

Samuel then turned to Mit who lowered onto all fours allowing Samuel to place John across his back face down…

"He is heavier than he looks!" said Mit giving a lighthearted chuckle – trying to lift the mood, and ease Samuel fears a little.

"Yes, he's a big lad," replied Samuel.

I guess we should leave now, Samuel said and lead the way out of the small cave onto the main path which had obstacles all over, but this was no worry for them for as Samuel walked the obstacles were just brushed aside as before.

As they turned right out of the smaller cave, Adrian who was half clambering over one of the rocks which blocked their path saw them, he was shocked by what approached him; he was frozen to the spot, unsure his eyes didn't deceive him, he closed his eyes and shook his head a couple of times, but when he opened his eyes to look it was still there! A ball of light so bright, and within it barely visible, due to the brightness, was the figure of a man, just calmly walking towards him!

Those who followed Matthias hadn't noticed his sudden state of shock and one by one appeared clambering over the rocks, only to freeze mid-motion at the sight before them…

Matthias hadn't moved an inch, he was still captivated, eyes lock squinting as he tried his best to look, into the light at the figure within…

Next to him, one of the men of the group emerged behind the rocks and on first sight froze, he could only mumble, "God save us what is that!"

On hearing his mumbles, Matthias's gaze was broken, "I'm not sure, but I think it means us no harm! Can you feel that?! The energy emitting from it is wonderful, feels like a summer breeze passing through me! Do you feel it?"

"Now you mention it, yes I do, it is quite soothing isn't it?" the man replied staring in an almost dazed-like manner…

Then a voice; "Don't fear me! It is me Samuel, you have nothing to fear, please continue, John requires urgent assistance please come quickly, I will light your way…"

Samuel is that really you? How have you come to be so?" Adrian asked in shock; as it was someone he knew, and had somehow transformed themselves, this was hard to comprehend…

"That's a question I will answer when we have time, but for now your assistance is required so please don't delay…"

And with that Adrian and those with him moved as quickly as they could, climbing over the rocks and shifting smaller debris away to one side.

By the time they had managed to clear the obstacles and set foot on the path, Samuel was only a few feet from them, they all watched as Samuel lifted the still unconscious John from Mit's back and lay him on the ground…

"He has been this way for some time now! Can someone please help him?" said Samuel most concerned for his friend, as he looked at John, he felt saddened, and in reaction to his emotional state his light began to dim…

Mit noticed this immediately, and stood on his hindquarters and walked to Samuel who had his back to him, and placed a comforting paw on his shoulder, "He will be fine, we have help now try not to worry… With your worry your light starts to dim! They will need your light if they are to help him!

Come on stay positive, we need your positive energy right now," said Mit in a soft warming tone.

Yes, you're right, he's a strong bugger; he will be fine!" smiled Samuel, and as he did his light radiated warm and bright, everyone could feel this amazing warmth throughout their entire being.

Samuels warmth filled them all with euphoria, the likes of which they hadn't felt since the early day of New Year's Eve, before the occurrence, which seemed so far away now…

They all felt positive and a sense of calm as they all set about their duties, one of the healers that was to see to John, turned to Samuel; "You look incredible, and your warmth is just what we all need, I'm sure John is feeling it two, he will be fine I'll see to that don't you worry."

Then she crouched down and took John's head in her hands and began to hum, after a few moments she smiled! "I see it, he will be fine, he as cracked his skull, and it is putting pressure on his brain, I just have to put the skull back as it was and that will release the pressure."

"That's wonderful!" Samuel said in such a thankful yet quiet voice.

With that she continued to meditate, picturing the parts of cracked and slightly missed place scull moving back into their correct location, then she seemed to speed up the healing process, the bone seemed to grow back together seem-less, you would never of known it had been broken, where the bone had been pressing on the brain it was slightly swollen, so she stitched the cut to his head then wrapped an Omiul leaf around his head, saying; "That's it he should be up and about in a few hours, just give the Omiul leaf a bit of time to do its job and heal that cut and reduce the swelling…"

While John had been receiving attention for his injuries the other four person group had now reached the king, as they slid down from of the rocks into the little area in which Matthias waited for them ready to lead them to the king, he greeted them so happily…

"Am I pleased to see you! Thank you for coming, he is over here, I told him not to move his ankle!" He then led the way.

Once they reached the king who had been waiting patiently, he was in good spirits and jokingly said; "I'm so pleased to see you I was getting terribly bored, and my backside is very wet and cold sitting on this damp ground, then gave a chuckle."

"Don't you worry my king we will soon have you out of here and in some dry clean clothes, now let's see that ankle," it was chirpy Judith, with her cheeky smile that could make anyone feel comfortable no matter the pain, she had such a warm jokey personality…

She then lifted the king's left leg and as she did the king grimaced as his ankle moved, she could see it was very swollen, she gently placed a hand on the soul of the king's foot and applied a little pressure as she moved the foot slowly up and down, again the king grimaced, "Can you move your toes for me?" she asked, and so the king did as she asked grimacing again as he moved his toes, "Oh you men all very big and strong, but a little pain from a bruised ankle and look at the faces you pull!" she said and gave a cheeky little smile to which the king couldn't help but chuckle and say, "It hurts quite a bit."

"Oh I can see that by your facial expressions, you should try child birth, that's fun!" she said sarcastically, again the king laughed, "You are a cheeky one you," he said as she gently massaged clove oil into his ankle and foot, which continued to make him grimace, Judith chuckled and gently shook her head, "Oh dear! All done, it will be a little painful for a day or two, but you must do your best to use the foot as normal otherwise it could become stiff and take longer to return to full movement."

"Thank you," said the king, "it feels much better! Thank you."

"That will be the clove oil it's very good, I'll massage more in later this evening, now let's get you up!"

She then looked to two of the strapping young men who stood to her right, "Yep; you to look strong enough! One each side of the king please, and lift him to his feet, thank you!" She then continued; "He will need you to help him balance, but don't take all of his weight he must try and use the foot as much as possible, he will probably moan a little, but pay him no attention! He's a man, it's to be expected!"

The two young men looked shocked by her words – this was the king she was talking of, the king looked up and could see the shock on their faces! "Don't be shocked lads, she is right after all, we are the weaker sex," he then laughed loudly, "Get me to my feet please, he then reached his arms up enabling the young men to crouch and place his arms around their shoulders, as they stood supporting his weight the king whispered to them; "She means no disrespect, she jests with us, she is a very bubbly cheeky one that one, and a very good healer, look at that cheeky round smiley face! Warm the heart of anyone."

Just as the king finished his words, the two men looked at Judith who must have overheard the king's words, and Judith being Judith, she gave them a squinted-eyed stare, she didn't mean it of course, but they didn't know that! she was such a tease!

"Ok maybe not!" said the king and chuckled...

"Don't want to get on the wrong side of that one!" he chuckled and in turn the two young men couldn't help but laugh with him.

And so, the three merrily made their way to the others of their group, and when they got there, Matthias said he was happy to see the king on his feet once more.

The king thanked him for his help, and promised he would be back to full strength in a day or two, but for now we need to regroup with the others that are with Samuel and John, then get out of here before the rest of the cave collapses around us!

Matthias agreed saying; "Yes I think we could be pushing our luck staying much longer." As the cave's roof continued to make cracking sounds and rocks fell around them, not masses just the old one or two, but this was enough to cause concern…

"Matthias then called out to Samuel, how are things with you Samuel? Is John going to be ok?!"

"Yes, we think he should make a full recovery, he is likely to remain unconscious for a few hours yet!" replied Samuel.

"Can we move him? Don't think it's safe to stay here much longer," Matthias replied in a calm tone.

Samuel turned to the healer that had seen to John, she had heard Matthias and nodded yes, then continued; "We will need to carry him, we need to keep his head up so the pressure doesn't build up on his brain."

"I can carry him again! Just lay him the length of my back, tie him to me so he can't slip off!" said Mit.

"That's a great idea!" said the healer, but what about getting him over those rocks which block our path, we could move them but that would take time.

"Leave the rocks to me!" said Samuel.

Samuel then called to Matthias and the king; "Can you get to us?!"

"Yes, we are on our way now, should be able to see us any moment now!" and as Matthias said this, he peered over the top of a rock; "Here we are over here!" Matthias called to Samuel.

On hearing Matthias's voice Samuel turned to him, "Is there room behind you if I move those rocks for you so you don't have to clamber over them with the king?" he asked.

"Yes, there is quite a bit of area for us to stand clear."

"Ok, I'm coming over so stand back!"

With that, Samuel said to the others, "I'll be back in a moment." Making his light even more intense, he walked towards the rocks which separated them from the king's group, as he did so, once again the rocks slid away making loud crunching and dragging noises until the path was cleared, and now the king could be brought to the larger group and they would proceed together.

Those of the group that had arrived with Adrian where shocked by what they witnessed, Samuel's power was incredible to them, it also helped them to feel secure in the knowledge they would soon be out of the caves with such a force with them…

They would have to proceed slowly due to the king and John's injuries, John had now been laid on Mit's back; and rather than tie him too Mit's back, two of the group would walk one each side of Mit placing a hand on John to stop him shifting around and falling off…

Samuel now said for everyone to walk behind him as he led the way, easily shifting the debris that blocked the path ahead…

And so they walked, cautiously watching the roof of the cave, as rocks and smaller but still dangerous debris continued to fall around them, having this miraculous light of Samuels made it much easier to navigate and avoid the falling rocks, as now they could see them as they fell, there were a few near misses nevertheless, but they managed to judge their movements, and in some cases where it was visible a rock had become dislodged and dangerous they would remove it with their minds.

They would spot the danger and safely bring it to the ground, rather than take the risk it would fall on them.

The group had been walking twenty minutes or so, they were nearing the exit of the caves, and the light which shone so bright from Samuel could now be seen by those who had remained outside the caves.

As they saw this bright light they began to feel unease, as the light was so bright they knew it could not be manmade, it could not be a manmade lantern of stick and fire! And after all they had been through, they did not know what to expect next from those caves, they did not know if the king and his group had been successful in blocking the caves, after the explosion they did not know if the king and his group still lived!

For all they knew even Adrian and his group had succumbed to the dangers within the caves…

And besides; none of them had anything which could burn so bright!

And this lead to group outside to fear this was something evil headed their way, they couldn't make contact with them as the caves wall's blocked their Telepathic ability, which just increased their fears, and so they began to move back, the adults clambered to the children taking hold of them and those in groups ready to flee, even the hundreds of rats were scared and ready to run for their lives…

Then from behind them came a whooshing sound, some turned in fear; thinking something horrible was approaching them from behind, but thankfully it was nothing to fear, it was Egum, Symphet and Saturn, and riding on Egum was Bogumill, he had brought men from his village with him, two riding Saturn and Symphet and hundreds more riding all manner of creatures, who were making their ways at speed, the cloud of dust from the approaching group could be seen in the distance getting ever closer.

As Bogumill and Egum landed, Bogumill leapt from Egum's back quite hastily, "Where is the king?" he said in a raised voice, he was so concerned for the king's wellbeing, unlike him, he was quite angry!

And unfortunately for her, the one in his path was Babbyah, she could see by Bogumill's facial expression and the way he had his fist clenched he wasn't best pleased with the situation.

And so Babbyah approached Bogumill, being the strong woman she was; "the king stayed in the caves to seal the entrance from Polaria, there was an explosion, so we don't know as to his wellbeing, but Adrian and a party went into the caves to find the king and those with him…"

As Bogumill listened to her words he just stared at the caves, taking in what she was saying.

As she continued; "We haven't heard from any of them since, and now there is a bright light which seems to be moving ever closer towards us!"

Bogumill became agitated saying; "Why did he not call on me, I would have gladly taken my men and sealed the caves myself! Instead we are now left to wonder if we have a king;" as he spoke, he once again showed anger in his demeanour, again clenching his fists.

"I understand your concern, we are all very concerned! But being angry will not help anyone, we have to think clearly you know this," Babbyah said in a calming tone and smiled at Bogumill, he knew she was right! "You're quite right, I let my worries get the better of me, I will calm myself, thank you I apologise, replied Bogumill, relaxing his shoulders and unclenching his fists looking Babbyah in the eyes, as he took his gaze from Babbyah to look back at the cave, there were gasps as the source of the light appeared from the mouth of the cave, although painful on their eyes they stared intently, they could just see the source of the light was the shape of a human...

"How can this be?" voices could be heard to say, and they continued; "is that a man? Could it be one of our kin? Is it a God?" And some people said nothing, some became even more fearful at the sight, no man as such power, "We should run," some said...

But then behind the light they could see John on Mit's back with members of the group each side of them, and then the king appeared being supported by another two members of the group which had left with Adrian, "It's them, they are alive!" shouted Bogumill, then a huge cheer rained out, HOORAY! they all shouted and began to run towards them...

As they approached Samuel and the group, Samuel dimmed his light and by the time they reached him and the group, he had closed his mind's eye and the light was no longer, and now the people could see who it was that held such power, "You had us worried for a moment, we thought the light was something terrible headed for us, how did you elevate yourself to such power?" some asked, wanting to know so they could try for themselves...

Samuel just smiled and said; I will tell you sometime but not now, the king and John need help!

When Bogumill saw the king he was happy he was alive, but had to say his piece; "My king you will be the death of me, why did you not call on me to aid you? Why is it I had to find out of the horrors you and yours faced from our dragon friends, you only had to say and I would have sent many men to your aid!"

The king looked to Bogumill and smiled; "I'm sorry old friend it all happened so fast, and we couldn't make contact as there is something on the other side of those mountains which blocks our Telepathy, so I couldn't call on you even if I wanted!"

The king then continued to Bogumill; he felt these lands were no longer safe for himself and his people, he continued that he thought it best that Bogumill and his people leave Bulgan and follow him back to Engypt…

Bogumill replied; "Why is it so unsafe that you feel we should leave our homes, you did manage to seal the caves, didn't you?"

"We did indeed, but your south is still open, and this enemy could easily work round and attack you from your south… it's not just you I fear for, every surrounding village is in grave danger I feel; I have never seen anything like these creatures they are pure evil, and as we stand we have nothing to defend ourselves, apart from our children and the dragons…" replied the king, urging Bogumill to leave with him…

The king then said; "We all need to rest and to take refreshments, it's been a horrible, long, terrifying day for us, but I will call a meeting with yourself Matthias and Adrian, we really need to plan for the future I fear there is worse to come! So, let us return to your home where we can rest," said the king to Bogumill with a very weary smile.

"Yes of course my king, you look tired!"

As Bogumill spoke his men arrived, some on horse, some on huge warthogs the size of men with huge tusks, and some even riding mammoths…

Once the riders had all arrived, they waited for orders to be given, they stayed mounted in expectation they would be continuing to the caves…

But no, Bogumill turned to his men and said; "There will be no fighting this day, let us be thankful for this, but as for tomorrow or the next I cannot say, so we will return home and be happy, the king and those with him will be accompanying us, you have shown true courage riding here not knowing what to expect, and thankfully it has been a joyous ending to this journey, thankfully our king is safe, it would seem we have some knew friends joining us," Bogumill said as he smiled and looked to Mit who was now surrounded by his kin; all so thankful he was unhurt, he no longer had John on his back, John had been placed on Saturn's back along with an healer, so they could be whisked back to Bulgan where he would continue being cared for; they were just taking flight as Bogumill welcomed Mit and his kin…

As Mit heard Bogumill's words, he stood tall on his hind legs smiled proudly, he never thought he'd see the day when cave rats would stand side by side with humans, and for a moment he actually thought why did we shy from these wonderful people for so long?!

As he stood looking at all the welcoming faces, and the other creatures that lived with the humans in harmony, and seeing them also welcoming them, he turned to Nibbles who stood feeling so proud of her mate, looking at him with eyes full of love and happiness; he said; "Look at this world, we have never seen it truly in the light of day, it is beautiful," as he looked around taking in all the beauty the world had to offer, such colours of all the different plants and trees; and to see the mountains reaching to the beautiful blue sky at the light of day was a pleasure to his eyes; he continued, "And to be part of this world and it's wonderful dwellers feels so right, we are no longer cave rats my love, we are something much more now, we are one of them!" and with that together they walked amongst the people and creatures feeling a true belonging for themselves and their kin as they received such warm welcomes from everyone, man and beast…

They didn't get to properly introduce themselves to everyone; as it was time for the now two thousand-plus group to make their way back to Bulgan where the king and his group would rest, they would be leaving at first light for Engypt.

As they journeyed back the riders dismounted the horses, mammoths and warthogs to walk side-by-side with the rest of the group and allow the creatures to walk at a steady pace without having them on their backs; so, they could relax. Their new friends the rats and their young were enjoying their new found home, especially the young rats running this way and that through the long grass stopping to smell the beautiful array of flowers beautiful pinks blues reds yellows, every colour imaginable, they smelled so sweet to them, they had never smelled anything so beautiful, or seen such colours; being nocturnal creatures due to their shyness...

The journey to Bulgan was a pleasurable journey, the people were speaking to one another and making new friends with the rats, none spoke of the day's events, they didn't want to spoil the moment, they would have plenty of time to remember those they lost, but for now they wanted to enjoy the togetherness on this wonderful warm sunny afternoon.

Even the adult rats had begun to let their guards down and mingle with the humans and the other creatures with them, even Egum and Symphet decided to walk along as part of the group and make the most of such a beautiful day. It was as though everyone somehow knew they may not get to relax like this and be with others in such a relaxed way for a while, the future was now unsure to them all...

As they walked one person among them who wasn't as relaxed as the others, his mind full of worries for his people, he wanted to forget even if only for a moment, but he could not; the king's natural leadership lead him to always think of his people first, and that included those of Polaria; even though they were no longer the people he once knew, he felt terrible, he felt as though he had slaughtered his own, he also knew he had to let it go, he had to face the fact he would probably have to do the same again, he thought about everything, his mind was going crazy, he was even thinking of ways to find out how far this change had spread, he knew the east, south and west regions hadn't be effected, he only knew Polaria had been affected, but what about beyond, further North beyond Polaria were many small settlements, there were still thousands of people to the North that may not as yet be affected.

The king was constantly thinking, his brain could not rest.

But even so he didn't let on, for the moment anyway!

The king would mention his thoughts to Matthias and Bogumill when the time was right, and so for now kept a brave face.

They had been walking many hours, and arrived at Bulgan at dusk, Bogumill and his people went and freshened up, while the king and his group made camp for the night and then freshened up ready to eat with the people of Bulgan.

The rats joined the horses, mammoths and warthogs as the people of Bulgan had left food for them all, a mixture of left over foods and fruits, the rats were enjoying their new diet, they were used to just eating bugs that roamed the caves, but now they were receiving nice rice, beans, assortments of vegetables and fruit; this is delicious said Mit with his mouth full of food, barely able to speak with his mouth bulging.

The others were too busy eating to reply at this time but nodded very happily.

Whilst the king's group were eating, the people of Bulgan who sat with them, were interested to learn what the group came across in Polaria, and some would ask in a roundabout way; "Was it what you expected, when you arrived in Polaria?" one asked Matthias, to which Matthias only replied solemnly; "No, it was not!" he then continued; "I'm sure the king will be informing you all this night, when he is ready!"

Matthias wasn't the only one being asked questions, but the group stayed civil with their replies, but none said what they had experienced, they didn't feel it was their place, and none had the heart to tell, how do you tell good people there is a strong chance your lives are in danger and will never be the same?!

This was the duty of the king.

They ate and drank until they were full, and when the king had his fill he looked to Matthias and waved him to approach, he then stood and turned to Adrian and Bogumill giving them a nod of the head, at which they stood and left the table making their way to the king.

"Our king has the weight of the world on his shoulders, I've known him a long time, and I don't think I've ever seen him look so concerned!" said Bogumill as he and Adrian approached the king…

Adrian replied "He will need all our support, what we experienced was horrific, and how we plan to protect our world from its spread! I wouldn't know where to start, but I'm sure the king will have ideas!"

"Well; I think we are about to find out!" replied Bogumill with a smile.

"Yes! Indeed," replied Adrian feeling a little anxious to hear the king's plans, he had seen with his own eyes what they were up against, and knew they needed weapons of some sort, steel was useless against these creatures, what do you use against an impenetrable creature! he thought…

Once they reached the king, he asked Bogumill if there was somewhere, they could go and not be disturbed…

Bogumill replied; "We could go to my home, no one will disturb us there."

"Good lead the way old friend," replied the king with a smile, and held out his left arm pointing for Bogumill to lead…

"Thank you once again for your generosity, you're a good man," the king said to Bogumill as they all walked to his home.

"My king, it is always a pleasure to have you visit, I just wished this visit didn't feel like your last to Bulgan, feels such a sad time, especially for you as you have suffered such losses and carry such weight."

"It is a truly sad time for us all!" replied the king, then placed his right arm on Bogumill's shoulder as he limped along, "Hopefully you and the people of Bulgan will only have to leave for a short period of time, just want to be safe is all, for all we know we may never see those things again!"

"Let us pray that is so," replied Bogumill.

The king smiled and continued; "So you will leave your home and join us in Engypt then?"

"I thought of what you said and from what Egum has said, I think you are right, we should leave, but I pray for only a short time, this is my home, and the home of my people; I will have to put it to them, it will have to be the people's choice, and they will need to know everything my king," Bogumill said sadly!

The king replied; "That goes without saying my friend, that's one of the reasons I want us four to be alone, so we can discuss the future, we need to make many plans!"

Once they reached Bogumill's home he opened the door and invited them in, it was a lovely little abode, it's walls were round; not square like most, it was timber framed with the inside lined with a beautiful reddish-brown clay, and a staircase which was part of the wall and followed it round and up to the landing and bedrooms.

His wife Ivana was home, she was putting their daughter Yoana to bed upstairs, Bogumill showed them to the common room, which was through a door to the right. He asked them to make themselves comfortable on the many beautiful handmade floor cushions, made from many different fabrics, they were patchworks, such beautiful works they were to, soft and comfortable lovely vibrant colours red and woven gold patterns for the adults, of which there were five, more than the household needed, obviously for when they entertained guests, and two yellow, pink and pale blue with embroidered animals on them for their daughter, and a guest of her age when required.

The cushions formed a circle around a beautiful hand-carved circular table; It had a circumference of six feet, it was a tree trunk that was sliced and stood twelve inches; and around its edge beautifully carved sceneries of woodland and mountains, with fine detail, and on the top of the table was a jug of water and a chessboard with beautifully carved chess pieces of wood.

"Please make yourselves comfortable, I'll be back in a moment just going to say goodnight to Yoana, and let Ivana know you are here," Bogumill said with a smile then headed off up the stairs.

He headed straight to Yoana's room and found his wife just finishing tucking Yoana in nice and snug, then kissing her goodnight, Yoana's eyes were closed as he entered the room, he slowly and quietly walked over to his wife as she turned, "Hello my love," he said with a huge smile as he embraced her and kissed her cheek, "Hello my handsome husband," Ivana replied and smiled.

"Daddy!" little Yoana said as she reached out her arms for a goodnight cuddle and kiss, she loved her daddy's hugs, and so Bogumill kissed his wife once more then sat on the edge of the bed leaning over Yoana, wrapped his arms around her and gave her a nice loving squeeze and kiss; "Night-night beautiful girl," he said so softly, then stroked her hair, "Night-night beautiful..."

He then stood turning to his wife; "we have company downstairs my love, the king wishes to speak with me! he has brought Matthias and Adrian along with him, he was saying we needed to be undisturbed! sorry my love there was no warning!"

"That's fine, I will make you all a nice pot of chamomile and honey tea so you can help yourselves, then I'll leave you to it, I was wanting an early night, are they ok? I take it the journey to Polaria went well?"

"No, it did not, I didn't want to say anything until I knew more, but unfortunately it did not my love, this is why the king wishes to speak in private, I will explain more too you in the morning, I will know more by then. I'd better get back to them, love you." Bogumill smiled and headed back to his waiting guests.

Ivana looked concerned by what he said but put on a brave smile and didn't let herself worry; she would have to wait till morning to find out exactly what all the secrecy was about. And so, she did as she said she would do, and went down to the cooking area of the house where the open fireplace still burned hot and put on a bowl of water for heating to make the tea.

While Ivana was waiting for the water to boil, she could just hear what the men were saying, she heard the king, Matthias and Adrian explaining exactly what happened to them, how the changed people just came out of the ash ground with amazing speed, how their strength was like no human, they were much stronger.

As she poured the water into the pot of chamomile and honey she couldn't help but listen intently; her head was now filling with terrible images as she listened.

The men were just explaining how Matthias's knife just broke; when Ivana knocked on the door and entered the room, as she walked in the king said, "Hello Ivana, how are you?" and smiled.

"I'm very well thank you, King Stephen, you have hurt your leg I see, she noticed his ankle had been wrapped with Omiuel leaf, and as she lifted her head to look the king in the eyes it was obvious to the king she was upset. He realised she had heard what they had been saying…

"You look upset, have you heard what we have been talking about?" said the king softly.

"Unfortunately, I have, the walls are thin, I'm sorry I did not mean to listen, but couldn't distract myself," she replied with a sadness in her eyes.

"It is fine, this concerns us all! Please join us if you wish, there are no secrets between us, what we speak of tonight I will be telling our people tomorrow, so please join us, you may have ideas of use in our situation," said the king.

And so, with that Ivana poured them all a cup of chamomile and honey tea, and sat next to her husband as the king, Matthias and Adrian continued to tell of the day's horrific events…

As they told of the horrible events, Ivana took Bogumill's hand and squeezed it tight, she was terrified by what she heard, the pictures in her head filled her with fear, and at the same time such sorrow for those poor people and what they had become. It was unimaginable that once wonderful people could be turned to monsters!

As the king told of how he and Matthias had to use the dragons to defeat the creatures, using the dragons fiery breath to burn them and drive them away to the blackened woodlands, Ivana was horrified; "That is awful! But you had no option, they would have surely followed you through the caves, and when done with you, on to us here?! You cannot feel you did wrong, you did what you had to for the sakes of your people, and I, as one of them am thankful to you," Ivana said with a voice of compassion and respect.

The king appreciated her words; "Thank you, it truly eats at me within, the horrible act we had to perform, but I do know deep inside me it was the only choice, and to hear you second that means a lot, thank you," he said with real sorrow in his voice, but managed a smile of gratitude.

The king continued to speak telling them how they had sealed the caves, "Not quite the way we planned, but nevertheless they are sealed!

"I do still feel that Bulgan isn't safe as you know!" the king said to Matthias, "and this is why I thought it best we all meet and discuss how best we inform the people; and how on soul do we move so many people such a great distance!

"We have to consider there will be elderly and the very young amongst us!" the king continued; he felt that not all of the people are going to be willing to give up their home, the land they have known their entire life so far!

He then asked Bogumill; "What will we do when we come across this situation?"

This was something the others; Adrian and Matthias, hadn't considered! and so they too looked to Bogumill waiting for an answer with a look of thoughtfulness as they pondered the quandary for themselves.

Bogumill replied; "You are quite right my king, and this is why we have to let it be the people's choice as to whether they stay or leave! If people do decide they don't want to leave then we can only except their decision, we can't force them, but we have to be sure they truly understand the weight of the situation! There can be no tentativeness, the people have to be made to understand their choice could be a choice of life or death, they must realise if they stay and are somehow attacked, we will have no way to assist them, they must understand that!

"And if I'm honest! I think we could find the older generation may wish to stay, this land is all some know, it is where they have always thought they would come to rest, and so, may choose to stay, wanting to be part of this beautiful land."

Then Matthias interrupted; "I'm sorry we cannot let people stay because of some dream of being at one with this land they love, although I understand what they feel for their homelands. But the death they face would be horrific, we can't let our people no matter age or love of home be left behind to face such a death! I'm sorry but sometimes one has to be cruel to be kind!"

"So, you are saying we force the people to leave?" asked Bogumill...

"Yes I am! Think about it, if someone's elderly mother and father decide they wanted to stay here because this land is all they know, then that child would feel an obligation to stay, and to make things worse; What then if they have young children themselves? Do we let young children stay and face having their life's cut short? I think not." He was most passionate in his tone!

"Strong words Matthias," said the king, the king felt Matthias was right and so; "I must say I agree with you!"

The king then sat with his back as straight as a board, and ran his right hand over his forehead and down his face as he took a deep breath, and then dropped his hand from his chin to his lap and said; "I have probably lost the entire northern regions and the millions of people who inhabited them to this evil! Not to mention those we lost today, God bless them! I'm sorry, we can't let another person die! We have to try our best to protect our people, and I guess some will not like the choices I make, but they will be thankful in the long run!"

The king then said; "We have to get all our people back to Engypt where we can best make defenses, and plan for whatever the future may bring. Matthias I have watched you fight and I have never seen anything like it, you have an natural ability and knowhow of combat, and it is for this reason when we do return to Engypt I would like you to teach our men and women what you know, I can't believe I'm saying this but we need to teach our people how to fight, we need to form and train an army!"

"Can you do this for me?" the king said nodding his head and looking at Matthias with the look of a man in desperate need!

Matthias without hesitation replied; "Yes my king, I will make it my life's duty to create an army for the defense of you and our people, but it will take time!"

"I know it will! But we must do the best we can with the time we have, whatever that may be!" replied the king, and continued; "We also have to find some sort of weapon of which we can carry, something that can do these creatures damage, we know steel is useless against their scale-like skin. we will need to consult with our alchemists, and hope they know of something!

Anyway, that is for later, let's get to the matter of informing your people," the king said as he looked to Bogumill and Ivana.

"Once we have informed them of the need to leave, how long do you think it would require for your people to make preparations to leave?! It's a huge task I know!"

Then Adrian asked Bogumill; "How many people of Bulgan are there?"

To which he replied; "Many, many thousands, spread throughout the whole region, some living in the mountains, it is hard to put a number to them!"

Bogumill then continued; "At a guess! I would say ten to fifteen thousand, it will take days to organise such an exodus!"

"It will indeed," said the king, he then continued; "It isn't just us humans! We have to save as many beasts of ground and air as possible to, I think tomorrow both me and you Bogumill should communicate with every living creature that lives in this region, asking them to join us here…"

Adrian then added; "If there are going to be so many and so much time needed to organise, I feel we should ask the dragons to assist us in patrolling beyond the mountains, so we can check the creatures haven't began to return, and let's pray they do not have creatures of the air that have been changed!"

"That is a great idea!" said Matthias, "It would be good to be able to see what is happening, for all we know while we sit here they may have returned, or worse still, could be working their way around the mountains! There are many smaller towns or villages that could be at risk of attack on the outskirts of these mountains."

"Ok, that's a great idea," said the king. "At first light, Adrian could you find two more riders for the dragons to assist you, and I will speak with Egum, you will be our eyes and ears!"

"With pleasure my king," Adrian replied proudly…

Ivana then asked if it wouldn't be a wise idea for Matthias to start training Bulgan's strongest and fastest men to fight while there would be days to do so, and while they train the king and Bogumill could speak with the alchemist of Bulgan!

She then continued; "It would make me feel much safer to know we have men and hopefully some weapons of which to defend ourselves!"

"You are right my love, it will be a slow journey due to our numbers, we will have to stop at night and so we could be vulnerable! It would definitely be best to try and find a way to defend ourselves before we leave, we can't expect the dragons to watch over us twenty hours a day!" said Bogumill looking at his wife very proudly for such a great idea…

The king smiled then said; "Considering we have never had to discuss such things I think we have brought a good few ideas to the table, and at first light we should act upon them! So to recap, at first light Adrian you are going to find two of the best riders we have to accompany you patrolling the lands around us! I will speak with Egum and ask him to meet you at the northern edge of the town with his kin, then me and you Bogumill will speak with the people, we will also ask for our strongest, fastest men and women to join Matthias, and then hopefully Matthias you will be able to test them and choose the best you feel to protect us!"

"I will my king," said Matthias confidently...

The king then continued; "Then me and you Bogumill will meet with your alchemists, and hopefully they may have an idea for weapons, whilst we meet with the alchemists can I ask Ivana to overlook the preparations for our journey, and please find people to assist you in doing so!"

"It will be a pleasure, and I have just the people in mind to ask," Ivana replied and smiled at Bogumill...

"Right, the hour is late, we should be leaving you now, let you rest in peace, rest well," said the king and looked to Matthias and Adrian, the three stood ready to leave, when Bogumill said they were welcomed to stay for the night and sleep on the seating cushions; which were plenty big enough and very comfortable...

The king looked to Ivana and said; as long as you don't mind, these cushions are very comfortable after all, and smiled.

"Settled then," replied Ivana, she then took Bogumill's hand and they together said good night to the king, Matthias and Adrian, who in turn replied; "Goodnight." Bogumill then left the room and headed to bed upstairs.

The three men made themselves comfortable wished each other a goodnight and in no time fell asleep.

While the king, Matthias and Adrian slept Ivana and Bogumill lay talking, well mainly Ivana, she was upset by the thought of leaving their family home, and the land she had known her entire life, do you think we will ever return, she asked Bogumill...

Bogumill placed his left hand on her face ever so gently. "I hope we can, I truly wish we didn't have to leave at all, but it is best we do, hopefully we are just being overly cautious, and we hear nothing more from these changed and we can return home in a matter of weeks!"

"At least by doing as the king wishes, we will be able to return hopefully in the knowledge all will be well, and we will at least have well trained men and women with the ability to protect us should we need…"

"Yes, better safe than sorry, hopefully we won't be gone to long!" Ivana replied, smiled then kissed her husband goodnight.

No one truly slept well that night, not even the people of Bulgan, the rumours had traveled fast and with them fear, which in a way wasn't a bad thing, it just meant that the people would be more agreeable to the king's suggestions, they would just have to be sure not to let fear lead to panic!

What sleep they did get was broken at sunrise by the sound of cockerels cock-a-doodle-doo-ing, and very loud it was, Ivana was the first to rise. She had been up long before the cockerels and had prepared breakfast for her family and their visitors.

When they had all woken they had nice warm bowls of warm water and towels waiting for them to freshen their faces, then they ate around the nice big table, it was a pleasant breakfast, everyone seemed in a positive mood, all wishing each other a good morning, Bogumill's daughter Yoana was surprised to see the king sitting at the family table, "Good morning King Stephen, it is nice to see you!"

"Thank you Yoana, it is very nice to see you again to, you look more like your mother each time I see you," replied the king with a big smile.

Yoana's mother Ivana was a tall woman with very long shiny black hair, with olive skin and big brown eyes, she was a truly beautiful woman, and Yoana did indeed look very much like her.

"Yes, thankfully my daughter gets her beauty from her mother and not me!" said Bogumill as he looked at Yoana and smiled with such pride.

"You can be truly thankful to god for that!" laughed the king.

"You're not that bad my love," Ivana said jokingly then kissed his head.

"Will Yoana be helping you today my love?" asked Bogumill.

"Yes, I thought it best she stays with me, she is very sensible and will be a great help today," replied Ivana as she poured the tea.

"That's great," said Bogumill as he turned to Yoana, "Your mother will be very busy today, you will see just how organised she is, you will learn much."

After a time, everyone at the table had finished eating and it was now time to get started, so everyone thanked Ivana for a lovely breakfast and letting them stay. "You must tell me some time who made those cushions, they were very comfortable!" said the king.

"Thank you, I made them myself!" replied Ivana.

"You have a gift, said the king, maybe someday I will talk you into making a couple for me, thank you once again, right, best be on our way!"

With that they all left the house together, Adrian said "See you soon!" and off he went to find two riders. Matthias the king and Bogumill made their way to a large open area of green, and on the field was a boulder which had steps calved into it, it had a flat top to it, and was used for announcements by Bogumill; it was high enough that a crowd could easily see who spoke from it, and so with the aid of Bogumill and Matthias the king was helped up the steps, his ankle was still a little painful so the help was appreciated.

The king asked Bogumill and Matthias to stay by his side while he spoke with the people, so they did as he asked, the king now closed his eyes and connected with every soul of Bulgan using his mind.

"Hear me my good people!" Every person stopped what it was they were doing and turned to see the king. "I need you all to join me on the westerly field at the speakers boulder, there is much I need to say, so please gather all your family members and come, you will have two hours to gather, I need every citizen of Bulgan here thank you…"

Once the people heard the king, they began to fetch their family members and friends, everyone made their best efforts to ensure all would be there for the king…

Chapter 7

The Energy Within

The king then asked Bogumill and Matthias to assist him down the steps. "Right best speak with Egum now then!" and with that the king called to Egum; Egum replied instantly, "Yes my king?" The king then asked Egum if he could help patrol the outer regions, to which he was happy to do, so the king then asked him to meet Adrian at the edge of Bulgan to the north, to which he once again agreed, the king thanked him, "Thank you my friend, please be careful don't take any risks!"

"We will be careful my king, I'll be off now to meet Adrian, we will keep you informed if we see anything!"

"Thank you," said the king, then in the distance from the easterly woodland he saw his good friends taking flight, as he did, he asked God to watch over them…

The king then asked his new friends the cave rats to as quickly as they could pass word to all the living creatures they could find, to join them at the speakers boulder on the western field.

No sooner had the king finished speaking when Mit gave a few loud squeaks and whoosh the rats ran in every direction seeking out every living creature, they looked everywhere, in caves, mole holes, all manner of places, and when they found a creature they asked that creature to also pass on the message, and so it continued…

While the people and creatures of Bulgan went about seeking others to be sure they would be at the field, the king, Bogumill and Matthias headed to the centre of the town where the alchemists reside in a huge building; this building was built different to all the others which surrounded it, this building was constructed of stone and brick, and stood three floors high; so around eighty feet tall.

As they approached its huge double doors which looked to be made of solid oak and stood ten feet tall; and each five feet wide, they must have weighed an extreme weight, but even so as they approached the door to their left silently opened, no creaking as you would expect of the hinges of such huge doors.

And when it was a quarter open, a young man stepped out wearing a black hooded robe, he took two steps to his right as he faced the king, he then stopped, stood feet together bowed his head, right arm by his side and raising his left and said…

"Good king, I am Dara, Boman is expecting you and awaits you in his laboratory! Please, you and yours enter, and I will lead you to him!"

The king was first to enter passing Dara who still stood head bowed and holding his arm out, he was then followed by Bogumill, as Bogumill passed Dara; "Nice to see you again Bogumill," said Dara head still bowed, then Matthias entered last; "Nice to meet you Matthias," Dara said, which shocked Matthias, as he had never met this person and no one had said his name, so he thought, how does he know my name?!

As he stood looking at the hooded stranger, his gaze was disrupted; "Please continue," Dara said, to which Matthias did and joined the king And Bogumill who stood in what was a huge hall, and in the centre was what looked like a water well, but this was full to the brim; and the liquid within it could be seen swirling around. It was a silver liquid, it was swirling one way then the other, it seemed to move of its own free will!

As Dara stepped inside clear of the open door it closed behind him without aid, the king turned to Dara and asked; "Is that Udriume?"

"Yes, it is, in its purest form, it rises from deep within the planet's lower crusts, there a few wells such as this! Your alchemists of Engypt have a well such as this, not quite this size though!" said Dara.

"Yes, I've seen it! But it is nothing the size of this! This must be what, twenty feet in diameter! Ours can only be five; replied the king looking shocked to see so much Udriume…

As they looked around there were three doors on each side of the main hall, and at the end was another set of double doors, the walls were silver and seem to slither!

"The walls are lined with Udriume I see!" said the king.

"Yes, the walls are entirely Udriume, the stone walls you see outside are to disguise, and help the Udriume take the form it as by becoming part of the stone, let's say the stone helps it maintain its shape while it is in its liquid state!" replied Dara.

There were two other alchemists working with liquids in glass containers. And on the shelves where plant like things, stored in square glass containers, but these things were moving! The head of one thing had what looked like tree branches coming from it, with tiny little leaves, and just below these tree branches were two tiny eyes!

The king was totally intrigued by this creature which as he focused, almost looked like a bark-covered lizard, it seemed to have front legs with a long body then rear legs and a long tail, the king wanted a better look and so walked over to gain a closer view!

As the king approached the glass container the creature within suddenly stood up on its rear quarters and pushed its tail into the soil, then held out its front legs to the sides closed its eyes and extended the branches on its head to obscure it!

"Unbelievable!" said the king, "What type of creature is this? It now looks just like a tiny tree!" he said as he chuckled!

With that Matthias and Bogumill both stepped closer for a good look! As they now crowded the little thing it started to emit loud clicking sounds, click, click-click, click, click-click-click, click! Then rapidly two of its branches swung out hitting the glass with a loud thud!

The three men leapt back with shock!

"Wow! Aah!" they shouted with the shock of the extremely sudden movement of the creature. "My God that thing is fast!" said the king clutching his chest, "Almost gave me heart attack," he laughed.

"Oh, that is a Treegum!" said Dara, who couldn't help but chuckle at the sight of these three big men jumping from a baby Treegum, which only stood twelve inches tall...

"Well I wasn't expecting that!" said the king, with a look of embarrassment!

"Yes, I saw that! You're lucky that's a baby, they can grow quite huge, some as tall as sixty feet when stood upright, but still just as fast, but they are quite armless unless threatened!" said Dara as he looked at the creature holding his gaze which somehow calmed it, it relaxed itself and sat back down on all fours.

"My king, gentleman if you care to follow me, I will introduce you to Boman!"

With that the men took one last look at the treegum, which gave them one little click, as though to say goodbye, and then they followed Dara, as they walked Dara informed them that Boman was quite eccentric but an absolute genius!

He then continued; "You may be a little shocked by his random behaviour, but please don't worry he means no harm, he is just very, shall we say hyper!"

On hearing this the three men looked to each other, the king asked Bogumill quietly; "Have you ever met this Boman?"

To which Bogumill replied; "No, never, this is my first time in this building! And I don't think he as ever left it!"

Matthias just sort of nodded his head and continued looking around at all the strange bubbling liquids in glass beakers, and plants; well if they were plants! after what they had just experienced!

They continued to follow Dara to the big doors at the end of the hall, when they approached them, they opened!

As they passed through into the laboratory, the doors closed behind them again unaided, as they looked ahead they couldn't see anyone in the room, there was a big pot, which seemed to be filled to the brim with bubbling Udriume hanging over a fire in the centre of the room. The walls were lined with scrolls, thousands of them, stored neatly in what looked like a huge cabinet which reached from floor to ceiling, it was made up of square partition one for each scroll, and was built into all four walls, it looked incredible! This dark wooden structure filled with scrolls. How does one get the time to read all of these? the king said; so much knowledge as he looked around.

There were no windows, the room was being lit by Udriume in the ceiling, which seemed to glow so bright it easily lit the entire room.

Then a voice from above and behind them! "Ah gentlemen, you have arrived good, good, good!"

As they turned to the direction of the voice, they saw this older oriental looking man; he must have been around sixty years of age; from what they could see of him, from under his hooded robe as he floated down to them; after picking a scroll from the top row of the cabinet!

"So-so pleased you are here," he said as he glided down reading the scroll he had half unrolled; as he came down to their level his feet did not touch the ground he was effortlessly levitating, multitasking, gliding around reading the scroll and at the same time pouring the heated silver liquid from the big pot into another much smaller pot, all with the power of his mind!

Not once did he make eye contact with any of them, but he could be heard humming as he read the scroll, the king Bogumill and Matthias looked at each other in silence with a look of confusion, Matthias shrugged his shoulders and turned his hands up as if to say I don't know what's going on!

This strange man had welcomed them, then nothing, it was as though they weren't there at all as he just continued going about reading the scroll.

Then! "My king could you join me?" Boman said as he glided over to a long workbench; and on the workbench he placed the small pot which he had just filled, next to the pot were three moulds, the moulds were long and thin, shaped like swords!

As the king approached Boman, the strange man turned to the king looked him in the eyes, and said; raise your right hand please! And so hesitantly the king lifted his hand, as he offered his hand to Boman without warning the strange man pricked the king's finger with a very sharp small blade!

"Ouch!" exclaimed the king; "What do you think you are doing?!" he said with a very stern look!

To which Boman replied with very short sharp words; "Shush! Sorry, has to be done!" staring intently at the king's now bleeding finger, the king looked back to Dara giving him a stern look!

Dara gave a confident smile as he lifted his hand up palms facing the king and mouthed, "Bear with him!"

So the king took a very deep breath as Boman now held his bleeding finger over the small pot of heated Udriume, he then squeezed it causing the king to flinch and blood to drip into the Udriume, as the blood made contact, the Udriume reacted starting to spin like crazy within the pot, the blood could be seen to streak and swirl, then suddenly with the pop of a bubble in its centre it stopped and settled, the blood had dissolved into the Udriume. "Excellent!" said Boman with a smile of achievement on his face!

He then proceeded to pour the liquid into the mould, and sure enough it was a sword, but the liquid did not set like you would expect!

The king looked at the mould seeing the liquid was not setting hard, and said sarcastically; much use that will be, am I supposed to pour it over an enemy?

To which Boman burst into laughter; "Pour it over an enemy, ha-ha, ha; no no-no, not at all!" and in a slow soft voice; "You have to tell it what you want it to do!" as he stared at it, then slightly turned his head right and peered at the king from under the hood of his robe...

"Touch it! Don't be afraid of it, it is not hot, it won't burn you!" he said and smiled...

"Ok!" said the king as he slowly placed his hand closer to it, as his fingers became only an inch or so from it; the king started to experience a tingling sensation in his hand and arm.

"It's tingling!" the king said; with a look of unease, and as he did Matthias and Bogumill went to take steps forward concerned for the king, but before they could Boman looked at them, "It's fine, the king is fine, this is the bonding, they are becoming one, and when it is complete, he will be able to tell the sword to do whatever he wants with just a thought!"

The king continued until finally he was touching the pliable liquid, he pressed his fingers into it, it was not wet, or sticky, and when he lifted his fingers to look there was nothing stuck to them as you might expect of a liquid, as he looked at his fingers, Boman told him to speak with his mind to it. He continued; tell it you want it to be a razor-sharp sword, solid and true...

And so the king once again placed his fingers on the sword, and as he did so he thought of the sword solid and sharp, no sooner had he thought it, the sword was no longer liquid, he placed his hand on the stem of the sword, and lifted it to look at it closely...

"One last thing to finish it with," said Boman, "please let it go it won't fall!" And so the king did, and like magic the sword floated and with that more Udriume appeared out of the smaller pot, and as Boman looked at it, it began to take the shape of a grip, the piece of the sword which is held in the hand, this piece was approximately eight inches long, it slid onto the stem of the blade and locked itself in place, the whole sword pulsated once, just a bright momentary pulse of brightness. The sword and grip were now one, then fine laces of leather wove themselves around the handle in a crisscrossed fashion, it looked like a work of art when it was finished. "Oh yes your need this too," said Boman, as a hard-black leather-bound sheath was made in moments before the king's eyes by young Dara; with just twists of his hands more of the Udriume was plucked from the big pot and with his mind it was manipulated into a perfectly fitting sheath, which Dara then bound with black leather perfectly, it only took moments and it was complete…

"Tell the sword to sheath itself!" said Boman.

And so, the king thought for the sword to slide into its sheath, and as he did, it did!

Boman continued; "You don't want to be holding it in your hand all day! So reach for it!" As the king lifted his right hand the sword shot into it…

"This is quite remarkable!" said the king looking at the beautiful detail of the sheath, the leather was embossed with the stem of a rose which wrapped around the length of the sheath, and at the top where the sheath met the sword's handle was an open rose and the words; "For those I love I give my sword."

In a soft low voice the king asked Boman if this weapon would defeat the changed ones, to which Boman said it would indeed, he then continued; "This sword is made of Udriume as you know, and Udriume is an living organism, it can manipulate itself into any shape you think of, and because it is a living organism, it's power will penetrate anything!"

The king then asked Boman how could he be sure of this. "You haven't seen these creatures!" he said shaking his head.

"Oh, but I have! I've seen your journey; I saw what you saw and felt what you felt! You see, the walls of this building are made of Udriume, and Udriume enhances our thoughts, it enhances our powers when surrounded by it as we are now! Nothing can block my Telepathic powers when in here, and this is how when you couldn't contact anyone from Polaria, due to the infected surroundings which are full of negativity and bad energy; which totally outweighed you and your group's positive energy, I started to see visions of you and your group at that time, and then of the future!"

The king had to ask; "What did you see of the future? Please tell."

Boman said he would tell them, but at this present time he had to get on with arming Matthias and Bogumill…

With that two pots and pins appeared before Matthias and Bogumill, "Please gentleman; I need your blood," said Boman as he drew more Udriume from the larger pot, and levitated it over to the pots in front of them ready to fill them once they had squeezed a few drops of blood into them...

And so, they held out their fingers, and with a grimace the needles pricked them and the blood was drawn; Boman and Dara then continued to repeat the processes of making the swords as they did for the king, and as they did, Boman began to tell them of what he had seen!

He told them that the future he saw was a world of war and death, and that it wasn't only Soul that would suffer from the effects of this humanity changing occurrence which took the people of Polaria from them. He began to explain how the changes to their world would also change Earth!

He warned that some people of Earth will change, not as the people of Polaria had, no!

But they would change nevertheless, he continued to point out, as the king already knew, the Earth and Soul were paralleled with each other, and so are the inhabitants of both worlds. Matthias was unaware of this and so was feeling confused trying to take in what he was hearing. Bogumill was aware of this connection as he had been on visits to Earth with the king, but what they were not aware of, was just how strong the connection between the people of both worlds was!

And so, when Boman informed them just how one life would affect the other, they became so, so overwhelmed with the weight of this new knowledge.

The knowledge that this parallel connection didn't only allow for one to experience deja-vu; and that the times they had had strange dreams which felt so real; as though they were actually – there weren't just dreams, but a true experience!

What they had experienced was their parallel selves real experience, for that moment they were actually seeing and feeling what their soul mate saw and did, the connection is that strong!

Boman continued to explain in more detail; telling them that the universe was made of pure energies, both positive and negative, when we draw on the positive energy life is happy, as we to are energy; our energy comes from the universe, and because our planet is paralleled with Earth we share the same energy, so if one draws more to the negative energy then that is passed to the other…

And because our life energy comes from the universe and is shared by two individuals, whatever happens to that energy will effect both individuals, so if one of those people that share that life force should become negative and full of hatred then so shall the other, because they share the same life energy or as some call it the spirit…

Matthias confused by what was being said, had to ask; "So you are saying on another world there is another me!"

"Yes!" replied Boman, he then tried to help Matthias understand and so continued. "We are connected to another world in another dimension to ours, in which we lead different lives, we will look different to our parallel selves, we could be white skinned here but dark skinned there, if we are male here we will be male there, the only thing that makes us different is our appearance, but as for our blood and life force it's the same, and god forbid you die here, as your parallel you will die there! If the connection is broken in one dimension then it will cease to be in both, and so both die!"

The king was feeling so very sorrowful and shocked at the realisation that the events of the days before would have cost lives on Earth to!

And so, in shock and feeling guilt the king asked Boman; "So those who perished at my hand yesterday, their parallel selves would have perished with them?"

There was a silence for a moment, as Boman didn't want to upset the king further, he could see the king's pain written on his face, he could see the king was thinking about the hundreds of people that would have perished at his hand on Earth, and yet they had done nothing to deserve such a death…

Boman thought carefully before he spoke, he would not lie to the king, but he had to make the king see that his actions were right, and not just for the people of soul, but also for those of Earth.

And so, he turned to Dara and asked him to continue with the swords alone for a moment. He then turned to the king, Matthias And Bogumill, and explained the effect of the catastrophe experienced on New Year's Eve.

He told them that the catastrophe which changed the people of Polaria will have also changed the people of Earth.

By whom he meant those which shared their life force.

He explained that where the people of Polaria had changed mentally and physically their soul mates on Earth will have had their energy changed dramatically to the negative, those on Earth wouldn't change physically; as the metamorphosis was brought about by a physical substance, which was absorbed into a physical body and changed that what makes us human.

That which caused this change can't be transferred to Earth, but the negative mental energies can, because it is energy, and it is the energies which make up our chakras, and our chakra is what controls our wellbeing.

These creatures are no longer humans in the way in which they think. They have no empathy no love, they only have rage and a thirst for blood! They have become pure evil!

"And I'm sorry to say, good king, that so their parallel would also have become full of hatred and evil! So with this in mind, you should not feel remorse for what you had to do to save your people, for you have also saved many people of Earth with your actions.

Those on Earth would have collapsed when the connection was cut, they would not have suffered, the spark that charges the heart would have instantly stopped and so would their lives.

The king had heard and understood, and in a way, it did ease the guilt he felt, but he would never be truly free from it.

The king already knew the answer but nevertheless had to ask; "So if one of our people here in this world dies suddenly then their parallel being would also die! Am I correct in saying that?"

As Boman replied he looked the king directly in the eyes, and placed his right wrinkle-skinned hand on the king's shoulder, and with a look of confidence said; "Yes you are right! That is what I have explained, and I can tell that you are now concerned as to the effects of battling these creatures is going to have with regards to losses. You now realise if you should lose one of your people in battle that someone somewhere on Earth is lost too! And this weighs heavily on you, you did not ask for this, you are not responsible for this, but as king you feel totally responsible for your people, as a good king should!"

The king took a deep breath as he felt the pressure of such responsibilities, and his face looking tired, as he replied; "I do indeed!" he said with a voice of strength raising his head straight and true as a man of discipline, "And I will face my responsibilities as king; doing my best to defend my people, and those of Earth in any way I can!"

"I know you will," replied Boman with a smile of respect for the king, he then said; "And this is why I and my alchemists will be doing our best to help you in this fight to defend against the spread of this evil through the universe! But, and please hear me and remember these words! No matter what! No matter your loss or gain, you as a people must stay pure of heart and mind, you must not let yourselves become filled with hatred for this enemy, or full of pride at your conquests over them; as these feelings are negative, the ego is negative and can lead to people forgetting the true reason they fight!

"And that is for good, for the love of peace, and not to polish one's self-esteem, this can lead to brutality and there for we become as bad as those we fight, and with that the negative will grow in the universe and this cannot be allowed to happen!

"We must stay positive even in battle, we must not carry rage or hatred, but a sense of release, for everyone you strike down you will have released their trapped pure spirit energies back to the universe, you must look at it as though you are releasing them from the bondage of evil.

"If you feel anger or rage you will be releasing negative energies into the universe and so on to your parallel you. And in doing so they will become negative and even as bad as those linked to the changed, you would be fueling more negativity on Earth, and so yourself and your parallel will become one of the enemy! It will be hard for it is a double-edged sword, for if your parallel you become hateful then you will feel that negative energy to, and things are going to change on Earth which will cause good people to struggle!

"And so, you will need to keep a pure mind and spirit, you will need to regularly meditate to keep your chakras in line and your energies positive, this will help keep you and your parallel strong against the attack of negative energies. And at the same time fill the universe with much needed positive at this time of such unknowing!"

Matthias feeling very apprehensive by what he was hearing couldn't help but exclaim his concerns; "We have to fight an enemy we cannot be angry with! It is humanly impossible surely! When you have people you know being hurt or killed one cannot help but feel anger, we have just been in that place! I understand what you say regards the changed being people trapped within a metamorphosis, and in an everyday situation I would feel sympathy for them. but they are not unwell being seen by a healer! No, they are very capable powerful killers and yet we are expected to face them and not be angry!"

Boman smiled and said; "I didn't say it would be easy, that is why I say you will have to meditate, clear your mind, and if needs be close your heart. I can teach you if you are unsure how this can be done! I can teach you to temporarily close off emotion, to put yourself in a state of not feeling with your heart, you will see your enemies as obstacles and nothing more, no feeling, no sorrow, no emotion, no hatred nothing just numb towards them."

"But I do not want to lose myself, I do not want to lose that which makes me human!" Matthias replied in quite a frustrated tone!

Boman replied understanding Matthias's concerns saying; "I'm not looking to change you as a person, it is just a matter of controlling your emotions I wish to teach. I wish to teach you how to put yourself in a state of control, a temporary state where you will not know fear, or anger! A state of pure focus where you will feel no emotion just pure energy, you will be able to feel the balance and therefore control it!

"When you feel the energies becoming negative you will feel it and be able to control it with your mind's eye, maintaining the balance of the chakra within, keeping them bright and balanced, this will control your emotions!"

Boman continued; "Trust me, trust yourself! You will not become a changed man, but you will become a stronger man, still loving and feeling the love of those around you, in fact these emotions of love and compassion will grow within you. you will even grow to feel a sense of release for your enemies when you strike them down, knowing their entrapment is over at the hand of your sword!"

Bogumill who was listening intently and had the same fears as Matthias and the king, truth be told, he was eager to learn, as he knew himself, and knew he would become angry very quickly! And so was eager to learn how to control his emotions, he and his people just as the rest of the people of Soul, apart from the king and his group, had never been faced with such emotion-provoking situations such as the threat of battle! None of them would know how they would truly react until the threat stood before them, so anything that could help them to focus and control their emotions would be a true aid to them he thought to himself!

And so Bogumill chirped up; "So when do we begin, and how do you intend to pass these teachings to our people; there are thousands of us here in Bulgan alone!"

Boman replied with a smile; "That will be the easy part, we will meditate together on mass, we will connect as one, our minds seeing and feeling as one, and this will happen in a day or two, but firstly we have to arm you all, these swords will be connected to you subconsciously, and have the power to enhance you in every way, it will multiply your energies and your abilities. These swords in themselves are pure energy, it will take practice for you and our people to master them, but when you have done so! It will feel as though it is an extension of you, both physically and mentally!"

With that, the king said it was a lot to take in; about which Matthias and Bogumill agreed, the king then continued; "Well we don't know what time we have, so we had better get on with it!"

And one after the other the four men agreed, yes!

Just at that moment, Dara approached; "Sorry to disturb!" he said bowing his head and raising it again; "The swords are finished and just require Bogumill and Matthias to bond with them!"

"Ok, thank you!" replied Boman...

And then with that he invited the king, Bogumill and Matthias to walk with him; "Please Gentlemen follow me let's introduce you two to your swords," he said smiling at Matthias and Bogumill who both eagerly replied simultaneously; "Yes." "Let's," continued Bogumill, and smiled at Matthias excitedly, who in turn smiled back and slowly shook his head; "Big child!" he said quietly to Bogumill, who just replied; "Yep!"

And so, the five men walked back over to the workbench where waiting for them where two beautiful sword blades, the handles and sheathes were also completed but could not be used until the two men had touched and commanded the blades to become solid and sharp!

And so with the direction of Boman the two men touched their blades and commanded them, and sure enough just as with the king's sword they reacted doing as commanded, now the two watched as the handles and sheaths were combined, both waiting with anticipation to hold them and feel it in their hand!

Boman noticed the king still held his sword in his hand; "You're still holding yours I see my king; wouldn't you like to rest your hand?"

"Well I haven't any other means to keep it with me!" said the king, he then continued, "I'll have to make a strap for it later, but thank you it is a beautiful thing!"

"Nonsense!" replied Boman staring at the king excitedly and smiling from ear to ear…

"Just raise your arm as if you are about to place the sword between your shoulder-blades!" he said then his eyes and mouth now wide open excitedly waiting for a response as the king lifted his arm bending it back over his shoulder and sighing as he did so not sure what to expect next!

"Now open your hand and release the sword!" Boman said getting ever so excited, raising his hands to his mouth…

And so, the king released the sword from his grip, and almost as if it leaped the sword stuck to his back instantly!

"Ha-ha-ha!" exclaimed Boman as he rapidly clapped his fingers together in front of his mouth; how wonderful, wonderful; you have bonded successfully! Truly wonderful I knew it would work!" he said to himself in a mutter!

The king was shocked! "It's stuck to me, and yet I can't feel it there!"

Boman replied laughing! "Do your legs or arms feel separated from your body?"

To which the king replied; "No, they do not, they are a part of me!"

"Well guess what! So is the sword now, it is part of your being, and will be till the day you die! This is why you can't feel it! But you know it is there just like your limbs," Boman said smiling, and feeling very pleased with himself…

"Well it's incredible!" said the king as he reached for the sword which unsheathed itself and shot to his hand; "Truly incredible!"

Matthias and Bogumill witnessed the magic of the sword and could not wait to try their own, and so once theirs had been completed they looked at each other nervously, Matthias told Bogumill he could go first if he wanted, But being the Gentleman he was Bogumill smiled and returned the courtesy; "Oh no after you good man," he said raising his left hand palm up next to Matthias sword, "Please you first," he smiled!

Matthias smiled a smile of nervousness back at Bogumill and then said; "Why don't we do it at the same time!" and chuckled…

"Ok! Sounds like a good idea to me!" replied Bogumill.

And together they held out their right hands ready to clasp their new swords by the handle; Matthias's sword glided beautifully into his hand, "Wow!" he exclaimed as he stared at his sword, it's tingling like crazy, the sensation is moving up my arm! Is that normal?" he asked hastily!

Boman replied to let him know it was totally to be expected, and not to worry, "The sensation will soon cover your entire body as the Udriume enters your body and bonds with you, you will always get a sensation whenever you hold the sword, you should begin to feel stronger as well, this is the Udriume enhancing your energies physically and spiritually…"

Matthias was becoming comfortable now as he started to slowly sway his sword in a figure of eight…

Bogumill on the other hand wasn't doing so well; as his sword lay on the workbench shaking, it looked as though it wanted to lift off of the worktop but something wasn't quite as it should be, Bogumill began to focus hard picturing the sword gliding into his hand, and as he did, with a great deal of thought, the sword lifted and sort of sputtered its way, lifting very slightly…

As Bogumill concentrated ever so hard the sword slid halfheartedly and incredibly slowly across the worktop.

"Yes it's working!" said Bogumill as the sword slowly slid across the worktop, it was heading for his hand, but it at this point it wasn't gliding or floating, more reluctantly dragging itself towards him, "I think mine is broken somehow!" Bogumill said, feeling quite uptight with the way his sword was behaving, but nevertheless he continued, focusing as hard as he could!

Now the others in the room were watching intently, willing Bogumill on, but now he could feel he was being watched! And so was starting to feel a little embarrassed by the situation, and as the embarrassment grew so did his frustrations, the sword was now at an sixty degrees angle dragging its tip across the work top and making quite a sound as it did so.

"My, it's being stubborn!" said Matthias as he chuckled at the sight.

On hearing Matthias's words Bogumill became angry with the sword; "Come here you useless thing!" he muttered under his breath, and as he did the sword just fell, only it's tip was still on the bench and so it fell to the ground, with a loud clatter…

"See it's broken!" yelled Bogumill.

Everyone was shocked by Bogumill's outburst, it was unlike the people of Soul to become so agitated, and so the king, Matthias, Boman and the young alchemist Dara all stood motionless and silent, as Bogumill muttered to himself, "What's wrong with it, damned thing!"

After a moment a voice broke the silence, it was Boman, "It is not the sword that is broken! It is you! You allowed your ego to interfere, you are not thinking pure, you are thinking negative, doubting yourself! And so you have become negative and angry, and the sword feels your anger and will not be held by anger, the sword works for good, positive energy, this is another reason you must focus your positive energies, I want you to meditate with me, I'll show you how to cleanse your energies, align your chakra and clear your mind."

Bogumill stood silent for a few moments, as the men looked on with concern!

"Will you meditate with me?!" Boman asked offering his hand, "I understand how you are feeling! This is all new and very daunting to you, you fear for yourself and those you love and this weighs on you, you cannot fight evil with anger! When you feel like this think of those you love and how you feel in their company, that good warm loving feeling that fills you with happiness, you must learn to hold these thoughts and feelings of happiness, and they will spur you on, this is what you live for."

And so Bogumill agreed, and as he did the king and Matthias asked if they too could join them, the king saying he thought they all could do with a lift of spirit.

Boman agreed and Bogumill smiled; his friends cared enough to join him, he thought to himself, and this alone ebbed away at the anger he felt inside.

And so together the four men stood in a circle, Boman instructed them to place their left hand on their chest over the heart, and their right hand over their forehead, the third eye.

He then asked them to close their eyes and breathe in through the nose slowly and deeply counting to six, then slowly exhale through the mouth.

They did this for approximately a minute, then Boman said for them to open their inner eye and look down their bodies seeing the colours of the chakras, he then said to see "they are bright and run centre line of the body, red, orange, yellow, green, blue, indigo and finally violet, the crown chakra; if they look out of alignment we will cleanse them and bring them back Into alignment! And if yours look to be aligned it is still advisable to do this meditation as it will help keep your chakra strong and keep them aligned!" and with that he then asked them to see with their third eye a bright white light from above, wash down over them, and as they did he asked them to repeat after him; "God I ask you to wash me with your cleansing light, wash me down with the energies of the universe, cleansing my energies, cleansing my spirit and aligning my aura making me strong and protecting me from negative energies which may try and claim me!"

Boman then said they should see the light washing over from head to toes, and as it does they should see the chakras brighten and pull into alignment; he then said; "Once they are aligned, see the light lift away upward and as it does see yourself shining bright, pure white. When you can see this, you will then say your gratitude, thank you lord for cleansing me keeping me pure, amen."

Once you have given your gratitude slowly open your eyes as you exhale!

Boman then opened his eyes, he smiled as he looked at the three men deep in meditation, they looked so at peace, especially Bogumill, earlier he looked as though he could kill, but now he appeared relaxed and Boman could see Bogumill's aura had changed; it was glowing bright orange, this was a good aura to see, this meant Bogumill had regained his self-control...

The king's aura was bright white with orange, this was almost perfection thought Boman, he then looked to Matthias.

Matthias's aura was orange and violet, this was also very good, these meant Matthias was self-controlled, courageous, benevolent and very intuitive, this would make him a great leader of men, as was the king…

As Boman looked the king was the first to open his eyes; and in a whispered voice; "Wow! I feel so light and full of energy! That felt wonderful! I have meditated before but not like that, seeing myself with such colour, it was wonderful I feel so relaxed! Thank you Boman," said the king.

Next to awaken from his meditation was Matthias, slowly opening his eyes he smiled; "Mmm! wonderful, I've always known how to draw on my energies, but I've never known how to realign them like that, so simple and so very effective! Thank you Boman!" he said with a look of enlightenment, feeling at peace within himself.

Now the three waited silently for Bogumill to awaken, this took several minutes, and when he did, he looked like a new man, his face and shoulders were now relaxed, he actually managed a big rugged smile which was nice to see, and so the king, Matthias and Boman smiled back.

In an almost whispered voice, the king asked Bogumill; "How do you feel old friend?"

To which he replied still smiling! "I feel wonderful, that was truly spiritually calming, I feel reborn, thank you for teaching me, Boman."

"I feel in control of myself, and truly relaxed! Can I try and pick up my sword?" he asked Boman and looked to his sword still laying on the ground with his right hand out, but before Boman could reply the sword shot from the floor, and then stopped in front of Bogumill just floating grip down tip up, just above his open hand, they stayed like this for a moment, Bogumill staring at his beautiful sword, and it would seem his sword staring back at him!

Then the sword slowly lowered its grip into his hand, Bogumill closed his fingers around the grip, he smiled as he felt its power begin to flow through him, "You're right! It really tingles doesn't it?" he said as he closed his eyes and allowed the sensation to grow throughout his entire body!

"You are becoming one, the sword will help to maintain your focus gaining you great strength," Boman said as he smiled and turned to the king and Matthias who too smiled happily for their good friend, he had conquered his anger...

After letting Bogumill enjoy the bonding for a few moments, Boman then said there was much to discuss, and that there was not much time to discuss the many matters in.

The king then replied; to which matters are you speaking?

"Well I understand you are looking to empty Bulgan of its people, you are wanting them to leave with you to return to Engypt with you!" said Boman curiously.

The king replied, telling Boman he and Bogumill thought it would be best as the changed are just over the mountains to the north and felt it would not be safe to stay here!

Boman informed the king he understood the thinking, but he then informed the king that they could not let the well of Udriume fall into the changed hands; if the changed have intelligence they could utilise the Udriume's power for evil, it could be used to enhance them just as it does the king and his people!

Bogumill was confused by hearing what Boman had said!

"I thought my sword wouldn't come to me as I was unbalanced and angry!" Bogumill said looking confused.

Boman quickly answered; "Yes that is right, the Udriume in this place as always been surrounded by positive energy thanks to myself and those who dwell in here with me, and also by the beautiful positive nature of your peoples that dwell all around this well, this well runs throughout the whole region of Bulgan deep underground, and has been fed beautiful positive energy absorbing it through the ground as you dwelled above unknowing such power lay beneath your feet!

"And so when it sensed your negative energies it would not respond, as it did not recognise such energies, but if it were that all the good positive people left this region and it became surrounded by pure negative energies, it would absorb that negative and so in time respond to it and enhance their negativity, making it very powerful!" As Boman spoke he became very concerned, he couldn't emphasise just how dangerous it would be if the changed were to gain the well…

The king Matthias and Bogumill looked at each other shocked by this news.

"So, what are you suggesting?" asked the king, he then continued, do you suggest we leave the people of Bulgan here to defend the well?

Boman replied; "Not just defend the well, but this region, with the right training Bulgan could be well defended as we are surrounded by mountains, and because we are quite central to the surrounding regions, this place is perfect as a forward defence, if we left this place then the changed would be able to easily unchallenged take the lives of those around us, beast and all!

Yes, you may be able to offer the people of Bulgan refuge in Engypt but at the cost of many lives in the surrounding villages and towns, you would never be able to evacuate the surrounding regions of all there many thousands of people in one mass exodus. But by staying here and training an army with these swords and the powers our people possess we could buy the surrounding regions time to evacuate!"

Matthias thought what Boman said made sense and so turned to the king saying; "I know it goes against our plans my king, but it would give us a chance to save many more people, we could ask the Birgumon to assist us, using this place as a forward defence they could easily watch out for any sign of the changed from above giving us early warning of their movements, and being so close to the northern regions of which they now inhabit, we could easily react as soon as word of them arrived, where as it would takes days to get men to aid from Engypt!"

The king was not a man who would willingly endanger the lives of his people or any creatures that lived in his world, but as he listened to the arguments put to him he could see it would be at an advantage to have forces in Bulgan, provided it could be well defended that was!

Even though Stephen was king, he would never make a decision without the agreement of others, he would always put the people's opinions and concerns above his own, and so he suggested they ask the people, saying; "If we are truthful with the people and they decide stay! then so be it!"

The king continued; "We four have not the right to rip families apart, if members of families decide they wish to stay and defend this region, then it will be their family members choices whether they stay with them or join us!"

At this Boman replied to the king he understood what the king was feeling; "My king this threat to our people doesn't differentiate between adult and child, nor male and female, human or beast, and so we will all be fighting, young and old, male and female will have to learn to defend themselves! It makes no difference where they are, I've seen glimpses of the future, I can't say when and where but I've seen, even our young fighting the changed, and they did not falter! And I believe this is due to training, I believe it's thanks to training our people now it will give them strength and ability for the future, there is no point in running from this place, or breaking up families thinking we would be saving the young and women or elderly, for no matter where we may be, we will be facing the changed in time! So I say the people of Bulgan stay! And I promise my king, I will secure the remaining cave entrance to the outside world! Only those we recognise will be allowed to pass.

The king looked Boman in the eyes for moment, then smiled a halfhearted smile, it was a smile of submission! The king's heart told him Boman was right, if they left Bulgan deserted then the changed would roam freely, and no matter where the king and his people might go, the changed would always be pursuing them!

The king then turned to Bogumill; "How do you feel about you and yours staying Bogumill?" the king asked knowing he would have to respect what Bogumill thought best, as he knew his people best...

Bogumill answered just as the king thought he might; "As I have said my king, me and my people love these lands, they are our home!" As he spoke the king could see he was emotional full of love for his home and its people, Bogumill continued; "And when I speak I know I speak for my people; we will stay, and we will do our utmost to stop the changed having their way.

"And I'm sure with Boman's teachings we will be controlled and true to the good, if or when we should face the changed! Rest easy my king this is my choice, and I will talk with the people alongside you today!"

The king placed his right hand on Bogumill's left shoulder and with eyes welling; "I feel you my good old friend, if I'm honest I would do the same for my home and people, no one wants to be a refugee, so I will stand by your decision, and support you, when I return home; Matthias will train many and return with them to support you, but I can't say how long that will take to have them ready, but I'm sure you will be able to hold them back until we can return!"

"Thank you, my king, we will not fail you!" Bogumill replied confidently!

Then Boman spoke once more; "With regards to training, the swords will guide you, they will lead your responses and enhance your instincts, those that wield them will just have to practice having faith in the sword, practice following its lead, and just remember to stay emotionless in battle!

"I will show you this day, but first we have to arm every man, woman, and child! And this will take time as we will need their blood, but I have started the process now," and with that thousands of tiny Udriume thimble-sized vessels appeared with just a click of Boman's fingers!

Boman then asked the king to speak with the people, and asked that the king told them to expect a small vessel too appear to them, and when it did, they needed to prick their finger and allowing a few drops of their blood to fill the vessel...

And so the king did as he was asked, which was made so simple as the Udriume of the building enhanced his Telepathic ability tenfold, he could   connect with all the people of Bulgan effortlessly, speaking with them all simultaneously, and when they all replied, the thousands of voices didn't cause him discomfort as they would normally when communicating with so many at once, the Udriume seemed to filter waves making them more manageable for the king's mind…

Once he had finished connecting with the people, he turned to Boman and informed him it was done, the people are aware and would do as he had asked!

With that Boman rolled both his wrists twice, then pointing his forefingers up and raised his hands quickly above his head! As he did the thousands of tiny vessels whizzed up passing through the roof of Udriume causing the Udriume to ripple as they passed through…

To all those people outside, the mass of tiny vessels appeared as a swarm, thousands of tiny shining vessels whizzing towards them, they were moving so fast in and out of the people it was amazing they didn't collide with anyone, they did cause people to duck down as they whizzed toward them, or in some cases run back into the door way they had just come from only to find the vessel chasing them as they yell, go away, and running! and as the people duck down looking up, or run out of breath from running, they would realise the tiny thing they had just avoided was actually for them; as it would just wait above them, waiting for them to stand and fill it with a prick of blood, and once the person had done filling, the vessel would whizz of back to the alchemists laboratory…

And as they started to return, the big doors of Boman's laboratory opened wide, then the four other doors in the hall all opened at once, and from them appeared four alchemists from each room, and with them thousands of the sword moulds, just floating, they drifted into Boman's laboratory filling it, there were so many; as well as filling the laboratory, they also filled the main hall…

On seeing just how full the rooms had become, Boman suggested it was time the king, Matthias and Bogumill leave saying; "Gentleman as you can see it's getting a little busy in here; Just avoiding one of the moulds as it floated past their heads, You, as I have much to be getting on with, so if you can avoid the moulds on your way out! Dara will show you the way, and thank you my king, we have made the right choices, and oh yes before you go, I've informed your alchemists of Engypt and they have already made preparations for your people's swords, they will just be needing you to connect with your people and inform them as to what is to be done!"

To which the king replied; "Do you mean the pricking of the fingers and the vessels?"

In quite a dismissive manner Boman replied; "Yes! Now if you'll excuse me, much to do, goodbye for now!" He then turned and started waving his arms around this way and that drawing Udriume from the big pot as the king, Matthias and Bogumill turned and followed Dara back into the main hall…

As they made their way through the mass of floating moulds, having to dodge this way and that, Dara informed the men; "When the people wake in the morning their swords will be with them, so when you speak with them today can you please inform them to touch the blade just as you did, and the rest will happen naturally!"

"I was going to ask how you would manage such a feat but I will just thank you instead, I will also be sure the people know what is to be done, thank you Dara," said the king as he reached the now open door which lead back out into the bustle of Bulgan…

As the three men turned left into the crazy streets of Bulgan; thanks to people running this way and that as the vessels still whizzed around, the king was wondering what was happening!

But soon realised as he saw one young man waving his hands around as if to swat something away, when in fact it was his vessel he was swinging at.

The three men couldn't help but laugh at some of the sights, one young woman dived headlong into a trough of water to avoid hers; not knowing what it was that pursued her…

There were those who had realised what the vessels were and had done as the king had asked them, and now they stood in laughter at the antics of those that had not realised, some were actually trying to calm some of those running and screaming by calling out to them, "Stop! It's nothing to fear, it's the vessel the king spoke of, stop running!" One very tall slim young man was shouting out to those who ran around like headless chickens; the very tall slim young man with his scraggly long hair had all but given up and began to laugh, as he did, he turned and made eye contact with the king.

For a moment he stood looking at the king still laughing, then he realised who it was he was looking at, and with that his laughter slowed, and he wide-eyed shrugged his shoulders holding his palms of his hands up with the expression of not knowing what to do next! The king smiled back at the young man raised his right hand showing the man his palm, sighed and mouthed leave it to me!

With that the king turned to Matthias and Bogumill; "I think it's best I intervene before someone gets seriously hurt!"

"Yes indeed," replied Bogumill, still laughing.

With that the king once more connected to the people of Bulgan; he told them to stop, they had nothing to fear, the things they are running from are the vessels he had spoken of, he then apologised as he did not expect them to appear in such a manner that would scare them; on hearing this the people stopped running around, the shouts of fear stopped and now people were beginning to laugh at themselves, how foolish they felt, after a few moments the laughter slowed and the people did as they were asked and began to fill the vessels, and after a hour or so everyone of age had given their blood as required and now went about their business as usual; which before the episode with the vessels was readying for the king and Bogumill speaking on the field.

Now that normality had returned, the king and Bogumill could now, as they made their way to the field, discuss how to approach the people of Bulgan regards the threat of the changed; and how it had been decided that Bulgan would now become a forward defence.

Bogumill was positive his people would understand and be more than willing to fight back against the changed, especial as with Boman's teachings they would see it not as a war! But more a fight to free those trapped by an evil.

He felt that would spur them to fight with the intention to free those they once knew, and the knowledge that those people may be gone in the physical, but their spirits made free by their hand, will hopefully keep them positive in times of battle and fear!

The king hoped Bogumill was right and went on to explain it wasn't fear they would feel but more terror, he then reminded Bogumill that himself, Matthias and those with the king's group had experienced first-hand the absolute terror, and yet they had made it!

The king then went on to explain how Boman was right with regards to remaining calm in the time of fear, he told Bogumill how when they were attacked he at first was fearful, but knew they had to fight back, he had to think clearly, if he and those with him had just panicked they would have perished!

The king remembered back to Bogumill; how somehow they didn't just run and scatter, how the group had actually pulled together, they had no weapons to fight back with, their only saving was the power off the children with them, and so they made the most of them drawing the enemy in so the children could destroy them; so yes I'd say as long as we can keep clear heads and not be dragged into unthinking anger we will survive!

The king then went on to say that he hoped that; Boman's teaching his meditations later would help everyone; "I think it has done wonders for you my friend, you had me worried earlier, we thought you was going crazy, but after the meditation you were the man I've always known!"

Bogumill replied saying; "The anger within me was uncalled for and I still don't understand why I became so, at least now I know how to calm myself thanks to Boman. His teachings will be a benefit to all of us!"

Then Matthias interrupted; "We are nearly at the field, look at all these people! it's amazing to see so many people, and creatures together as one like this."

As the king and Bogumill broke from their conversation and looked ahead now paying full attention to the way ahead of them, they were both astonished by the sight they beheld.

Everyone was there or arriving, there were thousands of people and thousands of creatures of all shapes and sizes, and as the king, Bogumill and Matthias made their way to the speaker's rock, the people and creatures would look to them and move aside clearing their path.

There were so many faces of all ages, both human and creatures, one of the most surprising to the three men was that there were; a- number of creatures they didn't even know existed until today. One in particularly stood out! They had met a youngster of such a creature earlier, and now before them stood in all its adult glory a treegum!

And it wasn't alone, there were hundreds of them in the distance, but could be seen over the crowd as they stood so tall even on all fours.

The treegum they first saw was standing just twenty feet or so ahead of the king; at his eleven o'clock, and my was it a wonderful creature; it was on all fours as the king approached; the king wanted to get close to it as he had never seen one before, apart from the infant earlier!

The treegum seemed very relaxed and at home amongst the humans and other creatures, which the king found strange as no one had ever seen one or even knew they existed, and yet it acted as though it had always been around them!

On all fours this creatures head with its huge tree branch extensions and leaves must have stood at least twenty feet tall!

Matthias and Bogumill who walked each side of the king were also in awe of the creature, "Wow look at the length of it!" said Matthias excitedly as his voice went from deep and manly to a high pitch. "That must be at least sixty or so feet!" replied Bogumill as he looked at it then across to Matthias.

As they got closer they could see its big eyes which were most odd! As one; the right was yellow, and the left was green, and they were looking in different directions to each other, rotating back and forth, behind its quite long snout, and it would from time to time open its long mouth slightly and its long thin black tongue would whip out have a quick waggle, then disappear back in its mouth, much like a snake would.

"It is a most peculiar looking creature isn't it?" Matthias said quietly to the king, as he watched its eyes rolling this way and that.

"Yes, it is indeed, but at the same time quite a beautiful thing; in a strange way, if you look into its eyes you can see it a gentle giant!" replied the king keeping his voice down.

The treegum with its tree bark skin, really did look like a tree with eyes.

In fact the king felt they were so well disguised it made the king think; to which the king had a theory as to why they were so comfortable around humans and the other creatures. "I bet we have actually walked past these in the woodlands and not noticed them as they blend in so well with actual trees," said the king as he smiled. "Quite incredible," he added.

As they drew closer, the Treegum began to click! very slowly at first, just the once, but as the three men drew closer still, the clicking became a little increased, click, click, click! On hearing this the king remembered the youngster in the glass container, and so stopped, feeling a little uneasy, and with clenched jaw, talking out of the side of his mouth he said to Matthias and Bogumill; "Boys, it is clicking!"

He didn't have to say anything more, Bogumill and Matthias stopped in their steps, now feeling very nervous and not daring make a move or lose eye contact with the creature; Matthias said; "That can't be good can it?!"

"No, I don't think it is, remember the little one, that clicked then lost its temper, I do hope this giant isn't about to do the same, we could be in massive trouble! " replied Bogumill as he ever so slowly turned his eyes to Matthias and the king...

Then suddenly more clicking could be heard, but now it was from every direction!

For some reason all the treegum began to click rapidly and very loudly.

As the clicking continued, it became faster and faster in groups of three rapid clicks then a pause, then again rapid clicking; Click-click-click, click-click-click, click-click-click!

As the clicking continued the people around the Treegum admiring the incredible creatures began to back away, the king could see the people becoming fearful and so quickly communicated to his people telling them to stay calm, and not to panic, he told them to slowly move away from the Treegum, but not to run...

And so, on hearing the king's voice his people slowly and calmly moved away from the creatures...

As the people backed away, the Treegum that stood before the king looked at him deep in the eyes, and began clicking incredibly fast, but the creature was manipulating its clicks to create a much lower tone, which it was continuing to manipulate into barely audible words. The words the king, Bogumill and Matthias could just make out to be; "Danger, you, circle! Danger, you, circle!"

It kept repeating over and over, the king turned to Bogumill and in haste asked; Is it my ears or is it saying danger, you, circle?"

As the king asked Bogumill, the creature began nodding as it continued the words, then the other Treegum began doing the same, saying "Danger, you, circle," as the hundreds of them started to move walking towards the humans and the other creatures, they were forming a huge circle around them, they were herding the humans and creatures into a bunched circle; and as they did several of the Treegum worked their way into the centre of the circle, and stood facing outward over the people and creatures within; looking toward those Treegum forming the outer edge.

As this was happening the people became very scared, and some were starting to panic thinking the Treegum meant to do them harm! But the creatures that were also being herded along with the humans were not fearful of the Treegum. In fact the opposite, some of the creatures such as horses, rabbits, even the cave rats which had not been rounded up, ran into the circle as if seeking refuge!

But the much bigger creatures such as the dragons, Birgumon and the huge cat-like Chu-Chun moved out of the circle. As the Chu-Chun moved they were making a low droning sound, showing their huge fangs and claws as they walked past the humans staring directly ahead of them facing the north...

Whilst being herded the king was constantly asking; "What is going on, what are they doing?!"

But neither Bogumill nor Matthias had an answer for the king; but then Mit came rushing out of the crowd, "My king, forgive me I have been searching for you, my Telepathic ability isn't as strong as yours, I've been needing to tell you, everything is not what it seems, the Treegum mean us no harm, they are attempting to protect us, they have sensed danger and have warned the other creatures who are heading to defend us!"

As Mit spoke with the king, the Treegum formed a huge dome with their bodies, they all stood on their hindquarters then dug their tails and rear legs deep into the ground like the roots of a tree; then stretched out their head branches, those Treegum who stood in the centre did the same reaching out to the Treegum forming the outer edge of the circle until they were all connected. They wrapped their branches together forming a huge woven dome of tree branches...

Mit continued as the king stood staring at the forming dome in awe, "They have sensed a very powerful negative energy full of darkness heading for us, it is due any moment now!"

Matthias quickly said; "My king we cannot hide in here we must assist them any way we can!"

To which the king replied in total agreement saying; "Well I guess this is the time we test our swords gentleman, but we must remember to keep ourselves in check, do not allow ourselves to become angry, we must not let them bring us to negativity, we must not feed them."

Then with a deep breath he asked his two friends; "Are you ready?!"

To which Bogumill took the king's right forearm with his, and Matthias took the king's left forearm with his left. And for a moment they stared, no words needed, then a nod of their heads and they turned and walked together towards the outer edge of the circle. As they did so the king connected to the people telling them not to fear, he told them the Treegum were protecting them and meant them no harm, and just before he was about to leave the safety of the dome, he told them they must not be full of hate or anger, he asked them to meditate on positive only, we can't fight these creatures with negativity, they feed on it, you will strengthen them against us, so please no matter what you see or hear please have faith in good.

Then with that the Treegum which stood blocking the way, opened its branches letting the three men out.

As the three walked out on to the fields the sun was bright and the air was warm being carried on a beautiful breeze. And for a moment they stopped and looked at their surroundings, they looked at all the beauty that surrounded them, the green grass, which was long and thick, speckled with flowers of which the smell was carried in the breeze.

And beyond, bushes of wild pai berries, lemon groves, apple and orange trees, with the backdrop of thick lush woodland and snowcapped mountains with freshwater streams running down; "It's beautiful isn't it?!" said the king feeling love for the beauty that stood before him.

"It truly is, my king," said Bogumill, hoping he would get the chance to walk through the wood once more…

Matthias smiled and then said how he thought it strange, how at a moment when they stood ready to fight in battle and could possibly lose their lives that the world looked so incredibly beautiful and made you want nothing more than to live.

He then smiled at the king and Bogumill and said; "Well at least it isn't raining!" then laughed!

The king replied to Matthias's statement about the world looking so beautiful at such a moment saying; "Yes, it is strange, but it reminds us what beauty it is we fight to protect; don't you think?!"

The king once again wanted to contact his family but knew if he did his wife would sense something was wrong, and that would lead to her worrying. And if anything happened to him this day he didn't want her last thoughts of him to be full of fear for him, he knew, she knew he loved her, and so would leave it at that! As for little May he quickly communicated with her, telling her not to fear, she would be safe, and to be sure to stay with her group, and so she did as her father asked, and rounded her group up so they would be together. He then said he would see her soon and that he loved her; she said she loved him too…

And so, after their moment of enjoying the surroundings and reminiscing, they turned to face the north and headed to where all the beautiful creatures of their world awaited them…

There were hundreds of creatures waiting for battle, although he preferred a better situation, it was nice for the king to see his old friend Egum and his kin were there to. And because the king had called for every human and creature to join him this day to speak with them, even Ti-at and hundreds of his kin were there waiting. It was incredible, the king never knew so many Birgumon existed, and as for Matthias, well he was in heaven; he was surrounded by his favorite creature in the whole world.

Matthias wish the circumstances were different, these Birgumon were in a very agitated state, they were pacing and flapping their huge wings and making very loud screeching sounds, they were in no mood to be petted.

As the king, Matthias and Bogumill walked to join the creatures and take their place beside them; the king thought it an idea to form groups, and so communicated with Ti-at to ask if it might be possible Matthias ride him; so they could work together giving the king and those with him cover from the air. This did seem logical to the king, Matthias and Ti-at, as the cave entrance to Polaria was sealed. So, the only way the changed could possibly gain entrance to Bulgan was from the air, or to climb the mountains. And as that was the direction every one of the creatures was facing, it seemed to be the case…

And so, Matthias full of pride mounted Ti-at and together they waited for the king to give them orders.

Ti-at then called for his kin to prepare to take flight as soon as the king gave the order. With this, the Birgumon stopped flapping their wings and moving around; they became silent, they just stood looking to the mountain's tops waiting for something to appear!

Now seeing the Birgumon who were gathered in the centre of the group had calmed, standing ready to take flight at an instant, the king turned his attentions to the Chu-Chun. The king had never been up close to a Chu-Chun; as they were quite reclusive creatures and would normally roam the thick mountainous woodlands, only seen very rarely.

And so, the king approached them cautiously, although he knew they wouldn't cause him harm, they did seem very fidgety, pacing around only stopping for a moment to look up at the mountains and giving a low gargled growl. These beasts looked quite daunting with their huge fangs and claws with incredible power and speed. Their armoured skin of scales which glinted a multitude of colours, which could be seen to shimmer in the sunlight, and yet at a distance they appeared to be one colour of a reddish-brown.

As the king continued their size was more apparent, on all fours their heads stood aligned with his shoulders; "Thank God these beasts are on our side!" the king said to himself.

Just at that moment one of the Chu-Chun turned and walked towards the king, as it did the king could hear its voice in his head, "Hello good king, I am Tanzin, and this is my pack! I sense your unease, please do not fear us, your kind and mine have lived in harmony for centuries, we have no reason to harm your kind, we are hear at your request, we will stand with you till the end if needs be; after all what I sense comes today will require every living creature to pull together as one, I sense incredible powerful negativity comes for us. But I'm sure as one we will prevail!" Tanzin said as he lowered his head in respect for the king. And in turn the king bowed his head in mutual respect; then spoke saying he knew the Chu-Chun were a peaceful breed and that he was very thankful for their being with him at this time, he then continued asking Tanzin to forgive him his emitting fear, and explained it was not fear more an admiration for such an incredibly powerful and yet gentle breed of creature such as themselves...

Tanzin chuckled and said; "Yes our appearance can be rather fearsome, and this is why we live high in the mountains away from other creatures who we may cause to fear us!"

On hearing this the king said the Chu-Chun were very welcome amongst his people and continued; "It would be a privilege to have you and yours visit us in the future. Did you not feel welcomed when you were amongst my people this day?"

"Surprisingly yes we did! In fact, your young children are very affectionate, felt comforting to have them touching us, stroking us, maybe when we are done here, we will return with you."

"Me and my people would be very happy to have you amongst us!" the king then chuckled; "Especially the children."

He then continued; "But for now we just have to get through today!"

And with that he asked Tanzin if he and his kin could form a row across the front of the group, and stop anything from passing, to which Tanzin agreed, with that they wished each other well; Tanzin returned to his kin and within moments they made their ways to the front, and formed a row.

Meanwhile the king and Bogumill approached the mammoths, and spoke with the herd leader whose name was Batoor, he was a total gentle giant; and was a good friend of Bogumill...

"Oh, hello my good friend!" Batoor said as he clapped eyes on Bogumill and ran his trunk over Bogumill's head.

"Hello old friend!" Bogumill said with a big smile at the affectionate welcome from the giant...

Bogumill held Batoor in high regard and didn't like the thought of this big gentle giant that; since a child Bogumill would go for long rides with and talk of all manner of thing, could be in danger this day. The king could sense Bogumill's fear for this beast and so asked if he would like to stay with Batoor? To which Bogumill replied to the king; "I'd rather he didn't have to partake in this at all. If anything should happen to him I would be heartbroken; he has been my friend since I was a small child, and is an old boy now aren't you?!" Bogumill said as he run his right hand over Batoor's trunk and looked him in his big gentle eyes!

Batoor trumpeted and shook his head; "You cheeky man, there's plenty of life left in this old beast yet! A hundred and twenty is still young I'll have you know!" then trumpeted loudly!

Bogumill laughed then told Batoor in a more serious tone; "My friend this situation we find ourselves in could be very dangerous, and I'd rather you be safe back with my family under the dome. There are plenty of others here who will be of great assistance, this is no place for you my old friend, the king has spoken of these creatures, and if it is them that come for us then they are very fast, and you I'm sorry to say my old friend aren't; this could place you at a disadvantage, these things have no mercy and will not hesitate to end you, and I could not bear that!"

Batoor looked at Bogumill, then gave him a shove with his trunk; "Don't be selfish! You'd expect me to leave you and my kin here, sorry I'm not going anywhere!" he said as he raised his head looking left and right in an almost sulking manner, "I'd be worried sick about you and them. No! I'm staying where I can keep an eye on you, you're not too fast yourself I'll have you know!" then stared Bogumill in the eye with a real stern look!

Bogumill shook his head gave a grunt then; "Grr, ok but I'll be right at your side," he then looked to the king, "Is it ok with you I stay and fight with Batoor?"

"But of course it is; I'll be riding Egum, so I will have your back from above!" replied the king with a smile...

He then wished Bogumill and Batoor good luck! And headed off to join Egum.

Bogumill mounted Batoor and lead him and his kin to form a line behind the Chu-Chun, as a second row of defence. As the Chu-Chun saw the mammoths they gave them a loud welcoming roar! To which the mammoths trumpeted back! And took their place just behind them.

This front line off defence with its sixty Chu-Chun and forty mammoths looked quite impenetrable. Well, the king hoped it would be, he was unsure if he was wasting time and even possibly wasting lives, as he did not know what was coming or if the teeth of the Chu-Chun would be able to penetrate the changed's armoured scaly skin. he hoped that the Chu-Chun being a living creature would be able to pierce the changed, unlike the man-made steel knife. We will soon see he said to himself!

As the king walked amongst the beasts making his way to Egum there were still many small creatures making their way to the safety of the dome. They were harmless creatures such as rabbits, squirrels, and white mountain foxes, even spiders looked to the safety of the dome…

One of the rabbits stopped the king to ask if he and his many kin could assist the king. The king smiled and told the rabbit, he was happy for his kind offer, but thought it best they take shelter!

The rabbit smiled and said; "Well if you change your mind just call and we will be at your side, we do have powerful teeth and claws!" the rabbit said as he showed them off to the king. "And we are very fast!"

The king thanked the rabbit once more; "Thank you, but for now you get to safety. I may have use for you in the future!" He then smiled and watched the rabbits disappear rapidly into the dome!

As the king finally reached Egum, who stood with his mate Symphet by his side and their son Saturn just behind them, they smiled at each other and said hello!

"It's so nice to see the three of you again," said the king reaching both hands up stroking the necks of Egum and Symphet.

"It is nice to see you to good king," replied Egum and gave the king a big smile, but behind the smile the king could see Egum was feeling a little insecure!

The king had known Egum his whole life and knew how to read his expressions. He had always been able to see into Egum's eyes and feel him, and so the king feeling empathy for Egum, knowing it was his family he was concerned for, and knowing if his own family was here at this moment, he too wouldn't want them in dangers way, and so said; "Egum, I want you and your family to go, I don't want your family in danger's path, we have many here, we will be fine I'm sure, so please don't feel you have to stay!"

Egum was happy for the king's offer, But to Egum the king was family, and he would never leave family to face danger without him. So, he told the king he would stay, but wanted Symphet and Saturn to leave the field and take refuge in the dome. To which the king agreed, in fact the king thought it a good idea, for two reasons; one was obvious, they would be safe in the dome, and the other, if anything should manage to pass the king's forces and get to the dome, the two dragons would be a great defence, along with the Treegum, and the thousands of people and other creatures within. They would at the least be able to buy the children a chance to escape!

Hearing this Saturn passionately spoke; "Father I'll not leave you! Yes let mother seek refuge, but I'm staying!"

"No!" said Egum in a raised voice; "You will stay with your mother and be sure if the worst should happen here, you must get the children to safety!" Can you do this for me, please son!

Saturn thought for a moment and realised if he didn't do as his father had asked, then his mother wouldn't leave them, he knew there was no way she would leave her child, and so grudgingly agreed with his father...

"Ok! I'll stay with mother, please come back to us! Both of you!" he said looking to the king as well as his father with tears in his eyes.

"Yes! You had both better come back to us, or I'll kill you myself," Symphet said trying to hold back the tears.

"We will I promise! I will not let anything happen to Egum, you have my word!" the king said putting on a brave face!

Symphet and Saturn smiled and shook the tears from their eyes, Symphet saying; "Your word is good enough for me, Stephen, and you be sure to watch over him, you big lump," she said looking to Egum…

"I will my love!" Egum said then opened his huge wings and wrapped them around Symphet and Saturn, and kissed them, saying he would see them soon, "Now leave before it's too late!"

He then backed away; "Go before I change my mind!" and with that Saturn and Symphet said goodbye to the king, "See you soon, God willing!"

And off they went looking back occasionally as they walked to the safety of the Treegum dome.

The king and Egum watched them until they had entered the dome, both felt very emotional; "We will see them again my old friend, I promise you," said the king trying to comfort himself and Egum.

Yes, we will, Egum replied with a determined tone, the king could feel the dragon's determination, and this filled him with confidence.

Egum then turned and lowered his head allowing the king to mount him, and together they waited looking to the mountain tops…

They had all been waiting for ten minutes or so, but nothing had appeared, there was an eerie silence, all of the beasts of the king's forces had become still and silent, and yet not a sound could be heard, not even a bird chirping or taking flight.

The king and those with him started looking to each other, shrugging or shaking their heads not sure what was happening. Were the Treegum's warnings incorrect, had they mis-sensed?

Everyone began to relax in the hope that the Treegum had been mistaken!

Just as the king rubbed his hands on Egum's shoulders, and was just about to say it looks like a false alarm, the Birgumon started to screech and flap their wings like crazy they had become extremely agitated very quickly, the king looked to the mountains tops has hard as he could, but couldn't see anything!

The Birgumon's eyesight was three times that of any other creatures or humans for that matter, and they had definitely seen something.

They were eager to get into the air, but the king told them to wait! He did not want to break up the forces, at least until he could see what had their attentions so!

Chapter 8

They Come to Test Us

After only a matter of several minutes the king spotted what it was that had set the Birgumon into a frenzy. So had Matthias and Bogumill!

And now not just the Birgumon were in a state of agitation; as what came towards them was now visible to all just passing between the mountain tops. The Chu-Chun began to hiss loudly followed by the mammoth's loud trumpeting, but none moved, they waited for their king to give the order!

As whatever it was approached descended following the mountain's face, they could then be seen to level at about one hundred feet; heading directly at the king's forces. The king shouted; "Hold!" as some of the Birgumon wanted to take flight!

Matthias who was on Ti-at's shoulders had to keep telling him to calm as he ran his hand on his neck, as the beast was eager to take flight and attack whatever it was that came towards them!

Whatever they were, they were of some size, as they still had some miles before they would reach the king's forces and yet they looked the size of a cat!

Now closer still they were some form of blackened bird, only twenty in number. Beneath four of them appeared to be something being held, whatever it was; was long as its ends drooped between the bird's talons.

Just at this moment, Boman had received word of what was happening on the fields, and instantly connected with the king, he looked through the king's eyes seeing what he saw, once he saw the creatures coming towards them he recognised those that hung below, and instantly said for the king to bring down those creatures now! "You cannot let the creatures hanging below reach the Treegum, bring them down now!" Boman said in a tone of shock at what he saw.

With that the king gave word to Matthias to attack! He also told Matthias that Boman said the creatures below must not reach the Treegum!

"They won't! We will bring them down long before they reach you!" said Matthias, he then told Ti-at, "It's time, let's stop them now!" Ti-at gave a loud cry; and with that took to the skies followed by all the Birgumon with him; all two hundred!

Watching the Birgumon take to the skies and their numbers far greater than that of the attacking creatures, the king thought surely, they are defeated!

Boman was still with the king, and said; that may be, but if one of those Mattatoids makes it to the ground it will be a handful. It is a snake-like creature with six legs, very-very fast, and worse still is it has huge fangs and two spikes on its tail; one each side, both its fangs and tail spikes carry venom. they are deadly and can inject venom multiple times!

He continued; "It was thought to have been extinct, so where has it come from?!"

Boman then continued; "If they make it to the ground those creatures you have with you will have no defence against it. you must not let those creatures with you attack the Mattatoid, it will defeat them; its venom is instant!"

"So how do we fight them?" the king asked.

Your swords will multiply any gift you have, it will also improve your physical ability giving you an ability to fight back in ways you have never imagined! it will have to be you and those with you that have swords of Udriume that face them!"

The king replied nervously; "There is only the three of us, and Matthias is airborne with the Birgumon!"

Boman replied with confidence; "Have faith in yourself and the sword will do your will, remember the sword grows stronger with positive energy, so see yourself prevailing and you will, you must not doubt, not for a second!"

Boman then said he had to get back to the production of the swords for the remaining people of Bulgan and the king's group, he then said to the king that he would prevail, keep faith! then he was gone!

"I can do this!" said the king to himself, and with that drew his sword in readiness…

The sword's power flowed through his entire body, and as it did it relaxed him. He became composed, focused, every sense was multiplied tenfold, he could feel the creatures that attack them, he knew their intent…

With that the king dismounted Egum, he instructed Egum, to burn the creatures from the sky, and so Egum left the king where his stood and headed to join the Birgumon and Matthias.

Egum would have to fly hard, as the Birgumon were almost on the strange creatures of black. Matthias could see them now and told the king what he saw ahead. He explained they look the same shape as the osprey of Polaria, but now they were much bigger; scaled and black!

He then continued to tell the king of the creatures below them, saying they looked like a huge snake but with legs. "They do not look pleasant at all," he said; but still calm in himself.

Then he and Ti-at commenced their attack; ordering his-kin to fly head long into the changed ospreys; taking them in their talons. But they could not easily pierce the flesh of the ospreys; as would be the case of any normal creature; their scale-like feathers were very tough and took great effort for the Birgumon's talons to breakthrough, but nevertheless they did. And once they had; they pulled them to the ground where they could pin them with their weight, stopping them from moving and then inevitably destroy them using their beaks and talons…

Matthias and Ti-at circled around the sky battle just in case one of the creatures managed to escape as they were swiftly being picked off. One of the creatures carrying a Mattatoid had done just that, and went into a steep dive making its escape, these creatures when in a dive could reach speeds that would almost match the Birgumon...

And this one had a head start, and the six Birgumon that gave chase could not seem to close the gap fast enough to stop it reaching the ground.

Just as the creature neared the ground, the Birgumon backed off letting it be; they had not given up, no!

They had seen Egum who had been following their attack and was still approaching from the south, and so he was heading directly for the diving creatures. And so the Birgumon opened their wings as wide as they could to grab as much wind beneath to stop them as fast as possible; the great dragon glided in exhaling flame as he did so instantly igniting the creatures, but he was not taking any chances and so followed them till they impacted on the green fields below. Egum then, once he was sure they were no more, turned back to the battle.

As the Birgumon fought the creatures some would try and get underneath them in an attempt to get at the Mattatoid, but the Mattatoid would lash out at them with its powerful long tail, attempting to impale the Birgumon with its spikes. On seeing this Matthias asked Ti-at to tell his kin not to risk being caught by the poisonous Mattatoid's spikes, and to only attack the osprey.

And so, they ceased, and continued to go for the osprey only. After a matter of ten minutes or so they had defeated those osprey which had been attempting to give cover to those that carried the Mattatoid. And now the Birgumon descended on the remaining two being sure to steer clear of the Mattatoid's swinging tail.

As the Birgumon swooped in taking turns to rip into the osprey they achieved their goal, and the ospreys soon fell with their cargo in-toe. The fall was a good hundred feet or so, they impacted the now black scale spattered field just ahead of the row of Chu-Chun and Mammoths with an almighty thud! a plume of dust and dirt as the ground they impacted exploded, sending debris in all directions…

All those of the king's forces, both above from the air and those who stood with the king, looked on, waiting for the dust and debris to clear!

The king who stood now amongst the Chu-Chun and mammoths was feeling very uneasy, his sword was pulsating energy throughout his body, as though preparing itself, this sensation was unlike what the king had felt before, it was very intense.

And so, the king listened to his instincts which seemed to be heightened with every pulsation from his sword, and so turned to Bogumill who was sat on Batoor and told him to ready his sword!

The king continued; "Something doesn't feel right! Please ready your sword and dismount."

Bogumill asked the king what was wrong and continued that they had won surely! But the king told him he felt it wasn't over! he described how is sword was emitting and energy he had not felt before, and so said for Bogumill to hold his sword and see if his felt the same!

And so Bogumill did as the king said, and dismounted Batoor, then reached for his sword which instantly leapt into his hand, the sensation was the same for Bogumill as it was for the king; "I must agree with you my king, my sword is pulsating rapidly, it is much different to before."

"I thought it might," replied the king, as he looked around him, "I think it best we move our forces back thirty or so feet, until this dust settles."

The king then connected with Matthias asking if he could see any movement where the creatures had impacted from above, but Matthias said he could not! The plume of dust is to dense I can't see anything at the moment; He said as he focused as hard as he could, and flew as close as he dared without entering the dust…

The king then asked Matthias to join himself and Bogumill, to which he agreed; swiftly he and Ti-at returned to the ground-forces, where he dismounted Ti-at and walked quickly to the king. Matthias was feeling most pleased they had defeated the changed creatures in such a swift manner. As he approached the king and Bogumill he held out he's hands in greeting for them both, and in return they gripped his forearms, "Good to see you back in one piece," said the king with a firm grip and warm smile.

"It is good to see you both," replied Matthias gripping their forearms tight with true happiness they too were well.

"Yours and the Birgumon's engagement of the enemy was incredibly swift, carried out perfectly, I must say;" Bogumill said with utmost respect for Matthias and the Birgumon.

"I must agree, but something tells me it isn't over yet, my sword is still pulsating, and that can't be a good sign!" said the king feeling a little apprehensive, still surveying the lands to the north…

Matthias replied in an attempt to reassure the king, saying; "There couldn't possibly be any-way those creatures survived that impact, surely!"

"I pray not, but I'm just not feeling confident at this moment, I can't explain it, but what I do know is if they still live, then only us three can fight them, they are two dangerous for the Chu-Chun that will just head straight at them. These Mattatoid are poisonous and very swift," said the king warning Matthias and Bogumill.

"So, let us pray they have perished, for our sakes!" said the king feeling quite apprehensive, but nevertheless willing to do whatever had to be done to protect those he cared for, human and beast…

Matthias agreed with the king, he had seen the way the Mattatoid would swing its deadly tail at the Birgumon, he knew if the creatures had been on the ground rather than hanging under another creature they would be quite deadly; being able to move freely, using their speed and power!

As the three men continued to discuss these creatures there could be heard a sound, it was like a cough! It repeated several times before it changed to a high-pitched roar, but not just one, but two, it could definitely be heard to be two separate roars as they differed slightly in tone and became simultaneous!

"Oh, good God no!" said the king fearing he was right, the Mattatoids still lived they had only been concussed by the impact!

What kind of a creature survives a hundred-foot fall?!" said Matthias as he gripped his sword tight!

With the king in the centre and slightly forward, the three men stood abreast swords in hand, best foot forward and lowered their stance bending their knees, and watched and waited...

In the shroud of dust and dirt the two Mattatoids had woken from their unconsciousness coughing the ache from their chests, and now clambered to stand on all six legs, smelling the air. And in the air, they had the scent of the king and all those with him as they lashed out their tongues to taste their scent...

Then with great agility they rushed out from the dust headlong toward the king within moments they were among them. As the Mattatoids ran at the king now only ten feet from him, one of the ghastly looking things with its huge fangs and dark-scaled skin glistening, leapt up and over the king's head, swinging its tail as it did, luckily the king was quick to react, as he crouched low, and then rolled right as the double spiked tail swung past his face missing him by only inches!

The creature landed directly behind the king, and turned left slowly staring at him directly, now the king had one to his front and one to his rear. He changed his stance to side-on so he could quickly look left then right without having his back to either creature.

The creatures seemed to have no interest in Matthias or Bogumill, or any of the creatures which stood a good thirty feet from them. No they wanted the king, like two assassins they had their target!

After the initial shock Matthias and Bogumill realised the king was in peril and quickly reacted, screaming and shouting waving their swords to distract the creatures, but the creatures didn't so much as look at them, and so Matthias and Bogumill ran and put themselves one either side of the king, between the king and the snarling, tongue lashing, tail wagging creatures before they could pounce at him!

Matthias shouted to the king; "Stay between us no matter what!"

It was at this point the king noticed four of the Chu-Chun slowly sneaking up on the Mattatoid. They slowly crept with their bellies barely off the ground, slowly-slowly sneaking up behind the Mattatoid nearest them. The king knowing what danger they would be putting themselves in, connected with them telling them not to proceed. He then told all the other creatures not to approach as they would be no match for the Mattatoid's poisonous tail and fangs!!

But still the Chu-Chun slowly approached!

The king; with teeth gritted, said they were fools, and knew he had to act quickly before the Chu-Chun pounced and surely died! So, he shouted at the Mattatoids, "COME ON! WHAT ARE YOU WAITING FOR, POUNCE, HERE I AM!"

As the creatures snarled and hissed the king looked to Matthias and Bogumill telling them to wait for them to pounce; then get behind them as fast as they could before the creatures turn, and hack their tails…

With that the king let out a yell "Damn you, your not have me today!" as he charged at the Mattatoid of which the Chu-Chun were sneaking up-on, as he ran at the Mattatoid they both moved in at him; diving at him with their mouths open and fangs extended and dripping poison, the king with total faith in his sword swung out with the blade as the Mattatoid closest to him lunged at him with its mouth open and tongue out tasting his sent; as the king swung his sword he caught the Mattatoid's tongue severing it, the creature let out a loud high-pitched screech…

At the same time Matthias did as the king asked, and ran up behind the creature and with a powerful swift motion raised his sword and brought it down slicing its tail off at the spiked tip, now the creature had no tail the Chu-Chun saw their chance and raced to finish the Mattatoid off. They pounced four-strong onto its rear quarters, ripping and biting at its back, as the Mattatoid turned its head right to strike at the Chu-Chun with its mouth, it exposed its neck to the king, with no hesitation the king drove his sword into its neck and pulled down which brought the creature down.

Now it was down unable to defend itself the Chu-Chun finished it…

Now there was only one Mattatoid to contend with, which was facing the king, the king was keeping the Mattatoid's attention swinging his sword and calling it to him, giving Bogumill and Matthias the opportunity to get behind it, and as they closed in ready to strike the creature suddenly turned on them. And as it did; its tail swung round hitting the king, luckily not with the spikes, they had just missed him, but nevertheless its tail made contact sending the king flying through the air spiraling and landing some ten feet on his left side. he impacted hard dropping his sword and grimacing in pain as he attempted to move or even breath! The pain grew stronger in his left side ribs; "Damn it!" he said feeling the pain trying to get back to his feet.

In the meantime, Bogumill and Matthias stood aligned, facing the creature, and above them Egum.

Egum could engulf the creature with flame, but the three men were too close to it; and if he were to attempt to set fire on the creature it would engulf them all. He would need them to get a distance between them and the Mattatoid, but they could not run from it, they would be no match for its pace.

As for the king he was struggling to get to his feet, and he had dropped his sword, this left him at a real disadvantage!

Matthias and Bogumill were unaware of the king's situation and were expecting him to be striking the Mattatoid's tail at any moment, which would make the creature turn then they could strike its neck. But no! The king was still struggling to get to his feet, "Why has he not struck the creature?" Matthias asked Bogumill, both staring into the eyes of the Mattatoid…

"I don't know, but I wish he would hurry!" replied Bogumill stepping this way and that as the Mattatoid moved its head slowly sizing them up…

Suddenly the Mattatoid lunged at Bogumill with its mouth open with incredible speed. Bogumill only just managed to step to his right as the creatures open lower jaw caught his left shoulder luckily only with its chin; sending Bogumill rolling along the side of its face and neck losing his footing and falling just in front of the creatures left front clawed foot. As he landed on his front, the creature lifted its foot; claws extended and lunged it forward at Bogumill who quickly rolled right just keeping ahead of the big clawed foot as it crashed to the ground narrowly missing him!

The creature quickly turned its head left and down; heading again for Bogumill with its mouth, as it did Bogumill lashed out with his sword in his right hand catching the Mattatoid's chin, gashing it! The creature let out a loud hiss! Then swung its rear round left bringing its body in line with Bogumill; it was now facing him head on!

In his haste to get to his feet Bogumill stumbled landing on his back, the Mattatoid was snarling showing its huge fangs and dribbling poisonous venom as it looked into Bogumill's eyes approaching him slowly!

While Bogumill still on his back scrambling away from the Mattatoid on his hands and heals of his feet, Matthias knew he had to act quickly. Just as he thought of running in at the creature; Boman's voice appeared in his head saying; use your mind, tell your sword to fly and it will!

With that Matthias held his right arm out straight wielding his sword pointing at the Mattatoid's head!

Bogumill was unable to move quick enough and the Mattatoid lunged at Bogumill. Bogumill knowing he was done;

just closed his eyes in expectation of a painful death; as he did, Matthias shouted "Head!" and with that his sword shot from his hand and penetrating the Mattatoid's head clean through killing it instantly! And as swiftly as his sword had left his hand it was back!

"Well I didn't know you could do that!" Matthias said in amazement looking at his sword as the Mattatoid fell landing it's head on Bogumill's legs, it was dead!

Bogumill feeling this sudden pressure on his legs having his eyes still closed tight was expecting all manner of pain, and so clenched every muscle in his body, his jaw so tight he almost cracked his teeth! All that now ran through his mind was his wife and daughter, he was so tempted to contact them but thought best not; as they would feel his pain, and so just lay waiting for the end, but there was no sharp stabbing of poisonous fangs into his flesh, then a voice; "Are you going to lay there all day?" Slowly Bogumill opened his eyes to see Matthias standing over him shaking his head and smiling!

"Come on you, let's get this thing off of you!" Matthias said as he crouched and took the Mattatoid's head in his hands…

Bogumill, now realising he was alive, was shocked; "What happened?" I thought I was about to meet my maker, how is it possible I'm still alive?! This thing had me!"

Matthias replied; "I'll tell you shortly, but first let's get you up." As Matthias spoke, he looked to the location of the king, he could see the king was struggling to get to his feet clasping his left side.

"Oh God, the king is Injured, let's get you up now, I'll lift the head and you slide out from under it ok?!" "Yes," replied Bogumill. And so, Matthias lifted the Mattatoid's head, freeing Bogumill…

As Bogumill got to his feet he too looked to the king. "My king; don't move we are on our way," he said fearing the king had been stabbed or bitten by the Mattatoid.

As the two ran to the king, Egum landed next to him. "My king you're hurt!" "Yes," said the king grimacing with pain, "I think I've broken my ribs." As he still clutched them, he tried to get to his feet, he was on his knees with only his right hand taking his weight, and every time he tried to straighten, he would yelp with pain.

Matthias and Bogumill quickly arrived fearing the worse; seeing their fear for the king Egum told them the king had broken his ribs and that he would be ok!

"Thank God for that, we feared you had been bitten or impaled by the Mattatoid, thankfully not the case!" Matthias said with a look of relief! and continued; "Broken ribs heal, let's get you to your feet," as he looked to Bogumill who stood to the king's left ready to place his hands under the king's left arm while Matthias moved to the king's right side, and placed his hand on the king's elbow and readied himself to lift once the king was ready.

"Are you ready my king, this will smart a little, so say when you are ready!

With that the king took a breath; I'm ready, lift away gentlemen," the king said bracing himself...

With that Matthias and Bogumill counted one, two, three, and lifted the king to his feet, he felt the pain and grimaced letting out a moan h-ah!

Once the king was on his feet Bogumill communicated with his wife; saying the king was injured and could she send someone with a horse and cart to fetch them.

Ivana replied; "Yes, I'll be as quick as I can."

"Thank you, my love, see you soon!" Bogumill replied with a smile and a real sense of good fortune he was still alive and able to speak with his wife; thanks to Matthias...

Bogumill then informed the king and Matthias that Ivana was sending a horse and cart to fetch them, to which the king said he was thankful. "Good thinking!" said the king struggling to stand!

The king continued they should probably make their way as best they could and hopefully meet the cart on route; as just standing there wasn't helping anything, and so the three with arms wrapped around each other slowly made their way with Egum in tow.

As they walked ever so slowly Egum chirped-up; "Don't you think that was a little too easy?"

"What was a little too easy?" asked the king inquisitively, trying to take his mind off the pain he was having to endure...

Egum quickly replied; "Their attack! We defeated them incredibly swiftly, almost too easily!"

Matthias quickly replied with quite a judgmental tone; "Maybe it was because they were just stupid bloodthirsty creatures, without intelligence easily led to their own deaths at the scent of human flesh!"

Bogumill thought on what Matthias had said, but then; "No! I don't think that the case; they showed intelligence, in the way they used the ospreys to transport the much deadlier Mattatoid. That is intelligence! But nevertheless, now it's been said I to must agree with Egum. Something doesn't feel right, their attack was to easily thwarted. At the same time, it would seem that you my king was their true interest! And let's not forget, they nearly had you!

No, I think they have intelligence, and I feel we will be seeing just how intelligent our foe truly is in times to come!" said Bogumill with a look of concern as he shook his head and bit his lips...

The king replied to Bogumill saying he hoped he was wrong; "If they are unintelligent then we can use our intelligence to beat them, if they come at us blindly then we can outsmart them, so let's prey they lack intelligence," the king said trying to smile a smile of hope...

Egum then said that he could have easily burned them, but because the king, Matthias and Bogumill were so close to the creatures he could not, as he would have killed them to.

And so suggested; "If they are attacked again then he and his kin should strike first with fire, before the enemy could get close, or they should at least strike the most formidable foe..."

The three men could see sense in what Egum spoke.

The king pointed out that they were all new to battle, and had much to learn, they hadn't even learned how to wield their swords properly yet!

And so, he continued that they would have to ask Boman to teach them the true potential of the swords...

As they walked Matthias was distracted by the Birgumon which still circled above them as though keeping a lookout…

"Look at them! Aren't they magnificent!" Matthias said with such awe of them…

The king looked to see, but struggled with every movement he made, even lifting his head caused him pain in his ribs, but still he looked as best he could, "Yes they are truly incredible creatures and we owe them much, without them today would have had a much different outcome I feel," he then turned his head to Matthias and said he could tell them to relax now, they should save their energies and return to the ground.

And so Matthias connected with Ti-at saying; he and his kin could relax, he didn't think they would see any more changed this day, Ti-at replied to Matthias in agreement, he said they didn't sense danger now but they would just scout for a few more minutes to be sure, then they would return to Bulgan…

Matthias agreed and thanked Ti-at for what they had done this day, saying; see you soon, "Thank you all, don't know what would have happened without you!"

Ti-at smiled and said; they were welcome.

As the three men and the huge dragon walked, they could see the Treegum retracting the dome they had formed over the inhabitants of Bulgan. They now began to take their usual form, and from within the masses, making its way towards them they could just make out a horse and cart. "Finally!" said Bogumill; "Let's stop here, the cart is on its way my king, no point in struggling on and causing you pain, let's stop here."

The king agreed, it was quite painful for him trying to walk even though he was being supported by Matthias and Bogumill, and so they stood and waited.

Within a couple of minutes, the horse and cart arrived, and they were greeted by Ivana as she brought the horse to a halt just in front of them.

She quickly dismounted the cart and ran to Bogumill wrapping her arms around him in a warm embrace; "God it's good to see you," she said to Bogumill as she held him tight then kissed him.

She then turned to Matthias and the king; "It's good to see you are all in one piece, but what have you done my king?" she said looking at the king's twisted stance.

"Think I've broken my ribs!" he replied, as he gave a sigh of disbelief...

Ivana looked at the king and said; "Well we will get you seen to, let's get you back where you can be seen to," with that she smiled a warm smile and asked Matthias and Bogumill help the king to sit on the back of the cart.

And so, they guided the king to the back of the cart where he turned his back to it, saying; "This will probably be easier if you lift me and sit me on the edge, thank you gentleman."

With that Matthias and Bogumill stood either side of the king bent their knees and joined hands whilst facing each other, Matthias's left hand gripped Bogumill's right hand, which was held just behind the king's knees, and their other hands were clasped together at the middle of the king's back to support his back while the king sat on their lower arms forming a seated posture, this enabled the two very strong men to lift the king straight onto the edge of the cart.

Once the king was as comfortable as he could be considering his injuries, Bogumill and Matthias joined him sitting on the back of the cart, legs hanging over the edge, keeping one hand each on the king's shoulders making sure he could not fall.

Ivana then climbed back on to the front seat of the cart, telling them to hold tight, and off they set at a very slow pace as the ground was quite uneven, and the three men were being rocked around which caused the king to grimace and moan with pain; "This is just my luck!" said the king shaking his head and chuckled followed by an ouch!

Matthias and Bogumill both let out a chuckle, and Bogumill couldn't help but say; "I think we need to wrap you in wool if there should be another battle!"

Matthias let out a big laugh! "Could you imagine that on the field of battle, this big ball of wool with just feet, hands and head barely visible running around? Ha-ha-ha!"

"I should think it would be quite a distraction for any foe!" laughed Bogumill…

"Ha-ha! Very funny," replied the king in a sarcastic manner, then started to laugh at the vision in his head; of him wrapped in a big ball of wool, "God forbid I fall over, I'll not be able to get up again!" he laughed!

And as the king laughed so too did Matthias, Bogumill, even Egum had a chuckle; Ivana just shook her head smiling and thinking to herself; do men ever grow up? as she looked back at the three men and a huge dragon besides themselves with laughter. One good thing she thought; at least they have high spirits, which was a very good thing considering.

It wasn't too long before they had arrived back at Bulgan, their laughter had stopped by this point, they were now just enjoying the scenery as it slowly passed by, the odd bump did make the king grimace a little but nothing too bad, on seeing the king in discomfort the people became concerned for him, they began to approach the cart asking is the king ok? Is he wounded? "My king are you ok?" one woman shouted with concern!

The king thanked the people for their concern and said he was fine, and that he had had a fall and damaged his ribs but he would be fine in no time, he continued; "So please don't be worried, I'm not going anywhere!" he smiled.

With that voices could be heard thanking god for the king's safe return, others would say thankfully the king isn't seriously injured to others and smile.

Then the questions started, the people wanted to know what had happened, what were the strange creatures? And were they in danger?!

The king asked Matthias and Bogumill to help him stand up on the back of the cart, and so they did as the king asked. The king, feeling pain as they helped him to his feet, did not allow it to show on his face, he didn't grimace, he wanted to appear strong wanting to ease the people's fears, and so did not want them to see his pain as he spoke with them.

He then informed them of what they had found in Polaria, and told them of the attack and the losses they suffered whilst there, he then continued to tell the people that they could expect more attacks, but they would soon be well armed to defend themselves as the alchemists had created a magical weapon for each and every one of them. The people listened intently, they did not become panicked by the king's words, in fact the opposite was the case, the people had a strong faith Good would always prevail over evil, and they also had a strong faith in their leadership…

And so they listened not with fear but unity, as the king continued; he continued to inform them that their lives would change now, they would have to learn how to fight, and now although unimaginable to them a few days ago; they now would have to form an army to defend the entire southern regions from the changed.

The king then said to the people they will not fight with hatred but with compassion, they must not become filled with negativity as the changed feed on it. He then told them to think of any battle the chance to free the trapped spirits of those they once knew, and not as the killing of a creature, for parts of their good spirit are still trapped within the changed form, and they will free it.

He then turned to Matthias and placed his hand firmly on his shoulder, and told the people to look to Matthias, he would be training them all in the art of combat, and that he had many skills and would teach them well with the aid of Bogumill. He then said that he had to meet with the alchemists, and then after he and his group he had brought from Engypt would be returning home, but would return when they had formed an army to support the protection of the southern regions. He then continued that together they will be ready no matter what may come! to which the people cheered and clapped.

It was incredible, these people were so strong, together they would all pull as one, and that makes for an incredible force to contend with, for any foe…

Once the king had finished speaking; the people chanted long live King Stephen, as he was help down from the cart by those below, again he felt the pain in his ribs, but did not let on.

The mass of people continued to cheer and chant for their king, but now also for Bogumill and Matthias, chanting they had faith in them and together they would survive; "With faith in God and you we will survive, we will stand together forever!" they chanted repeatedly.

As the king, Matthias and Bogumill made their way to the alchemist's laboratories the people reached to touch them, whether it was just a touch of the hand or their clothing, it was enough to feel empowered...

And so, the three men continued to walk slowly through the crowd of people taking time to thank them for their support. After some time, they reached the alchemist's building, once again the door swung open and once again there was Dara waiting to greet them. The activity within was incredible, the three men watched with wonder at the moulds, swords, sheaths, handles and globules of Udriume whizzing around at speed, it was like a production line in there. The moulds would settle on the benches the Udriume would fill them, then the tiny droplets of blood which had been supplied by the thousands of people would be dropped into the Udriume; this would bond the sword to their users' DNA, so only they could wield its power.

Then the sheaths would lay on top of the mould and then the sword's handle on top of that. As the Udriume would have to be touched by its user for it to harden, then the handle would almost magically become part of the sword once touched, there were thousands of swords awaiting their dispatching, and each had an instruction; (Touch me I am yours to wield).

"Welcome back my king, Matthias, Bogumill, it's good to see you all once more. Boman is aware of your arrival and will be with you momentarily."

"Thank you," replied the king and smiled, Dara could see the king was in discomfort, and said he could see the king had damaged his ribs, to which the king replied he had indeed, with that Dara asked Matthias and Bogumill to support the king's weight, and so they did as asked and stood each side of the king placing an arm under the king's armpits and braced.

Dara said he was going to heal the king, but it would be momentarily quite painful; and so, asked the king if he had permission to proceed. "Yes of course," said the king, he then looked left then right at Matthias and Bogumill who took the king's weight, Dara then asked Matthias and Bogumill to lift the king slightly, just enough the stretch his ribcage.

As they lifted the king slightly the king let out a loud yelp "Ah, ah!"

Dara then placed his hands on the king's left ribs and as he did Dara's hands lit up so brightly, pure bright white at first then the colour changed and began to pulsate through many different colours, red, orange, yellow, green, blue, indigo and violet, all the colours of the chakra.

As they pulsated and changed the king began to feel real pain, so much so he began to yell; "Ah-ah-ah" and beads of sweat ran down his face. Matthias and Bogumill became shocked at the response to Dara's actions, with a raised voice; "What is happening?!" asked Matthias, most concerned.

"Not long now," Dara replied eyes closed in a state of meditation.

Then suddenly cracking sounds could be heard coming from the king's ribs, the king passed out, and now Matthias and Bogumill struggled to hold the king's entire weight; with teeth gritted "Please hurry!" said Bogumill, he is heavier than he looks.

After five minutes or so Dara's hands stopped glowing! It's done!" he said, and then placed his right hand on the king's forehead and said; "Wake!" and as he pulled his hand away the king's eyes did open, and in a subdued state the king asked "What happened?" as he took deep breaths, eyes opening and closing as though very sleepy! He then began to support his own weight, Matthias and Bogumill now let him go, he was a little unsteady but soon regained his faculties, and quickly realised he had no pain. "You fixed my ribs, thank you so much, feels like they had never been broken, you are a gifted healer Dara," said the king still a little dazed.

With joy Matthias said that the king had them worried for a moment; "You were yelling with pain, I almost thought Dara was killing you, you cried out so loudly! but thankfully all is well, that was an incredible experience Dara, you could have warned us!"

Dara smiled; "Well I did say it was going to be painful!"

The king placed his right hand on Dara's right shoulder as he faced him smiled and said; "You did indeed, but my God man that was awful, the word excruciating would have prepared me a little better," he then laughed, and thanked Dara again.

It was then that Boman entered the main hall, "My king, Matthias, Bogumill you made it. I'm so happy! Matthias did you like the way your sword did as you told it bringing the Mattatoid down?"

Matthias smiled and said to Boman; he wished he had told them the swords could be used in such a way earlier, it would have made things much easier, they would not have had to get so close!

Boman replied; "I said these swords will do whatever your will, but I didn't have time to go into detail, but now you know these swords will do whatever you imagine and more, remember practice makes perfect, so the more you practice the more you will learn."

The three men knew they still had much to learn about the power of their swords, and the king said they would practice daily and so would everyone who held one.

Boman said that daily training would be a must, and they would need to learn every skill possible, they would also realise inner skills they had never imagined they held, and that the swords would release their innermost strengths, he then continued; "They will need to be strong in days to come," today he felt was a test, he said he felt that something was controlling the changed and that the small party which was sent this day was just a scouting party, a way to see their strengths and weaknesses!

So, with this in mind, he said if there should be another attack; he felt it would be a much bigger assault, but they would be ready…

On hearing Boman's words Bogumill agreed, he to thought it was too easy to defeat the changed, and that the numbers were too small to be a real threat, he continued; we need to get training as soon as possible! When will the swords be ready?

Boman replied, "They are on schedule and will be dispatched this evening, and I thought it best I communicate with everyone whilst they sleep before dispatching them. I'll tell them what is to be done when they receive the swords, so you need not concern yourself with this task my king, I know you need to be on your way as soon as possible back to Engypt, you have much to do! Also as you may have noticed I have put a little instruction with every sword, this should help the people remember what I would have said whilst they slept."

The king replied with a smile; "It would seem you have everything in hand Boman, that makes me feel at ease about leaving for Engypt. When I get back to Engypt I have to then ready for a visit to Earth, god knows the effects all this has had on the people there!"

The king's facial expression changed to one of concern as he thought of Earth; "I just pray things aren't too bad there, the people of Earth are not as strong as us mentally or spiritually, and so could be easily lead by any change in energy the universe may have suffered since the catastrophic events of New Year's…"

Chapter 9

They Have Found Us

Boman looked at the king; and just as he was about to speak, his words became muffled, and it seemed as though the vision was fading, It was as though Sato was losing his connection with us as we began to float upwards slowly at first looking down on the main hall with all the commotion of the swords creation, and the five men stood in conversation, then the vision passed through the roof of the building and continued accelerating now, up-up-up, now we could see Bulgan surrounded by mountains; and beyond to the north, the lands that were once Polaria, now blackened, before we could focus on Polaria and catch a good look at the land and see if there were changed, there was a haze and then we were surrounded by colours, we were in a tube of colour shooting backwards, then suddenly it stopped and just darkness...

Then Sato's voice, in a whispered tone; "Everyone quickly! Open your eyes but be still and quiet; we are not alone!"

And so one by one we opened our eyes, as I opened my eyes the first thing I noticed was it was quite dark! and I could just see Sato with his forefinger on his lips, he then mouthed; "Be quiet!" then he removed his finger from his mouth and stared at my sword which was rattling around, I looked back to Sato.

Sato gesturing with his hand making a clasping motion and mouthing take your sword! so again I looked back to my sword and held open my right hand into which the sword silently glided, I clasped it tight wondering just what was going on!

If Sato said take my sword, I was doing as I was asked, as for him to ask meant something was wrong.

Next to wake was Syrah, before she could speak Sato placed his hand over her mouth, the look on her face was of shock! as Sato held his hand covering her mouth, then once she realised all was not well her eyes filled with sorrow, it hit her! Sato was never wrong his senses were very strong and he sensed danger! her heart sank as she slowly shook her head and muttered "Please God no!"

Syrah then calmly looked through the dim light to a large dark wooden cabinet; which stood against the far wall of the Dojo at the opposite end of the hall to the door of which we had entered. As she looked at the cabinet, she became very focused as she opened one of the double doors of the cabinet, and from within she drew out three swords ever so quietly they glided towards us. One she took for herself, one she placed at Aashif's crossed legs, and the other she placed in front of Jasmine's still crossed legs.

Aashif and Jasmine had not fully regained consciousness yet, and so Syrah whispered to them to be quiet and stay calm, both looking a little dazed and sleepy, they both slowly nodded their heads and looked around the room trying to regain their bearings; after a moment or two they looked at us, Jasmine asked Syrah with a whisper; "What's going on?" as she blinked trying to focus her sleepy eyes.

Syrah replied with a calm demeanor, whispering; "We need to stay calm, it would seem Sato as sensed we are not alone in the building! The changed may have found us, and so now I will need you and Aashif to pick up yours swords and slowly stand!"

Although she had never been shown this particular sword before; as Syrah, just as Sato had hoped we would never have to use them, and so kept them a secret, hoping to show us when we were older and teach us all their powers, but no that was not going to be the case. the time had unexpectedly come for her just as for me to finally learn of the swords, and now it looked as though we would have to learn about the swords as we used them.

As Jasmine grasped the sword she felt its power, but she was not shocked, she said she had dreamed of this sword, like it had been calling her, she continued that she had seen herself holding this very sword, it was easily recognisable to her as it had red silk woven into its handle, just as she had seen in her dreams…

She had instantly bonded with the sword, she felt its power running throughout her, the power was so strong she began to emit a glow of energy, like a shroud around her. The colours that emitted from her seemed to roll and pulsate as it moved around her; with shock Syrah said it was incredible! "You are a very powerful conductor of energy, this is so very rare, very few have this power! You can manipulate anything that has energy!"

Jasmine slowly got to her feet looking at her body as it glowed! "This is incredible!" she said excitedly, "Why have I never seen this, or felt this before?" she asked and looked to Syrah.

"All I have time to say at this moment is the swords enhance our powers, bringing dormant powers to the fore!" replied Syrah.

"You look incredible!" I said in wonderment…

Then Aashif asked; as he reached for his sword; "Will mine do the same for me?" he asked with eyes wide open with excitement.

Syrah looked at Aashif thinking what to say as she did not wish to disappoint him, but she had to be honest!

"Your sword is made from Udriume just as ours are, but it wasn't created with your DNA as Jasmine's and Jacob's, as theirs were commanded by the king of our world, and the blood of our now king and princes was used in their creations, their blood is of the same line as Jasmine and Jacob, me and Sato were sent here to defend Jasmine and Jacob and their swords gifted to them by our king before he perished in battle, as did our queen! You will be able to use the sword, as you have wonderful good energies, and so it will let you fight evil with it, but as for powers! It will not enhance you, but these swords are the only thing that will penetrate the changed, nothing man made can hurt them, they are shrouded by evil, they will feel you hit them and kick them, but you will not cause them damage as you would a human, so look after it with your life!"

Syrah went on to say to Aashif; "It's just as well you are the finest swordsman I have ever seen, that is your gift my son."

"That means so much coming from you!" replied Aashif with a face full of pride.

"Enough talking!" said Sato; we need to be ready something is coming; we must stay together!

"Can't we just leave via the fire exit?" Aashif whispered as he looked to the door, which was in the left corner of the room, on the same wall as the big cabinet.

"No!" whispered Sato, where would we go, they would just come after us, no we make a stand here and now!

"Listen!" whispered Syrah.

Just as Syrah said listen, the door in which we entered the room and parts of the wall exploded into pieces, the force of the explosion knocked us all to the ground, sliding us all across the floor where we ended up slamming into the rear wall hard! I bashed my head almost knocking me unconscious, I was dazed and had dropped my sword, but I quickly opened my hand and my sword returned swiftly.

We had all suffered cuts from the flying debris, poor Aashif had a piece of wood from the exploding door; an inch-long splinter hanging from his left cheek, where it had pierced his face, he too was dazed as were all of us...

Jasmine and Syrah had clashed heads, and were both holding their heads, and looking at each other with dismay, both covered in dust and debris, but apart from banging heads, they only suffered superficial cuts, more like scratches really."

"Are you ok?" Syrah instantly asked Jasmine, concerned she was seriously hurt, Jasmine replied; "I'm fine it's just a bump, are you ok?!"

With that Syrah said; "Good, yes I'm fine, let's get to our feet now!"

Sato seemed to be unhurt and was standing with his back against the wall and his sword in his right hand, the tip facing down as he held his arm out approximately twenty inches from his hip...

It appeared that Sato was not knocked to the ground but somehow just slid on his feet still standing across the floor with the force of the explosion, he was stood calmly waiting for something to appear through the dust. He was almost zoned out, his head tilted forward, his eyes piercing the dust almost staring through the lids of his eyes as his head was at such a tilt...

I quickly got to my feet sword in hand and stood by his right side, his energy was so immense I could feel it whilst I stood next to him, it felt incredibly powerful yet calming, suddenly in my head visions of all my training in swordsmanship and martial arts running rapidly like a fast forwarding video took my breath away, and when they had stopped I felt so ready, calm and focused for whatever may come.

Then Syrah stood to Sato's left sword in hand and ready. She to ever so focused, as she stood sword in her right hand, she raised her left hand out in front of her fingers point up and slowly bent her knees slightly lowering her stance.

And by Syrah's side stood Jasmine, she had dropped her sword, and so as she stood next to Syrah, she opened her right hand, to which her sword suddenly appeared. Now that her sword was in her hand she shuddered as it once again super-enhanced her powers and she began again to emit a colourful shroud, she was ready, she was calm and focused.

Then by my side Aashif slowly took his place whilst touching the splinter of wood which was still embedded in his left cheek, as I turned to look at him, I noticed the splinter in his face, he was grimacing as he placed his fingers on it and gripped it tight, just as he took a grip of the splinter two huge figures appeared as the dust began to settle, and in the dim darkening light, they slowly approached us with their legs slightly bent torsos leant forward arms out wide, hands open wide, fingers extended and claws readied to strike, these two creatures with black and shiny scaly skins, had small almost horn-like things, about two inches in length which circled their heads, they were quite daunting as they approached, one had yellow eyes and the other red, we had nowhere to go! we would have to fight them here and now!

Then Aashif let out a loud cry; "Come on then!" as he pulled the splinter from his face and throwing it to the ground, then raised his sword over his right shoulder both hands gripping the handle tight; then charged at the disfigured manlike creatures, as he ran at the one on the right as we faced them, he got within striking distance, but the creature which had yellow eyes just raised its left arm and without making actual physical contact just brushed Aashif aside, throwing him into the wall...

As he impacted the wall hard he fell to the ground, it looked as though he had been knocked unconscious. Seeing this Jasmine shouted; "Aashif!" and then suddenly the lights began to switch on and off rapidly, it was Jasmine she was pulling the electric energy from the lights and wall sockets, like continuous lightning bolts the electrical energy sparked its way across the room from every point there was a light or socket and made contact with Jasmine's left hand; the light she emitted became so bright, electric blue and silver, she pulled her left hand back bending her left arm backwards then swiftly swung it forwards fingers wide open, as she stretched her left arm out ahead of her the energy she had drawn shot from her fingers...

It impacted the creatures sending them sliding backwards, but they still stood, they just slid backwards on their feet, and as they did, they stretched out the claws in their toes and stopped themselves!

As they came to a halt, the changed with red eyes pulled its right arm to its chest then pushed it away fast, and as it did it unleashed an energy which formed a shield in front of them deflecting the electric energies from Jasmine. The two clashing energies sent sparks shooting out with incredible loud sparking noises, popping and snapping as the electricity flowed over their shield of energy…

And together they walked towards us; the one with the shield in front of the other!

Sato told Jasmine to continue, saying she was slowing them, and this would enable us to get behind them and attack…

And so, as Jasmine continued to release electricity on them, we moved forward. As we did Aashif regained consciousness, he shook his head then clambered to his feet a little dazed but ready to have another go at the changed.

And so, he joined me on my right side and together we approached the changed from the right, Sato and Syrah approached them from left…

We moved swiftly moving in and behind the changed that had the yellow eyes, which was shielding behind the other. But now it turned to face me and Aashif, and as it did it fired its claws at us, instinctively I dodged the claws as they shot past me. Aashif with two swift left then right motions of his sword deflected a couple of projectiles, then he dropped low bending his legs and rotated right lashing out with his sword as he came into line with the changed's legs, but the creature was fast and leaped over Aashif's sword, and as it did it unleashed a kick with its right leg catching Aashif in the face sending him spiraling backwards!

As Aashif fell backwards I realised attempting to attack this creature with just my sword wasn't going to work, I had to use my energies to force it back then attack with my sword…

So, I focused seeing my mind throwing the creature against the remainder of the wall they had passed through, then throwing my left hand forwards; with clenched fist I released an energy which was visible, it looked like a shockwave as it left my fist…

My shockwave impacted the creature's chest throwing it hard against the wall, with the impact the already damaged wall collapsed under the weight of the creature impacting against it, sending the creature crashing backwards, the loosened bricks fell on top of it…

And so; I, Sato and Syrah saw our opportunity to finish it off, and as we ran at it; swords ready to strike, the creature let out an almighty ear-piercing sound! The sound was like a bellow, it carried such an impact, an actual physical impact hit the three of us knocking us backwards and sending bricks and debris along in its wake which narrowly missed us...

As I looked back to the creature's location; it was already upright and heading towards me, making a fast beeline towards me!

I was still on the ground on my front looking over my shoulder as the creature made its way towards me, quick thinking I looked at my sword which I had dropped, and so with my left hand reached for it not to grip it! but to guide it! with my arm stretched towards it, I looked back at the creature which was only six feet or so away from me, and so swung my arm back pointing at the creatures chest, my sword launched with great speed heading directly at its chest, but the creature swiped it away with its right hand, slamming it to the ground; the creature cut its hand in doing so and let out a yelp!

I quickly reach for my sword again, this time taking it in my hand and scrambled to my feet!

Sato and Syrah almost as one with me also jumped to their feet, and turned to face the creature, then suddenly the creature cried out and almighty gargling scream as the tip of a sword appeared from its chest!

It was Aashif, he had managed to regain consciousness and get behind the creature whilst it was focused on me; he had driven his sword into its back and drove it through killing the creature, as he withdrew his sword the creature fell to its knees then onto its front with an almighty thud... Stood there in shock at his actions was young Aashif, sword still in hand and a look as though he had done something wrong, he was a truly gentle, fun-loving guy in different circumstances, and the realisation he had just killed a living creature hit him hard, he wasn't excited or happy at his actions, no, he was quite saddened although he knew he had to do what he did to save me!

As we all looked at Aashif, ourselves quite shocked his eyes became distracted!

He began to look passed us, and around the room, then with a voice full of anguish; "Where is Jasmine?!"

On hearing his words, we turned, Jasmine should have been behind us! but she was gone and so was the red-eyed changed!!!

To Be Continued

CPSIA information can be obtained
at www.ICGtesting.com
Printed in the USA
LVHW021556041119
636282LV00004B/879/P